Dear Reader,

Welcome to and .... of Duets!

Duets #31

It's babies and more babies, beginning with popular Kate Hoffmann and *Three Babies and a Bargain*. What's a single woman to do when she has to play nanny for three little mischievous nephews? Why, she strikes a bargain, *and fast,* with gorgeous handyman Nick Callahan! Next, Silhouette Romance author Sandra Paul delivers *Baby Bonus?,* a humorous tale about a sexy bank security expert dealing with five pregnant tellers—and one beautiful manager, Jessica—who have no time for his stuffy rules!

Duets #32

In *Tryst of Fate* talented Isabel Sharpe pens a delicious tale about an author who suffers lust-induced writer's block every time he encounters the woman of his dreams. Should he marry her or give up writing? Then Carrie Alexander is back with book two in THE COWGIRL CLUB miniseries. Three lifelong female friends love horses and—what else?—cowboys! *Counterfeit Cowboy* is a galloping good read!

Be sure to pick up both Duets volumes this month!

Birgit Davis-Todd
Senior Editor & Editorial Coordinator
Harlequin Duets

"So what's the plan, Rosemary?"

"Today's plan is to get you back in touch with your senses," she said.

"Sounds good." He rolled onto his back, hands behind his head. "I like being stimulated."

Rosemary sent him a prim look, which was about as opposite from how she was feeling as dried-up soyburgers are to the real carnivorous, finger-licking, fat-dripping variety. "Close your eyes and concentrate. Imagine your body is nothing but a nose. Then tell me what you smell."

"I can smell you."

Rosemary jerked back, halting her slow instinctive lean toward his seductive voice. "That about wraps up smelling."

"We're done already?" Jordan opened his eyes. "It was like my whole body became one giant nostril. I swear."

Rosemary tried to fix him with a furious glare, but it was hard, considering his sly and repentant little wink, whereupon she became a flood of hormones and forgave him instantly.

For more, turn to page 9

Counterfeit Cowboy

"Not so fast, Ms. Molly."

"I want to go see the kittens." Molly pulled on Raleigh's hand.

"Give me a good-morning kiss," he said, his eyes coaxing her, "and then I'll let you go."

"Is this blackmail? It's cold out here."

He drew her closer. "I call it a warm-up."

Warm-up? "You're pretty sure of yourself, hmm, wrangler man?"

"When it's right, I don't fight it."

Knowing she was wanted, toasted her inside and out. "What about the boss's rule against fraternization?"

Raleigh chuckled. "Shucks, ma'am, I don't call it fraternization. Not you and me."

The words filled Molly's heart to the brim. Just over two weeks in Wyoming and she'd found three of her Cowgirl Club goals: open skies, hard work and—she brushed her hand over Raleigh's iron-hard thigh—tight jeans.

As the recipient of such good fortune, she would be miserly not to give some back.

For more, turn to page 197

HARLEQUIN DUETS

ISBN 0-373-44098-7

TRYST OF FATE
Copyright © 2000 by Muna Shehadi Sill

COUNTERFEIT COWBOY
Copyright © 2000 by Carrie Antilla

Tryst of Fate

ISABEL SHARPE

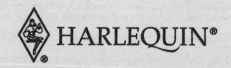

HARLEQUIN®

TORONTO • NEW YORK • LONDON
AMSTERDAM • PARIS • SYDNEY • HAMBURG
STOCKHOLM • ATHENS • TOKYO • MILAN • MADRID
PRAGUE • WARSAW • BUDAPEST • AUCKLAND

Dear Reader,

Like my heroine Rosemary, I grew up bouncing from one torrid crush to another. And, like Rosemary, I spent so much time dreaming about the perfect romance that the guys I knew didn't stand a chance (not that they were exactly lining up outside my door). Luckily, by the time I met my husband, I'd learned some of the lessons Rosemary eventually learns, so I didn't let him pass me by. In fact, I announced to my friends, ten seconds after I first saw him, that he was the man I'd marry. Poor guy. I'm not sure he knew what hit him.

Ten years later he's learned to tolerate my impulsive nature as I've learned to appreciate his more practical approach to life. If he and I are anything to go by, Rosemary and Jordan have a bright future ahead!

I hope you enjoy their story. Online readers can write to me at IsaSharpe@aol.com.

Isabel Sharpe

P.S. Look for my next Duets novel in January 2001.

To my wonderful friends, Mom and Dad,
for giving me unfailing love, unwavering support
and a lifetime of summers in Maine.

1

NEW YORK CITY spread out before them, bejeweled and mysterious, twinkling in the darkness, inviting and exciting as an amusement park ride to a child allowed out past his bedtime.

Well, as much of New York City as you could see from the top of an eleven-story apartment building on East Ninety-Seventh Street. Certainly a twinkle or two could be detected between other buildings, and there were some nice bright neon signs across the adjoining parking lot advertising beer. Very close to being a perfect romantic evening. Fine for a first date.

Rosemary sighed rapturously and stretched her arms open to embrace the scene before them. "Don't you love the city in the moonlight..." a breathless pause, then huskily "...Rob?"

"Moon's good," said Rob.

Rosemary sighed again, only not so rapturously this time. Her co-worker was the strong silent type. Well, silent anyway. Maybe not that strong. Slender you could call him. But nice. Nice went a lot further than strong. Nice you could live with. Nice you could turn into forever. Strength you could always hire if you needed heavy lifting.

She tipped her head dreamily. "Up here noises are muted and softened. You can almost imagine the city as a meadow, chirping and scurrying with—"

"Rats," said Rob. "Meadows have a lot of rats."

"...rats." Latest sigh. A cool summer breeze slid over Rosemary's cheeks, which certainly ought to be flushed in anticipation of a kiss—or two—and stirred her long, auburn hair, which should be cascading down her back like a silken curtain right about now. If he'd care to mention it.

On cue, he came up close behind her, put his hands to her shoulders and slid them down the length of her arms, bared by her flowing sundress. Rosemary tried hard to summon the delicious sensuous shiver she ought to be experiencing. She nearly got it. Pretty close.

"Rosemary..."

She smiled. The warmth of his hands at her waist contained the promise of romance.

She was ready.

Because she'd grown up having crushes on half the boys in her class and Batman and Alan Alda and most males in between, fictional or otherwise. She'd read romance novels by the ton, dreamed herself into every heroine role, watched and waited, though mysteriously stayed dateless.

Then she'd gone to college and discovered Literature and Intellect and Feminism, which she misinterpreted to mean she should fall in love with a career instead of a man, since the saying went that women need men like fish need bicycles.

But then recently, as she approached the end of her twenties, she'd gotten more in touch with who she really was, not what they tried to make her in college and she realized she was closer to her real self in grade school when she dreamed all those dreams of Mr. Right.

Because there wasn't anything wrong with wanting love. So with a successful, rewarding career under her belt, she declared herself ready to find the bicycle she'd spent all those years thinking she shouldn't want.

Only it seemed most bicycles for a fish her age were either broken, secondhand or interested in other bicycles. Tonight at least she had a chance. Rob was so nice, after all. And the night so romantic.

"Yes, Rob?"

Rob inhaled to speak. His hands crept down to fumble greedily at her seating area.

"Rosemary, your ass is awesome," he whispered. "I mean, it makes me totally nuts."

Rosemary froze.

Rob froze behind her.

For the first time since the city was founded, for one horrified moment, absolute silence fell. New Yorkers everywhere stopped, traffic stopped, airplanes hung suspended. No one moved. Or breathed.

Or so it seemed.

Rosemary moved forward, away from Rob's hands. She held herself stiffly, looked out at the bleak, aging, dirty landscape, which the moon and stars and a thousand miracles couldn't make romantic tonight. And she sighed again.

Men couldn't get it right. They couldn't. Well, ninety-nine percent of them couldn't, ninety-nine percent of the time. In her experience, only one had ever gotten it right. One. Steve Judson, back home in Lazy Pines, Maine. That night at the continuation of their high school graduation party, in John Langley's basement. Incredibly, for one of the few times in all the years she'd adored him, she'd actually been talking to Steve. He'd been so close. She'd seen the fine doe-brown stubble on his chin, inhaled the exhilarating scent of his maleness and his aftershave.

Then that booming crash of thunder, and sudden pitch blackness, and pretend-terror screaming from the girls. Then the arms around her, the kiss pressed to her mouth with perfect aim as if he had night vision, like a tiger. Her head had started to spin, but not from the smuggled-in beer; her body had begun to melt in little buttery rivulets around her; her loins had heated to the point of no return, except that she was too inexperienced to understand what that meant really, and the kiss had gone on and on until she'd simply ceased to exist except in the pure passionate beauty of the pressure of his mouth and the clean manly taste of him.

Then someone had come in with a flashlight; he'd released her and stepped away. The lights had come back on and she'd been left to stare at him, dreamy, astonished, wildly aroused and head over heels, while he had to pretend nothing had happened because he was with someone else that night.

That night, that man, that time, that place. Never repeated, with Steve or any other man, though Rosemary kept hoping it wasn't too late. When you knew something like that existed, it was crazy to pretend you could settle for anything less. Anything like poor Rob, hovering behind her now, probably scared and sheepish. Slender and silent and scared and sheepish. Poor Rob. Rosemary sighed yet again.

And what a senseless tragic waste of a perfect romantic summer evening.

THE FOLLOWING MORNING, Rosemary strode into the offices of *I Am Woman* magazine, half an hour late. As usual. So in essence she was right on time. But considering how many extra hours she worked fact-checking stories, especially the two weeks before each issue's monthly deadline, she couldn't find any guilt in her heart. And besides, this morning she had to wait forever for a subway—a sweltering sardine can packed with other people's sweaty bodies.

Yech. She still wanted to wash.

Then she had to pass the construction site down the street and endure the whistles of the guys even though she wasn't wearing anything remotely provocative, unless they thought blue-and-white striped shirtdresses worn over commuting sneakers were the ultimate in sexuality. Then a gust of hot July wind had blown dust into her contacts and she'd bumped into people while trying to open her streaming eyes wide enough to get them out, when of course quite sensibly, the last thing her eyes wanted to do was open, in case they let more dust in. And the people she bumped into had been furious and rude and told her to watch where she was going, damn it, and she'd just felt like some people deserved to have anvils fall out of the sky onto their heads.

Thank goodness she'd decided to take some time off soon to get out of the city, maybe after this issue's deadline was past, though she still hadn't made the reservations for her trip to Paris. Something kept holding her back. She hadn't yet figured out what, but maybe she would. Maybe soon.

Rosemary went to her cubicle, dumped her purse on her desk and waved across the room to Rob, who scuttled sheepishly around a corner to avoid waving back. Poor Rob. She made herself a cup of green tea, rich in cholesterol-lowering, anticancer, antibacterial polyphenols, steeped five minutes, one sugar, no milk, and changed her commuting sneakers for brown sandals, frowning at their scuff marks.

Two sips into the green tea, she picked up the phone, ready to embark on another fascinating trip through someone else's expertise. The rest of her tea would sit and get cold as it always did and she'd throw it out, and whatever vermin lived down the office sink would be free from cancer, cholesterol and bacteria for the rest of their little buggy lives.

"May I speak to Ms. Trimble, please?" Rosemary made a face at the telephone. She loved her work, but Ms. Trimble was the most difficult and defensive author who had ever lived, probably who ever would live. "This is Rosemary Jenkins, researcher from *I Am Woman* magazine. How are you?"

Ms. Trimble was fine. Of course she was fine. But

already the edge had begun in her voice. She could make, "I'm fine, thank you" sound like, "Go to hell you slimy invasive yodeling parasite."

Rosemary braced herself and asked a few pointed questions about sources in Ms. Trimble's latest article. Ms. Trimble sputtered and bristled, then she huffed and she puffed and she blew her ego up. Rosemary's ears listened; her mouth kept asking the questions. Her pen sketched a picture of herself and Rob on top of her building, surrounded by a meadow full of giant rats. One rat had a particularly nasty expression on its face and under this rat she wrote, "Ms. Trimble." Then on the top of the picture, she drew a man flying in for the rescue in tights and a flowing cape.

Not that she was the type who needed rescuing. She could make her own life happen, thank you. But something had been churning in Rosemary for a while, besides the desire to find the man who was Her Destiny. Some very deep and basic longing that wasn't being nurtured in the hot dusty crowded lonely city. Some longing for peace and simplicity.

The kind of life she'd had in Lazy Pines. Where people were who they seemed to be, and most of them seemed kind and generous and helpful. Old Mr. Cudahy, with his stories full of wisdom, and dear Dolores Thompson, never without caring advice no matter what your problem, and sweet Mavis Tattersall down at the Anchor Barn, who embodied love for her neighbor with a zeal few could match.

Where if you passed a construction site, the men would tip their hard hats and respectfully ask how your family was, and if the wind blew hard, it blew the scent of pine and the sea, not dust and grit and who knew what. And if you bumped into someone, they said, "Oh, pardon me, my fault entirely," and wished you the happiest day possible instead of cursing you all the way back to your ancestors' ancestors.

That kind of place.

She finished annoying Ms. Trimble-Rat and hung up with a long sigh, part relief, part yearning. One more swallow of lukewarm polyphenols, and she got up to go to the office library and confirm the sources for the article. But of course, as it always did when she needed to go anywhere, her phone rang.

"What…Rosemary? It's Dad. Am I calling at a bad time?"

"No time you call is bad." Rosemary plopped into her chair, leaned back and smiled at the ceiling. Every call from her father began with the same exchange.

"How was your date?"

"Not so spectacular." Rosemary peered around to be sure Poor Rob wasn't within earshot.

"This fellow not your Destiny, eh?" Her Dad chuckled. "Speaking of which, I saw Steve Judson yesterday."

Rosemary pushed away her annoyance at her father's teasing and sat bolt upright. "Steve? In town? Was he—does he—is he—"

"Easy does it. He just moved back to Lazy Pines, to coach football over at the high school. Still single, too, from what I gathered. He asked how you were."

The sensuous shiver Rob had failed to arouse cascaded through Rosemary's body without the slightest hesitation. Steve. Back in Lazy Pines. Asking how she was. "What did he say? Exactly?"

"He said exactly, 'How is Rosemary?'"

"But *how* did he say it?"

Her father gave an exasperated sigh. "He said it like he wanted to know how you were."

"But like he *really* wanted to know? Or just like—"

"Rosemary, he wanted to know how you were. I said you were fine. He said 'Give her my love.'"

His love. *Oh wow.* "How have you been, Dad?" Rosemary did not want to change the subject. She wanted to know if Steve still had that one adorable dimple in his right cheek; if his body could still inspire its own religion; if he still thought about that night in the basement; if he regretted never mentioning the kisses or pursuing her afterward, though of course he couldn't with that girlfriend he had at the time, or sort-of girlfriend. Who knew with Steve, who was always so kind and courteous and attentive to everyone? Then he left town for college in Massachusetts, and Rosemary left town for college in Connecticut, and they got involved in their lives. Until recently, keeping him a distant fond memory had been okay. For the most part.

But she had to change the subject on the phone with her father, because passionate longing could become extremely embarrassing during a normal conversation.

"I'm fine." Distant fumbling sounds came over the phone. "Yesterday I found sea rocket on our front rocks. Never seen it there before. Where's my...oh, here it is."

Rosemary grinned at the elegant, balding, mustached picture of her widowed father she kept on her desk. He personified the absentminded professor—even in retirement when he was technically no longer a professor. Especially when he was writing a book, which he currently was, on edible marine plants. "Sea rocket. That's great, Dad."

"So…how are the plans coming for your trip?"

"My trip." Rosemary got the same wave of impatient irritation in the pit of her stomach she got every time she thought about having to organize the trip. "Oh…fine."

"Haven't planned it yet, eh? Look, why traipse around some foreign—"

A loud crash came through the receiver. Rosemary tensed, then relaxed when she heard her father's patented foul language, which sounded sort of like, "Danga-blastin-racka-fracka," only all mumbled under his breath like an angry cartoon character.

"What was I…oh yes. Your trip. Why don't you come up and traipse around here instead?"

Rosemary frowned over at the wall on her left. Give up the chance to see Paris? The City of Lovers? The city she'd dreamed of visiting since girlhood?

She frowned at the wall on her right. Give up her certain meeting with Jean-Jacques or Jean-Claude or Jean-Whatever on the fabled banks of the Seine?

"And—" her father's voice turned sly "—you can find out exactly how much love Steve wanted to send."

Rosemary's breath came in with a gasp and went out in a soft "Ohh." She stood up out of her chair and clutched her free hand to her head, feeling as if she were about to announce her own salvation to her office mates.

In the space of one phone call she had the possibility of Lazy Pines and Steve all at once. Like Dorothy in *The Wizard of Oz*, happiness could be lying right in her own backyard. With no jet lag or visas or language barrier to complicate matters. She might just as easily find what she'd been longing for in good old Lazy Pines.

And maybe she'd discover Her Destiny was the one man she'd never stopped dreaming about.

Steve.

RYAN WALKED into the small immaculate house, motioning his partner, Jennifer, to check the kitchen while he went toward the bedroom. The body was here, just a matter of time until they found it. He couldn't tell why he knew; just an instinct that Death had been recently and very well rewarded.

He pushed open the bedroom door and took a deep breath; his gut tightened with familiar sickness before professional interest took over. White female; early thirties; gunshot to the head; dressed in black and white; everything in the room spray-painted black or draped in white sheets so the only sources of color were the victim's blood and the lifeless red bird nestled between her crossed arms.

The Cardinal had struck again.

Jordan Phillips scowled at the screen and saved the document to his hard disk. Nice visual; he liked the idea of the black-and-white room with the two red symbols of death, but the scene still needed something. The whole book needed something. He checked his watch. Thursday, six o'clock, August 2. A week behind in his extremely tight schedule.

He got a beer from his small kitchen, popped off the top, took the first swig, and gave a loud sigh of exasperation. Over the course of the next several weeks, his hero detective, Ryan, would have to hunt and trap the Cardinal with his lovely new partner, Jennifer. The book had to be finished by late fall or Jordan risked losing his contract and the momentum he'd started with the recent release of his first thriller.

The doorbell rang; Jordan rolled his eyes. What new delight awaited him this evening? Another vaguely legitimate charity? Another attempt to convert him to the religion-of-the-week? Or, best yet, the opportunity for an extended chat with another of Lazy Pines' scintillating citizens. If he hadn't absolutely *had* to move back here…

"Hello and good evening to you, dear." Old Dolores Thompson held up a basket of pink-and-green wooly things, consulted a worn piece of paper on which must be written her appointed speech, and cleared her throat.

Jordan sighed, ruffled his hair, and took a long swig of beer, trying to look as menacing and degenerate as possible to cut her visit short. He had to work out what to do about Ryan and Jennifer. There was no chemistry between them. Ryan even sent Jennifer away so he could discover the body alone. He never would have done that with Ada, his partner in the first book. Ryan and Ada had been so hot for each other their guns had singed their uniforms.

"We, the Lazy Pines Daughters of Charity are raising money for the annual Lazy Pines Talent Show. The proceeds will go to them not so fortunate than what we are ourselves. We are selling these most adorable crocheted doilies for the mere and measly sum of only five dollars to whoever so wants to assist us in our noble adventure."

Dolores smiled, obviously relieved to have gotten the speech out, and craned her neck to peek past Jordan into the tiny house his parents let him use. No doubt she hoped to glimpse something writerly and vaguely pornographic that would keep the Daughters titillated for weeks on end.

Jordan put his beer between his thighs, pulled his wallet out of his jeans pocket and extracted five dollars. The real trouble was that his new heroine, Jennifer, didn't grab him the way Ada had. He pictured Ada, auburn hair massed behind her, slender body strong and graceful, hazel eyes snapping with light and intelligence.

From the moment he started writing that first book, he knew Rosemary Jenkins would be the perfect model for Ada, partner and sometimes-lover to Ryan. Rosemary had the look he wanted, the energy, the determination. Purely an artistic choice—or so he'd fooled himself into thinking.

"Here." He handed Dolores the five, then raised his hand to stop her reaching into her little basket. "Forget the doily."

Dolores's features expanded into astonishment. "No doily?"

He shook his head. The problems began when he noticed Ada becoming more of the book's focus than Ryan, when the descriptions of her became more tender, more loving, more erotic. When the lines between Ada and Rosemary, Ryan and Jordan had begun to blur. "I've got tons of doilies."

"You do?" Dolores frowned in confusion. "Did one of the Daughters already—"

"No, no. You're the only one." Jordan had decided immediately to make that first book an emotional spring-cleaning. Exorcise the hold Rosemary Jenkins had kept on him for the last decade-plus. Indulge his passion in a private on-page affair, then put her in an envelope and send her off to his agent. At the end of the book when Jordan couldn't bring himself to kill Ada off, he had her request a transfer—to make sure Rosemary got as far out of the realm of possibility in fiction as she was in real life.

"Then how?"

He stared at Dolores. Was she still here? "How what?"

"How do you have so many doilies, dear?"

Oh, that. "I, uh, I make my own, Dolores."

Dolores's painted-on eyebrows shot up.

Jordan put his wallet away, retrieved his beer from between his legs, yawned and scratched his belly. Time to end this particular visit. "Yeah, I sit up nights in my living room—naked usually—and I just crochet my little heart out." He leaned forward; Dolores shrunk back, eyes the size of quarters. "We writers have our little quirks, you know? But Dolores…"

He leaned closer; she practically did the limbo to get away from him. "Don't tell anyone," he whispered.

Dolores shook her head so the wrinkly skin on her neck waved back and forth like a rooster's wattle. "No, dear…not a soul," she breathed.

"Good." He winked. "Bye, Dolores. Come back soon."

"G'bye." She turned and hobbled off the front stoop and down the street as if the Furies were chasing her.

Jordan chuckled and went back inside, then wandered out onto his back porch, wondering how long before the Daughters of Charity came by after dark to watch him crochet in the nude. People in Lazy Pines had nothing better to do with their narrow minds.

He sat down on an overturned crate and watched the gulls wheel and dive for their dinner at the mouth of the Soonadee River. Maybe he should bring Ada back. She and Ryan worked so well together. The current between them had carried the whole first book along….

He scowled at his idiocy. He wasn't going to go through that emotional upheaval again. Nor was he going to have his career hijacked by some woman he hadn't seen in ten years. He and Rosemary hadn't even been more than friends, though they'd always been close. The one time he'd kissed her, when the power went out at John Langley's party, she thought he was someone else. When the lights came back up she'd been all misty-eyed, staring at that megamuscled mini-brain jock, Steve Judson, as if he'd just proposed marriage.

At that moment, Jordan hadn't had the heart to bust up her dream-come-true. He'd tried a few days later, though. Even tried to kiss her again, when the words didn't come out the way he wanted. But he hadn't aimed right and the kiss had gone wide. She'd laughed and shied away and said those words he most hated to hear, "But Jordan! We're *buddies*."

Jordan scowled, took a long swallow of beer, and, just this once, allowed himself to remember. His mind went back over that first kiss like an underprivileged kid set loose in a toy store with a thousand dollars. She'd been incredible. Her mouth smooth and warm and sweet—the heat had come on between them full force in an instant, like somebody had struck an entire box of matches at once. Explosive. Searing. He'd been hard-pressed not to rip her—

"Hi Jordan, whatcha doin'?" Five-year-old neighbor, Casey, took a flying leap off his back porch next door and ran over to stand at the border between their properties. He held up a figure bristling with weaponry. "I gotta new Power Brute Attackeroid, wanna see? My mom says I can come over, but only if you say okay."

"Okay." Jordan forced his thoughts back into G-rated territory and smiled at his precocious neighbor. Saved from senseless mooning by youth and molded plastic.

Casey hurled himself across the grass and up onto Jordan's porch. "See? He's got super power action laser weapons, and...um, um...a thing here that makes his kill light go on." He pushed a tiny button, hands trembling with excitement; a dull red glow went on in the creature's chest. "Isn't that cool?"

"Way cool." Jordan reached over and rubbed his hand over the spiked tops of Casey's blond hair. The boy was the only thing in this suffocating town he enjoyed.

"My dad got it for me 'cause I kept my room clean for a whole calendar page." He swooped the figure around and made a series of loud explosion noises, followed by the shrill dying screams of countless victims.

Jordan grinned. Testosterone in action, aged five.

"Hey, Jordan? My mom said you left Lazy Pines a long time ago and...um, um...she wants to know how come you're back, but she told me not to ask, but I wanna know, too, so I decided to ask anyhow."

Jordan considered his beer bottle. How did you explain to a young boy that the minute you became physically involved with a woman you could no longer do what you loved most? "You ever heard of writer's block?"

"I can't write so good yet. And I gave my blocks to my baby brother. He can't build with 'em, but he likes to knock down stuff."

"Well, writer's block is like...it's like..." Jordan struggled to put the concept into a five-year-old's realm of experience. "It's like having a broken TV when there's something on you really want to watch."

"You couldn't watch TV? My mom doesn't let me so much. I hate that."

Jordan smiled and tried again. "I couldn't write my book in the city. There were too many...distractions." He gestured out at the flat marshy land behind his house. "Here it's quiet."

Quiet. Dull. Life-suppressing. What he wouldn't give for a Red Sox game at Fenway Park right now, with forty-three thousand of his closest friends. But at least here he could work. When his writing ability had ground to a halt barely one scene into his second novel, he knew something had to change or he'd blow what his agent had called an extremely promising career. By sheer trial and error he'd figured out what caused the sudden block.

Karen. Susan. Barbara. Elizabeth.

At first he hoped it was the lack of sleep that inevitably followed a night of carousing. Then he tried to blame it on some hitherto unknown allergy. Alcohol? Perfume? Latex? He even gave lingering-Catholic-guilt-over-premarital-sex a shot, since he often experienced emotional restlessness and a vague feeling of remorse along with physical satiation. But that wouldn't explain the times the block came before the sexual relationship had begun.

In the end, he realized he could only be in denial so long. Those morning-after hours in front of the keyboard, in near-panic over his blank mind and stuttering fingers finally convinced him of the need to face the truth. If he wanted to keep writing, he had to cut to the chaste.

"Hey, Jordan? How come you look kinda cranky today?"

"Because I don't think I like the woman in my book." Even after he'd composed pages of character backstory—Jennifer's whole life prior to the book's opening—in the end, she was still flat to him; he didn't really like her.

Casey regarded him solemnly. "Is she bad?"

"No, she's not bad. But I can't seem to get to know her. It's hard to write about strangers."

Casey frowned. He fingered his toy, flew a few quiet bombing raids, then lifted his face back up to Jordan. "How come you don't write about some lady you know?"

"I tried that, Casey. But it's hard writing about women you like, too." The options were poor. Rosemary was out of the question. If he picked a different woman from his past, the block could come back. There were no appealing women in Lazy Pines—which was exactly the reason he'd come back here.

"I liked Zoe but not anymore because she sat on my head at recess. You could write a story about a girl you don't like."

Jordan stared at him. Blinked. Stared some more. His rusted brain screeched slowly back into action. As Casey would put it—*Duh.* "Caaa-*sey!* Diiinner."

The woman's voice made Casey scoop up his Power…Beast…whatever and dash back to his own yard, calling out a cheery "See ya later" over his skinny shoulder.

Jordan waved, chugged the last of his beer and went back inside, bursting with renewed energy. Of course. Someone he'd never been intimate with, someone he'd never want to be intimate with. No risk of bringing on the block that way. Someone local, preferably, so he could observe her in action and record her characteristics more accurately. That shouldn't be too—

"Ha!" He clenched his fingers and pumped his fist in the air. Mavis Tattersall, manager of the Anchor Barn. Perfect. A sour witch who hated his guts, but she had a certain earthy appeal that would suit Jennifer to perfection.

Most important, she was not Rosemary. Nor would she ever be.

He grabbed his notebook and set off for the Anchor Barn, adrenaline shooting through him. Like it or not, Mavis would rejuvenate Jennifer and save his fledgling career from the dungheap.

2

JORDAN STRODE down Main Street, wincing at the muddy dead fish smell of low tide permeating the town, trying to merge Mavis and Jennifer in his mind. The transfer of images had the potential to work well, but he'd need to be careful describing the character. Mavis's contribution had to be well disguised so none of the locals would recognize her. The last thing Jordan needed was to supply more grist for the Lazy Pines gossip mill. He'd had a tough enough time being back among these suspicious, hostile people without alienating them further.

Luckily, he had excellent experience in that regard. His description of Rosemary had been masterfully deceptive, if he could allow for a little immodesty. Her own father could read the book and not recognize her. Of course, her father didn't recognize himself occasionally, but the point stood.

Jordan chuckled as he turned the corner onto Ripley Way, past the line of apologetic Colonials, trying not to stumble on the uneven cracked sidewalk. Every news-hungry tongue-wagging vulture in town would read about Jordan Phillips's youthful infatuation with Rosemary Jenkins and not have a clue what a rumor feast they were missing. Not a clue about the dark, passionate secret he kept in his heart.

That is, he used to keep in his heart. Until he got rid of it.

He pushed open the bell-jangling door to the Anchor Barn and walked inside. Mavis Tattersall stood behind the cash register, talking to old Mr. Cudahy, in the booth nearest the door. Jordan eyed her carefully and congratulated himself on his insight. She was perfect. Blond hair done in a gravity-defying style—he'd change that of course; body slightly thick—he'd slim her down; a little past the age he wanted—no problem.

Her features were plain, the set to her jaw stubborn and almost angry, her lips a tough line, her expression cold and merciless. Pretty good material for a hard-boiled detective.

But her eyes made her perfect. Blue and deep, imbued with a sensuality she'd probably change if she could. Those eyes would intrigue Ryan; make him want to search beyond the make-my-day attitude to find the woman beneath.

Jordan, however, just itched to get her down on paper so he'd have to spend as little time in her medicinal presence as possible.

He moved forward; Mavis looked him up and down as if he had a visible sexually transmitted disease. He looked her over in return, keeping his mind open to whatever descriptive images flew into it.

"Pornography," Mavis snapped. "You'll go straight to hell. I'd pray for you if I didn't know it was a waste of my time."

"Nonsmoking," he responded acidly, banishing the first descriptive image which involved Mavis and an airborne broomstick. Apparently his first book had already stirred some interest among Lazy Pines' residents. No doubt he'd have more prissy reactions to look forward to. He didn't need to ask what she meant by pornography. The passionate love scene between Rose—he caught himself—Ada and her lover, Ryan, had plunged Jordan into a fevered sweat that lasted over a week. Good thing Mavis had no idea he wrote the book about Rosemary or she'd sic an exorcist on him.

"You can sit there." Mavis slapped a menu into his hand, and gestured toward a booth near the rest rooms as if she'd rather escort him personally through Satan's gates.

"Thanks." Jordan ignored her and started toward a table with a view of the river, where he could watch her tend to her duties.

"She's an innocent girl and you made a slut out of her." Mavis's booming voice stopped him in his tracks.

"Excuse me?" He turned and gaped at her sour, Grinchy frown. What the hell did she mean by that?

"You heard me." Mavis's eyes shot hostile beams that could probably dislodge wallpaper. "I have nothing more to say to you."

Jordan sighed, even as he noted the particular shade her eyes turned when angry. People like her made cannibal aliens from Mars look like the cast of *Father*

Knows Best. He took another step toward his chosen table and felt a weak tug on his sleeve.

"Author, author!" Old Mr. Cudahy raised a trembling hand in salute.

Jordan nodded tightly. The old man was always either in this booth or leaning on the counter at Howard's General Store across the street. Jordan's theory was that he vaporized into some other dimension when he left either establishment.

"Liked your book." Mr. Cudahy regarded him somberly, his pale eyes watery under their wrinkled lid topping. "Reminded me of the time my fourth wife went to the Lazy Pines masquerade dressed as a doughnut, and no one knew who she was. But I know her and I knew."

Jordan took in a deep breath and reminded himself that he, too, might end up this way someday and he'd hate any young man to be thinking what he was thinking right at this moment. "I'm not sure I can see the connection, Mr. Cudahy."

"You got her down just right m'boy. Jumped out like she was standing in the room with me."

"What are you—"

"Rosemary, m'boy. Rosemary. Who do you think?"

Jordan stared. Behind him, Mavis humphed loudly. Jordan stared some more, unable even to turn and see what expression Mavis used to accompany her humphs. A sick feeling launched an invasion of his stomach. Old Cudahy couldn't tell you what day it was half the time and he'd seen Rosemary in the pages of Jordan's book as if she'd been labeled. Was that what Mavis meant when she—

"Hello, young Jordan!" Billy Deemer, who wasn't older than Jordan, but was several times his width, ambled over from a booth across the room, beaming as usual, and slapped Jordan on the back. "Loved your book. Very thrilling. Very exciting. Had to go for my inhaler a couple of times. Know what I mean?" He elbowed Jordan in the ribs.

Mavis humphed so loudly her vocal cords sounded in danger of rupturing.

Jordan redirected his stare at Billy, every hair on his body standing up in apprehension. Had Billy recognized Rosemary, too?

"Oh, come on, Mavis, love. We're all adults here." Billy winked at her and chuckled, then turned abruptly to Jordan again. "And what a fine portrait of our Rosemary. You caught her exactly."

Jordan clutched at the back of a booth seat to make sure something still existed firmly as he knew it, and mumbled something unintelligible even to his own ears. The urge to run screaming out of the restaurant pummeled his instincts.

How had they guessed? How had they all guessed? Rosemary had been totally transformed. Altered beyond any possible recognition. Jordan had told no one of the inspiration for Ada. How had they—

"She's back in town." Mr. Cudahy's head wagged up and down as if he'd forgotten how to turn his nod mechanism off.

"That's what I heard!" Billy joined in the nodding,

setting off a chain reaction in his astounding cascade of chins. "Her father's very happy. Told me so himself."

A river of cold sweat began to form on Jordan's body. Rosemary? Back in town? Just as the book had come out and everyone seemed to know?

He forced himself to breathe normally. For crying out loud. This was not the end of the universe. Rosemary was just a woman he'd had a crush on, years ago, and had kissed once in a dark basement. If she found out about the book, she found out. She'd be flattered and that would be the end of it. Like he kept telling himself, he'd gotten her out of his system.

"Fact is…" Mr. Cudahy's eyes flew beyond Jordan and his lips twitched. "Fact is, she's not only back in town."

"Nope." Billy slapped his enormous thigh and chuckled. "That's not all."

Jordan resisted the urge to roll his eyes. He wouldn't even ask what the hell they were talking about. The people in this town personified irritation.

"Well, hello there, sister!" Mavis's voice rang out in a way Jordan had never heard before: warm, welcoming, even affectionate. Who on earth could bring on that kind of a transformation?

He swung around, intending to register carefully the change in Mavis's face, and stopped when he saw who had come into the restaurant.

Thick auburn hair topped a slender body; extraordinary hazel eyes crinkled into the smile her full lips directed at Mavis; long graceful arms flung wide as if to embrace the whole town.

Jordan's breath rushed into his body, as if opening his mouth had ruptured an internal vacuum. Somewhere someone had turned on an electric instrument that seemed to be ringing directly into his ears. The invasion in his stomach increased to a full-scale war involving every emotion he was capable of feeling.

He forced himself to blink and look again.

Right in front of him, full of life and light and air and motion, in the way he'd spent years observing and months trying to capture and preserve on paper.

Rosemary.

ROSEMARY TURNED from sweet, loving Mavis, absolutely bursting with the warmth and joy of being back in Lazy Pines, and tilted her head at the tall, dark, brown-eyed, wavy-haired man staring at her as if he'd left most of his brain cells behind when he walked into the Anchor Barn.

"Jordan Phillips!" She hugged him, somewhat surprised when his arms hesitated, then pulled her into an embrace that didn't feel like glad-to-see-you, but more like thank-God-you-survived-the-nuclear-blast. "My old buddy!"

His body flinched; his arms released her. She smiled up into his eyes, which she had forgotten were so intense, like he was thinking profound and probably passionate thoughts all day long while the rest of the world wondered what was for dinner and whether they'd make the bus home or stand out on the platform and get rained on.

In fact she'd forgotten a great deal about Jordan which was too bad because he'd really been one of her best friends at Lazy Pines High. For a while she'd even wondered if he was Her Destiny, before she'd realized of course Her Destiny lay with Steve. "I didn't know you were back in Lazy Pines."

He mumbled something she couldn't quite understand about his parents' house and writing and quiet, and she wondered if maybe poor Jordan had started doing drugs after she knew him and not stopped in time, or maybe he'd been in some accident and sustained a touch of brain damage.

"Jordan has written a novel, Rosemary. It came out only last month." Darling, jolly Billy Deemer moved forward to greet her and nearly smothered her in a rather off-smelling embrace that made her wonder if he'd been having water trouble in his house again. Funny how she remembered him smarter looking.

"A novel! That's wonderful. I can't wait to read it." She smiled at Jordan again, a little concerned this time because he did not look at all well and she was worried he'd have some kind of seizure or pass out right onto the floor of the Anchor Barn, which, let's face it, wasn't quite as clean as it used to be.

"How's your father?" Jordan asked as if he were very, very anxious to change the subject. Perhaps he was embarrassed about the book he'd written. Maybe the characters hadn't come out the way he'd hoped.

"He's fine. Though yesterday he tried to make a

blueberry dessert gelatin out of Irish moss for his book, and didn't quite rinse the fish taste out.''

She glanced surreptitiously around the restaurant to find Steve, hoping Jordan didn't notice her doing so. You never knew what kind of mood swings people with brain damage could suffer. She should recommend a dose of motherwort or a nice cup of skullcap tea to calm his nerves. But her father had told her Steve came here often to eat, and Rosemary would rather engineer a ''chance'' meeting than have to call and announce her arrival like some prodigal princess returning.

''Terrific book.'' Wise, dear Mr. Cudahy nodded his head like one of those little animals people put in the back of their car, grinning as if he had a secret he wouldn't share with the rest of the class no matter what the teacher threatened. ''You should read it. It'll surprise you. Like the time my third dog Rex hid in my closet and jumped out at me after dark. Nearly swallowed my teeth.''

''Hmm.'' Rosemary scanned a few more booths. Mr. Cudahy named all his dogs Rex. She remembered the surprising one. Somehow, though, the story had seemed more riveting the first several times she heard it. Her eyes lit on one broad-shouldered blond-haired man near the front window. If she could just edge a little closer to the—

''Looking for someone?''

Rosemary started. Her eyes jumped right back to Jordan's which were looking directly into hers as he waited for her answer, and her own eyes couldn't help wondering how they thought anything else could have been worth looking at. "Well, no, not exactly…that is, yes. Steve Judson."

"Steve." His usually sexy mouth scrunched up into this tight-looking line that didn't make him look angry really, but extremely frustrated and a little disgusted. Rosemary took another quick peep over his shoulder and determined that the large blond man couldn't be Steve because she felt no pull, no energy, no sense of Her Fate emanating from him. All she could sense was that if he'd been stupid enough to order the Admiral's Platter, he'd just have to live with the indigestion later.

"Steve's probably still at football practice with the kids."

"Of course." She nodded up at Jordan, then just stood and stared because she couldn't think of anything she'd rather do right at that particular moment. Had she not known that Steve waited for her somewhere in this town, she would have shivered and gotten rather warm from the way Jordan was staring back at her. As if he wanted to devour her whole. Perhaps he needed a woman. There were probably several he'd find attractive in Lazy Pines. Mavis, for one. Maybe Rosemary could help him land Mavis.

Her excitement rose, the more she thought about the match. They'd be good for each other, Mavis and Jordan, with Mavis so dear and loving, and Jordan so kind, and thoughtful, and intelligent, and talented, and sexy, and very, very good-looking, and gentle and dangerous all at once—the kind of guy who would look really really great in a white, billowing-shirted pirate costume, holding the mast with one hand, pointing toward the enemy with a sword in the other, and—

Rosemary reined herself in. Mavis. He'd be great for Mavis. Mavis was already coming over for lunch the day after next. Rosemary could invite Jordan right now and launch her matchmaking plan while Mavis escorted a tourist couple to a table on the other side of the Anchor Barn.

"Jordan," she smiled innocently, "why don't you stop by the house sometime day after tomorrow? Around lunchtime? Mavis will be there, too."

"I'd like that." He tipped his head slightly, and grinned his gentle, dangerous, pirate mouth into a grin that made him very close to breathtaking and nearly irresistible. Rosemary had to exhale quickly to keep from saying, *Oh my Lord.* She'd absolutely have to rethink her prognosis about the brain damage.

And if it weren't for her blissful future with Steve, she might be tempted to rethink her idea of finding Jordan any woman that wasn't her.

ROSEMARY WAFTED along the length of the widow's walk on top of her father's house. Well, she wasn't exactly sure she wafted, but she was sure on a warm, summer, full-moon night when you wore only a cotton nightgown and the sea shimmered restlessly in front of you, and the shadows in the woods behind you were etched in silver, that wafting could be the only way to go.

She lifted her arms high to embrace the white light, which shone here in Lazy Pines unhampered by build-

ings and city wattage. She lifted her arms to embrace
the night and the world and the moonlight and all her
fellow men because finally, finally her dream would
come true. Tomorrow she had a date with Steve.

She'd called him, fingers shaking with nerves and
eagerness as she punched in his number, her voice
tremulous and husky after hearing his deep tone over
the line.

His voice, however, hadn't sounded quite as tremulous and husky in return as she had expected, but then
perhaps he had been a little taken aback by her call.
Midnight might be a tad late, but on a moonlit summer
evening, there simply wasn't a better time to make a
date with Destiny. Of course he'd agreed readily to see
her. Of course he'd felt the undercurrent running between them of what this meeting truly signified. The
rest of their lives. Together.

Heavy running footsteps sounded behind the house,
where the road wound around the point and passed by
her father's place. Rosemary crouched down and
peered out between the railings of the fence. Of course
it was Steve running over to see her, moments after
hearing her voice on the phone, tremulous and husky
as it had been. Who else, driven by the insane desire
to see her again after so many years? And who could
blame him? Their passion would light the night like a
second sun.

Rosemary squinted into the darkness at the figure.
Definitely male. Definitely built. Definitely stopping
opposite the house. She could hear the heavy quiet
breathing of a body used to exercise, see the bright

moonlight glistening on the hair and skin of a naked, rather magnificent chest and torso.

A light breeze fanned her at just the right moment to cool her suddenly heated cheeks.

Jordan.

Why had he come? Why was he stopping here? She stood suddenly and leaned over the railing.

"Rosemary." His whisper floated up to her and made her feel just a little weak-kneed and shivery. Imagine how she'd feel if it had been Steve as it was supposed to be. She'd be very glad of the railing to keep her from pitching off the roof.

"I'll be right down." She stopped in her room to pull on shorts and a shirt, a little giddy and eager to see her buddy, then ran downstairs and out the door.

He still waited outside, in the same place he'd been before. A shirt now covered his upper body; at a distance the darkness still covered his face. Rosemary walked toward him, inhaling the scent of balsam pines, the salty sea and then the not-too-strong male scent of Jordan, which smelled sort of dangerous and exciting in the near-darkness. Mavis would be a lucky woman. She deserved a man like Jordan.

"Hi," Rosemary said, sort of out of breath and heart-thumpy. "What are you doing out this late?"

"Couldn't sleep."

She nodded. He had that look on his face again, the one where he came across as held-in-check carnivorous, but in a sexy tiger way, not a greedy hyena way like so many men. She'd really better get busy setting him up with Mavis before he got so desperate he came on to her instead.

Rosemary turned and started up the rough pebbly road next to Jordan, trying not to become too overwhelmed at the thought of him coming on to her. One day away from realizing Her Destiny, such thoughts were quite unseemly. But walking like this next to him was bringing back an almost overwhelming longing for memories of the time they spent together as schoolkids.

"Jordan, do you remember that night we had to walk up and down this road for hours, in the dark just like this? The night a few days after graduation when I bet the boys baseball team I could drink faster than they could?"

"I'm surprised you remember anything about that night."

"I remember the air, soft and dark like it is now, I remember you trying to keep me quiet, and I remember an overwhelming urge to do the Charleston."

"I had bruises for days." He chuckled and leaned in so their shoulders met and stayed pressed together for a few steps, which managed to be brotherly and affectionate and thrilling all at once.

"I remember how sweet you were to take care of me when I'd been so stupid, and I remember…" Rosemary's feet stopped involuntarily in the middle of the road as if they could stop the path of her thoughts by not moving. That was the night Jordan had tried to kiss her. When she'd been so full of Steve's kiss from the party a few days earlier that the idea of kissing anyone else had seemed like heresy, especially her buddy, Jordan. But now with the same soft air and shadowy trees whispering in the moonlight, the memory seemed ready to ambush her in an entirely new way, one that left her a little shaky and warm in places Jordan hadn't ever warmed before.

He turned and kept walking, and Rosemary started her feet up again, wondering if he was remembering the near-kiss, too, and what he thought about it now. But since she had to hurry a few steps to catch up to him, he obviously wasn't prepared to go into it in any depth at the moment.

"What brought you back to Lazy Pines?" He asked the question, not casually, not conversationally, but reverently, as if he still couldn't quite believe she strolled along next to him here, as if her coming back were the greatest gift he could imagine.

Rosemary sighed. Jordan Phillips could get a woman more than a little dizzy if she wasn't careful. If she didn't already have a clearheaded idea of the who and where of her future. "I needed a break from the city. I needed to come back to be among generous, honest, loving people living straightforward, purposeful lives."

He gave a snort of laughter not at all suited to the occasion. "You know anyone like that here? I'd love to meet them."

"You've met them. You just don't know them. There's a big difference. If you were just a little nicer to people you could probably find out."

He made another scornful noise and Rosemary let the subject drop for now. She'd make sure he understood about Lazy Pines some day.

"Why did *you* come back?" She'd asked him before, at the Anchor Barn, but he'd had that temporary brain damage and hadn't been too clear on the answer. "You hated this place the whole time we were growing up. I just about dropped my drawers when I found out you live here."

A sigh came out of him when she said "drop my drawers" that competed with the swish of the waves in the bay and sounded a bit like longing. Really, he'd been single too long. And with his body exerting this strange kind of pull that kept her bumping into him on every other step, she was starting to think she'd been single too long as well.

"I came back because I couldn't write in the city."

His voice sounded gentle and deep in the gentle deep night. His stride matched hers; the moonlight lit the woods around them eerie white like a stage light. Oh gosh, Mavis would have it so good.

"Mavis likes to write, too."

"She does?" He did not sound particularly impressed. In fact he sounded a little astounded, which proved how little he knew Mavis and how much he would grow to like her.

"She writes poetry. She wrote a poem for me on my eighteenth birthday, would you like to hear it?"

"Sure."

He did not sound particularly enthusiastic. But he would love the poem, and Mavis as well someday.

Rosemary cleared her throat, found a patch of moonlight in which to do justice to Mavis's lovely words, and put her hand over her heart. "'Friend, friend, you are my friend. When I have things to talk about, you are always there. Friend, friend, you are my friend. And I thank you. A whole lot.'''

Silence fell in the deep gentle darkness of the woods and it struck Rosemary that she had not really thought about that poem in the last ten years and maybe it had lost a bit over time. "Back then it meant a lot to me."

"I'm sure." His words came out a little strangled sounding.

Rosemary frowned. Shared love of writing would not be what would bring Mavis and Jordan together. Something else, then. "You should get to know Mavis better."

"Believe it or not I'm trying."

"Oh." His statement surprised her so much she couldn't say more. Had he already picked Mavis out for his own? Had Rosemary merely been an antenna for the interest passing between them?

"What does she spend her time thinking about?"

His question surprised her further, and delighted her. At least it would have delighted her if she wasn't suddenly feeling something a little like jealousy, which was ridiculous of course. After all, she and Jordan were taking this midnight stroll in the gentle and deep woods just so she could get him interested in Mavis. And lo and behold, he was already.

"Mavis thinks about…" Rosemary swallowed. Dear, lovely Mavis, with so much love for her fellow beings. What the heck did she think about? "She thinks about her fellow beings and what they like to…that is, what they like to…eat.''

"Eat?"

Rosemary grimaced at a nearby stump. He did not sound as if his fires of love had been kindled quite yet. He sounded as if Mavis matched curtain-hanging in the thrill category. "She also likes to watch golf on TV."

"Ah." They walked on in silence for a while, Rosemary desperately trying to think of something that would make Mavis sound utterly enticing.

"She has a nice garden at her house." The sea rhythm swished hypnotically; Rosemary's hand bumped Jordan's, and bumped it again, a nice warm hand she wanted to hold for the rest of their walk. "With Johnny-jump-ups and daylilies and—"

"What does she look like when she's happy? I've never seen her happy."

"When she's happy." Rosemary cast her mind back to try to hook some memory of sweet loving Mavis being happy, and came up empty. This would never do. If she was going to convince Jordan of Mavis's role as His Destiny, she'd have to come up with something. "Well, when she's happy, she…uh, smiles, and…" a vision of Jordan grinning at Rosemary in the restaurant popped into her mind, "her eyes crinkle at the corners and turn down at the edges like the whole world was put there for her to love and laugh at, and you can't believe how much you want to dive into that smile and hold it and keep it next to your heart until you—"

Jordan's face hit a patch of moonlight and Rosemary

realized she was getting a little carried away. In his view anyway. He looked a bit glazed over, like he couldn't quite imagine Mavis happy in just that way.

Rosemary sighed. Neither could she.

"Okay." He shook off his glaze and seemed to make a concentrated effort to focus on Mavis. "So she *is* happy sometimes. What makes her happy?"

"Ohhh gosh. Well, clean tables, hot food, full customers with good credit...." Rosemary wrinkled her nose. Mavis sounded a little narrow when one described her too exactly. Maybe exactness wasn't quite so necessary at the moment. "Then there's things like world peace, and discussing the true nature of man's propensity for—"

"What makes you happy, Rosemary?" He'd passed the patch of light and his question floated to her out of the anonymous darkness.

Rosemary heard herself make a little sound, kind of like a small gasp, but not of horror so much as astonishment that one little question said in a deep gentle voice in the moonlight could make her want to change Destinies immediately. She took control and made herself remember the kiss in the basement. Steve. Tomorrow she would see Steve and feel ten times what she felt tonight; ten times the longing, ten times the—

Jordan stopped and turned and took a step closer, his face illuminated by a new patch of moonlight. He touched the back of his hand to her cheek, causing the kind of explosion in her body she'd only experienced once before.

"What makes you happy?" He whispered the question this time, causing the most astonishing reaction throughout her system, like the finale of the world's biggest ever fireworks display, only more.

What made her happy? At the moment, with the Fourth of July going on inside her, there was only one response. Only one thing that could make her this happy, with this kind of wild excitement, and only one other that had made her even more happy, ten years ago. The memory of that other time with Steve as well as the blissful and fertile future Jordan had with Mavis would keep Rosemary from answering the question now as she instinctively wanted to, which was to look him straight in the eye and say, "You."

"Well, I don't know. Happy? Gee, uh, ice cream, Ferris wheels, nuclear disarmament…that kind of stuff."

He nodded, his face white in the moonlight, eyes black and blazing. Rosemary's fireworks increased and burned hotter until she experienced a near-total internal meltdown.

"Jordan." She felt and saw and heard him swallow at the sound of her voice, then he opened his mouth and answered, "Yes?" in the husky and tremulous voice Steve really should have been using on the phone.

"You know before, when I said I came back to Lazy Pines to get away from the city and see people I love?"

"Mmm?" He gave the impression "Mmm" comprised the current extent of his vocabulary, but he managed to imbue the sound with so much tenderness, Rosemary just wanted to die of it.

"It wasn't true, not really, not totally anyway." She let out a long, wavering sigh, which caused him to inhale, as if her breath merely transferred into his body across the cool night air between them. "I came back...to see if my Destiny might lie here in Lazy Pines after all."

"I see." His tone was gentle still, teasing now, but his gaze carried inside her where it must be enjoying the current orange-hot display of burned-out and melted sparklers and Roman candles. "Do you think it might?"

"I don't know right now." She half smiled, and tried to keep the wistful longing for what she would never have with Jordan Phillips off her face. "But I'll tell you tomorrow."

3

"I TOLD YOU, I was home Tuesday night." John "The Bomb" Donalds folded his arms across his chest, more protective than defiant.

Ryan exchanged glances with Jennifer. Were they finally getting close to the information they needed?

Jennifer smiled calmly. "Where were you Tuesday night, Mr. Donalds?"

Ryan suppressed a grin. If anyone could make the jerk crack, Jennifer could.

"I was home." The voice came out hoarser this time. A fidget; a swallow; a muscle jumping in his cheek. They almost had him.

Ada let her—

Jordan pounded the backspace button on his keyboard. Not Ada. Jennifer. Ada was the last book. Jennifer this one. Jenni-bleeping-fer.

Jennifer let her smile droop, then spread it on again, wider, sweeter, pushed back her long, auburn—

"For crying out loud." Jordan gestured impolitely toward the screen. Blond. Jenni-bleeping-fer was honey-bleeping-blond. Ada had been auburn.

Jennifer pushed back her— Jordan curled his lip,

unable to banish the picture of Rosemary pushing back her damn auburn hair.

Forget the hair.

Jennifer pushed back her chair. Ryan sent her a look of triumph. She had the bastard. She had him right where she wanted him. Like a worm dangling on her—

Jordan made a sound of disgust. What kind of cliché cesspool was that? He exited the document without bothering to save his work. His muse had deserted him, and he knew exactly why.

Last evening after a futile attempt at work, he'd been unable to relax, unable to sleep, unable even to summon the heart to sit naked in his living room when he heard the Daughters of Charity whispering outside his window. Besides, he didn't own a crochet hook.

Finally, his body twitching with nervous unproductive energy, he'd given up attempting anything even remotely constructive inside, and had gone out the back door for a jog. The entire way to Rosemary's, his brain had been screaming at his legs to take a different direction. What could he possibly gain by going past her house? Whereas he knew exactly what he had to lose— everything he'd spent the past five years working toward.

Jordan sneered at his Fred Flintstone screensaver and strode out of the house, pulling the creaky old door shut behind him. Rosemary had no right to come back now, just when his life had teetered back into balance. No right to walk into the Anchor Barn and render him as stuttering and speechless as a choking parrot. No right to hug him, spread her scent over and around him, and completely erode his mind's ability to protect itself from autoinduced idiocy.

Jordan struck down Main Street, heading for town to make sure he wouldn't repeat his mistake of last night. He'd foolishly indulged his desire to jog past her father's house, to spend a moment gazing at her window, maybe give in to a memory or two....

Nothing prepared him for the sight of Rosemary on the widow's walk in a drifting white nightgown, bending down toward him in the moonlight like Juliet herself. Nothing had prepared him for how it would feel to walk beside her again, enjoy the provocative—and often mysterious—way her mind worked, relive the natural rightness of their being together.

He'd been caught off guard once again. Now he had consequences to pay—a morning where his characters and his words were as flat and uninteresting as... as...flat, uninteresting things.

On impulse, Jordan walked into Howard's General Store and nearly bumped into Howard, bending over to unload lightbulbs from a box on the floor.

"Oh, hello there, Jordan." Howard straightened, took off his cap and then replaced it. "Haven't read more than a few chapters of your book, son. Must say it's a good 'un, though, so far. Like the parts with Rosemary 'specially. You done her just 'bout right."

Jordan nodded his thanks, resigned by now to his fate. He might as well be grateful that so far everyone had accepted his passionate tribute without comment.

Either they had a higher level of respect for him than he imagined, or they were even denser than he thought.

He glanced around, not really sure why he'd come in, and strolled over to examine the battery display case, still where it had been since boyhood, when he came in regularly to refill his flashlight for after-bedtime reading.

The worst part about last night—worse than his transformation into Testosterone Man the minute he saw Rosemary, worse than the torture of the occasional contact between their bodies and hands as they strolled down the road, worse than her hazel eyes glowing with moonlit earnestness while she recited Mavis's horrific poem—had been her reference to seeking Her Destiny here in Lazy Pines.

She might very well be talking about a change of life-style, away from the hectic pace of city life, but her eyes in the Anchor Barn when she'd been searching for Steve, told the ancient and powerful story of woman on a man hunt. If she'd felt half of what Jordan felt during their long-ago kiss, knowing Rosemary, she'd stop at nothing until she determined whether she and Steve were meant to be together. What that entailed didn't bear thinking about.

He picked up a package of batteries, turned it over absently, and wandered down the adjacent aisle. But when and if Rosemary found out Steve wasn't the phantom kisser, she'd be determined to find out who was. Granted, several men had been in the room at the time, but if she ever came after Jordan, his career could be in serious danger. He hadn't sweated and strained, braved dozens of rejections, and worked himself to near exhaustion over the past five years only to throw it away, even on someone like Rosemary.

"Why hello, Jordan! Someone just gave me a copy of your book. I so look forward to reading it."

Jordan greeted Dolores Thompson wearily, hating the fact of small-town life that required chatter everywhere he went. "I hope you enjoy it."

"Oh my, I'm sure I—" Her eyes darted to the shelves opposite, and back to Jordan, several times.

Jordan followed her glance and felt the slow, delightful boil of mischief overtake his frustration. He'd inadvertently wandered down the aisle with the art and craft projects. Facing him were dozens of skeins of yarn in brights and pastels.

He reached up to a soft blue. "Do you think this color would look good on me? I want to start a vest after I finish my set of happy elf pot holders."

"Well, I—I—" Dolores's gaze skittered up and down his body, then rested firmly on the yarn. Her wrinkled cheeks grew pinker by the second; her breathing accelerated. "It's a l-l-lovely color, Jordan, dear. You should enter the talent show with something you've... I—I—oh my, it's awfully hot. I believe I'm going to have to sit down."

Jordan led her over to a chair Howard kept in the store for bored spouses and bought her a ginger ale from the cooler near the front door, contrite for teasing her. He had no idea she'd react that dramatically. "Are you all right?"

Dolores took a long swig from the can, rapidly fanning herself with her free hand. "I'm fine now, thank you, dear. Just overcome, reliving a few memories of my youth." She winked up at him and for a second her vague eyes snapped into a sly, seductive focus that would have been a total turn-on in a woman a third of her age.

Jordan's jaw dropped. *Go, Dolores.* "Ah, me." She took another sip and sighed. "You know, sometimes I think it would be a lot easier on everyone if women and men lived separately and only got together at night when they...had to."

Jordan chuckled. "Amen to that."

He couldn't have put it better himself. The trouble with his writing today merely put into crystal perspective what role Rosemary should play in his life: None. After lunch at her place tomorrow—he couldn't resist the opportunity to observe Mavis outside the restaurant—all other contact would have to be kept minimal. That way, even if Rosemary discovered Steve had had a stunt double, she'd be less likely to pin the role on her "buddy" if Jordan was out of target range.

Jordan patted Dolores on the shoulder and said goodbye. She gazed at him with a still slightly dewy-eyed expression as he left the store, two things firmly resolved in his mind. First, for the sake of his career, he'd tell Rosemary he was leaving town. He'd pack up his car, drive off very publicly, and sneak back into the house to chain himself to his computer until she was safely home in New York.

Second, one of these nights, if they kept coming

around, he was going to show the Daughters of Charity some serious crocheting.

ROSEMARY PAUSED at the entrance to the Gilded Clam Shell Restaurant for the deepest, longest, most calming breath she could manage. She'd had several cups of skullcap tea already with little effect beyond the predictable one of causing numerous trips to the bathroom. Some things were just too important, too earth-shatteringly huge to be soothed, even by skullcap. In just one moment, one swing of the door, one step inside, she'd be with Steve.

She put her hand to the door, ready with all her heart and mind to be reunited with the one man she'd ever truly loved, and—

"Rosemary?"

Steve's voice behind her caused an immediate stoppage of all internal functions, followed by a roar of their resumption, kind of like when the Red Sea must have hurled itself back together after having been parted and quiet.

Rosemary swung around and put her hand to her eyes to block the sun setting romantically behind his towering figure. "Steve."

Oh, he looked splendid. Tall, blond, massive, masculine, handsome face almost glowing in the yellow light behind him.

Steve. At last. She could barely keep the tears back, barely keep from throwing herself at him and sobbing out her joy.

He stepped forward and took her into his arms for a

quick hug, which kind of smashed her up against the concrete of his chest, and she hurt a muscle in her neck from trying to hug him back and squeezing too hard.

But no matter. He was Steve and he was here and they were going to have a wonderful evening and end it on some glorious moonlit walk wrapped in each other's arms, confessing their undying retroactive love.

"Wanna go in? Great chow here, I'm starved."

She smiled in agreement and wondered whether he'd said things like "wanna" and "chow" in high school, which didn't exactly make him sound like a literary genius. But no matter. He was Steve; he was here, and he was hers.

They walked in and settled into a cozy booth with a view of the river emptying into the bay and a view of the pines and a view of the gulls and the herons and the rest of their lives together, and Steve grinned that special slightly goofy grin across the table at her and made her insides all contract and squeeze together with bliss, or they would have except they didn't seem particularly inclined to.

No matter. He was here and she was here and so on and so on.

"Steve, it's so good to see you. I've…thought of you often over the years and wondered how you were." She let him see in her smile and in her eyes exactly what direction her thoughts had taken when they concerned him, and waited for him to return the favor.

"I'm fine, fine. Doin' great. Football keeps me busy."

Rosemary tried not to notice the lack of returned favor and ignored her brain which commented a little unpleasantly that not much had changed; football always kept him busy. "I heard you'd been drafted by the New England Patriots."

"Yeah. Then I messed up my knee bad. I had a bad fall, popped out the bone, tore out a bunch of ligaments and stuff. You shoulda saw it." He whistled. "Big mess. They said I'd never play again. And they were right."

"Oh, Steve, I'm so sorry." Rosemary laid her hand on his bulging Popeye forearm which rested across the table so temptingly close and wondered if her love would be enough to cure his knee problem, meanwhile trying not to think about how empty and pale his blue eyes seemed compared to some other dark, vibrant ones she'd been lost in recently.

"Yeah, but I'm okay with it. I like coaching the kids. I got a great team here."

"Oh?" Rosemary put a smile on her face since it didn't seem to want to register one the natural way, and cocked her head as she did when her dates called for listening.

And she listened. Through the soup, the steak, the potato, the second steak, the salad, the pie, the second pie, the third pie, and finally, to end it all, the badly suppressed and thoroughly satisfied after-coffee belch.

Football. She could name every kid on his team, their yards last season, their chances this. She'd eaten one bite to his several, watched the food enter his mouth, watched its transformation into small particles as he continued to talk while chewing. She could only hope not to be party to any more of its long and perilous journey.

But now the food had been eaten, the check paid, the restaurant exited. The night was still young, the shore close by, and Rosemary Jenkins would find Her Destiny or die trying.

She knew for certain Steve had just been nervous in the restaurant—one of those people who talked too much when excited. Even now he was probably berating himself, thinking what a bore he'd been, talking nothing but football when all the time he'd been wanting—no, *aching,* to reach across the table for her. What agony it must have been, counting the minutes, filling them with chatter, until he could get her alone outside where they could be unobserved and no longer separated by a cloth-covered table.

Which, as a matter of fact, was exactly where they were right now.

"Wanna go bowling?"

Rosemary swallowed. She'd simply pretend he hadn't said that. Knock it out of the evening's record entirely. "I thought maybe we could take a walk along the shore to watch the sunset."

"Hey, I'm there. Great idea."

They walked along a path through the wooded shore behind the restaurant, and Rosemary felt in her entire being that the magical moment finally approached her. She took Steve's hand and he didn't seem to mind, even when she had to squeeze his to keep him from letting go when he tried to loosen his grip.

They walked along to a place where the trees thinned and the restaurant owners had built a tiny screened-in gazebo for bug-free sunset-watching, which was thankfully empty of randy teenagers at the moment. Rosemary and Steve sat together and stared out at the sea, and Rosemary thought she'd die of internal happiness when Steve put his arm along the back of the bench behind her. At last. At long, long last.

"Hey, this is cool. I didn't know this was here."

"I used to come here a lot...." She was going to say, *to talk endlessly about everything with Jordan Phillips,* but at the thought of Jordan her insides suddenly began ballroom dancing lessons and she thought it best to keep his name out of the proceedings until she taught her insides a thing or two about True Destiny.

"Steve." She scooched closer until their thighs touched from knee to hip, and turned to face him, causing what she hoped were wild and barely controllable tremors of desire to race through his body. "I think we should talk."

"Yeah?" He looked puzzled. "Have we been doing something else?"

"I mean about us." She reached out and traced the line of hair that went up and around his fine, large ears.

"Us." Steve seemed to have no trouble controlling those tremors of desire. Though he did lean slightly away from her exploring finger, which meant she must be making his control job a lot harder.

"I mean about that night all those years ago, when you and I...when we..." She left the sentence dangling, tantalizing in the soft night air, for him to finish, and embellish and act upon.

"We what?"

Rosemary scrunched her mouth in frustration. Instead of giving in to his tremendously strong love for her, he stared at her as if she ought to be filling out health history forms in a mental clinic. "Oh, Steve, you didn't...you couldn't have forgotten."

He frowned and looked as if he were trying very hard to remember something he knew for a fact had never happened. "Are you talking about you and me?"

"Yes." A spark of hope lit inside her. The memory had returned.

"Together?"

"Yes, Steve. Together." She smiled a tender indulgent smile and leaned toward him, lips parted, ignoring the fact that something approaching panic had flitted onto his features.

"But Rosemary."

"What is it?" She'd leaned so close to his somewhat square face, she could whisper the words, which she did, whispering being so much more romantic and all, and closed her eyes so he'd know he could finally kiss her again as he must be dying to.

"We never...I mean, I don't know what you mean."

Rosemary's eyes flew open. A certain amount of exasperation landed into her romantic aura. Maybe she should have slipped him some superstrength ginseng. "At John Langley's graduation party. When the lights went out. You kissed me."

"I kissed you?"

Rosemary inhaled and exhaled. Sharply. Sad to say her true love currently exhibited more signs of Density than Destiny. "Yes. Kissed. Me. On the mouth. Yum."

"Rosemary, you've made a mistake." He shook his head rapidly, looking as if he'd sat on a hornet's nest and thought it impolite to move off. "That couldn't have been me."

She stared, her mouth hanging open, and thank goodness for the screens or something would have flown right in and she wouldn't have noticed because her entire world had just caved in. "I was talking to you at John's party. The lights went out. You kissed me. What do you mean it couldn't have been you?"

"I'm sorry, Rosemary." Steve shifted around on the bench, rubbed his huge hands up and down his thighs. "You see...uh...well the thing is..." He held his breath, wiped his brow, squinted at the sky, frowned at the sea.

"Yeeees?" Rosemary's astonishment became colored by distinct irritation.

"The thing is..." Steve scratched his neck, blushed crimson, took in a long breath, and finally turned firmly toward her. "I never would have kissed you, Rosemary."

"Whaaat?" She had never heard anyone gasp out a word, but her *whaaat?* came positively surfing out on a shocked inrush of air.

Steve gave an apologetic half grin and blinked a few times. "I said I never would have—"

"I know, I know what you said. You wouldn't have kissed me in a billion years, even if someone threatened your entire family with a bazooka.'' She wondered if people felt this way when their homes were crushed by volcanos. Sick and empty and flattened themselves. ''But why not, Steve? Why not?''

''Because…'' He shrugged and smiled sheepishly. ''Because, Rosemary, I'm gay.''

''MAVIS, COME IN!'' Rosemary greeted her friend warmly, or as warmly as she could considering everything in the universe stopped making sense last night. Considering she'd made a big mistake coming to Lazy Pines when Jean-Jacques or Jean-Claude or Jean-Whatever probably stood on the bank of the Seine right now wondering what the hell was keeping her.

''I'm so glad you could come to lunch today, Mavis. Would you like something to drink?'' Except that even though it wasn't Steve, *someone* had kissed her that night so long ago. She couldn't have merely imagined a kiss that could send her into orbit and back without knowing she'd been gone.

She poured out a glass of iced chamomile, lemon balm, lavender and fennel tea and handed it to Mavis with a nice smile, which counted as pretty amazing considering she felt like growling and gnashing her teeth. For all she knew, her kisser had left Lazy Pines long ago, and she'd missed out entirely on that one-in-a-million love she knew was possible. Maybe he'd moved to Paris and now stood on the bank of the Seine wondering along with the Jean-Whatevers what the hell was keeping her.

''Cracker?'' She handed Mavis a platter, trying to

remember, as she'd been trying to remember all morning, who else had been at John Langley's party. She'd made a partial list, and intended to find out which of the men on it still lived in Lazy Pines and if they'd mind very much if she showed up and kissed them. Because if she'd been that wrong about Steve, she'd never trust her instinct again and would have to reenact the scene to know for sure.

Jordan, of course had made the list, since he'd been at John's party and of late had certainly been disturbing her atomic structure, but honestly, when he'd tried to kiss her that one night ages ago, it really had been a platonic disaster. Then there was Timmy Johnston who always teased her, but he kind of looked like a cranky reptile, and nothing in Rosemary's body had ever reacted sensually to cranky rep—

"Rosemary!" Mavis grabbed her shoulder and shook gently. "Where are you? I've been talking to you for the last minute. You haven't heard a word."

Rosemary sank onto a beige wing-back chair in the house she grew up in and sighed. All the loneliness and emptiness she'd come to Lazy Pines to banish now had the potential to become more powerful than she was. "Oh, Mavis. I'm so miserable. This guy I thought I loved isn't who I thought."

"You mean Steve." Mavis took a sip of iced tea as if she'd just mentioned something everyone knew, like what day of the week it was.

"How on earth did you know?" Rosemary didn't quite remember telling anyone about Steve except her father.

"Come on, we grew up together."

"Oh yes." Rosemary nodded, but she didn't see how growing up with someone enabled them to read your mind. "Well, he turned out not to be himself, and now I don't know who is."

"You don't?" Mavis put down her tea and stared as if she couldn't imagine how Rosemary had become so dense.

"You do?" Rosemary stared back. This was getting a little weird. "Mavis, you absolutely have to tell me who he is, now that he's not Steve."

The doorbell rang. Rosemary jumped up. "Jordan's here. Mavis, give. Now."

"I think you'll find out very soon." Mavis picked up her tea and took an infuriating know-it-all sip.

Rosemary scowled at her friend. When Mavis got that piggy priggy look on her face there was absolutely no point trying to change her mind.

"Okay, okay, I'll bring him in." Rosemary marshaled all her forces to regain control and walked calmly to the front door. She'd waited this long to discover Her Destiny, she could last through lunch. Besides, there was Mavis's happiness to think about—her happiness with Jordan. If Rosemary had to wait for her own eternal bliss, at least she didn't have to make all her friends wait, too.

"Hi, Jordan." She opened the screen and nearly sucked the words back into her mouth. He stood there, innocently enough, but his dark gaze shot out of his smooth-shaven face and his arms and neck showed strong and long out of his white shirt and he just didn't have any right to look like that and be her buddy.

"Hi, Rosemary."

And there they stood while chemistry buzzed and clouded around them, and Rosemary was starting to think that whoever kissed her at the party could go jump in the Seine because she might just want to launch an immediate and unplanned attack on Jordan Phillips.

"Hi, Jordan," Mavis said rather coldly, and since she'd come up to stand behind Rosemary, Rosemary was forced to bring herself under control for the second time in the last two minutes.

"Hi, Mavis." Jordan nodded to Mavis, and looked her over too carefully for Rosemary's taste even if she wanted the two of them to be happy and entwined forever. Or at least she thought she did.

She settled the two intendeds into her living room and got Jordan a glass of tea and sat down to begin Matchmaking, Part One, which started with Mavis throwing Jordan a rather poisoned glare.

"Mavis and I were talking about love," Rosemary announced, to get the ball rolling in the right direction.

"Really?" Jordan moved his chair closer to Mavis, still examining her minutely. "Have you ever been in love, Mavis?"

Something in his gentle tone caused Mavis to unclench her lips and remove some of the poison from her glare. Rosemary couldn't blame her. Unfortunately, since Jordan had directed his attention and gentle tone at Mavis instead of her, all the clenching and poison had the bad judgment to enter Rosemary's body, double strength.

"Once," Mavis snapped, only the snap didn't really sting. "Though it's not really your business."

"No, it's not," Jordan agreed smoothly. "What happened?"

Mavis hesitated, mumbled a little, then proceeded to tell him, which took an endless amount of time in Rosemary's estimation, and through it all Jordan watched, and seemed to drink in every word and gesture and inflection, while Mavis performed a gradual thaw under his thoughtful study.

They were falling for each other. The plan was going even better than Rosemary had planned.

Hurray.

Then in the millionth or so episode of Mavis's story, when she and the lost love had been arguing about serving pickled herring or mussels on a platter of catered canapés, Rosemary looked over at Jordan, and he interrupted his perusal of Mavis and looked back at her, and she just knew.

Because when he looked at her, his eyes suffused her entire being with warmth and excitement, and who else but the man in John Langley's basement had ever made her feel so gloriously conscious of being alive and well and living in a Total Woman's body?

She couldn't of course be wrong, except that she'd have to find out for sure, which meant she'd have to kiss him immediately, which meant absolutely that Mavis would have to shut up and stop hogging Rosemary's Destiny for herself.

"Well, Mavis. I'm glad you could come by today. I hope you'll come again soon." She meant to smile politely at Mavis, but her eyes seemed to be unable to leave Jordan's, which were exhibiting a similar paralysis in her direction.

"I thought we were going to have lunch," Mavis, or someone that sounded like Mavis, said. Rosemary couldn't really tell if anyone else was in the room, or indeed if even the room was still in the room because she'd stood up and taken a step toward Jordan and he'd stood up and taken a step toward her and right now that was all that could even remotely be considered important in the universe.

The voice that probably belonged to Mavis mumbled something else and then seemed to fade out in the direction of the front door, which left Jordan and Rosemary alone in her father's book-strewn living room which was exactly, *exactly* what she wanted. Because she just had to kiss him or she'd probably swell up and explode with longing.

One of them must have moved first, and one of them probably deserved credit for doing the kissing and one for being kissed, but all that mattered was that in a very short second they crossed the room to each other and their mouths joined in a rush of impatience and they kissed and kissed again until the kiss encompassed both of them in the same potent miracle as the first time, but now so many years later.

Then when she was afraid she would explode after all from the sheer ecstasy of it, his arms slid around to encase and embrace her in a strong and secure and utterly dangerous pirate embrace that made her want to surrender entire ownership of her being for the rest of time. There simply could be nothing more wonderful than wanting to keep kissing Jordan Phillips until you turned blue and passed out or starved to death from lack of food.

Except that the kissing suddenly seemed to be over.

"Rosemary, I don't know how this happened. I never intended to—"

"It was you." She put one hand to his cheek, touched the wavy hair that hung down on his forehead with the other, dreamy and light-headed and a little scared by all the feelings. "Oh, Jordan, it was you all the time."

"What was me?" He looked a little shell-shocked which pleased her immensely, even if his answer didn't.

She put her hands on her hips and glared. "Basement. Storm. Me. Don't you dare try to—"

"Okay, okay, it was me." He sighed up at the ceiling as if the admission nearly cost him his life. "But that was a million years ago, and since then—"

"Ten. It was ten years. And it might as well have been yesterday for the way you just kissed me."

"Okay, ten years. And yes, the kiss was...nice. But—"

"Nice? Jordan, it was amazing...it was wondrous...it was...it was *Destiny,* don't you see?" Her voice cracked just a little on the word, but not so much with awe as with a strange kind of tension she didn't understand.

"No, don't say that." He put up his hands as if to ward her off. "I can't be your Destiny."

"Why not?" She pushed away the strange tense feeling and scowled fiercely. If he told her he was gay, she'd deck him.

"Because." He took her shoulders and gazed down at her face with a look so tender and warm, she felt as if he'd kissed her all over again and she knew he was definitely not gay. "Because I'm leaving tomorrow for a few weeks to do some research."

"But you'll be back." She took a step forward and looked up very earnestly into his face so he'd understand that such a little obstacle meant nothing, then put her hands against his chest to feel his heart beating strong and fast and alive under her fingers.

"I can't be with you. When I'm with a woman, I can't write. I need to write, Rosemary. I live to write. Plus, I quit my day job last month so I'll starve if I don't write."

Rosemary frowned. At least being gay was believable. "You're trying to tell me if you make love to me you won't be able to work?"

"That's right." He managed to look genuinely anguished. "Not a single sentence worth printing."

Rosemary frowned harder. Why didn't she run into men with simple problems, like hidden wives, or ancestral vampirism? She didn't believe any kind of psychological problem could separate a man from the woman fated to be his. But if *Jordan* believed it to be true, she might as well kiss Her Destiny goodbye.

Unless it was just an excuse…

She tipped her head up toward him and parted her lips, as if inviting another kiss. He swallowed hard and made a frustrated groaning noise. "Believe me, if there was any other way…"

His voice came out croaky and strained and his face became suddenly set in stone as if he didn't dare allow any of what he felt to show. Rosemary backed away and hid her relieved smile. No excuse. Jordan truly believed women were the source of his trouble.

Her mind instantly spun into fact-checker mode. Her father's computer was upstairs in his study. If Jordan planned to leave tomorrow, she had the rest of this afternoon and all night to find out everything she could about writer's block, causes and cures. Which meant if she was going to help him, which she desperately wanted to do, for both their sakes, right now, she needed him out of her way.

"Okay, well, I certainly don't want to cause any problems for you."

"You don't?" Surprise and a disappointment he probably didn't want to feel cracked through the stone of his face.

"Of course. I know how important your writing is to you. You'd resent me terribly if I tried to impose myself between you and your work. You know—not today, not tomorrow, but soon, and for the rest of—"

"I can't believe you're taking this so…well." He said "well" as if he meant "lightly" and Rosemary had to fight to keep from flinging herself back into his arms to tell him she took nothing as seriously as she took being together for the rest of their lives, and as soon as she figured out how to cure him of his trouble, they could begin.

"Well, gosh, Jordan. We've been buddies for so long, it's probably best we stay that way, right?" She ushered him to the front door, poor shell-shocked pirate, and waved him cheerily out onto the front stoop.

"Yeah. Buddies." He smiled as if he'd just eaten something that deeply disturbed his digestive functioning.

Rosemary sent him a sparkling smile to hide her agony of sympathy, and closed the door on his stupefied and somewhat mournful expression, telling herself over and over that she was doing this awful thing to help him in the long run. She leaned back against the heavy wood and took a deep preparatory breath. Okay. Battle stations.

If she had to stay up all night, forgo food and read every word on the entire Internet, she'd find a way to help Jordan Phillips regain his confidence. And in the process, make sure he could fulfill his role as Her Destiny.

4

"BUDDIES." Jordan turned right onto Main Street. His feet thudded on the dusty ground with each step; he raised the left side of his lip into his best Billy Idol sneer. *Pals. Compadres. Amigos.* Just a couple of old high school chums. He spat into the dirt and instantly regretted the rather disgusting if effective gesture.

Buddies.

Never mind the continent stilled when their eyes met. Never mind the world caught fire when they touched. Never mind the universe exploded into sensual fireworks the second their lips joined.

Buddies.

He increased his pace, arms pumping at his side, working his frustration through the muscles of his limbs. Of course, staying away from Rosemary *was* what he wanted—what he said he wanted. For the sake of his writing she had to be kept out of his sight, out of his mind, and definitely out of his arms. So he'd accomplished his goal. Just not quite the way he expected.

At least she spared him the elaborate charade of pretending to drive off on a trip somewhere tomorrow. Obviously she wasn't as determined to turn the basement kisser into Her Destiny as he thought. Or at least as much as she implied that night in the moonlight when she still thought the phantom face-sucker was Steve. After Jordan's pitifully weak protests just now, she gave up the idea of Jordan-as-Destiny without so much as a regretful blink.

How could she give him up so easily after that kiss?

His walking rhythm stopped so abruptly, he almost fell over forward. *Maybe she liked kissing Steve better.* She'd had a date with him last night—she must have found out he wasn't the one from John Langley's party. Who knew what kind of research had gone on in pursuit of the truth? He curled his fingers into fists and tried to banish the picture of Steve's dry thin lips in contact with Rosemary's full ones. Maybe she was even relieved Jordan wasn't eager to be part of her life. Let her off the hook so she could go back to Steve and have his pea-brained, bullet-headed, no-neck babies.

Jordan began to walk again, slower this time, forcing himself to a natural stride. So be it. He'd worked through the rejection already—denial, anger and depression. Now he could go home and write. Get on with the career he'd have to work hard to build. Whatever feelings the kiss had revived would fade naturally. Maybe his hard-on would even abate some time this month. Before the end of the year, anyway. For sure. No problem.

He reached his house and leaped up the front steps. Come to think of it, everything had worked out for the best. Only his pride had fared badly—a slight case of being hopelessly pulverized. Nothing he hadn't suffered before. Experience had taught him that his ego would get its shape back, like one of those stretchy squishy stress-relief dolls.

Jordan walked into his house, headed straight for the computer, sat down and turned it on. He rubbed his hands together and waggled his fingers to limber the joints while he waited for the machine to go through its groaning, creaking loading sequence.

When the beast was ready, he looked through the file directory and paled. *Oh no.* He'd finished a chapter that morning. That meant today of all days, after he'd been in intimate contact with a woman—with *the* woman—he'd be encountering that horror of all horrors: The Blank Page.

Jordan gritted his teeth, closed his eyes and scrubbed his hands through his hair until he thought it had been suitably punished. *Don't let it get to you. Don't give the fear any power.* Just because he'd kissed Rosemary Jenkins did not mean the block would come on today. Instead of a creative meltdown, he could just as easily stretch his hands over the keyboard and not look up until hunger made him realize he'd worked through dinner. That could happen, too. Easily.

He licked his lips and opened the new file. C-h-a-p-t-e-r F-i-v-e. He typed the words slowly, deliberately.

Underlined them.

Made them bold.

Switched to all caps for a new look.

"Damn." Jordan brought his fist down on his mouse pad, shooting the mouse off to dangle forlornly by its electric cord tail. He couldn't face it. Couldn't even face finding out if he was blocked or not. What if he sat down and all he could type over and over was, *I still want you, Rosemary. I am a masochistic, idiotically romantic, repulsively optimistic horse's rear.*

He pushed back from the screen, leaped out of his chair and headed for the front door. A beer at the Anchor Barn. Or two. That's all he needed to restore his equilibrium. The anxiety would *not* get the better of him.

He reached for the doorknob, just as the doorbell rang. Adrenaline fooled his stomach into thinking he'd dropped twelve stories toward the earth's center. Rosemary. Changed her mind. Didn't change her mind. Might or might not have changed her—

He yanked open the door.

"Hellooo." Billy Deemer looked as if he'd attempted to run one twenty-sixth of the Boston Marathon and nearly expired. He held up a pudgy hand and wiggled his fingers in a cutesy greeting that didn't help the condition of Jordan's stomach.

"Billy. What can I do for you?" He tried not to make the words sound like, "Get the hell off my stoop," without much luck.

"Well," Billy panted, "I was just wondering..." He mopped his streaming forehead with a yellowing handkerchief and looked past Jordan into the house. "Whew! I'm beat. I walked all the way from—"

"You were wondering?" If Billy wanted to come in he'd have to wait until Jordan grew old and died.

"Wondering if you knew what was wrong with our Rosemary."

Alarm flashed through Jordan's body. "Something happened to her?"

"Well, as near as I can tell, she invited Mavis for lunch, then didn't give her any." Billy opened his mouth wide a few times to try to replenish his oxygen faster. "You were there, too. Did she give you something?"

"No." *Yes.* A kiss on the mouth and a kick in the groin.

"Hmm. Not like her. Not like her a-tall. And she won't talk to anyone. Mavis went by there herself. I went with her." He beamed so brightly his sweat seemed to glow. "She asked me to. Lovely girl, Mav—"

"And?" Except for the fact that Billy made a great sunshade, Jordan really wasn't interested in his continued company.

"'Can't talk to anyone,' Rosemary says. 'Busy,' she says. 'Researching.'"

"That's her job."

"Something to do with building."

"Uh-huh."

"Well, we assume. All we could hear was something about blocks. Rider's blocks. You know what those are?"

Jordan swallowed. His eyelids rose until his eyes were practically forced out of his head. "Rider's blocks?"

Billy's eyes narrowed suspiciously. "Heeey. You do know what those are. Mavis said you might."

"Look, Billy, thanks for coming by." Jordan backed

into his front hall, hand on the door, mind reeling.
Rosemary was closeted with her father's computer researching writer's block. If he knew Rosemary, which
it turned out he did after all, she was doing everything
in her power to figure out how to cure him. Which
meant her abrupt dismissal had merely been an attempt
to get him out of the way. Which meant, Steve notwithstanding, she was as determined as ever to have
her high school kisser become Her Destiny. Which
meant he was outta here. "I have to go pack. I'm going
away for a few weeks."

"Oh?" Billy frowned in confusion. "Mavis said
you'd—"

Jordan closed the door on Billy's bemused expression and spun around to face his living room. A fascinating mixture of euphoria, dread and panic churned
a path of destruction through his insides. Euphoria because Rosemary had not gone rushing off to conceive
mental-midget minijocks with Steve. Dread because
she could seriously inhibit his writing if he allowed her
close to him in any capacity. Panic because he wasn't
sure how much longer he could feel euphoria and dread
together without spontaneously combusting.

Only one thing was certain. One fact remained that
he could cling to while the rest of his being undulated
into uncertainty.

He was "leaving town" first thing in the morning.

JORDAN BROUGHT OUT his last suitcase from the house,
packed with laundry and a few small kitchen appli-
ances for more weight. He loaded the case into the back

seat of his car beside two other bags and a briefcase he hoped looked like a laptop, and closed the door. Mrs. Robinson came out of her house across the street and he waved enthusiastically to make sure someone saw he was leaving.

She stopped in her tracks and stared as if he'd forgotten to put pants on. Or underwear.

"I'm off for a few weeks," he called. "I'll see you when I get back."

She gave a quick nod, stuffed a letter in her mailbox, and backed into her house, eyes glued on him, wide with apprehension.

Jordan shook his head in disgust. Lovely neighborhood. Such warm delightful people. He had no idea what Rosemary saw in the residents of Lazy Pines, except that they always seemed to change personalities when they saw her. Probably because Rosemary's family had lived here for generations; Jordan's parents moved to Lazy Pines when he was an infant, and left when he graduated high school, though they kept the house for occasional summer visits. A mere eighteen years in this town made him practically an alien life form.

Casey burst out of the house next door and came running over. "Hey, Jordan, are you leaving?"

"For a few weeks."

"Weeks? But you said you'd be here when my Super Power Blastoid Space Kit came in the mail, so I could show it to you." His voice caught; his eyes got slightly moist and red around the corners; he sniffed and wiped his nose stoically.

Jordan grinned and drew the boy close, kneeling down next to him. "I'll tell you a secret."

Casey's eyes shot wide open. "What?"

"I'm only pretending to leave so I can work and no one will come by to bother me. I'm going to drive away now, and sneak back when it's dark."

"Coool." Casey grinned as if Jordan had invented the universe in only five days.

"So the minute your super…thing comes, you knock on my back door, okay?" He held up his hand.

"O-*kay*." Casey gave him a high five.

"Caaa-*sey!* You come back here and finish your breakfast."

"Aw, *Mom*." He ambled back to his house, turning to give Jordan a thumbs-up sign before he disappeared behind his glaring mother.

Jordan forced a smile on his face and gestured to his car. "I'm going on a trip."

Casey's mother nodded sourly, and turned to go inside, then did a double take, stared behind him and before Jordan's eyes, became a different person. "Morphed," as Casey would say. Her eyes lit up; a warm smile curved her mouth. She even seemed taller and several pounds thinner.

The nerve endings on Jordan's body began to prickle. He'd seen that change come over people in this town before. It could only mean one thing. Light footsteps sounded behind him, running up the sidewalk. He stepped out from behind the car and caught her as she barreled into him.

"Oh, Jordan," Rosemary gasped out. "I was so

afraid you'd have gone before I could—'' She broke off, panting. "I ran all the way…I was up all night. You—you have to—''

"Shhh. Catch your breath.'' Jordan took hold of her shoulders. Rosemary was flushed, disheveled; her chest heaved with the effort of taking in enough air. Her scent rose off her warm body and wafted to him in the still-cool morning air.

He took his hands off her shoulders while she struggled to regain final control of her breathing. Man, he'd love to make her breathless like that. Only her gasps would be those of surprise at the sensations he could induce in her; her cheeks would be flushed with pleasure; her eyes bright with desire; her hair disheveled from his—

"Stop!'' He yelled the word out loud before he could put the impulse on hold.

Rosemary jumped and put her hand to her doubtless already hammering heart. "Stop what?''

"Nothing. Just trying to patch a brain leak.'' He grinned weakly, furious with himself for wasting all that time trying to be pleasant to his ungrateful neighbors. If he were in the car right now on his way out of town, he wouldn't have to deal with the current need to put various body parts on ice. "I'm about to leave.''

"Oh, Jordan, you absolutely, *absolutely* can't leave now. Look.'' She clutched his arm earnestly with one hand and fished out a piece of paper from her skirt pocket with the other. "Look at this.''

"Paper.'' He nodded politely, wondering how the hell he could get out of this conversation, out of this town, out of this incredibly titillating mess without ruining his chances of finishing Chapter Five. "Very nice. Very...papery." He edged toward the driver's side of his car.

"Stop. Listen to me." She held the paper up as if it contained the only code that could defuse a nuclear weapon holding the country hostage. "Do you know what's on this paper?"

"No, Rosemary." Jordan opened his car door. The sooner he left, the better. Staying involved too much risk. "And I don't have time to—"

"Ways to make love." Her tone became low, husky and intimate. "To me. As much as we want. For the rest of our lives."

An electric wave swept across Jordan's body. He froze, one leg in the car, ready to escape, the other refusing to sever any connection with soil that Rosemary also inhabited.

She moved a step closer. Her hair brushed his bare arm; she tipped her head up toward his face. "Any place. Any time. Any position. Anything we want."

He opened his mouth to stop her, but all that came out was a hoarse groan that sounded like a lovesick moose.

She waved the paper in front of his face; he screwed his eyes shut to block out what might be written there. Even reading the words could set him back when he sneaked home that night to work. There could be some seriously provocative material on that paper. Highly charged. Erotic. Dangerous stuff.

He opened one eye slightly, like a kid cheating at a

guessing game and focused on the scrawled phrases. "How to Grow Like A Tree." He frowned and opened the eye slightly wider. "Herbal Happiness and You." His other eye joined the now-frantic search for immoral propositions. "Meditate Your Way to Peace: In This Life Or Your Last One."

"Are you sure that's the right piece of paper?"

"Of course it is." She snatched it back defensively. "These are your cures."

He sighed, trying to feel relieved instead of disappointed. "Rosemary, I really appreciate what you're doing, but I have tried everything. The only thing that works is chastity. I'm on an incredibly tight schedule with this book and I can't afford to backtrack. I also have a very important business meeting this afternoon in Boston, and I have to leave now."

He forced his left leg to abandon their common ground, closed the car door, and fumbled for his keys in pants suddenly too tight to admit any pocket intruders. Thank God he'd managed to sound coherent and decisive with that last speech. Two of the very last things he was feeling.

He found the keys, jammed them into the ignition, started the car and turned to wave goodbye to Rosemary. She wasn't there. He twisted his neck around to see if she'd gone back toward the road. Nothing. He rolled the window down and stuck out his head. Still no sign of—

The passenger door opened behind him. He whipped around to find Rosemary slipping into the seat beside him. "Jordan, this stuff is new...it's wonderful, and it's all nontraditional. I'm sure you just had some doctor give you medication or some shrink tell you it was your mother's fault. This is the total mind, body and spirit approach, treating the individual as a whole instead of—"

"Rosemary, I'm sorry." He ran his hands over his face. If she didn't stop leaning toward him in that scoop-necked sundress he'd promise her anything. He had to get her out of his car. "I'm sure it's interesting, but—"

"I've developed a three-phase plan. We can start tomorrow and be done in two weeks." She leaned closer, eyes pleading. "I'm sure you can spare a few hours here and there for two weeks."

"No, I can't." He reached across her and opened her door. "Now will you please—"

"The first phase is nourishing the body." She leaned away briefly to shut her door. "We can take a picnic out on Seamen's Delight, and get started."

"Rosemary." He reached over and reopened her door. "As much as I like the sound of anything involving you and delighted semen, the bottom line is I have to get to Boston or I'll be late for—"

"Jordan, remember in high school when I desperately wanted to be on the cheerleading squad?" She pulled her door shut again.

He sighed and let his body thunk back against the seat. "Yes."

"Remember how I was too embarrassed to show my girlfriends my tryout routine and you sat and coached me on it over and over until I was brave enough to audition?''

He nodded. Was there any possible way he could forget any detail that involved her? Especially that time, when she'd turned to him, above all her many friends, for help. He felt like he'd been knighted. He'd walked around in a dizzy haze of pleasure for three weeks. The Chosen One. Until he realized she just wanted to be on the squad to get closer to Steve. ''I remember.''

''You believed in me. And that gave me the courage to try.''

He bit his lip to keep down a chuckle. Now would not be the appropriate time to mention he'd just wanted the chance to spend hour after hour alone with her in a tiny room watching her shake her pom-poms.

''You were a true friend. Now I want to help you succeed the way you helped me.''

''But you didn't even make the first cut.''

She waved away his objection. ''Because I was a dreadful cheerleader. But you're a great writer, and I bet you're a great lover. And you can't spend the rest of your life trying to separate the two. You can't spend the rest of your life running away from your—''

''Destiny, I know.'' He grinned at her and nearly swallowed his tongue when she met his eyes and smiled back. A warm smile. A sexy smile. With eyes that for an instant held a touch of…fear? He pushed away the obviously false impression. Rosemary was afraid of nothing. He'd never met anyone so entirely, occasionally irritatingly, sure of herself.

The worst thing was, he wasn't so entirely sure she was wrong this time. He couldn't run away forever. Well, he could, but he was starting not to want to anymore. And a certain auburn-haired, hazel-eyed, slender sprite was starting to be the reason.

"I believe in you, Jordan, and what you're trying to accomplish." She edged closer to him on her seat. Her voice had dropped to that seductive whisper that turned his brain to dryer lint. "Please. Let me help you have it all."

"Rosemary." He swallowed. He'd be taking a huge risk.

"Let me return the favor." She put one knee next to the gearshift, one arm on his headrest, and half rose out of her seat toward him. "Let me be a good friend to you the way you've always been to me."

"Rose—" He swallowed again. On the other hand, she might be worth a huge risk.

"Two weeks." She put her other knee next to the gear, her other hand on the steering wheel and leaned closer. "Just two weeks."

"Rrr—" The dryer lint had completely replaced his brain cells. He was in danger of giving in.

"It's all I ask." Her mouth was barely an inch from his. Her scent filled the car, invaded his body and made the lint into the Springtime Fresh brand. He was lost. He was going to agree.

"Say yes," she whispered against his mouth. "Let me help you. Please, Jordan."

"Yes." He reached to pull her against him. "Yes."

Her arm slipped off the steering wheel; she fell back

before he could catch her. The loud blare of his car horn penetrated the entire neighborhood for a good fifteen seconds before he and Rosemary managed to extricate themselves. By that time several nearby houses had emptied themselves of occupants, all crowding around the car in answer to a perceived call for help.

"Jordan, Rosemary, watcha doin'? Workin' on an act for the talent show?"

Great guffaws all around. Jordan rolled his eyes.

"Lots of stuff in the car. Goin' on a trip?"

"Trip, hell, that's no regular trip."

"Glory be, it's finally happening. Must have been that book he wrote."

"Quick, someone go tell her father."

"Your book?" Rosemary looked at Jordan blankly. "Tell my father?"

He looked blankly back. "I have no idea."

"Roger," someone shouted. "Get 'round quick and tell Rosemary's father."

"Tell him what?" Roger shouted back.

"Whaddya think?" The original shouter spoke over the crowd's collective groan of exasperation; Roger was obviously the fourth to last person on earth to know.

"Tell her father Rosemary's eloping."

5

ROSEMARY PULLED ON a worn pair of cotton pants and a cotton top, looked at herself in the mirror and frowned. Maybe she should have suggested they picnic on the shore instead of on an island. She couldn't very well wear beautiful flattering clothes when she'd be climbing into boats and sloshing into freezing ankle-deep water landing at Seamen's Delight. But her outfit definitely lacked something in the suggestive category. In the fall-madly-in-love-and-follow-me-to-the-ends-of-the-earth category. One of those categories vital to her and Jordan's future.

She tied her hair back, making sure a few tendrils did that wispy thing around her face that tendrils were supposed to do, and decided that was as good as it would get. She considered putting on makeup, but makeup on a face set over worn cotton clothes made it look like someone had given you the wrong head for your outfit.

She sat on the bed and gave in to a few jitters, not quite sure why she was nervous about this picnic. After all, she was merely following the plan, merely trying to make sure Her Destiny fell into place as destinies were destined to do, except that hers seemed to need an extra push or two in this case. But somehow when her life plan had involved Steve, it had all been so easy and clear. When it was Jordan with whom she would sail off into the sunset, things were a little more complicated. And a little scary.

But of course she was doing absolutely the right thing today with her plan to rid him of this ridiculous idea that women were blocking his writing. Because someone who was destined to write was destined to write. Period. And someone as…omigosh, *amazing,* as Jordan, would absolutely, absolutely not be destined to remain alone.

So Rosemary would cure him.

But she would make sure to do so platonically, because if he thought kissing her would bring him writing trouble, then just from the power of his belief it probably would. So no matter how tempting Jordan looked or acted or simply *was,* Rosemary would behave herself. Not like she had in the car trying to convince him to go along with her curative plans, but she'd been desperate then, and she was no longer desperate. Now she had a plan and a willing plan-ee, and her life was bang on target, silly near-panicking nerves notwithstanding.

She smiled bravely at her reflection, readjusted a few wisps, and headed downstairs, where the picnic basket waited. In fact the basket had been waiting forever, at least the nonperishable stuff. She'd packed it last week the day she'd convinced Jordan to come on this picnic, when everyone thought they were eloping. Her father still hadn't quite shaken off the idea.

Rosemary reached the first floor and experienced a tremendous buzz of pleasure when she heard Jordan's deep rich voice in response to her father's higher, breathier one. No question but there was powerful magic between them—her and Jordan, that is. As soon as Jordan was over his little problem, they would have to spend some serious time wrinkling his sheets. Preferably the very second he was cured. The entire town would probably be flattened by the force of their love-making, but so be it. Some things you just had to be selfish about. Lazy Pines could rebuild.

"Marriage is a sacred and serious step, son." Her father's voice came through the half-closed door of the kitchen, and Rosemary just had to stop and listen because she could imagine exactly what kind of squirming Jordan was doing right at the moment.

"Uh...yes. But I think you—"

"Rosemary is a determined sort of person. She's the kind who—" A crash interrupted him, followed by the sound of liquid sloshing off the table, and her father's colorful nonsense swearing originally patented by Yosemite Sam and his ilk. "She's the kind who'll have you doing something you didn't think you wanted to before you even notice you started. Where's that fragga bracking mop?"

"I think it's a little premature to be talk—"

"Her mother was like that. But I never had much fight in me anyway, where she was concerned at least. You, however, you'll have to...have to..."

Rosemary smiled tenderly. Finishing sentences was

not her father's strong point. Maybe that was why he never let anyone else finish theirs, either.

"I can handle Rosemary."

Rosemary raised her eyes to the ceiling, then closed them, smiling. Something about Jordan's deep male voice assuring her father he could handle her made her want to burst in the room and demand to be handled immediately. She'd have to work hard to keep this picnic about food and The Cure when she wanted it to be about entwined limbs and fluid exchange.

"That's what you think, son. And I can understand that. But she'll railroad you into... I remember the time she decided we should all take ballroom dancing lessons. All our family and all of Steve's family, when The Daughters of Charity were giving lessons. None of us wanted to, we all refused, then found ourselves there on the first day learning to waltz. Still not sure how it happened." Another crash, this one sounding like her father had opened the broom closet to check for the mop and the entire contents had hurled themselves onto the floor. "Danga-blastin rinka franka... But you know what?"

"What?" Jordan sounded extremely weary, as if he wanted to leave the house and leave the town and leave the earth's orbit to go somewhere totally peaceful and sleep for about a hundred years. Rosemary would go into the kitchen soon to rescue him, but she wanted to hear what her father was going to say.

"We all loved ballroom dancing." Her father said the words as if he were the priest atop the mountain finally revealing the meaning of life to the sweaty blistered pilgrims who'd climbed up to see him. "We all loved it. That's Rosemary for you, son. That's my Rosemary."

"Thanks, I'll remember."

Rosemary could practically hear him mutter to himself, "Whatever the hell you just said." She pushed open the door in time to catch the last trace of exasperation on Jordan's face before it lit up when he saw her. Only lighting up wasn't a very good way to describe it. His expression did clear, and become more pleasant. But there was also this darkening, intensifying of his features that sent thrills absolutely skittering all over her body. And she in her dreadful boating clothes that wouldn't turn on a sailor who'd been in solitary confinement for six years.

"Hi, Jordan."

"Hi, Rosemary."

They stayed there, grinning like brainless goofs for a long enough time that her father cleared his throat and left the room before Rosemary had as much as a second to glance at him and say hello.

"Are you ready?"

He nodded, took in a long breath and let it out, as if her question might have been asked for an entirely different reason than going on a restorative picnic.

They left the house, Jordan carrying the basket containing his cure for the day, and walked down to where her father kept his skiff. They lugged the little boat down to the water, not far since the tide was nearly high, loaded it up with their picnic supplies and clambered in.

Jordan insisted on rowing and Rosemary let him so she could sit and watch his shoulders and arms and back doing their work under the clinging cotton knit of his shirt, the whole time pretending to be carried away by the scenery with various, ''Ohs,'' and ''Ahs,'' and ''Oh *mys*.''

Shameless, really.

They landed on Seamen's Delight, deserted as usual, and tied up the boat to a fallen tree on the shore. Rosemary climbed up a nearby ledge and stretched her arms wide at the view of the mainland on one side and the ocean on the other. Cool breezes blew her wispy tendrils around, and great white piled-up puffy clouds sailed contentedly overhead.

''Oh gosh. This has New York absolutely beat.''

''Beautiful,'' he said reverently, quite possibly meaning her as well as the scenery for the way he was staring at her.

Rosemary led the way to her favorite picnic spot, on a rocky outcropping at the high end of the island, with a view of open ocean. The ground was soft with moss; the woods fragrant with pine; wild blueberries, cranberries, raspberries and blackberries grew around them; gulls wheeled; eagles swooped; seals barked and belched their battles on a nearby ledge. Before them the sea stretched out, an endless, restless expanse of blue and green, dotted by lobster buoys and cormorants and loons and really everything you could hope for to ''nurture the senses,'' which was the title of today's cure. Too bad someone couldn't package and sell a "virtual" Maine coast experience. Crime would drop one thousand percent everywhere.

"So what's the plan, Rosemary?" Jordan stretched out on his side, head resting on his palm, grinning at her with a combination of wariness and excitement that made him look tremendously alive and male and not at all like someone whose love life had been asphyxiated by his own neuroses. More like that pirate that made her shiver and, recently, feel just slightly vulnerable and confused, which was not something she was used to.

"Today's plan is to get you back in touch with the basics of being human—taste, touch, sight, smell and hearing. I read all about it in a book I found online called, *Anxiety Attacks: The Sense-ible Approach.*" Truth to tell, she thought it sounded a little too New Age-y, especially when Chapter One was called, "The Body is a Huge Finger," but she had a job to do, and only limited materials and knowledge. "To get you away from the idea that the conscious mind is the ruler of your being. To scale back your complicated modern life into its true essential components."

He blinked. One eyebrow lifted. "When do we eat?"

"Not yet." Rosemary reached into the basket and unfolded the pieces of paper containing her notes, aware his dark eyes followed her every movement. If he kept that up she'd have to practice some of this stuff on herself. "First we have to stimulate your basic senses."

"Sounds good." He rolled onto his back, hands behind his head, sunlight dappling his body and face, still watching her. "I like being stimulated."

Rosemary sent him a prim look, which was about as opposite from how she was feeling as dried-up soyburgers are to the real carnivorous finger-licking, fat-dripping variety. "First we will work on your sense of smell. Close your eyes and concentrate. Imagine your body is nothing but a nose. Then tell me what you smell."

He grinned at her again and closed his eyes obediently, which left Rosemary free to examine his body leisurely, which meant she had to remind herself over and over again of her decision to keep things platonic during the course of The Cure.

"I can smell the sea, the pines, a little mud, old leaves, a dead fish or two, the freshness of the air...." He frowned as if concentrating on an elusive odor, then his lips spread into a slow smile. "And I can smell you."

"Me?" Rosemary sniffed her clothing. Had she pulled out an already-worn shirt this morning?

"You smell like all things natural, fresh and beautiful—open, sun-drenched flowers; warm homemade bread; hot spices and sweet spices, ripe fruit, earthy, female—"

"Okay, Mr. Author." Rosemary jerked her body back from its slow instinctive lean toward his seductive voice. "That about wraps up smelling."

"We're done already?" Jordan opened his eyes.

Rosemary scowled at his deliberately innocent expression. "I think you'd better leave me out of this, given your little woman problem."

"I guess I got carried away." He sat up with a patently fake dazed expression on his face and pushed his hands through his hair. "But it was like my whole body became one giant nostril. I swear."

Rosemary tried very hard to fix him with a furious glare, but it was hard considering she couldn't blame him for making fun of the method, and still harder considering he gave her a sly and repentant little wink, whereupon she became a flood of hormones and forgave him instantly. "I guess you don't want to try any of the rest of it."

"Of course I do." He nodded earnestly. "I wouldn't be here if I didn't want it to work. Just don't ask me to become a nose again."

"Okay, I promise." She examined her papers, wondering which category could keep them the furthest out of trouble. "The next one is hearing. Close your eyes and concentrate on what you hear, minimize your other senses. Think for a while, then tell me everything you hear."

He closed his eyes. The breeze tugged at a lock of dark wavy hair and moved it across his forehead. His dark lashes rested against his cheek, making him look like a little boy asleep, except that the rest of him had very little in common with boys and everything in common with—

"I hear the quiet lap of the waves and the gurgling rush of water over the rocks. I hear wind whispering through the pines, seagulls calling after lobster boats, the irritating whine of a mosquito, an occasional loon. And…'' He frowned. ''And…''

Rosemary rolled her eyes. Not again. Was he going to tell her he heard the beating of her heart? The whirring of her brain? The rumbling of her stomach?

His eyes shot open. ''I hear people going at it like wild monkeys.''

''You hear—'' Rosemary gasped. She heard it, too. Just over the next rock ledge back in the woods. Sort of a strange moaning, rising, dreadful sound that should be like that tree that kept falling in the woods with no one around. Instead, there she was, with Jordan, feeling a little sick with embarrassment to be caught so nearby, while the moaning rose and rose until it finally hit a bizarre crescendoed peak and dwindled down to a soft, ''Ahhh.''

Making as little sound as possible, they scooped up the picnic and crept back down the path to the beach where they left the boat. They crossed the sandy cove, climbed to the other side of the island and found a large flat rock which was almost as good as the first one, though without the wonderful freeing view of the ocean spinning out into the horizon.

Jordan flopped down. ''I take it you didn't expect they'd be part of my training.''

''My goodness, no. I wouldn't…I mean I could never…I mean, I wonder who they were?''

Jordan shrugged and Rosemary got out her notes again, feeling rather flushed from thinking about what those people had been doing and how she and Jordan could have started a tidal wave or two if they'd been inclined to follow suit. But she couldn't let herself think that way. She had her patient to look after, so she scanned her list carefully.

"The next exercise uses your sense of touch. Close your eyes and I'll give you things to identify by touch alone." She handed him a rock, still warm from the sun. "I'll start with an easy one."

"A rock." His fingers turned it over, explored the edges, grasped it in his large palm so that it nearly disappeared. "Smooth. Warm. Hard."

Rosemary swallowed. She would never, never make it. Any second she'd have to hurl herself into the icy water or she'd attack Jordan and beg him to pleasure her.

"Cor—" Her voice came out a thick croak and she cleared her throat. "Correct."

She picked up a nearby clump of moss, with a tiny forest of red-tipped lichen on its surface and moved toward him, wondering if he was still smelling all those beautiful and poetic things in her, only stronger now that she was so close to him. He put out his hand, fingertips outstretched, and came into immediate and intimate contact with her breast.

For a second, neither of them moved. His hand was warm and male and seemed to be exactly the right size, as if it had spent the last twenty-eight years growing and replicating cells to fulfill this unique and marvelous purpose.

Then, as if a nuclear explosion had gone off between them, they both flung themselves backward and away from the contact.

"I'm sorry." He crossed his legs as if he were hiding one of those little male indiscretions, only in his case not so little if the glimpse she'd had was accurate.

"No, *I'm* sorry. I should have put it in your hands so you wouldn't have to grab for it."

His eyebrows shot up. "You—"

"The moss! The moss, I mean. Oh, Jordan." Rosemary sighed and flung her papers to the ground. "Maybe sensory stimulation wasn't such a good idea. Let's just eat."

"Sounds good. Sense-ible even." He smiled and she smiled and that strained look that had begun to ease off his face got right back on when the smile and their eye contact wouldn't quit.

Rosemary broke away first, and retrieved the picnic basket.

"What's for lunch?"

"Broccoli, flaxseed, kale with dried soybeans, whole-grain organic bread, tofu cheese and green tea with Siberian ginseng and tincture of passionflower."

"Oh." He winced. "Do I get fries with that?"

"It covers all the basics for health in one meal." Rosemary looked at him the way a teacher looks at a student she knows will fail the course. "If you eat this way all the time your anxiety levels will drop."

"If I eat that way all the time I'll stage a commando raid on the Anchor Barn and head for the deep fryer with a straw."

"Well, the principles are sound. No caffeine, only monounsaturated fats used sparingly, high fiber and Omega three oils, herbal stress remedies, and then—"

"Rosemary." He accepted a plate of food and looked at it mournfully. "If I do this, I will be doing it only for us. And if I do this for us...well, let's say this sacrifice will make Romeo look like a self-indulgent egomaniac."

Rosemary's jitters began again, a little stronger this time, when Jordan said, "for us." She speared up some broccoli and crunched away, making herself wonder if she should have consulted her father on any seaweed remedies so she wouldn't have to wonder why Jordan was making her feel so odd and restless. She glanced at him, as he painfully chewed on a mouthful of kale and soybeans and her heart relented. Okay. No seaweed.

They ate in silence for a while. Rosemary watched surreptitiously as Jordan put food in his mouth and his strong jaw chewed it, granted, using most of its strength to do so. She watched as his strong hands used the fork, and his strong throat swallowed the food. Then he looked up and caught her watching him and that strange almost panicky feeling in her stomach grew worse, which bothered her a lot because until she'd known Jordan was Her Destiny, she'd never felt anything like this around him.

She pulled herself together and remembered on this occasion she was a doctor of sorts, and doctors couldn't allow themselves any panic over their patients in case the panic communicated itself to them.

"Did you ever just decide not to have the block? Sit down at the computer and say, 'I refuse to have the block today, because it is destructive to my well-being and darned inconvenient in the process?' "

He laughed. "I wish it were that easy."

"How do you know it's not? Did you ever try?" She frowned. "You complicate your life too much, Jordan, emotionally, I mean."

He leaned forward, his dark eyes radiantly intense. "And you simplify yours too much. What you do with negative feelings I haven't a clue, but I suspect someday they'll burst out and you'll go nuts and hack up your neighborhood with a cleaver."

"No." She shook her head. He was definitely wrong. "To acknowledge unhappiness is to give it power."

"The white-and-white world of Rosemary Jenkins."

He said the words without bitterness, only somewhat gravely and maybe a little enviously. He put down his plate and stared out at the sea and the sky and Rosemary wondered how he could make such a simple and glorious thing as life so twisted and sad. Twisted and sad, and somehow burdensome. She looked at his vital handsome face taking in the vista before them and probably turning it into beautiful and poetic words, and she wished she could help him see how much better off he'd be if he spent more time living and less time worrying about doing it properly.

But first she had to deal with the block.

"How did it feel when you made love to these…these…women?" She tried very hard not to make "women" sound like "wanton sluts from hell," but it sounded like that anyway.

"How did it feel?" He raised his eyebrows. "Damn fine, thank you."

Rosemary gritted her teeth and poured him a glass of Siberian ginseng tea with tincture of passionflower. Then poured herself a double. "I mean, what struck you as unusual in how you felt that might give us a clue what caused the block?"

He sat up and took a sip of tea, cast her a look of mild alarm and smiled weakly. "Mmm. Those people in Siberia must be very calm."

"Jordan, I asked you—"

"Okay. Let's see. How did it feel to make love to *all* those women?" He put his glass down and stretched out lazily. His face took on a dreamy, remembering expression; he chuckled and "hmm'd" softly. Then sat up abruptly as a large wet stalk of broccoli made vehement contact with his forehead. "Okay, okay."

He removed the broccoli from his face and tossed it back onto Rosemary's plate. "I remember feeling extremely restless, like I wanted to pace all night."

"Did you?"

"No. I also had this horrible urge to ask them to leave immediately after."

"Did you?" She tried not to sound hopeful.

"No. I wanted to be alone. But I didn't want to be alone. I wanted...something."

"What?"

"I don't know. The longing was horrible, but I didn't know for what. Then after they'd gone I'd be confused, and guilty, as if I'd done something wrong."

"Do you think you did?"

"No. Then I'd go to the computer to write, and nothing decent would come. Nothing. Not a sentence. Sometimes not a word."

"Ah-ha." Rosemary nodded rapidly, hoping he would think she'd taken in the entire scenario and immediately pinpointed the problem so his confidence in her ability to fix things would cure his problem all by itself.

"You understood?"

"Well…" She looked at him with a pained expression. "Not quite yet. But I'm close."

"Not a clue, huh?"

"Oh, Jordan." She sighed and looked at him with longing. "But it's only the first day of The Cure. We've only talked about your body…that is, the care of your body."

"Will you take care of my body, Rosemary?" He grinned at her, reached over with one arm on either side of her waist, and amazingly, half lifted her and brought her close so she ended up sitting right next to him. "Like when I had pneumonia in eleventh grade and you came over every day to read to me, bringing chicken soup and my homework? You made my dismal sickroom into paradise every afternoon for two weeks."

"Oh, Jordan." She kind of sagged toward him and he put his hand up to her head and pulled her down to him and kissed her. But not the kind of kiss he'd used in her father's living room, when she'd practically climaxed from the sensual power of it. This was a sweet, sad, tender, beautiful kiss, so soft and slow she felt every possible nuance of it, and even though it didn't last all that long, it seemed to go on forever. And because it was so sweet, there could be no other reason for giving it except that Jordan really, really cared for her, and the panicky feeling in Rosemary's stomach just erupted.

She reared up, poured herself a huge glass of tea, though a lot of it splashed on the rocks, and gulped it, her hand shaking. Then she turned to Jordan with an apologetic smile she was sure didn't go far in concealing her confusion. What was going on? What was happening to her?

"Are you okay, Rosemary?" He propped himself up on his elbows and watched her carefully.

"Sure. Fine." She turned her face out to the bay and pretended great interest in her Siberian ginseng and passionflower, because to do otherwise would be to show Jordan something that was of no use to his Cure.

Namely, that in her quest to help pull him together so he could become Her Destiny, Rosemary was in danger of falling apart.

6

"LET ME CHECK my records." The convenience store manager pulled out a worn ledger. His chair creaked; a truck rattled by outside. He scanned several pages, then several more.

Ryan flicked Jennifer a stony glance which she returned, also without expression. The tension weighted their faces, their guts, put moods and emotions on hold.

"Here we go." The manager cleared his throat. "Ray Browder. December 13, 1999." He turned the book toward the detectives and punched the line with his dirty thumb. "Ray called in sick that day. Said he had the flu."

Ryan clenched his jaw to try to fend off the disappointment, the crushing sense of failure. He and Jennifer thanked the manager, left the store, got into the car, and started down the street, without looking at each other or speaking. As if not interacting could somehow erase the truth of what they'd just heard. The truth that set their investigation back weeks if not months, and put the lives of young women in the city back into jeopardy.

They had the wrong man.

JORDAN HIT the save button with a chuckle of satisfaction. He'd made it through Chapter Five. He was still alive, still breathing; he hadn't turned into a drooling head-banging idiot. The pages didn't exactly write themselves, but he'd fought off panic over the parts that didn't go well, reminding himself there was no such thing as instant perfection in a first draft. Either Rosemary had accomplished something with her bizarre ideas about nutrition and sensory indulgence, or coincidence had paid a timely visit.

He'd spent the time between her seductive persuasion in the car and the picnic, filled with dread and self-recrimination. He never should have agreed to go. Why was he tempting Fate this way? His writing was suffering badly enough already. Bla bla bla. Moan moan, complain, complain.

By the time of their adventure on Seamen's Delight, he'd hit bottom. Unable to write, unable to sleep, unwilling to go, unwilling to cancel. Finally he'd faced himself in a figurative mirror and been disgusted. When had he turned into such a snivelling neurotic wimp? Whatever strange and wonderful cures Rosemary had up her sleeve couldn't possibly be worse than hiding at home until she left. He had "nothing to fee-ah but fee-ah itself." So he'd ditched the fee-ah, and allowed himself to relax around Rosemary, open up about his trouble and not feel ashamed, flirt a little and enjoy a faceful of broccoli. Even allowed himself a kiss—and got to watch *her* nearly lose it for a change.

He grinned and stretched his arms and shoulders, stiff from hours at the keyboard. Her uncharacteristic loss of composure could mean only one thing: Rosemary was actually suffering from real feelings. Not the wild cinematic emotion she decided in junior high would lead to Her Destiny. But honest, confusing, suddenly vulnerable feelings. The kind that if all went well, led not to the ring-down of the curtain on happy-ever-after, but to a lifetime of deep satisfaction knowing you chose the right person, even during the bad times.

Not that he and Rosemary would necessarily end up facing the altar together, though she came closest to the kind of woman he'd want up there with him. But at least he could introduce her to something more than basement kissing and Steve worship. Something other than the fantasy take on male-female relationships she'd protected herself with for all these years. Her childhood had been tough with her mom dying young and her father barely able to take care of himself. She deserved to find real happiness with a real man. And if Jordan could keep his block under control, that real man could very well be him.

He opened a new file and typed, "Chapter Six." No point wasting the positive energy he had going right now in his work. If he had to eat flaxseed and kale to get his books, his life and his feelings for Rosemary back on track, so be it. Something was certainly working.

He consulted his outline and frowned. Ryan and Jennifer were supposed to return to Ryan's apartment and have wild, furious sex, driven by the frustration of their recent discovery. In the outline it had seemed like a good idea. Now the thought of them turning to each other this early in the book seemed contrived and unnatural. But what instead? Have them go straight to Lieutenant Baker and admit failure?

"Jordan?" The light tapping on his back screen could only be coming from one source.

"Come in, Casey." Jordan shook his head. He didn't want Ryan and Jennifer to see their lieutenant yet. They had to rehash all the facts of the case, try to find out what they could have overlooked so they could report something more hopeful than total catastrophe.

"I found this outside and I thought you might need it." Casey held out a milk bottle top, his face serious, not meeting Jordan's eyes.

"Oh, you did?" Jordan grinned and ruffled the spikey tops of Casey's hair. Excuse number fifty-seven to come see Jordan. "Well, thank you, Casey. I've been missing this."

"Yeah?" The boy's face lit up. "Whatcha doin'? Can I help?"

"Sure." Jordan gestured to his screen. "The people in my book were going to go home and…make the bed. But now I'd rather have them do something more…"

"Fun?"

"Yeah." Jordan nodded gravely. "More fun. But they still have to figure out a problem while they do it, so whatever it is can't be too fun or they'll get distracted."

"I'm a pirate," Casey announced solemnly. He put the plastic top over one eye, squinted to hold it in place, and peered around the room. "They could go to the playground. It's okay and everything, but not exciting like Patty's Pizza Palace. Besides, I was at the playground today and there were big kids there. Maybe as old as your book people. They had fun, but I don't like big kids."

"Why not?"

Casey let the bottle top fall and folded his arms across his skinny chest. "Because big kids think they know *everything*. Like grown-ups."

Jordan laughed and swiveled his chair to look directly into Casey's face. "You know something? Grown-ups don't always know a whole lot more than you."

"No way."

"It's the truth. Kids like you know better how to be honest. You know how to fight and forget about it afterward. You know when and how to unwind when you're under stress...."

Casey's brows drew down. "Understressed?"

"Under stress. It means frustrated...." Jordan turned his head to one side and frowned, his thoughts clamoring for attention. Images of Ryan and Jennifer floated into his creative consciousness...at a kid's park, hesitantly circling the play equipment, talking out the timeline of the case, awkwardly trying out a swing, a slide, then going slightly out of their minds on the seesaw.

Nice. He liked the idea. But how would an adult reacquaint him or herself with that kind of childlike release? Ryan had the capacity to enjoy a playground romp, but Jordan couldn't see him initiating it. Could Jennifer? Conceivably. Possibly. Maybe...

Jordan jumped to his feet. "C'mon, Casey. Let's go ask your mom if we can go to the playground. And take Mavis, too."

"Mavis? What for?"

"Because." Jordan raced with Casey out of the house and down the porch steps. "I want to see how she swings."

ROSEMARY RECROSSED her legs for at least the tenth time on the wait-for-your-table bench in the Anchor Barn, and glanced at the clock for at least the hundredth. Twelve-thirty. Her father was supposed to meet her for lunch at noon. She'd even pinned a note to his tweed jacket, the one with elbow patches, before he went off on his daily foraging trip. Her father still wore a jacket and tie every day, even down to the shore, as if he couldn't quite internalize the concept that he'd stopped going to the college each morning.

She stood to read the notices on the community bulletin board again. The Daughters of Charity were still looking for acts for the annual talent show; Myra Crestall was offering childcare, in her home or yours; there was a baked-bean and pie supper at the Advent Church five o'clock Saturday; Jim Tobin had a snowblower for—

"Hello, dear. Your father late again?"

"Dolores!" Rosemary turned and greeted dear Dolores Thompson with a hug. "I haven't seen you yet this summer. You look wonderful."

"Thank you, dear. Where's your father?"

"He probably got distracted gathering sea blight."

"I see, yes." Dolores squeezed her wrinkled lids shut, nodded rapidly, then popped her eyes open again. "Will you be entering the talent show? I'll never forget the year you entered as a child with that darling song...what was it?"

Rosemary sighed. One tiny disadvantage to being in beautiful freeing Lazy Pines was that some people wouldn't let best-forgotten chapters of your life molder and rot away as they should. "'A Hundred Bottles of Beer on the Wall.'"

"Ah, yes. Remarkable performance. Maybe you'd win this time. Is Jordan entering?"

At the sound of Jordan's name, the jitters, which had left her alone for quite a while today, took a frantic lap around Rosemary's body and set her off again. "No, I don't believe he'll enter."

"Too bad. Betty Newcastle won with a lovely crocheted afghan one year. Though I think she usually keeps her clothes on."

Rosemary frowned. "I don't think I see what you—"

"Oh my." Dolores put shocked fingers to her lips. "He hasn't told you. Well never mind, dear. I'm sure he will when he's ready."

A strange bewildered feeling crept over Rosemary, as if with this conversation she had been transported even farther from a physical universe where things made sense and people behaved in logical and predictable fashions. "He'll tell me what?"

"About the nude crocheting, dear. At night, in his living room. None of the Daughters has been able to catch him at it yet, but we'll keep trying. That's not the kind of thing you'd want to miss. With Jordan looking the way he does, I mean." Dolores's voice dropped to a whisper; she sidled up closer. "I hear you're trying to help him with his...suffering."

Rosemary smiled brightly, she hoped, and nodded confidently, she hoped, while assigning the crocheting story to old age and misunderstanding, and wondering how on earth Dolores knew about The Cure. Maybe people in Lazy Pines had some collective unconscious through which they transported information to each other's brains. Or maybe Rosemary had told someone and forgotten, which wouldn't surprise her these days.

Truth to tell, she expected a minor nervous breakdown to come knocking on her door any old time now. Jordan's next session was Saturday evening, two days away, and she had to regain control of this need to run back to New York and reimmerse herself in work and daydreams. Because how could she help Jordan rein in his neuroses when hers had grown to where she needed to spray them with weed killer or they'd choke out her sanity?

And why was she panicking anyway, when The Cure had shown every sign of working, and therefore Her Destiny could be realized as soon as the end of her vacation, in not even two weeks? Jordan told her yesterday Chapter Five was on its way to being done. Which meant she should be bodysurfing on waves of bliss, not near drowning in trepidation.

"What are you going to try out on Jordan for your date with him Saturday?" Dolores put her hand on Rosemary's arm and smiled affectionately right up into her face.

A tiny prickle of irritation interfered with Rosemary's answering smile. Her collective unconscious theory was gaining ground. Every person in this town seemed to know not only what was happening to her, but when. She nudged her smile into sincerity. Dolores was merely acting out of love and concern for Rosemary's happiness, as she always had. "I'm prescribing Yoga to help reduce his stress and relieve his anxiety."

Dolores stabbed a finger toward Rosemary's chest. "Downward-Facing Dog Pose."

Rosemary couldn't help starting just a little. She could have sworn Dolores said—

"Downward-Facing Dog Pose?" Old Mr. Cudahy shuffled past them, and eased his body into what was essentially his personal red padded vinyl booth. "An insult to dogs everywhere. Join me?" He patted the table in front of him.

Rosemary shook her head. Wonderful Old Mr. Cudahy, with his stories full of infinite wisdom, could push her right smack over the edge today. "I don't think—"

"Of course we will." Dolores strengthened her grip on Rosemary's arm and half dragged her to the table. "Come on, dear, it'll do you some good until your father gets here."

Rosemary gritted her teeth, surprised at herself for the merest hint of uncharitable thoughts toward her dear, dear neighbors in Lazy Pines. But she didn't want them to do her any good. She wanted to have lunch with her father and talk about seaweed, go home and bury her head under her covers until she ran out of oxygen, and forget all about Jordan and his problems.

Because she could barely identify her own at the moment, let alone handle them.

But she found herself settled against the glass-and-wood partition dividing the booths, with Dolores wedged firmly next to her, probably in case she tried to escape, and Mr. Cudahy grinning at her across the table like a person who managed to survive a brainectomy.

She closed her eyes and inhaled deeply, even more surprised at herself for turning on her friends when they were just trying to help.

"Downward-Facing Dog Pose is wonderful for stress relief." Dolores beamed. "Hatha Yoga, I believe. Did you come across it yet?"

"No." Rosemary sighed, still wondering how she could make a break for the door. "I was going to have him Grow Like A Tree."

"Hmm. Grow Like A Tree is effective, but Downward-Facing Dog Pose is better. Watch." She left the table, bent at the waist, and landed on her arms in an astonishingly flexible pose that made a triangle of her body with the floor.

"In my young days I could rub my nose on the hardwood and see if it needed sweeping." Her words came out slightly thickened as if the blood were rushing down into her vocal cords and making them hard to maneuver.

Rosemary tried to close her gaping mouth and failed, her astonishment obviously needing to run its course a little longer. Dolores must be pushing eighty-five, and she'd folded herself up like a collapsible bed.

"When my wife and I went on our first date, I was so scared I couldn't button my shirt."

Rosemary slid a glance over at Dolores, who'd sat down next to her again, to see if Dolores still thought the earth was revolving properly, because with Mr. Cudahy's comment, Rosemary was sure it had spun into another dimension.

"Downward-Facing Dog Pose will help rejuvenate his mind, and refresh his body." Dolores made the announcement with a touch of ecstatic mania, like a TV housewife extolling the virtues of detergent.

Rosemary whimpered. She was apparently alone in her quest for normal bearings in the universe. Dolores hadn't caught on to Mr. Cudahy's shirt tale because she was too busy posing dogs.

"My fingers just couldn't manage the buttons. Had to open the front door with my shirt hanging open."

Rosemary's left eye began to twitch. If she hoped to survive the week intact enough to guide Jordan through his pain, she had to get out of here. Now. "Mr. Cudahy, I don't see what—"

"It's normal to be nervous, Rosemary, dear. It's always terrifying." Dolores looked around the restaurant. "I wonder where Mavis is."

Rosemary stared at Dolores. Had these people always been this strange and vague and alarming or had Rosemary changed? "What is always terrifying?"

"Course she'd had the very same problem with buttons that evening, so she had to find a dress with a zipper."

Rosemary gave up and dropped her head into her hands.

"Everyone is frightened, trust me." Dolores patted her shoulder. "I declare, Mavis isn't here. Look, there's her mother taking over. Always thought Mavis's mom was sweet on your father, Rosemary."

"What are you talking about? Frightened of what?" Rosemary's voice came out sounding a little hysterical.

"Even my fourth dog Rex got scared when we brought that bitch over to breed him. Hid under my bed for two solid hours."

"The feelings are so new, and strange, aren't they, dear?" Dolores shook her head sympathetically. "And you feel so helpless."

"How did you—"

"Menus?" Mavis's mother, nearly a carbon copy of Mavis except that the years had softened the hard lines of her face, handed menus all around.

"How do you know what I'm feeling?" Rosemary had two choices. Burst into tears or start doing the Cha Cha on one of the Anchor Barn tables. Either was eminently possible.

"Special today is the scallop plate, with a soup or salad. How's your father, Rosemary?" She smiled warmly; Rosemary could only gape dully. "I'll be back to take your order in a few minutes."

"Have you read Jordan's book, dear?"

"I—"

"Finally got Rex out and ready and then the bitch got one look at him and *she* went under the bed."

"His book? No." Rosemary practically moaned the words. Surely this was some bizarre German surrealist movie. Surely someone would pop up very soon from under the table, waving a monocle, shouting, "*Nein, nein, das ist nicht vat I vanted. Vee do eet again.*"

"I'd read it if I were you." Dolores gave a knowing smile. "I'll bring by a copy. You might learn something."

"What could I—"

"Then we got the bitch out from under the bed and they finally made it. And you know what?"

"What?" Rosemary almost screamed the word.

"My wife and I were married for fifty-three years."

"What are you—"

"Ready to order?" Mavis's mother smiled at Rosemary again, her pen poised. "You tell your father I said hello and don't be a stranger. Last time I saw him he took one look at me and ran his bicycle into Howard's front door."

"You see?" Dolores patted Rosemary's shoulder. "You shouldn't worry. Everyone's the same. Everyone's afraid."

"What are you all talking about? *What is it I am supposed to be so afraid of?*"

"My dear, I thought it was perfectly obvious." Dolores clutched her heart as if her surprise might kill her off. "You're afraid of falling in love."

"WE'RE GOING to the *park?*"

Jordan smiled nervously at Mavis's incredulous expression. "Yeah. I thought we could—"

"This was the adventure? Playing on a swing set? *This* is what you had me leave work to do?"

"Your mom seemed perfectly hap—"

"You've always been a strange one, Jordan." She folded her arms across her chest and gave him the patented Mavis Glare. "Don't know what Rosemary sees in you."

Jordan got out of the car. He should have known Mavis's inner child had reached middle-age long ago.

"What's the matter with *her?*" Casey scrambled out of the back seat and gave Mavis a five-year-old look of disdain that could stop a charging beast. "Don't you like to have fun, Mavis?"

"Of course I like to have fun."

"So come *on.*" Casey rolled his eyes at Jordan. "My baby brother is like that sometimes. You give him something he really wants and he says, 'No.'"

Jordan grinned and bent to look at Mavis through the driver's side door. "Are you coming?"

Mavis sighed and unbuckled her seat belt. "Okay, okay, I'm coming. But I have to be back at work in half an hour."

Casey turned and rushed over to the swings. "Mavis, come give me a push."

Mavis hesitated, then stalked over to stand behind him; she gave him a tentative shove, almost as if she'd forgotten how swings worked. Jordan's mind snapped into writer's mode. He walked closer, noted her hesitation and awkwardness, then a gradual return of proficiency—even grace. Her glare softened, her eyes shone; the tight lines of constant strain around her mouth disappeared.

"Higher," Casey yelled. "Higher, Mavis."

Jordan took in a quick breath. He had a sudden painful longing to be playing here in the park with Rosemary. Watching her on the swing, sun bringing out the red lights in her hair, eyes sparkling with energy and exhilaration.

There could be a lone kid playing in the park when Ryan and Jennifer decide to stop there. Or maybe the kid's mom asks Ryan and Jennifer to watch him while she goes home to change her baby's diaper, or maybe she left something on the stove. The kid could ask Jennifer for a push.

Jordan sat on a swing next to Casey, who squealed in excitement as Mavis pushed him higher and higher. Jordan chuckled; his heart swelled at the joyous sound. His fantasy of being here with Rosemary grew to include their own little version of Casey.

Jennifer could push the boy on the swing; Ryan could swing on another nearby. The kid's laughter would ring out; they'd join in helplessly; the sick mood of their disappointment would fade; hope and determination to crack the case would take its place.

He backed up and let himself glide back and forth on the swing, glancing over at Mavis. Her cheeks were flushed, thin mouth curved upward. Her eyes met his and she—

Jordan almost fell off the swing. She smiled at him.

One of Lazy Pines' residents actually smiled at him. Bring out the camera and record the event for posterity.

"This was a good idea," she said shyly. "I'm having fun."

Jordan blinked. He couldn't be hallucinating—everything else about the day had been completely normal. But here it was, right in front of his eyes: Mavis Tattersall was being pleasant to him.

"Hey, Mavis, let's go on the slide now. C'mon, Jordan."

Jordan shook off his shock and followed. The three of them played on the slide, each taking turns. Their fun was silly, frantic, breathless. The longing in Jordan's heart grew. He wanted this. He wanted this with Rosemary. He wanted her and their children to be playing in this park together someday, so the fun he, Mavis and Casey were sharing could be enriched by the love of a real family.

The fantasy scene mixed with Ryan and Jennifer's, Mavis and Casey's. It grew, flourished, filled him, until he was fumbling desperately in his pockets for the pencil and notebook he always carried with him. Energy and feverish excitement coursed through his veins. He sat on the down end of a seesaw and scribbled page after page, jerking each one up and over the spiral binding as he filled it.

The block was gone.

He looked at his watch, practically foaming at the mouth to get home to his computer. "We should go. It's one-thirty."

"Oh lordy, I lost track of the time. I do have to get

back.'' Mavis laughed, then bent down and put a hand on Casey's shoulder. ''Thank you, Casey, I don't know when I've had such a good time.''

''I *knew* you'd have fun. Jordan said you would, too, right, Jordan? I remember.'' He grinned proudly. ''You said you wanted to see how Mavis swinged so you'd know if you could get her home to your bed to make it.''

Mavis's jaw dropped. Jordan froze, at a complete loss how to deal with the situation. ''Uh, Mavis, it's not like it sounds. He meant 'make the bed'... That is, what I *said* was...''

Jordan clamped his mouth shut. He couldn't begin to explain. After Mavis's outraged reaction to the sensual way he'd portrayed Rosemary in his last book, he'd only make it worse if he told her the truth about her and Jennifer.

''And you practically engaged to Rosemary,'' Mavis snapped.

''I...just wanted to be better friends.'' Jordan pasted an earnest look onto his mortification. The lame line was the best he could come up with. ''That's why I invited you here. Because you're close to Rosemary, and...her friends are—''

''You wanted to be friends? Well, I've got news for you, buster. Friends don't—'' she glanced at Casey ''—make each other's beds.''

''That's right.'' Casey nodded vehemently. ''My mom says you have to make your *own*.''

Jordan stifled a roar of frustration. ''Look, Mavis,

he's a child. He got you confused with a scene I was explaining from my book.''

"Oh no, I didn't.'' Casey turned a hurt look on Jordan. "I understood. And that's exactly what you said.''

Mavis drew herself up, resoured with vengeance. "See?''

"Mavis, I swear, it was noth—''

"I have only one thing to say to you, Mr. Jordan Phillips.''

Jordan blinked wearily and sighed. His fifteen minutes of being tolerated in this town were obviously over. "Yes, Mavis? What would that be?''

She leaned closer until he could smell the deep-fried smell of the restaurant and see the large pores of her makeup-caked skin. "This little attempted 'adventure' of yours is going to be all over Lazy Pines like barnacles on a boulder.''

7

"CALMING POSES, calming poses... Here's another one. Sitting Forward Bend." Rosemary gaped in disbelief at the picture of the woman folded so completely in half that she was using her own shins as a face rest. Such a position had to be a physical impossibility; the photographers must have used stunt legs.

Jordan would be here in twenty minutes for his Yoga lesson, and she already had a nice array of poses ready, so he could certainly skip Sitting Forward Bend. In fact, most people who had actually been wired with hamstrings in their legs could cheerfully do without it as well.

She tossed the book onto her already book-piled bed, on top of the copy of Jordan's recent release, which she'd picked up along with the Yoga manuals. Because, aside from being very, very curious, in her new role as His Future she should certainly read every sentence he ever wrote.

Rosemary glanced at the clock for only the zillionth or so time in the last hour—6:42 p.m. Jordan would be here in eighteen minutes, and she was ready. Emotionally and physically ready. She'd spent the entire two days since that surreal non-lunch at the Anchor Barn

trying to sort out her feelings. Finally she had con-
cluded that Dolores and Mr. Cudahy with their poses
and under-the-bed dogs and buttonless dates were way
way off base.

Because how could she be afraid of falling in love
when of course she must already be…that way…since
Jordan was Her Destiny? You couldn't have someone
as your Destiny and not be…that is, not
feel…terribly…*strongly* about them. So of course all
that stuff was no problem. She and Jordan would date
for a while, probably not too long, become engaged,
get married, have children, and live until death under
the bright happy sunshine of Those Life Has Favored.
Because to admit things could go otherwise was to give
unhappiness power that it should never, ever have.

In any case, she needed to do something to further
their relationship because everyone in Lazy Pines had
recently been treating her as if she'd been suddenly and
tragically injured, so Dolores and Mr. Cudahy and
probably Mavis's mother must have told everyone all
about what they thought Rosemary's problem was with
that *L* word.

It was a little much to bear.

The doorbell rang. Rosemary jumped and the air
whooshed out of her lungs before she could gasp it
back in. Jordan was early.

She walked down the stairs, step by step, trying not
to grip the banister as if she needed one of those stair
elevators installed. She reached the first floor, walked
down the front hall, one foot, then the other. Because
with all the crazy tumbling going on inside her, emo-

tions bouncing one way then the other, her mental captain had decelerated airspeed and turned on the fasten seat belt sign.

She reached the end of the hall, took a deep breath, put her hand to the knob, twisted and pulled.

"Dolores!" Rosemary slumped against the door jamb. All that gearing up in vain for her next encounter with Destiny had removed the support her muscles needed to stand.

"Hello, dear. I brought you that copy of Jordan's book I promised you."

"I got one—this morning—when I was at the bookstore." Rosemary's heart began resuming its regular rhythm, though the captain kept the seat belt sign on in case he encountered any unexpected turbulence.

"I see." Dolores leaned forward, her voice a loud whisper. "He's not here yet?"

"No." Rosemary shook her head. "No, not yet."

"Good. Because I wanted to talk to you."

"Uh, Dolores..." Rosemary searched quickly for an excuse since it had taken her two days to restore her equilibrium last time Dolores talked to her and she didn't have two days this time, only about fifteen minutes.

"I wanted to make sure you didn't let that little business bother you, about Jordan and Mavis."

"Jordan and Mavis?" Rosemary frowned. Had they been fighting?

"Oh!" Dolores put three fingers to her lips. "I've done it again, haven't I? He hasn't told you."

"Hasn't told me what?" Rosemary tried not to roll

her eyes in case it looked like she wanted to kick Dolores off her father's doorstep, which she just about did. "Let me guess. *Coed* naked needlework this time?"

Dolores shook her head. "Men are the way they are. I'm sure it meant nothing."

Something about the way Dolores said "Men are the way they are" made it sound as if Rosemary, being a woman the way women were, would need to hear more about this than she did the crocheting. "Exactly what meant nothing?"

"His little…indiscretion." Dolores gave Rosemary the exact same I'm-sorry-for-your-terrible-loss look the whole town had been giving her for two days.

"With *Mavis?*"

"I told you, such things mean nothing to men. Don't you—"

"*Jordan and Mavis?*" Rosemary's mouth refused to close; her brain refused to transmit anything remotely articulate to her tongue, as if it couldn't quite grasp that this much shock was going to have to be dealt with.

"Read that book, dear, don't worry. Love is what counts. Jordan knows all about love."

"With *Mavis?*"

"Oh no, dear. His heroine."

Rosemary hated women who screeched, but there was no denying she was about to be a prime offender. "*Her, too?*"

"You make sure you read it." Dolores patted the book she carried. "Trust me, dear. It's all there. Ah, here comes Steve. My, doesn't he look grim."

Rosemary dragged her gaze from Dolores's wrinkly face to take in the sight of Steve's huge frame lumbering up her father's front path. He had a dark, slightly sullen look on his face, like a kid who had his Halloween candy stolen and would be forced to fight to get it back.

"Hello, Dolores. Hello, Rosemary." He spoke stiffly instead of producing his usual cheerful shout. "Uh. Rosemary, can I talk to you?"

Dolores gave Rosemary's cold limp hand a pat. "I'll just be off then, dear. Goodbye. Don't forget to read the book."

Rosemary nodded absently, and looked up into Steve's cranky but dear and familiar face with something like wistful longing. Her life had been so peaceful and uncomplicated when he'd been her future. Someone like Steve would never have problems requiring flaxseed and Downward-Facing Dog Pose, nor would he sneak off with one of her best friends the minute she lifted the block that prevented him from doing so. She loved Steve. In a nice way, that left her heart calm and protected.

"Come on in." Rosemary reached out for his hand and tried to pull him into the house so she could enjoy his soothing presence inside and maybe cry on his shoulder a few times, but she'd forgotten that Steve was made of some kind of iron so she rebounded back from her pulling effort and stayed on the porch.

"I can't come in, Rosemary." He shifted his weight from one foot to the other, one hand shoved in his rear pocket. "I was just on my way to— Well, I figured I ought to tell you first."

"What is it?" Rosemary squeezed the huge comforting hand she hadn't wanted to let go of and now was glad she still held. Because if he dumped any more bad news about Jordan on her, Rosemary was going to drop to her knees and beg him to marry her in spite of his total lack of sexual interest in women.

"I'm on my way to punch Jordan in the nose."

Rosemary's mouth immediately dropped open, as well it should for all the practice it was getting. "You're—"

"I feel bad, since he's your friend, but Mavis's brother asked me to, and Mavis's brother is...well, he's—" He blushed and averted his eyes.

"Yes. Okay. I understand." Rosemary dropped his hand. She really, really didn't want to hear about how someone as splendid as Steve was in love with someone else. Her ego could only take so much in ten minutes.

"Okay, well, I just thought I ought to let you know." He turned to leave.

"Steve." Rosemary put a hand on his arm, knowing better this time than to try to stop him with any sort of physical force. She really couldn't let him go punch Jordan in the nose. For one thing, Jordan would be on his way here, and as much as he deserved to be punched in the nose, he really should be punched in the privacy of his own home where he had access to wet compresses and 911.

Plus, since the picture of Jordan and Mavis in varying degrees of physical contact had just started to penetrate the shocked fog of Rosemary's brain, she was starting to think that the kind of revenge Steve would exact should really be up to her. Rosemary had never actually punched someone in the nose, unless you counted the smack she gave Sally Plappinger in fourth grade for stealing her Ho-Hos, but she was starting to think she could probably manage to punch Jordan's nose without the slightest misgiving, after he had the chance to tell his side of course. One thing she had learned on this latest visit to Lazy Pines, much to her surprise, was that its residents were not necessarily involved in an exclusive love affair with the unvarnished truth.

"Would you do me a favor, Steve?"

"Sure, Rosemary, anything." He looked down at her with obvious affection, and Rosemary gave another wistful sigh and hoped Mavis's brother would be able to make him as happy as she could have. "Would you mind punching Jordan in the nose tomorrow? He's coming over today and I'd rather he was not physically damaged."

Steve's scraggly brows drew down as he considered her request. He scratched his head. Cocked it to look up at the towering pines behind her father's house.

Rosemary stifled a surge of irritation. This was not a request for the latest techniques in brain surgery.

"Yeah. Okay. I don't have a problem with that."

"Thank you, Steve." Rosemary squeezed his arm. "I really appreciate it."

The crunching gravel sound of footsteps coming up

her father's path made Rosemary's breath jump back into her body and her internal electricity nearly overload. She peered around the iron football-playing mountain in front of her and caught sight of Jordan striding toward the house, confident and eager, smiling except for the briefest distasteful sneer at Steve, and sexy-as-hell, his dark hair and just-shaven face set off by a white T-shirt and navy sweats. Fury mixed with her attraction into an internal conflagration that could make toast of her father's house in about fifteen minutes.

"Hey, how's it goin'?" Steve stepped off the porch to shake Jordan's hand.

"Hi, Steve." He glanced at Rosemary, back at Steve, then at Rosemary again, and grinned a little stiffly. "Hi, Rosemary."

"Hi, Jordan." She managed to introduce enough ice into her tone in spite of the sensual fire raging through her body, to make his grin turn distinctly worried.

"I'm on my way out, but I'll see you tomorrow. Okay?" Steve slapped Jordan on the shoulder, waved to Rosemary and walked down the path toward the road.

Jordan leaped lightly up onto the porch next to Rosemary, and frowned at the male giant striding away. "Am I seeing him tomorrow?"

"As a matter of fact you are." She opened the front door. "Come in, Jordan. We have a lot to do."

He caught the door behind her head and gestured into the house. "Lead the way, Dr. Jenkins. I'm game for anything today. I have no idea what kale and soybeans have to do with writing, but it's working. I'm on a roll, for the first time in months.''

She pictured him tapping at his keyboard at lightning speed with Mavis's scent still on his fingers. "So I gathered.''

"I finished Chapter Six this afternoon. I have Chapter Seven outlined already, and at this rate..." His voice dropped down to become low and husky. He took her shoulders and fixed her with a gaze that would melt diamonds. "I could be ready to give up the monk's life soon, Rosemary. Very soon.''

Rosemary had to gulp and remind herself that all rumors taken into account, he was quite possibly evil spawn from hell and she'd be risking her humanity coupling with him. "How soon?''

"I'm not ready to risk it yet. But maybe in a few—"

"I mean like 'soon' as in 'the future' or some kind of 'soon' that means 'already happened with Mavis?'''

He gave a groan of disgust. "Rosemary. You can't possibly believe that I—'' He looked at her face incredulously. "You believe it. Come on, Rosemary, *Mavis?*''

He looked so aghast and bewildered that she could possibly have considered him and Mavis as a couple, that Rosemary's heart gave a tremendous lurch of hope. She folded her arms. "Convince me.''

He told her the story, and she couldn't claim to be able to keep it all straight as it involved swings and slides and little Casey Arbin and unmade beds, but she gathered Jordan was quite sure nothing had happened between him and Mavis.

"So you and she…I mean it existed only in Casey's mind?"

"Not even there." He grinned. "Nothing in Casey's mind but straightening sheets and blankets."

"I see." Rosemary squeezed her eyes shut. Joy and relief ran through her so hot and wild that she thought she might just expire in the middle of her father's living room before she'd had the chance to have Jordan Grow Like A Tree.

Which proved once and for all how right she'd been and how wrong Dolores had been about her feeling any fear of falling in…of falling for Jordan. Because of course she was delighted to be so crazy about him. And doubly delighted that The Cure seemed to be working so well. Because she and Jordan could now speed along to the part where their wonderful future together started.

She opened her eyes. "And Mavis?"

"Thinks I'm a lecherous creep." His eyes rolled in exasperation, then focused on her and turned, obviously hoping for some sign she believed him. "What do you think?"

She grinned and gestured to the Yoga gear. "I think it's time to get started."

Jordan exhaled as if he'd been holding his breath since he walked into the house several minutes ago, and held out his hand. "Let's go."

She and Jordan gathered the equipment they'd need for his lesson, and brought it outside and down to the tiny patch of sand on her father's shore, which he proudly called "the beach." The sun was starting its final descent behind the horizon, and the air was soft and golden and still, the sea a glassy pool. A seal poked its nose out of the water, swam a short distance, and dove under again with a soft swish.

Rosemary and Jordan arranged the candles and mosquito coils and exercise mats on the sandy spot, which had virtually disappeared under all the gear by the time they were ready. Rosemary got out her lesson plan and consulted it.

"We'll start with Hugging A Giant."

Jordan looked apprehensively behind him. "Is Steve coming back for this one?"

Rosemary shook her head, and reminded herself to warn him after the lesson about Steve and the punch in the nose. She couldn't do it now or she'd risk ruining his peaceful flow of Tho Energy. Or so the book said. "No, you have to imagine this giant."

"Fine by me. I don't think I'm Steve's type." He grinned, clearly unaware of what he'd said.

Rosemary smiled back, wondering what he'd do if she told him he'd probably be surprised by Steve's type. But that was Steve's business, and Steve could choose his own moment to tell. She and Jordan had more important things to focus on right now.

She had Jordan stand up straight and arrange his arms in a circle out in front of his chest as if he were hugging a giant, or a beachball or Rosemary nine months pregnant.

"There. Now, breathe deeply and try to clear your mind. Do you feel your Tho flow?"

"My huh?"

"Your Tho energy. The book says this pose is supposed to make your Tho flow more peacefully." She studied him anxiously. "Does it?"

"Hmm." He shot her a mischievous look. "Yeth, I think tho."

"Good. Now hold that pose and banish all tension from your body." She looked him over critically, then wished she hadn't when it occurred to her that his body looked incredibly tempting and beautiful, strong and lean, white and navy, and very male among the grey sexless rocks turned almost golden in the light.

"I bought your book the other day." She spoke to break the spell drawing her closer to him, then wished she hadn't when her statement apparently severed his Tho flow completely. In fact he was looking at her with something approaching horror.

"Oh?" He said "Oh?" as if all other words had deserted him, which meant either he'd been able to banish more tension than she'd thought, or he'd just been delivered a family-size dose.

"Dolores came by today to talk about it, too. She said something about your heroine. Is that one Mavis, too?"

"No." He shook his head back and forth several times, as if he wouldn't have to say anything more as long as he kept it wagging along. "No."

"Is she just out of your imagination, then?" Somehow she managed to ask the question as if the answer didn't matter at all, as if she were asking him whether he conditioned his hair. But the truth of the matter got closer to her being ready to scream with the need to find out what Dolores meant by Jordan "knowing all about love."

"I'd…rather not go into it. Maybe after you've read the book."

Rosemary nodded as if she deeply respected his privacy concerning the matter, but decided immediately that she hated his heroine's guts and would for the rest of time.

"So." He smiled, clearly anxious to change the subject. "What's next on the program?"

Rosemary consulted her list, deciding she'd read his book as soon as possible so she could begin her hate-fest right away, and picked out the next pose. As the light peaked into orange and red, then faded to maroon and indigo, and the air cooled around them, Jordan Grew Like A Tree, Looked Over At Sheep and Lifted The Earth. The nervous edgy laughter that came with the early trials faded into grace and earnest concentration as Jordan held the poses and Rosemary watched, and coached and savored the sight of him. Finally, as the light was all but fading from the sky, amid the flickering candles and smoking mosquito coils, the final pose was ready to be attempted.

"Downward *what?*" Jordan looked at her incredulously. "I thought examining sheep was bad. Where do they come up with these titles?"

"Downward-Facing Dog Pose. To relieve anxiety. You put your hands down and kind of lean on your arms."

Jordan pushed his fingers through his hair. His dark eyes caught the candlelight and reflected it back. "I'm beat. You show me this one."

Rosemary nodded and stepped onto the mats. She leaned forward onto her hands, trying to imitate what she'd seen Dolores do. "You lean forward like this, and—oh!"

The mat under her hands slipped forward over the damp sand while the one under her feet slid in the opposite direction. At the same time, strong arms circled her hips and held her lower half back against a hard male body. A hard male body shaking with suppressed laughter. At least that's what she hoped it was.

"I wonder." He cleared his throat and tightened the contact between her rear and his groin as she struggled to walk her hands closer to her feet so she could stand up. "I wonder if this is why they call it Dog Pose."

Rosemary finally managed to stand, flushed and breathless. "Good thing you weren't thinking of Looking Over At Sheep."

"One thing I do know," he whispered into her neck. "I am definitely Growing Like A Tree."

"Oh, Jordan." She turned around and lifted her head to meet his bending down to kiss her for the third time since she'd come to Lazy Pines. Only this kiss wasn't lustful or sweet, but somewhere in between, encompassing both, and making her head spin with pleasure and her body definitely, definitely needy and soft and liquid from wanting him.

His hands crept under her shirt and made warm circles on her back, chilled from the now sunless air. Rosemary pressed herself impossibly closer, trying to lessen the nonexistent space between them as if she were trying to climb into his body to fuse them completely. Trying to push him away from the sweet kisses and over into the realm of the lustful so she could turn off her mind and its awareness of what she felt and become only a body, swept away by the passion and desire and the sheer poetry of the moment.

But at the same time she was trying to meld them together, Rosemary started to feel resistance from Jordan. Resistance and a need to keep the kisses sweet and tender, and filled with feeling, and it occurred to her that he was trying to avoid the physical and she was trying to avoid the emotional.

And she just suddenly wasn't sure if they could ever get it right.

Their kisses slowed and shortened, became awkward and apologetic. Rosemary buried her head in his shoulder and Jordan wrapped his arms around her tight, and there, unspoken in the soft, still, now black night was the fear that they might not manage to be together after all, at least not now—and quite probably neither of them wanted to believe it.

"Rosemary." His deep voice resonated through his chest under her cheek and through her head and down through her body. In spite of her frustration, the sound still made her tingle all over. "I'm sorry. Maybe I'm a coward, but I can't...it's too soon. I've only just thrown off the block, and I want to make sure it's really solidly gone before I...before we can..."

"Go at it like wild monkeys?"

He chuckled. "Actually I was going to say, 'make love.'"

Rosemary's body jerked slightly when he said "make love," even though she tried not to let it and Jordan certainly felt it because he pried her face off his chest with a gentle hand and made her look at him. "There's got to be more to this than fireworks and dreams of happy-ever-after, Rosemary."

"Of course." Her voice sounded bright and brittle and slightly manic. What was he talking about?

"I want to be very sure you understand that. Because when we make love—"

Her body jerked again and he frowned down at her and she smiled through teeth that were starting to chatter and said, "Hiccups."

"When we make love, it might not be some beautiful rapturous cinematic moment."

"N-n-no?" She frowned. Of course it would be. How could passion that had been delayed as long as theirs be anything but an explosive perfect union?

"It's going to be real. It's going to be you and me. It may also be arms in the way, embarrassing noises and moments of extreme clumsiness."

She shook her head, started to shiver, and giggled, even though it made her feel like a dopey schoolgirl, but she wasn't really sure what she could be expected to say except to point out how wrong he was.

"I'm serious, Rosemary."

"Of c-c-course." She couldn't quite figure out how she could be so cold and shivery with the soft night air and Jordan's warm body so close to hers. But something was shaking her insides like she was castanets in the hands of a Flamenco dancer. "I'm not a v-v-virgin. I know what s-s-sex is like."

"The point is, the physical aspects of making love should be secondary to the emotions we're expressing."

Rosemary shivered harder. "You mean—"

"Making love shouldn't be the most important thing between us. Whether we ever do or not shouldn't affect what we feel for each other."

He looked so serious in the glow of the candlelight that a horrible fear started to creep up Rosemary's body. "Jordan? Do you have some kind of physical…problem or something? I mean beyond the block?"

He nodded and looked at her gravely. "I should have told you sooner."

Rosemary gasped, her mind already trying to figure out how she could help him. "What—what is it?"

"Well…" He looked at her even more gravely. "I have enough manly seed backed up to blow your head off."

Rosemary burst out laughing, weak with relief—selfishly maybe, but she couldn't quite handle having to effect another cure at the moment. Jordan kissed her, and she felt warmer again, and slightly reassured.

"I just don't want you to be disappointed," he whispered.

"Oh, I couldn't be," she whispered back. "Sex with you will—"

"Rosemary." He looked at her very, very seriously, even more seriously than when he was kidding and trying to look serious. "At the risk of sounding like Mr. Rogers, can you say, 'making love?'"

She laughed again to hide her panic. "No monkeys?"

"No." He shook his head, not laughing. "Say, 'Jordan, when we make love, I'll—'"

"Omigosh." Rosemary's eyes shot open. There it was again, that horrible noise. "I hear them again."

"What?"

Rosemary pointed off to her left down the beach where the awful sound was coming from. "The real wild monkeys, from Seamen's Delight."

Jordan opened his mouth as if he were going to accuse her of chickening out on saying "make love," when his mouth snapped shut and she could tell he heard it, too. That weird rising moaning noise they'd heard on the island. The sickeningly private sound of people doing simply and naturally, if somewhat strangely and definitely too loudly, what Jordan and Rosemary seemed to have endless trouble accomplishing.

She wanted to throw up.

"Let's go back to the house," she whispered. Anything to escape that dreadful crescendoing moan of someone approaching the apex of his or her sensual experience.

The experience that Jordan and Rosemary, on this candlelit beach in the soft sweet night air, seemed further than ever from sharing.

8

_____

"JENNIFER," Ryan whispered. "I...want you."

"Oh, Ryan," Jennifer whispered. "I...want you, too."

"Here..." He unbuttoned three of her buttons, "and now."

"Oh, Ryan. Oh yes. Here...and now."

Jordan stared at the screen, disbelief and horror rising into his throat. *I want you here and now?* He wiped out the passage and steadied himself, wondering if he ought to Look Over A Few Sheep if things didn't fix themselves soon.

"*Jennifer,*" Ryan whispered. "*I...really* want you."

Jordan deleted the sentence with hands that were starting to shake.

"*Jennifer,*" Ryan moaned. "*Oh, Jennifer. I want you more than...*"

Jordan swallowed. More than... More than...

"*More than...anything.*"

He closed his eyes and pushed his chair away from the keyboard. This couldn't be happening. Not after he'd finally thrown off the block; not after he'd allowed himself to kiss Rosemary at the picnic on Seamen's Delight and suffered no consequences. Not after he'd practically torn himself in half to keep from making love to her down on the shore last night. He stared at the words on the screen, blurred but recognizably horrible, even from a distance. It couldn't be happening.

He went into his kitchen and poured himself a big glass of iced skullcap tea, tossed back a handful of soy nuts and changed into sweats. He stood in the middle of his living room for twenty minutes and Hugged A Giant for all he was worth, until he'd fought off the panic and restored some kind of order to his mind.

There. That was it. Maybe he'd been hungry. Maybe his Tho energy, whatever the hell that was, had taken a little vacation. He sat down again at his keyboard, keeping fear at bay. He could do this. He could have his book and eat Rosemary, too—

He winced. Rephrase. He *could* manage to write and have a relationship at the same time. He could.

"Oh, Jennifer," Ryan moaned. "You are so…great."

A light sweat broke out on Jordan's forehead and under his arms. He deleted the sentence. Calm. Calm. He would stay calm.

"Jennifer," Ryan said.

Jordan's breath started coming faster; his fingers grew tense, heavy. Calm. Stay very, very calm.

"Oh, sweetheart, Jenny," Ryan uttered.

Jordan gritted his teeth; his eyes set into a hard glare. He was calm. He could do it. He could. He could—

"Jen, you ignorant slut, I'm gonna do you like a wild monkey."

He smashed down his finger on the final period,

shoved back his chair and banged out of the room, half wanting to curl into fetal position and cry, half wanting to punch something or someone until they begged for mercy. This couldn't be happening. Not now. Not after he'd been so close to having it all.

Maybe all he needed was a little inspiration. Maybe if he could find Mavis, watch her interact with someone, watch her move, watch her fry clams, *anything*.

The doorbell rang. He flung open the door, ready to vent his rage and frustration on whatever Lazy Pines idiot stood there.

Billy Deemer. Perfect.

"What do you want, you—"

Billy Deemer charged up the steps like a furious rhinoceros and sank his hugely fat fist into Jordan's solar plexus with all his considerable momentum behind the punch.

Jordan's mouth shot open, quite reasonably expecting air to rush into the vacant chamber. However, air had apparently no intention of doing so. He crumpled to his knees, hands at his stomach, feeling close kinship to his goldfish Sparky the day he'd jumped out of his bowl and perished on the kitchen table.

"*Sinner,*" Billy shouted. "*Adulterer! Fornicator!*"

Doors opened. Neighbors came out and stood on their front porches, arms folded in silent support of Billy and his crusade against evil in Lazy Pines.

Jordan pulled himself up on the doorjamb and faced Billy, having finally convinced his lungs to refill with air. "I take it...you've been chatting...with Mavis."

"For *shame*." Billy drew himself up so righteously that all but two of his chins disappeared. "For *shame*."

"Billy!" Mavis's shout and pounding footsteps sounded down the street. "Billy, no! I just talked to Rosemary."

Jordan dropped his head in his hands and groaned. Terrific. Mavis knew about Jennifer. That ruled out any more research to help unblock him; his last hope.

"Billy." Mavis reached him, gasping, and grabbed his arm. "It's okay, I misunderstood. He's writing his book about me this time." She turned a beaming face up to Jordan. "Isn't that right, Jordan?"

He nodded mutely, wishing a nice little lava flow would cover the entire town.

"Isn't it exciting?" Mavis positively glowed. With her eyes alight and her cheeks flushed she looked years younger and nearly attractive—the way she'd looked in the park before all the bed-making nonsense began. She smiled up at Jordan, then shocked the hell out of him by rushing up the stairs to give him a laughing bear hug.

He hugged her back, flattered by her excitement in spite of himself. Mavis wasn't so bad. The lava could take her last.

"Imagine that, Billy." She flung herself down the stairs, dragging Jordan after her. "A whole book about me."

"I'm imagining." Billy's brows drew down into a ghastly frown. "And I just imagined the part where you have sex with this *monster*."

He drew back his arm with speed seemingly impossible in a man his size, and punched Jordan again.

Jordan repeated his kneeling tribute to Sparky the gasping goldfish, incredulous that he could have been punched twice in one morning and not seen either one coming. Apparently circumstances had decreed it was time to punch a man while he was already down.

"Billy!" The sound of a slap being deposited on a fat cheek resonated through the neighborhood. "How dare you punch my author."

Billy stared at Mavis like an injured puppy. "But, Mavis," he whimpered, "he was going to have sex with you and I—I—*I* want to."

A shocked murmur ran through the block as people crowded closer to see Mavis's reaction.

Jordan staggered to his feet and decided now was as good a time as any to make his escape. Tweedles Dum and Dee would be taking up everyone's attention; he could leave this public hell and go back to his own private one.

He'd gotten two steps into his house when the phone rang.

"Jordan, it's Marty. I've got good news."

"Oh?" Jordan brightened hopefully. Maybe good news from his agent would get Jordan's Tho flowing again, like a mighty river.

"Charles Andrews had an accident, and he's going to be late finishing his book, so you've been moved up in the schedule! Isn't that great?"

"Moved up?" Jordan's hopeful brightness began to dim. "How much moved up?"

"Two months. But if you need an extra week or two that should be no problem."

Jordan barely heard the rest of the conversation, barely responded, barely took anything in. Two months. The two punches in the gut he'd already taken this morning had nothing on this one. He'd just caught up on his original schedule, and now, blocked again, he would have to accelerate to a pace that would strain him at his best.

Two months.

He clenched his fists at his side. He'd been an irresponsible fool, risking his entire career for the sake of a few kisses on the beach. He should have been more careful; should have known the block hadn't lifted permanently. He should have known it would take more than flaxseed and Lifting The Earth to cure him. Should have known his feelings for Rosemary were too powerful a force to toy with. But she'd carried him away with her optimism and determination, and her eyes and body and soft mouth and—

He smacked his fist into his palm. He had to stop this. Had to stop thinking about her. Had to stop seeing her, talking to her, allowing any thoughts of any possible future with her to endanger what he had to do. They had one more date on Monday. He'd tell her then. Finally end the chapter of his life she'd inhabited for over a decade.

He'd rent out his parents' house, rent another one farther up the coast. Leave Lazy Pines. Leave its memories. Find some other town inhabited by married and old people who didn't know him; who would leave him alone.

A charge of energy fought with his pain and won. Good. He'd made the right decision. Enough having other people try to change who he was and what he was doing. Enough trying to conform to someone else's idea of his Destiny.

From now on, Jordan was in charge of his own.

A commotion outside brought him to his door. He intended to close it; close out the silly rumble of the people of Lazy Pines, trying to revive Billy Deemer after Mavis had apparently decked him; close out once and for all any interference in his life and his work.

But somewhere far down the block, he heard Rosemary's voice shouting in panic, "Wait! No! No! Steve!"

His body went into fighting alert. What the hell happened? What the hell could Steve be doing to Rosemary? What the *hell* had gotten into the residents of Lazy Pines this morning? Thank God he'd soon be rid of them all.

Jordan Phillips would be taking no more punches.

He stepped out into the bright sunshine and clear air, confused by the sight of Steve coming up his front steps. He turned to look for Rosemary. Why had she been—

"Sorry about this, man."

"What—"

Jordan looked up, just in time to glimpse Steve's massive fist, a microsecond before it connected with his nose.

ROSEMARY DRAGGED along the path through the low shiny-leafed cranberry plants next to her father's house, searching for ripe berries. Her father wanted to make cranberry-seaweed bread, and Rosemary volunteered for the job of picking cranberries because picking cranberries was a lot more fun than having a nervous breakdown staring at the wall. How she was going to pass the afternoon she had no idea, except maybe she could read Jordan's book and hate his heroine for a while.

Tonight she had another Cure session where she would teach Jordan to unlock his creativity through the power of meditation and positive visualization. And after all she'd gone through in the past two weeks: finding out Jordan was Her Destiny, trying to cure him, kissing him on Seamen's Delight, hearing those people doing it in the bushes, unblocking him, kissing him on the beach, hearing those people doing it again, watching poor Jordan get punched in the nose yesterday...

After all that, she couldn't shake off a thoroughly uncharacteristic and completely unwelcome feeling of dread. A feeling that tonight was going to be a make or break, do or die, latex or door-slamming moment in her and Jordan's relationship. That after tonight she and Jordan would know whether their future lay together or whether Her Destiny had been a lousy stinking liar all these years.

All of which was making her drag through the cranberry plants because she absolutely *hated* when things didn't go well, or smoothly, or with any degree of logic or decency. Everything she'd worked so hard to accomplish for her and Jordan had succeeded, and there wasn't a thing to show for her success. The more she and Jordan got together, the more progress they made, and the further apart they grew.

It didn't make sense.

And the further apart they grew, the more she started to wonder if somehow she would have been better off going to Paris and eating croissants and rabbit in a wine-and-mustard sauce with Jean-Whatever and his brother Jean-Something-Else. Because nothing could be worse than coming face-to-face with your very own custom-designed Destiny and discovering it might not fit you.

"Rosemary!"

Rosemary turned her head only enough to bring the owner of the voice into visual range. Billy Deemer. Hurray.

"Rosemary, I'm so glad I found you."

"Hi, Billy." She tried to inject enthusiasm into her voice, but her voice was not prepared to enthuse. "What can I do for you?"

He mopped his brow, which glistened with sweat in the cool morning air. "I wanted to apologize to you for punching Jordan."

"To me?" Rosemary shrugged. "Shouldn't you apologize to Jordan?"

"Uh...probably." His eyes grew round and glassy. "But I'm scared of him."

"Oh, Billy." Rosemary sighed and gave up cranberry gathering. "Believe me, I understand."

"I mean, he's so smart, and intense, and talented, and..."

"Good-looking," Rosemary added glumly. "And don't forget sexy."

"And I'm just fat and dumb."

"Billy!" Sympathetic outrage flooded Rosemary's body. "You are not just fat and dumb. You're lots of other things, too."

Billy sank down dejectedly onto a handy boulder. Rosemary groaned and pinched herself for punishment.

"What I *meant* was, you have a lot to offer, Billy. You're sweet and funny, and gentle and kind, and…" She looked at Billy, hoping he'd break in so she wouldn't have to admit she was running low on adjectives.

"I guess I am all those things. But Mavis never…no matter how much I…well, love just shouldn't be this *hard.*"

Rosemary gaped as if he'd just told her the meaning of life, which she thought he just might have. "Say that again."

"It shouldn't be this complicated." He gestured helplessly. "When two people really like each other and really want each other, they should be able to be together. Period."

Rosemary kept gaping. For some reason she might someday be able to piece together, Billy Deemer was making sense. Mostly. There was one part in there…

"Mavis…wants you?"

"Yes." Billy and his chins nodded emphatically. "A couple of times we've even…even…*you* know."

Rosemary nodded, willing the image of Billy and Mavis coupling to leave her alone for the rest of time.

"She's wild." He sighed and stared wistfully off into the woods. "A regular sexual dynamo."

"How sweet." Rosemary forced a sick smile, aware something was raising its hand frantically in the back of her mental classroom, yelling, "Oh, oh, oh."

She looked at Billy speculatively. "If you don't mind me asking, when you and Mavis...'*you* know-ed,' was it ever on Seamen's Delight? Or down on our shore?"

"Oh no, never there." Billy blushed and shook his head. "It was in the kitchen at the Anchor Barn one time, and..."

"Okay, never mind." Rosemary smiled through the disappointment that she hadn't solved the mystery of the wild monkeys, and made a mental note never ever to eat at the Anchor Barn again.

"But then afterward, it's always, 'I don't know what I want, Billy...I'm not ready for commitment, Billy...I have too many things to work through, Billy.'" He wiped his brow and upper lip despondently. "It shouldn't be that way."

"I understand." Rosemary flopped down on the ground, not caring if her rear thwarted the seaweed bread potential of any cranberries. "More than you know."

"If people like each other and want each other, and one of them is just too pigheaded and messed up to admit it, and I'm not talking about *me* here—" he jabbed himself in the chest with a pudgy thumb "—then what I say is..."

Rosemary rose onto her haunches, hardly daring to

admit she was looking to Billy Deemer for confirmation regarding her and Jordan and her potentially deceitful Destiny. "What do you say?"

Something came over Billy's face Rosemary had never seen even hinted there before. It took her a minute to recognize, but then it hit her. Determination. Pride. Courage.

Wow. *Go, Billy.* "To hell with her." He smacked his thighs, causing them to ripple in impressive aftershocks. "I have a lot of love to give. I want to get married someday. I want to have lots and lots of little Deemers."

"Good for you." Rosemary applauded and winced at the image of all those little Billys overrunning Lazy Pines, and winced harder at the image of her having possibly to deliver the same speech to Jordan tonight. Because Billy was putting into words what she believed right down to the very core of her being was the absolute truth. And she didn't have to look very far past Mavis and Billy to see another couple with the very same unfortunate set of circumstances.

"I'm not waiting around until Mavis finally realizes I'm the best thing that ever could have happened to her. Because what if she never does?"

Rosemary listened and thought quite possibly all the unhappiness she had never given any power in her life might be about to dive in and claim its natural place in her universe.

"Because, damn it, I want to be *happy,* but I don't think I'll ever be happy with Mavis. And I think I finally know why."

"Why?" Fear crawled a slow clingy-legged insect path up Rosemary's spine. Because if Billy knew what she thought he did, which she knew as well but hadn't had the nerve or the desire or the plain honesty to admit to herself, then tonight would be her and Jordan's very last tango together.

"Because..." Billy leaned forward, and looked into her eyes with his very, very blue ones, and for the first time ever, Rosemary could see the fine and gentle and wonderful things Mavis must see in him. "...either you're pregnant or you're not."

"Uh, Billy?"

"What I mean is, all this talk of commitment and emotional luggage and uncertainty is just her way of saying, 'Forget it, I'm never going to be with you.'" He leaned closer, wagged his finger in Rosemary's face, and fixed her with a wise and very mournful basset-hound-type expression that made Rosemary's body absolutely brace itself for the blow she knew was coming.

"Because either you love someone or you don't, Rosemary. It's just that simple."

9

JORDAN SAT on the edge of his bed, staring at the clock—7:50. Rosemary was due in ten minutes and he hadn't yet settled on the best way to tell her. How did you break it to someone who had staked their whole future on you that you were sorry, but their life plan didn't suit you?

He pushed himself off the bed and slammed his hands against the wall, leaning his forehead against the cool wood as if in supplication for advice or comfort. He was doing the right thing. He had to keep telling himself he was doing the right thing for both of them. Because when that doorbell rang, and Rosemary burst in and filled his parents' little house with her joy and energy and freshness, perspective would become a scarce commodity as it always did when she was around.

Somehow, when he planned all this, the idea that he actually wouldn't be able to see Rosemary again hadn't sunk in. He still wasn't sure it had. Even during the ten years they'd been apart, he'd carried her with him—dreamed about her, written about her. Now, when his lifelong desire to have her as a lover instead of a friend was closest to being realized, he'd have to deliberately, artificially sever their bond.

He felt like Jordan at seven years old, standing on the playground after Jason Archer cheated at soccer, screaming that it wasn't fair.

The doorbell rang. He braced his body and mind, reminded himself of everything at stake, and opened the door.

"Hi, Jordan."

"Hi, Rosemary." He stood there, holding the door open, drinking in the sight of her. She'd left her hair down so it fell in soft undulating waves around her face and over her shoulders. Her skin glowed rosy and smooth in the early evening light. She wore a loose flowery dress of some thin material that would probably cling to her body when she moved.

He stared at her, trying to make himself understand that he wouldn't be able to make love to her tonight, or ever. It didn't seem remotely possible.

"Can I come in?" She grinned at him, a little apprehensively. He nodded and moved aside, aware something was different about her tonight, but not yet able to place it.

She came in and stood quietly, arms at her sides, looking at him with an expression he couldn't quite decipher. Not quite longing. Not quite fear. Not quite Rosemary.

"Would you like something to drink?" He asked the question to break the strained silence, though he wasn't sure he had anything but water in the kitchen.

"No, I'm fine." She nodded and stretched her lips again, clearly not enjoying the smile.

Jordan gestured to a chair and she sat stiffly. He stood like an idiot in the middle of the room, for the first time in his life uneasy around her. All the unsaid things between them bumped around his head until he felt he'd go deaf from the silence. What was she thinking? Had something of his mood communicated itself? Did she suspect anything of his changed plans for their future?

"I'll just get myself something." He went into the kitchen for a glass of water, and an escape from those strangely lifeless eyes. Damn. He dreaded hurting her. He dreaded hurting himself. He had to focus on positive things. Like his writing, his career. The fact that Rosemary would now be free to marry someone who could better fulfill her romantic notions of love and marriage, like Steve. Someone who didn't have to struggle so hard to be himself that he couldn't give her what she needed. Rosemary and Steve would be good for each other.

He put the glass down on the counter to avoid flinging it across the room. Right. Rosemary and Steve. Who the hell was he kidding? He'd be hard-pressed not to show up at the altar and enlarge Steve's nose for their wedding album, the way Steve had enlarged his.

"I read your book."

Rosemary's voice carried into the kitchen, entered Jordan's ear canal and completely paralyzed him. How the hell could he convince her he was serious about breaking up when his passion for her was all over every page?

"Oh?" His throat managed to croak out the syllable though he feared letting go of the dishwasher in case he collapsed on the floor.

"Yes." Rosemary appeared in the kitchen; he tightened his hold on the water miser button. "I liked it, mostly."

"Mostly?" His ego couldn't help being a little stung.

"That heroine." Rosemary shook her head. "She was totally unbelievable."

Jordan's fist clenched suddenly and the water miser cycle started humming behind his jeans.

"I mean for one thing, you couldn't at all tell what the hero saw in her. She was always bossing him around, trying to change him. If I'd been him, I would have told her to get lost."

Jordan let out something between a laugh, a groan and a cry for help, wondering if there was some kind of limit on painful irony in life. This about pushed it. "I think we better meditate."

"Did I insult you?"

"No. You're absolutely right." He let go of the dishwasher and pushed Rosemary gently back into the living room. He just wished she wasn't.

"I loved the rest of it." She looked up at him, eager to please, obviously afraid she'd hurt his feelings.

"I'm glad." He managed a grin. "Let's get started."

"Okay..." She took up a cross-legged position in the middle of the floor and patted the rug in front of her to show Jordan his designated space. "Sit here, across from me."

He sat. He was being a coward. He shouldn't let her stay a minute longer than necessary to explain his new life plan and her noncasting in the costarring role. But the scent of her hair had reached him as she walked ahead of him into this room, and he wanted to savor every second of their last night together. Even if it took him the rest of his life to cool down.

"We'll start with a relaxing meditation exercise, and proceed to positive visualization."

Jordan nodded, aware that if she wanted to wait until he was relaxed to start the visualization, she'd probably need a walker to leave his house.

He closed his eyes and stayed still for the required relax-and-clear-his-mind time, every muscle and brain cell screaming with tension. He opened his eyes to peek at the clock, sure it was past midnight. Eight-thirty.

"Now." Rosemary's voice, low and dreamy, ratcheted Jordan's suffering up several notches. "Imagine you are sitting at your desk. Your mind is clear and light. You are feeling confident and secure."

She opened one eye, obviously hoping confidence and security would be radiating from his peaceful body, and instead caught him staring hotly, wanting to bend her over backward and give her rug burn.

Rosemary frowned. "Close your eyes and concentrate."

He closed his eyes and concentrated on banishing the thoughts that could make *Hustler* magazine his only future option of getting published. He had to end this nightmare. He had to tell Rosemary what he'd decided.

"Now. Imagine you are going to write. You pick up a pen, and—"

"Computer."

"What?" Her voice was distinctly disapproving.

"I write on my computer." He gave a silent groan. What the hell was he doing? The longer he dragged this out, the harder it was on both of them.

"Okay. You are sitting at your computer. You decide you are going to write a new book, about a hero's quest. You type, 'Chapter One.'"

"Uh...usually I do some kind of character sketch first." His torment increased. Character sketch? What the hell did she or anyone else care about character sketches when the most important decision of his life had to be put into practice?

"Fine. You are writing a scene from the *middle* of the book. A battle scene. The hero is involved in a spectacular battle."

"Against what?" *Tell her. Tell her, you fool.*

"Against the Gorgonzola Galaxy Fighters, how the heck do I know? You're the writer."

Jordan opened his eyes and watched her. She sat as if in a trance, eyes closed, hair clouded around her face, describing the battle and his magnificent ease in chronicling it on-screen. Occasionally she'd gesture into the air as if she'd forgotten all about total body relaxation and was entirely lost in the space war.

His body contracted into painful tightness. His throat

thickened into a tense fiery mass. He had to say it. There was no holding back.

"...and just when things looked the worst for Captain Roquefort and his cheesy crew of—"

"I love you, Rosemary. I love you." His voice broke on the words—not the ones he'd intended to say, but he'd been incapable of saying anything else.

Rosemary opened her eyes, which widened into a kind of joyous panic when they saw what must be a look of furious desperation on his face.

"The block came back." He clenched his fists as if he could pummel it into submission. "It makes me sick that life has played this cheap trick, and forced me to choose between the two things I love most in this world."

"Oh, Jordan, sweetheart." She waddled forward on her knees, face glowing, and laid her hand on his arm. "You'll be able to write again, I know you will. Maybe you just need a short break. Once we're married you can move in with me and find a job in the city for a while. Or I know! You could write for *I Am Woman* magazine until your block goes away. They're always looking for writers, and you—"

"Rosemary." Her touch was torture. Her loving gaze was agony. Her faith that he'd choose her was worse. "I can't."

"You can't? Well maybe you could find a job—"

"Rosemary, I can't be with you."

"You mean in the city? But you can't want to stay in Lazy Pines."

He shook his head. "I had to choose. If we got married I'd be happy for maybe a month before I slowly started to go crazy. I *have* to write, Rosemary. It's something I've needed all my life. And now I'm on the cusp of having the kind of life I've dreamed of since we were kids.''

"I remember." Her lips barely moved; she whispered the words as if they'd slipped out inadvertently into the midst of her shock.

"If we got married I'd resent you within six months, a year, tops. I don't want to do that to you."

She looked at him with bewilderment, but also more understanding than he expected. "You love me...and that isn't enough. Is that what you're saying?"

"It's not enough. I wish it were."

She stayed close beside him, hand still on his arm, looking up into his face with that same strange look of sad, wise, maturity he'd seen earlier but not been able to identify.

"Well, I think love *is* enough, Jordan Phillips." She got to her feet and started pacing the room. "I think you're very, very wrong. And I think for the rest of your life you'll regret doing this. Because...either you love someone or you don't. It's that simple."

He took two steps toward her and planted himself to interrupt her pacing. "Do you love me?"

"Of course." She looked earnestly at his chin. "Of course I do."

"Say it."

"You want me to say it now?" She met his eyes incredulously. "Now that you've told me you're dumping our future down the toilet?"

"Yes." He grabbed her shoulders. "I want you to say it now."

"I think you're asking a lot."

"Rosemary, this may surprise you, but no, I'm not. You don't want love. You want romance. You want perfection. Well this is me." He flung his arms out. "I'm tortured and I'm flawed and I love you, and giving you up is the hardest thing I've ever had to do. It will eat me alive until I'm so old I have nothing left inside to be eaten. So the least you could do, to give me one bit of happiness before I go away and shrivel up, is to tell me right now, right here, that you love me."

"The *least* I could do? As if I've done nothing? Haven't I been trying to help you all this time so you could write and we could be together?"

"You've tried to make me over into Steve, Rosemary." He spoke through the heaviest, dullest, weariest pain he'd ever experienced. "I'm not Steve."

"You're selling me short, Jordan." An angry flush spread up her cheeks, making her eyes sparkle even more brightly. "I know you're not Steve. Quite frankly, not even Steve is Steve."

Jordan stopped and frowned at her. He wasn't? "He's not?"

"No. And if you could look one inch beyond your own needs for a minute you'd see that I've been trying to help *you*, not Steve, because I really don't think I can cure what ails him even if I wanted to which is beside the point because I *don't*. I want *you*."

"Why?" He got the word out through clenched teeth, not sure he wanted to hear her answer.

"Because…because we *belong* together. Because we're destined for each other. Because when we kiss it's like an atom bomb went off in the next room."

"Don't you see, Rosemary?" He took hold of her shoulders, fighting the despair that threatened his normal functioning. "That has nothing to do with me. With who I am."

"Of course it does." She hunched to shake off his grip. "What else could it possibly be about?"

He dropped his arms from her shoulders, smoothed her hair away from her face, brought his hand down to cup her cheek, and used every ounce of will and strength he possessed to keep from bringing that face he loved so desperately up to his. "You'll find another Steve, Rosemary. Someone who can be your Destiny. Someone who truly believes love conquers all."

Tears welled up in Rosemary's eyes and seared wet trails down Jordan's heart.

"It does, you know. I really do believe that." She swallowed convulsively. "Love does conquer all… You just have to let it."

They stared at each other hopelessly. Frustration seethed through Jordan's system. How could they be so close and so many light-years apart?

"Goodbye, Jordan."

He followed her miserably to the door and opened it silently. The cool night air flowed in, along with the peaceful rustling animal night sounds of Lazy Pines. "Goodbye, Rosemary."

"… Uh, Jordan?" Rosemary turned her beautiful tearstained face back to him, her lips trembling.

"Yes, Rosemary." Every atom in his body screamed at him to change his mind when she asked, take her back when she begged him, not subject himself to the years of pain and loneliness he now faced, not make the biggest mistake of his life.

Rosemary pointed to the bushes outside his living room window. The rustling animal noises increased along with some urgent whispering.

She smiled and inhaled shakily. "It sounds to me like you got some naked crocheting to do."

RYAN WOKE UP and got out of bed; Jennifer still lay in it. He dressed in an old T-shirt and jeans with holes from rusty nails from that warehouse. He and Jennifer had gone over it yesterday with a fine-tooth comb, looking for the final evidence that would tie Hostetler to the Cardinal. They had found nothing. He went downstairs and poured a bowl of cereal. The skim milk had gone sour. He made a face and poured it down the kitchen sink. Now there was nothing for break-fast….

JORDAN BENT his head and left it dangling over his keyboard. One week. One week since he'd made his brilliant decision to remove Rosemary from his life. A week and a half since he'd been able to put together a decent paragraph. He'd started the summer with a promising career. Started August with a career and the hope of having Rosemary in his life. Now, three weeks into the month, he had neither.

Beer. He shoved back his chair, strode into the kitchen and yanked open the refrigerator door. Empty. He swore and looked at the clock. Ten-thirty on a Saturday. The Anchor Barn would be jammed with locals, especially tonight after the Daughters of Charity Talent Show, but beer was beer, and he needed one.

He grabbed his keys and set off down Main Street, dimly lit by occasional streetlights, the humid air swirling grey with fog. Saturday. Tomorrow Rosemary would go back to New York. Maybe then the block would lift. Maybe knowing she was out of town would somehow cement into his brain the idea she was out of his life, cement the hole in his heart, and allow him to get on with his existence.

Maybe. If only he could accept, as she did, that love was enough. If only he could agree all he had to do to conquer his block was believe he could. But it wasn't his way to ignore facts and repercussions and operate based solely on what he *wanted* to have happen. Life was too complicated. Too much was at stake.

He pushed open the door to the Anchor Barn and stopped. What the hell was he doing? Rosemary could be here. He scanned the crowd anxiously.

"She's home with her dad tonight."

Jordan heaved a sigh of relief and grinned sheepishly at Mavis. "Anywhere to sit?"

She gestured behind him. "Big group there just leaving twenty-three. You can have that table. I don't expect many more coming in tonight."

"Thanks, Mavis."

"Jordan."

He turned back toward her, dreading her sympathy.

"I put up some blueberry jam yesterday." She put her hands on her hips and regarded him like a stern but affectionate sister. "You can come by any time...day or night. Any time you need some good homemade jam."

Jordan thanked her, touched by her offer of support in spite of his cynicism. Mavis was okay. As long as you didn't offend any of her quick-fisted protectors.

A boisterous roar erupted behind him as the group leaving table twenty-three pushed by and surrounded the register.

"There he goes again."

"Mavis, that man'll kill himself for you."

"Heard he even enrolled for correspondence classes at the university."

Jordan craned his neck in time to see Billy Deemer, lit by the Anchor Barn lights, huffing past the window on his twice-daily jog through Lazy Pines in an attempt to improve himself for his beloved. By the sparkle in Mavis's eye and the color in her face, Jordan might give Billy some pretty decent odds. Totally unexpected, but decent.

He sat down and ordered two beers from the waitress, responding to her sympathetic smile with a resigned nod. By now, privacy was a dimly remembered luxury.

"Hello, Jordan, dear." A light hand rested on his shoulder. "Mind if we join you?"

Jordan closed his eyes, then turned around with what he hoped was an apologetic smile. "Actually I was kind of hoping to be al—"

Mr. Cudahy and Dolores Thompson pulled up chairs, sat down, and fixed him with the same sorry-for-your-pain look he'd been suffering through all week.

"You'll *never* guess who won our talent show tonight." Dolores sat back and glowed as if she knew the results of the Oscars weeks before anyone else.

"No, I'm sure I won't." Jordan tried to smile politely, tried to beat down the feeling he was trapped for eternity with Dolores Thompson and Mr. Cudahy in some kind of existential Anchor Barn hell.

"Well." Dolores daintily slapped the table. "We were all *sure* the winner would be—"

"Sometimes I'm afraid to leave my house." Mr. Cudahy nodded gravely at Jordan and shifted in what must be a startlingly unfamiliar chair.

"I'm...sorry to hear that." Jordan rubbed tense fingers through his hair. How blunt could you be about asking polite elderly people to get the hell away from you?

"Oh yes, indeed." Dolores nodded at Mr. Cudahy as if he were the wisest man she'd ever known. "We don't ask for these things to happen, we don't want them to happen, but they seem to happen anyway, don't they?"

"I'm sorry." Jordan's voice came out sounding slightly strangled. "But I was really hoping to be—"

"I hate cars and buses, you know, dear. Airplanes,

too, and trains. I'm practically afraid of them. And I'd always wanted to see the world." Dolores patted Jordan's hand. "Most peculiar, but there you are."

"That is peculiar." Jordan glanced down at his beer, wondering if they'd leave if he started crying into it.

"Oh!" Dolores clapped her hands. "I got sidetracked by our little lecture. I must tell you who won the—"

"Hi, guys." Steve pulled up a chair and sat, a strained expression on his face.

"Of course I always have my chair here, and Howard's counter across the street. That makes it easier to get out." Mr. Cudahy looked to one side, frowning as if he couldn't remember if he just said the words or only thought them.

Jordan mumbled several expressions unsuitable for the ears of minors. Maybe he could casually admit to a contagious plague.

"I'm sorry *you* didn't win the talent show, Steve, dear." Dolores shook her head mournfully at him. "But you did kick that football awfully far."

"It was a good shot, wasn't it?" Steve looked marginally more cheerful.

"It certainly was." Dolores leaned closer and put her hand on his shoulder. "And don't you worry about that other little trouble. Ruth Alexander is just getting a little too old to duck as fast as she used to. I'm sure she'll recover nicely."

Steve glanced over at Jordan. "Didn't see you there tonight. What's up?"

Jordan gripped the neck of his beer, trying to stop

the rising tide of sarcasm springing to his lips. "Well, gosh, I tried and tried to arrange my entire calendar so I could see the Lazy Pines Talent Show, but I just couldn't swing it."

Silence fell over the table. Jordan sighed. He hadn't meant to be cruel. But he *really* wanted to be left alone.

"I guess maybe you have other things on your mind than who won." Dolores spoke kindly and made Jordan feel even worse.

"I'm sorry. I wasn't—"

"I was just telling Jordan about my fear of transportation." Dolores turned to Steve. "The minute I step into anything on wheels I can't keep a thing down."

Mr. Cudahy nodded his agreement. "Some days I just lie in bed and stare at the ceiling and don't move. Those days I'm glad my fifth dog Rex has his Ever-Feeder."

"In bed all day?" Steve frowned. "What do you do when you have to…"

"Oh, that." Mr. Cudahy raised his finger like a witness about to crush the prosecution. "Depends."

Steve frowned. "On what?"

"Look." Jordan suppressed a roar of frustration. "I appreciate that you are trying to cheer me up, but I really need to be alone, so I'm going to take my beers, and go over to the—"

"Actually, I came over here to tell you something, my man." Steve rubbed his nose with a huge thumb and forefinger. "I lied about how I stopped playing football. I didn't mess up my knee so bad that time. I coulda kept playing. I coulda kept playing with the pros.''

Jordan stared at him. He was getting used to the surreal nature of the conversation around him. And for once he was interested in something the big jock had to say. ''Why didn't you?''

''After I signed, every time I was ready to go out onto the field, my muscles would lock, and I'd get so scared I wanted to die.'' He shook his head slowly. ''It was weird. I mean, like, I'd been playing football all my life, and loved it. Then suddenly it started scaring me to death, and I didn't have fun anymore. It stunk.''

Jordan felt his first twinge of human empathy toward Steve. He sure as hell knew what that felt like. ''What happened?''

''Nothing.'' Steve shrugged dejectedly. ''I quit and came here to coach.''

''I stay in bed or I come here to my chair or I go to Howard's.'' Mr. Cudahy made his announcement and blinked solemnly. ''That's it for me.''

''I never became a world traveler. I never even leave Lazy Pines.'' Dolores spread her palms in surrender. ''And I always wanted to see Paris. Maine, that is.''

The three of them sat and stared at Jordan as if they dared him to make sense of anything they'd said in the past fifteen minutes.

Jordan rubbed his hand across his chin. It made sense, all right. He'd love to report that his heart swelled with charitable sympathy, but right now all he could think about was that he'd be damned if he allowed himself to end up like any of them.

Steve reached across the table and covered Jordan's hand with his. "Fight while you still can, man. Or you'll regret it. Forever."

"You can choose to fight or choose to give up. It's that simple, dear."

It's that simple. Rosemary's voice came back to Jordan from their last meeting, *Either you love someone or you don't....* Either you fight or you don't.... Make black-and-white choices about grey matters and by sheer persistence make sure they work.

It was crazy. A life philosophy based on nothing but childish stubbornness. With absolutely nothing going for it—except it was the only thing he hadn't tried.

Something that felt very much like hope welled up through Jordan's system. Something approaching determination threaded its way through the hope.

If he could manage to look at his life that way, adopt the Rosemary Jenkins outlook, instead of choosing between Rosemary and writing, he could make his own choice. Rosemary and fighting whatever caused this strange anxiety, or staying trapped forever, wishing he could change the past, like the Three Nutsketeers across the table.

He became aware of Steve's hand still covering his, and narrowed his eyes. Steve blushed and jerked back his arm.

Steve? Jordan stifled the mad urge to chuckle. Was that what Rosemary meant when she said even Steve wasn't Steve? Maybe Jordan could have wasted a little *more* time being jealous.

He shook his head in wry amusement. How could

he ever think he could sweep Rosemary from his life? He was even starting to see through her eyes. The business with Steve had been a complication Jordan had invented. *It's that simple. Either you love someone or you don't.*

"You see we're all...everyone in Lazy Pines, we're all involved in your past and your future, Jordan, dear. We all care very much about you."

"Are you kidding?" He gaped in disbelief. "I've always been treated like a bag of manure."

Mr. Cudahy cleared his throat emotionally. "But you're *our* bag of man—"

"Oh no." Dolores shook her head so hard her neck became a wobbly blur. "No one treated you like a bag of manure, dear. You've just always behaved like one. People think you don't like us."

He looked around again at their faces. Mr. Cudahy's confused affectionate grin; Steve's dull earnest smile; Dolores Thompson's soft pleading eyes. Could everything really be explained that easily? All the years of isolation living here fixed merely by being nicer? All the angst and confusion of facing his demons erased by deciding they would disappear? Was life really all that simple if you just decided it was?

Jordan grinned and shook his head wryly, the hope and determination going for broke this time. Okay, she'd won. He'd try out the Rosemary Method and decide to have it all.

He smiled the first real smile he'd managed in what seemed like years. Odd as they were, the faces across from him felt strangely like family.

"So." He laughed and smacked his palm on the scratched wooden table. "Who's going to tell me who won the Lazy Pines Talent Show?"

"YOU WON?" Rosemary clutched the mug of coffee her dad had made her, and stretched her eyes open as wide as their red-rimmed lids would let her. "Dad, that's terrific! What did you do?"

She asked the question with more than a little guilt because, being his daughter, she should know what he entered in the talent show. She should have gone tonight, in fact, but she'd been busy sitting on her bed crying. Because nothing made sense anymore. She loved Jordan and she couldn't be with him. He loved her and he gave her up. And worst, in the midst of her agony over losing him, she'd been horrified at a traitorous tiny bit of relief, because the emotions when she was with him had gotten so complicated and terrifying and hard to control. What kind of hypocritical wacko did *that* make her? She *loved* him for heaven's sakes. And she hadn't even been able to tell him.

"At first I wanted to sing *'O sole mio.'* Anna—that's Mavis's mother—loves opera. It's her favorite aria." He blushed. "But even after I practiced every day for some time, I couldn't sing it very well."

"I never heard you practice." Rosemary studied her father's back as he stood, stirring something on the stove. She'd never heard him sing a note her entire life. He must really be fond of Mavis's mother.

"Oh, I went far away, believe me. I never was much

of a singer. The point is, I was going after a fantasy, not what I was really meant to do.''

Rosemary's eyes narrowed. "This is starting to sound like a lecture.''

"Fantasies are wonderful things, but you have to remember that's what they are. I couldn't just open my mouth and sing because I wanted to. Singing takes years of hard work and dedication.''

He opened his mouth and launched into the most horrific wailing version of *'O sole mio'* the world had ever heard.

Rosemary gasped. The sound was painfully familiar. "Dad? When you were practicing, did you ever go out to Seamen's Delight? Or down on the shore?''

"Yes.'' He peered at her over his shoulder. "How did you know?''

Oh my goodness. As if this entire week hadn't been strange enough, Rosemary just found out her father was a wild monkey who practiced scales that sounded like weird sex.

"Never mind.'' She stood up and went over to inspect the greenish-brown glop he was stirring. "So, what did you win with? And what is that?''

"This is going to be kelp-and-Irish-moss ice cream. I won with my mixed seaweed bread. A recipe I've been developing for years. At first it was terrible—but I knew that seaweed bread could be the best damn thing anyone ever tasted. And because I had that vision for my seaweed bread, I worked and worked until that loaf became the finest loaf you'll ever eat from the sea. And I still may not be done. For the rest of my life,

Rosemary, I might have to adjust and fine-tune and tinker with that recipe. But as long as my vision of that seaweed bread is fine and true, it will last me a lifetime.''

Rosemary grimaced. ''This is definitely a lecture.''

''Just *wanting* to sing is not enough.'' He gestured with the whisk and left a dotted trail of brownish-green cream across the stove. ''Anything worth its salt takes work. Plenty of it, some painful.''

''So I've been trying for a singing career with Jordan,'' Rosemary looked at him mournfully, ''and I ought to be making him seaweed bread.''

''Yes.'' He turned to meet her eyes. ''Did you read his book?''

''Uh-huh. With that dreadful heroine who had to have everything her way.'' Rosemary took the whisk from her father and nudged him out of the way. ''You should stir with a more circular motion. And I think your heat is too high. You don't want the eggs to curdle or you'll have—''

She froze. Then dropped the whisk as if it were suddenly red-hot.

''Me!'' Rosemary turned to stare at her father incredulously. ''That—that horrible manipulative woman is me.''

Her father grinned and rescued the whisk. ''The whole town recognized you.''

''He must hate me. The whole town must hate me.'' She closed her eyes; her stomach sank, pulling her mood even further down along with it. She must have known underneath that Ada was her. Because it all made sense right away once she admitted it to herself. And here she'd told Jordan that Ada wasn't good enough for Ryan, and he must have thought so, too, because he gave Rosemary up.

Rosemary pressed her hands to her face. Every negative emotion she'd managed to keep out of her life for the past almost-three decades attacked her all at once. Her bubble hadn't been burst, it had been run over with a tank. Who the hell did she think she was, telling anyone what they should do with their life? She'd been a complete pretentious idiot. If she had a dog it would probably growl and bite her.

"I'm a total fool."

"That's my no-shades-of-gray Rosemary." Her father shook his head. "Everyone else who read the book could only see the love in each word."

"But Ada's so…irritating." She clenched her fists at her sides, wanting to stop feeling hurt and mortified, and curl up in fetal position for the rest of her life. "How can he love her? How can he love me if I'm that irritating?"

"No one is perfect. No one is going to make anyone blissful every second of the rest of their lives." His vigorous stirring sloshed seaweed custard onto the gas flame where it immediately filled the kitchen with an odor like burning hair. "I adored your mother, even though she drove me crazy sometimes—and I know I did the same to her."

"Mom did?" Rosemary wrinkled her nose and waved at the air in front of her face. "But I never saw you fighting, or—"

"You were young, Rosemary. You saw what you wanted to see."

"I guess I still do." Rosemary moved back to the table and slumped into a chair, eyeing the coffee distastefully. She felt like she'd woken up from a twenty-eight-year blissful dream to discover the world was really her worst nightmare. "I always thought you and Mom were perfect for each other."

"We were." He lowered the flame under the pot and turned toward her. "That's my point. But perfection should never be the goal. If you hold out for perfection you might as well give up hope right now."

Rosemary took a slug of the coffee, figuring she might as well ruin her body since herbal tea hadn't exactly brought her undying happiness. Had she been trying to make Jordan perfect? He certainly thought so. She thought she'd just been trying to help him. But tonight, with her rosy lenses distorted by spiderweb cracks, she wasn't so sure of anything anymore. Except that she loved him, and she couldn't figure out how to get past their problems, and having him and losing him terrified her equally.

"Dad...were you scared when you married Mom?"

"Of course, honey. The unknown is always scary, even if you're sure you're doing the right thing. But if you don't hold your breath and dive, you'll never find out one way or the other."

Rosemary nodded, drinking in his reassurance. A curious tingling heart-pounding sensation began in her chest, which she wasn't entirely sure was the coffee. Her father had been scared. And if she'd stopped being full of herself long enough ago, she'd have realized that Dolores and Mr. Cudahy and his somethingth dog Rex had been scared, too; they'd been trying to tell her the same thing way, way back then, on Thursday.

"Falling in love isn't an end, Rosemary, it's a beginning." Her father smiled tenderly and spilled half the ice-cream base he was pouring into a narrow jar. "If I've failed in one thing raising you, it's that I haven't managed to make you see how you've always gone to extremes. If you're not the best you must be the worst. If Lazy Pines isn't paradise then it must be hell. If your love with Jordan isn't everything you thought, then the whole thing is over. Nothing in life is that simple, Rosemary. Nothing."

She stared at him as if he were the relic she'd been seeking on a lifelong quest. Her world was still upside down, but from its new position, things were starting to look a little clearer. *Nothing in life is that simple.* She *had* always viewed events and emotions in black-and-white terms. Things either were or weren't. You were pregnant or not. Maybe she and Billy Deemer had oversimplified a little. Maybe Jordan didn't deserve the yes-or-no ultimatum she gave him.

"Love...isn't enough." She couldn't help sounding wistful. You couldn't give up a lifelong dream without at least a little wistfulness.

"No." Her father grinned, and ran a custardy hand through his graying hair. "But it's a damn fine start. I think you and Jordan could be very happy together. But it'll take a whole lot of...of..."

"Seaweed bread." Rosemary crossed the kitchen

and flung herself into his arms. She clung to his familiar strength and the musty tweed professor scent she'd treasured since she was a girl.

Determination flooded her body. She could make this work. She could go to Jordan right now and tell him she'd wait. She'd wait as long as it took until he— until *they*—could work through his problems whatever way he thought best. Even if it meant being apart for a little while. She'd wait. "Thank you, Daddy," she whispered.

"It's late. Go upstairs to bed and think about—"

"Upstairs? Now?" She laughed and pulled away, her heart singing a damn sight better than her father could. "No way. I have to go see Jordan."

"Rosemary, no one can change their life philosophy in one evening...." He chuckled. "Though I suppose if anyone could, it would be you. But I think you'd be better off sleeping on this until you're sure."

"Oh, Dad. Don't worry." Rosemary threw her arms around his neck and kissed his cheek. Joy was positively racing through her, minutes after she'd been so sure she'd never feel it again. "I've never been more sure of anything in my life."

10

ROSEMARY WALKED UP Jordan's front path, heart still pounding from nervousness and her brisk hike through town. The house was dark; the front windows closed against the chilly, humid night air. She went up to the front door and rang the bell, shivering on his stoop, partly from the damp, but mostly from the excitement.

No answer.

She knocked, pressing her ear close to the door to hear anything inside—the slightest sound. Because he absolutely, absolutely *couldn't* be anywhere but home waiting for her tonight, though he might not know that's what he was doing. She squinted at her watch in the dull foggy glow of the streetlight. Just after midnight.

She rang the doorbell again, wrapped her arms around her chest and bounced up and down with impatience. *Please, don't let him be away.*

No answer.

She leaped off the stoop and hurried around to the back of the house. Dark there, too, inside and out, with no light from the street, and no noise. She'd have to see if there was a way to break in, gently of course, because it was cold and she didn't relish the idea of presenting Jordan with the love of his life half-dead from hypothermia. And she'd be damned if she'd go home without accomplishing her mission after having come so far—physically and emotionally.

She scanned the windows in back of his house, eyes by now adjusted to the darkness. Much too high. Too much risk of ending the evening in a Lazy Pines hospital bed instead of Jordan's. She continued around to the south side where his bedroom was. No lights; no sounds; no open windows.

Back to the front, then. Maybe one of the living room windows, easily in reach, was unlocked. She pushed through the front bushes and tried one of the three. Locked. She pushed to her left, snagging her sweater on the prickly evergreen branches and swearing softly and not at all daintily.

The lights in the living room snapped on. Rosemary ducked immediately on adrenaline instinct, forgetting she *wanted* Jordan to see her.

He was home. Her heart began pounding from joy instead of fear. Jordan, her love, Her Destiny, was home. In one second, she'd rise and reveal herself, put in motion the reconciliation that would last their lifetime.

She closed her eyes to savor the moment. *Here. Now. It all starts here and now. Jordan and Rosemary.*

Tears welled into her eyes; she rose, her vision half-blurred, and peered into the living room.

And saw Jordan, sitting just-showered in a rocking chair, stark naked, crochet hook busily twirling a soft blue yarn.

Her tears increased, but this time because she was laughing hard and slightly hysterically. Oh gosh, he was beautiful. Even crocheting. He was priceless and he was beautiful and she'd wait for him until she was ninety if that's what he wanted. She tapped on the window, unable to resist the sight of his face when he saw her.

He yawned, stretched mightily, and made a big show of scratching where polite people don't.

As soon as her giggles released their hold enough to let her, Rosemary called his name. Then tapped on the glass again. "Jordan."

This time he glanced over at the window, arm raised for another good scratch in a brand-new not-so-tasteful place. His eyes met hers. He froze. Then moved faster than any human had ever moved since time began, she was sure of it. The ball of yarn practically flew off the ground and served a purpose usually reserved for fig leaves.

He held up a finger to indicate she should wait—as if she'd come to see him crochet and might now leave—and backed out of the room with an endearingly mortified smile, desperately clutching the yarn to his most manly parts.

Rosemary struggled through the shrubbery up to his front door, stomach muscles tight and exhausted from laughing. Poor Jordan. Thinking he'd finally given the Daughters of Charity what they craved and finding his first undressing for the love of his life done with considerably less sensuality than he might have liked.

His door flew open.

"Rosemary." Jordan stood there, in sweatpants and, Rosemary was pretty sure, nothing else. The sound of him saying her name with so much joy, combined with the beautiful dark-haired, magnificent-chested sight of him made her feel a little dizzy and slightly wobbly and completely wonderful.

"Hi, Jordan. I forgot my crochet hook. Do you have an extra?"

He grimaced and grinned. "When I heard you snooping around, I thought you were the Daughters again."

"I did ring the bell, but you must have been in the shower." She pointed to his still-wet hair and smiled, and he smiled back, and they stood there for a little while just drinking in the sight of each other, until Jordan must have remembered she was standing outside in the damp, chilly air, because he invited her in.

She stood in his living room, as she'd stood there before, but now suddenly with Jordan's chest bare and muscled and nicely shot with hair, and the rest of his body only covered by one thin layer of cotton, the living room seemed an awful lot smaller than it had ever seemed before.

Rosemary took a deep breath. If she wanted to tell him all the important and inspiring things she'd learned about herself and about them, she'd have to do it now because with him looking like that and staring at her as if she were a deer cornered in a lion's cage, she had a feeling very soon there would be little time for talking.

"Jordan, I've been a fool."

"No, I've been a fool."

"No, me." She put her hand to her chest. "I was bossy and insensitive, and you were right, I was trying to make you into my fantasy image of what I wanted, only I didn't realize."

"No, Rosemary, you were trying to help me. I'm the fool. I was too afraid to trust what we felt for each other."

He looked so mournful and contrite, Rosemary wanted to wrap herself around him and hold him forever, but she was currently too astonished.

"But what about your writing? What about resenting me forever?"

"I'd hate myself forever if all I had was life without you. The writing will take care of itself someday. I know that. You taught me something very important, Rosemary." He took hold of her shoulders and slid his hands up to cup her face. "Either you love someone, or you don't. It's just that simple."

She frowned and stepped back. Just when she'd figured it all out, he was making things complicated again. "Actually, you were right before. Love isn't enough. It's only a beginning."

He drew a frustrated hand across his forehead. "So I guess what we've figured out is that life is either simple or it's not, and love may or may not be enough."

"I guess that's it." She shrugged and gazed at him earnestly. "All I know is I'm willing to do whatever it takes so we can be together, Jordan. If you want me to be away from you for a while, I'll go."

He moved closer again, devouring her with a dark, hungry look. His sweatpants had taken on a new and intriguing shape. "Do I look like I want you to be away from me?"

"Oh, Jordan." Rosemary pressed herself against him, joy careening through her system. "My father said I should take tonight to think things over, but I couldn't wait to see you."

He kissed her, and his mouth was soft and strong, his chin and cheeks rough and masculine against her face. "I wanted to come see you tonight, but I thought I ought to wait until morning." He laughed and kissed her cheek and temple, his mouth leaving warm tasted spots on her skin.

"I rush right in where you fear to tread," she whispered. "Which proves I'm the fool."

"I'm no angel, Rosemary, but I do love you." He raised his head and stroked the hair away from her forehead, a question, and faint fear in his eyes.

Her heart swelled with tenderness and an eagerness to say the words. "I love you, Jordan."

He pulled her to him and kissed her again, but differently this time. Fiercely, possessively, as if her words had spurred him on to so much feeling he couldn't stop trying to capture it with his mouth against hers.

His hand slid down the length of her back and pressed her hips close to him. Close to the hard, male part of him that seemed intent on finding her of its own accord, even through the sweatpants.

He took her hand and led her into his bedroom where

the bed waited as if it were made for this occasion and had suffered the weight of his body alone for many years only because it knew this moment would finally come.

She sat on the bed; he stood before her, cupped her chin and turned it up so she was lost in the dark, passionate strength of his gaze, and out of the blue, Jordan asked her.

"Rosemary, will you marry me?"

Rosemary nodded. She nodded because her throat was too full of tears and happiness to be able to produce something as simple and delightful as "yes," but Jordan seemed to be satisfied with the look on her face because he spilled her back onto the bed and covered her body with the long lean length of his.

He kissed her again, and this time the kisses held reverence and joy and the knowledge they'd be together for the rest of their lives, fight whatever battles needed to be fought, and win them together.

But right now, Rosemary wanted his body.

She opened her legs so his sweatpant-encased hips sank between them and she treasured the hot pressure of him against her eager and by now ready sex.

She hooked her legs around his so he was trapped against her, and pressed her cheek to his cheek, and slid her hands down to cover his amazing backside, and pushed up against him in a rhythm that was nearly her undoing before they even got to the good part.

"Rosemary." He untangled himself and set about undressing her, with reverent gentleness. Then as her body came into his view, finally free and aching to be his, his gentle and reverent movements turned more toward those of that dangerous pirate who hadn't had a woman for much much too long. And who'd never had this one, who loved him to distraction and would be his wife someday soon.

Rosemary countered by pulling off his sweatpants and bending down to taste him, to feel with her mouth what she wanted in her body, and he bore it, groaning, for a few minutes, then gave a frustrated pirate roar and tumbled her on her back again.

This time he slid inside her, direct and true, as if he were meant to find her no matter where she was. He fit exactly inside her and she gave a long shuddering sigh of bliss at the feel of him filling her.

His rhythm was slow and sweet, and he gazed down at her while he rocked so she knew she was all he could think about, and care about and love at that moment, which was all she could do as well. Then his strokes became harder and faster and put into her body a hot urgency she knew would soon give way to waves of release.

And when it came, it came for both of them, magically and simultaneously, lips and limbs entwined, rising together; rising, then frozen for the burning wave to sweep across, then coming down and coming down until they rested, breathless and sighing and still occasionally pulsing together.

Rosemary lay under him, clasping him hard against her, fighting to stop the silly helpless need to cry that came from having been so afraid she'd lost him and now so, *so* happy to find him again.

Jordan lifted his head. "Remember when I said sex the first time wouldn't be some magical cinematic moment?"

She moved slowly beneath him, tears successfully banished by the sight of his dark, handsome, equally happy face. "Mmm?"

"Wrong, huh? Jordan making simple things complicated again?"

She smiled. She felt like purring. Like a cat full of food and milk who'd been brushed for three hours into blissful dozing ecstasy. "Don't worry. If you want bad, awkward sex, I could always find a way to—"

"Don't bother, really. Thanks, though. Fantastic sex is perfectly fine." He rolled off her, drew her to him and kissed her forehead. "I'm sure I can get used to it."

Rosemary fit her body to his, stroking his chest and savoring the feel of his arms pressing her close. She and Jordan deserved this. They'd worked their way to each other through long odds. Everything was open and clear between them. Except...

"Jordan...am I really as bad as Ada?"

"Bad?" He lifted his head and stared at her in genuine astonishment. "Bad? There's nothing bad about Ada. She's my masterpiece, my inspiration, my salva—"

His eyes widened; his body tensed; he stared up at the ceiling as if a lightning bolt could come down at any moment and strike him senseless, or as if it already had.

"Oh, *man*." He rose up onto his elbows. "How

could I not have thought of this before? I'll bring Ada back. *She'll* find the evidence to connect Hostetler. Or maybe she stumbled across it, working on another case. She and Ryan can catch the Cardinal together.''

Rosemary looked at him, hardly daring to breathe. Was this it? The end of his block? Had he finally dared to believe he could have love and writing, too?

Jordan bolted up to sitting, eyes electrically alive, hair tousled by their lovemaking. ''I can see the scene. Ryan is poring over the notes. There's a knock at the door. He looks up. Ada's already leaning into the room. She'll say something snappy, smart. Ryan'll feel every emotion known to man all at once. He'll be hard-pressed not to jump her right there at the station.''

He rose from the bed as if he were being drawn to his computer by a force stronger than himself. Rosemary moved out of his way, laughing breathlessly. He was back. Better than ever. The block was gone now, forever, she was sure of it.

She watched him type, watched the muscles in his back and shoulders play while he worked. Watched him, eyes earnest, bright, small frown of concentration on his brow. And felt like the luckiest and proudest woman alive to have a man who'd fight toward her in spite of the terrible risk. And felt honored to be Ada, who played a part in helping him after all.

She dozed a bit, awoke to find him back beside her, hands skimming over her body, ready to go again.

''I think making love to you is all I need for inspiration,'' he whispered against her throat. ''Those other women were just bad substitutes. No wonder my brain wouldn't work. It was like putting leaded gas in a diesel car.''

She touched his hair, arched herself up against his mouth on her breast. "Very romantic."

He grinned. "I'll come live with you in the city, Rosemary, since my work is now portable again. But on one condition."

She pulled his head up and gave his lower lip a soft sensual bite. "What's that?"

"We come back here to raise our little ones."

"You want to come back to Lazy Pines?" She stared at him, mouth gaping entirely unsensually.

"Of course." He gave her a what-else-could-you-possibly-think look. "I love it here. At least recently."

Rosemary laughed and turned to fit her body against her future husband's. "As long as we teach our kids what we've learned from this experience."

"You mean that you should always follow your heart?"

"No, not really..."

"Your heart's desire is in your own backyard?"

She shook her head.

"Life is simple unless it's complicated?"

"Close."

"I give up."

She sat up and started counting on her fingers. "Name all your dogs Rex, never sing when you could be baking seaweed bread, always make your bed alone, never trust that a wild monkey is who you think, hug your giant every day, and never *ever* assume you know more than a naked crocheter about his own—"

He kissed her mouth. "Yarn balls?"

"No." She smiled up at the man who would be forever in her heart, forever in her mind, and hallelujah, forever in her bed. "About his own Destiny."

PLAY
RUN FOR THE ROSES

...and you
can get

FREE BOOKS and a FREE GIFT!

Turn the page and let the race begin!

PLAY
RUN
FOR THE
ROSES

and get
THREE FREE GIFTS!

HOW TO PLAY:

1. With a coin, carefully scratch off the silver box at the right. Then check the claim chart to see what we have for you — **2 FREE BOOKS** and a **FREE GIFT**—**ALL YOURS FREE!**

2. Send back the card and you'll receive two brand-new Harlequin Duets™ novels. These books have a cover price of $5.99 each in the U.S. and $6.99 each in Canada, but they are yours to keep absolutely free.

3. There's no catch. You're under no obligation to buy anything. We charge nothing — ZERO — for your first shipment. And you don't have to make any minimum number of purchases — not even one!

4. The fact is, thousands of readers enjoy receiving books by mail from the Harlequin Reader Service®. They enjoy the convenience of home delivery...they like getting the best new novels at discount prices, BEFORE they're available in stores... and they love their *Heart to Heart* subscriber newsletter featuring author news, horoscopes, recipes, book reviews and much more!

5. We hope that after receiving your free books you'll want to remain a subscriber. But the choice is yours — to continue or cancel, any time at all! So why not take us up on our invitation, with no risk of any kind. You'll be glad you did!

Visit us online at
www.eHarlequin.com

Counterfeit Cowboy

CARRIE ALEXANDER

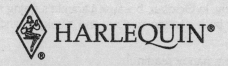

HARLEQUIN®

TORONTO • NEW YORK • LONDON
AMSTERDAM • PARIS • SYDNEY • HAMBURG
STOCKHOLM • ATHENS • TOKYO • MILAN • MADRID
PRAGUE • WARSAW • BUDAPEST • AUCKLAND

Dear Reader,

A confession: I bought my first Harlequin romance because of the gorgeous stud on the cover. He was a magnificent creature—sleek, sculpted muscles, deep chest, flowing mane...ah yes, what a horse!

I was thirteen and horse crazy. If there was an actual man on the cover, I don't recall. So it's only fitting that all these years later I should write a boy-meets-girl-meets-horse trilogy for Harlequin Duets. This time, though, my emphasis is on the other kind of gorgeous stud....

Grace, Molly and Laramie started The Cowgirl Club as horse-crazy ten-year-olds. Fifteen years later, Grace found her very own *Custom-Built Cowboy* (Duets #25) and moved to Wyoming. What's The Cowgirl Club to do but follow?

When Molly Broome applies for a job at the wacky, disaster-prone Triple Eight Dude Ranch, the first cowboy she meets—in the dark—is Raleigh Tate. The head wrangler is as handsome and smooth as a movie cowboy and maybe just a little too good to be true. Is Raleigh the *Counterfeit Cowboy*...or is he the blue-eyed hero of Molly's dreams?

Don't forget to look for the third book, *Keepsake Cowboy*, in October, because Laramie's going to inherit both a rodeo cowboy and a unique ranch house.

Till then, happy reading!

Carrie Alexander

Prologue

"THIS IS WAY COOLER than Camp Skowhegan." Grace Farrow gathered up her curly copper hair and secured it with a banana clip. She snapped the elastic of her bikini bottom and settled into a chaise longue. "Now that we're fifteen, camp seems so jejune, doesn't it? Positively *de trop!*"

Laramie Jones winked at Molly Broome and said, "Whatever that means."

Molly chuckled. "Someone stop her—she's speaking French again."

The trio had met at a camp in Maine five years before and instantly formed the Cowgirl Club, bonding over a mutual love of cute cowboys and all things horsey. This was the first summer they'd skipped camp, but Molly had kept the friendship going by inviting Laramie and Grace to her house for an official Cowgirl Club weekend. They were sunbathing by the turquoise pool in Molly's backyard in Darien, Connecticut, with bottles of diet cola, a bag of chips, tubes of sunscreen and well-thumbed, grease-spotted copies of the latest fan magazines at hand. The boom box was playing The Cowboy Junkies, their new discovery.

"Whaddaya know? My French classes have finally taken hold." Grace put on her sunglasses and struck what she imagined to be a sophisticated pose, like photos she'd seen of Brigitte Bardot at Cannes. So what if her cropped cartoon T-shirt and the streaks of white zinc oxide painted across her nose and cheeks didn't suit? "Someday I'm gonna have killer *je ne sais quoi*."

Laramie grimaced. "Cowgirls don't need je ne say what."

Molly watched enviously as Laramie tucked her long black hair beneath the cowboy hat she was rarely without. Today she'd paired it with a halter top made from two knotted red bandannas (Molly would never dare!), cutoff jeans that showed off long tanned legs (which seemed to have grown another inch over the past year, whereas Molly was still plagued with baby fat) and a scuffed pair of Tony Lama cowboy boots. Laramie simply didn't care when Grace had announced that the cowboy look, except maybe for Santa Fe style, was, like, totally out of fashion.

Molly wished that she had the *je ne sais quoi* not to care. She cared too much, about everything. Sometimes it was sort of suffocating, always being the good girl. But she was too chicken to try anything else. She was stuck with brown eyes, brown hair that was neither curly nor straight, a totally boring nuclear family and an inbred goody-two-shoes complex.

"Cowgirls need cowboys," Grace said. She nudged Molly. "Are there any on the loose in the suburbs of Connecticut?"

"Well, no...but my mom said we could rent videos." Even though the only boy she'd ever kissed had been Jason Gugliotti behind the bunkhouse at camp, movie cowboys were still about as far as Molly was willing to go. Maybe there was something wrong with her; a normal teenage girl wouldn't prefer John Wayne to Jason "Frenchy" Gugliotti.

"How about *Young Guns,* plus the sequel even though it's not as good? Or maybe *The Man From Snowy River*." Molly glanced at Laramie, who was the real force behind their cowboy obsession. "What do you think?"

"I can always watch *Young Guns* again. Lou Diamond Philips is such a babe. For an older man." Laramie leaned back in her chair and studied the house, a white colonial with green shutters and manicured hedges. "It's nice here, Mol. Thanks for inviting me."

Despite Laramie's words, she felt a little out of place. Not only did Molly have a perfect house, she had a perfect family—a father, a mother, two big brothers, a little sister, even a funny grandpa who'd watched every western ever filmed. Molly was the luckiest girl on earth, but as far as Laramie could tell, her friend didn't even know it. "Are your folks rich?" she asked, keeping it nonchalant.

Molly shrugged, then carefully tucked her loose bra strap inside her tank top. "My dad says we're comfortable."

"Whatever that means." But it was clear to Laramie. Uncomfortable was living with your nutty, nosy, dingbat mother in a one-bedroom Brooklyn walk-up. It was knowing that there was no place in the world that was your own. Except maybe for Laramie, Wyoming, which would seem a million miles away if it wasn't for the Cowgirl Club.

Grace piped up. "I think it means that your dad's stockbroker didn't get him in on the ground floor of Microsoft!"

All Laramie knew about Grace's parents was that they were important and rich—really rich. Grace lived in a fancy Manhattan apartment and took jumping lessons at a city stable on the bay mare that had been her fifteenth birthday present. "How's Dulcie working out?" Laramie asked, preferring to talk about horses, a subject she was more familiar with than stock shares, even though owning either was far out of her reach.

"Dulcie's the best, way better than a pony." Grace took off her sunglasses and sat up, cross-legged, her freckled limbs pink in the sunshine. "Hey, guys, what about having the next Cowgirl Club sleepover at my house? We can rent horses by the hour for you two and go riding together in Central Park!" Always full of enthusiasm, she gave her hands a clap and held them out to her friends. They were cowgirls, one and all!

Molly linked fingers. "That would be really great."

Laramie swallowed. "Sure," she said, giving Grace's palm a casual slap. "Anytime."

Not one for half measures, Grace grabbed Laramie's hand and squeezed it tight. "Look out, world! The Cowgirl Club's moving to Manhattan!"

1

"HOLY COWBOY..." Molly Broome murmured to herself. She sat up a little taller, her neck extended, the root of every hair on her head tingling as if she'd just seen a ghost.

Not a ghost. A cowboy.

But what a cowboy!

Molly leaned closer to the window to get a better look at the horse and rider galloping alongside Shane's pickup truck. Straight out of the movies, she thought, then made a face at herself. Even after a week in Wyoming, she couldn't get over it. The majestic Rockies, the panoramic valleys, the picture-perfect ranches with their white-faced cattle and barbed-wire fences were all like something out of the movies. Only the cowboys had been a disappointment...until this one.

The beginnings of a rainstorm spattered the glass. Molly took her eyes off the horse and rider to search the unfamiliar dashboard for the switch that controlled the windshield wipers. The gravel road she traveled was worn down to the ground and pitted with small boulders; the rain, turning to sleet in the frigid mountain air, made it all the more treacherous.

Nevertheless, Molly's gaze returned to the cowboy as she eased up on the accelerator. His horse, a flashy black-and-white Appaloosa, was keeping pace with the pickup truck, galloping across the open, flat land of a winter-sere pasture, its long flowing tail as glossy as the feathers of a crow.

The cowboy himself was not so showy. He wore a brown hat pulled low over his forehead, heavy gloves and a buttoned oilskin duster that revealed a pair of plain brown leather chaps when the coattails snapped in the wind. Between the rain, the low-slung cowboy hat and a raised collar, Molly couldn't make out much of his face beyond glimpses of a rock-cut profile and unshaved chin.

It didn't matter. After a lifetime of watching westerns with her grandpa Joe, she was so attuned that she could make up the cowboy's story and character in the blink of an eye. He was a lone wolf. A solitary soul who drifted into a frontier town with nothing but a horse, a rifle and an iron will. He'd leave the same way, unexpectedly, but definitely at sunset, after he'd won a showdown with a gang of outlaws and saved a young widow and her failing ranch from the evil intentions of the local cattle baron.

Fifteen years of membership in the Cowgirl Club had also primed Molly for romance, so it was natural for her to picture herself as the widow. While her rounded figure might have been better suited to lace collars and cotton print dresses, she'd rather be—at least in her dreams—the kind of widow who wore buckskin pants and scandalized the neighbors by ropin' and ridin' better'n any cowboy. Only the lone wolf could tame her, his passionate kisses making her remember how good it felt to be a woman...until the discreet fadeout that was the standard in vintage westerns. Fortunately, Molly's imagination was vivid; she could take it from there. And, my, how she'd sob when her mysterious cowboy got on his horse and loped off into the sunset....

Molly flounced a bit on the seat and let loose with an enthusiastic "Hoo-whee, cowboy" as she glanced once more at the lone rider. As if to acknowledge her admiration, he lifted a gloved hand and tipped the brim of his hat.

Caught gawking! Molly snapped her mouth shut so fast she almost bit her tongue. Her cheeks grew warm with self-consciousness, but the cowboy merely laid the reins against his mount's neck and touched a heel to its flank. With a flick of its tail, the Appaloosa wheeled around, sleek muscles moving beneath the spots blanketing its hindquarters as it cantered over a rise and disappeared.

Molly slowed the pickup to a crawl and craned her neck after them. There was no Technicolor sunset, only a stubbly brown pasture, a rim of chalky mountains and a sky bleak with a cold, hard November rain.

So much for fantasies.

The pickup truck had drifted to the left, following the direction of Molly's yearning heart. One of the tires hit a submerged rock, jolting her back to attention. She tightened her grip on the steering wheel as the tires slithered in the mud, spinning uselessly for a second or two before they found purchase and sent the truck shooting back up onto the crown of the road. Out of the corner of her eye, Molly caught a flash of something pale—and possibly moving—in the ditch she'd narrowly avoided.

She stepped on the brakes and checked the rearview mirror. Sleet pelted the deserted gravel road. Probably all she'd seen was some crumpled trash, whipped by the wind. What with the hard rain and her new corduroy coat and the fact that she was on her way to the Triple Eight Dude Ranch to talk herself into a job…well, it didn't make sense for her to slog around in the mud on the off chance that *maybe* she'd seen *something*.

Something squirming. Something alive?

Molly sighed and got out of the truck.

The sleet tattooed her face with icy needles. Shivering, she turned up her collar and walked quickly back the way she'd come, scanning the drab horizon for any sign of the cowboy. Nothing, not even the thud of receding hoofbeats. Looked as if one of them had been smart enough to go in out of the rain.

Trying to avoid the muck, she veered toward the side of the road and scanned the ditch. At first she saw only muddy runnels of rainwater coursing among the slick boulders and straggling clumps of weeds. Then a flicker of movement. A piteous cry came from the depths of the ditch, so weak the only reason she heard it over the drumming of the icy rain was that the countryside was entirely still otherwise.

Rabbits? Kittens? In New York, one didn't rescue half-drowned kittens unless one was Audrey Hepburn and looked good even in wet clothes and drenched hair. But Molly was in Wyoming now, with a strange new life beckoning her from the ruins of the old. Dismissing thoughts of the beige coat and potential job interview as unworthy, she scrambled into the ditch, trying to keep back on her heels. The gravelly slope skidded out from beneath her in a slippery slide of gritty muck. She landed on her backside with a squishy plop that foretold a hefty dry-cleaning bill.

"Glug," she said, hoisting herself up, turning her palms all to mud. Losing sight of both the kittens and any hope of maintaining her dignity, she pushed back her damp bangs and squinted into the stinging rain. Heaven knew she was no Audrey Hepburn even in the best of circumstances.

With a piteous cry of her own, Molly spotted the abandoned kittens. Stepping carefully, she got close enough to squat and gather up the poor, bedraggled things. She cradled them to her chest. Three kittens, all skin and bones and matted white fur beneath splatters of cold mud. They clung to the front of her coat like burrs, mewling in tiny bleats that made her chest get all tight and achy. "Okay, babies," she crooned. "You're safe now. I've got you."

After she'd checked over the area in case she was missing the rest of the litter, Molly clambered out of the ditch and trotted back to the pickup through the driving rain, clutching the crying kittens inside her unbuttoned coat to keep them from getting any wetter or colder. She'd left the engine running, so the cab's interior was nice and warm. With an apology to Shane McHenry, the rancher who was both the owner of the truck and the fiancé of her best friend, Grace Farrow, Molly stripped off her muddy coat and wadded it up on the passenger seat as a bed for the kittens. They huddled together, shivering little balls of wet, dirty fur.

"What the heck. In for a penny..." Molly tugged her blue cashmere sweater off over her head, thankful that she'd dressed in layers. As soon as she'd set foot on the McHenrys' Goldstream Ranch, she'd realized that she'd packed the wrong wardrobe, even though the clothes she'd brought were her most casual. Her jeans were okay, and some of the tops she wore when riding in the city, but her dresses were still hanging in Shane's sister's closet and this was the first time she'd dared to wear the cashmere sweater and corduroy coat. And look what had happened!

"That's Wyoming for you." Molly rubbed the kittens with the sweater. Their little pink mouths opened and closed with a chorus of mews. She took one to her chest, gently massaging its matted fur and thin layer of skin. "Poor baby," she said, puffing her warm breath into its teensy face, trying to coax its eyes open. It burrowed against her shirtfront instead. "Can't say I blame you, little kitty. The world seems like an awful place just now, doesn't it?"

Molly patted the cat. "Yeah, I know how you feel."

She swiveled around to stare out the window again. Not a soul in sight, not even a movie cowboy. She'd seen very few houses and only one other vehicle since she'd struck out on the gravel road, and according to the odometer she'd traveled nearly five miles! Fancy going five unpopulated miles in Connecticut, where she'd grown up, or New York City, where she'd lived ever since college.

It was like Grace said—Treetop, Wyoming, was a whole 'nother world. Which was fine for Grace—she'd deliberately chosen to make the drastic change from New York to piddly little Treetop. That was, if stowing away in the back of a cowboy's horse trailer on the night of your engagement to another man counted as a rational choice.

Molly shook her head, smiling fondly. Grace Farrow was a law unto herself. Her own case was different. Oh, it was true that she'd gone along with Grace and Laramie Jones, the other founding member of their self-styled urban Cowgirl Club, when they talked of the glory of cowboys and the prospect of someday making their own adventures in the West. And Molly had embraced the ideals of their club slogan—Hard Work, Straight Talk, Open Skies And Tight Jeans!— perhaps even more sincerely than either Grace or Laramie.

It was just that she'd never quite been able to put herself here. In fantasy, yes. In reality? Well...

Despairing, she looked in the mirror. Lank brown hair plastered in dripping rat's tails against a round, mud-smeared face. Dark eyes that betrayed her worry and uneasiness. Maybe even a touch of panic. Normally she was a firmly middle-class, straight-arrow, well-groomed, gainfully employed, extremely calm and reliable sort of person, resistant to change because that was the way she'd always been.

She wrinkled her nose at the description, yet acknowledged its accuracy. No sirree—Molly Broome and the ruggedly alien Wyoming countryside did not mix.

The kitten lifted its wobbly head and blinked open a pair of round blue eyes. Molly's heart melted. She sighed with what felt a lot like a kind of giddy, nothing-left-to-lose happiness, regardless of her present circumstances. Which made no sense at all. And she always made sense.

She held the kitten up to her face; the pitiful thing weighed less than her thumb. "How'd we wind up in this fix, little bit?"

Well, she couldn't speak for the kitten, but losing her job in a company-wide downsizing and finding herself with a dwindling bank account and a future that was suddenly as wide open as a wheat field had done it for her. Grace, newly ensconced at Goldstream and loving it, had persuaded Molly to come for a long visit over Thanksgiving week. She'd said there was no better place than the Rockies to put your life in perspective, and Molly had been at such loose ends that she'd agreed.

Given that her vocation was corporate party planning and her avocation was cooking, she'd gladly taken over production of the McHenrys' Thanksgiving dinner for ten. The meal had been such a success that Lilah Evers, the wife of Shane's hired hand, had told Molly that she should apply for a job at the Triple Eight Dude Ranch. Lilah had heard through the grapevine that Mrs. Peet, who ran the ranch's main lodge, had broken her leg in three places and was going to be laid up for six months. Once prodded, Molly had conceded that it wouldn't hurt to go on a look-see. She had no better prospects.

However, she hadn't imagined arriving in such a bedraggled state. She put Little Bit down with the other two kittens, considering whether or not she should turn back. It was the shivering animals that decided her. They had to have shelter and warm milk. According to the directions Shane had pinned to the visor, she was nearing the Triple Eight.

She put the truck into gear and with another spin of the back tires, continued on her journey. It may have been the previous lack of traffic, her rusty driving skills, or even a preoccupation with the chance that an ideal movie cowboy was also heading to the Triple Eight that caused her to neglect checking her rearview mirror.

Whatever the case, Molly Broome completely missed the sight of a car behind her swerving on the icy road to avoid her truck, losing control and slamming nose-down into the muddy ditch.

"WHATCHA WANT?" demanded the little old lady who opened the door to Molly's repeated knockings. "I ain't got time to bother with the likes of you. Can'tcha see we're all in an uproar here?"

Molly blinked her wet lashes. She couldn't see much. The storm was worsening by the moment. She'd run from the pickup to the porch of the massive log lodge without stopping to take in the place. There'd been only a quick impression of a great expanse of roof

that came to a peak against the roiling clouds of a darkened sky.

Thunder rumbled in the distance. "Cat got your
tongue?" the woman asked, peering suspiciously at
Molly from around the edge of the door. Her hair was
too yellow and her diamond earrings too large to be
the real thing.

"As a matter of fact..." The kittens were bundled
into the sweater and muddy coat clasped to Molly's
chest. She could feel them squirming.

"You're here for the job." The woman swung the
heavy wooden door open. "We was told to 'spect you.
Man's in the barn, seeing to the horses, but he'll be
along directly."

Molly stepped inside, wondering what "'spect you"
meant. Neither *inspect* or *expect* made sense. Lilah's
advice had been to just show up and tell Cord Wyatt,
the owner of the Triple Eight, that she was ready to
work. Molly had thought to bring along her résumé,
but they still weren't 'specting her.

"You may's well take a seat," the woman said. She
waved a sponge at a lumpen assortment of upholstered
chairs and couches scattered throughout the dimly lit
lobby. "I got drips to catch."

"There's one," Molly said, pointing. Fat drops of
water were falling from above, pooling on the var-
nished pine floor near a registration desk stacked high
with bound newspapers.

The elderly lady cackled and set a tarnished silver
punch bowl beneath the leak. Water drops hit the bowl
with tinny-sounding plinks and plonks, joining the
drip-drop symphony.

Remembering with nostalgia the time she'd heard
Handel's *Water Music* at the Met, Molly looked
around, absorbing her new surroundings. She was far

from a symphony hall. A variety of bowls and buckets had been placed throughout the large, dark lobby. If the stack of containers in the cart the woman was pushing toward a wide, curved stairway was any indication, every ceiling in the lodge must leak.

Molly's stomach sank. Employment with such a ramshackle operation would not be a feather in her résumé.

"Um, excuse me?" If she could quickly take care of the kittens, a clean—make that muddy—getaway was still possible before anyone showed up to interview her.

The woman turned back, scowling. "You still here?"

"Yes." Molly hesitated, momentarily nonplussed by the sight of the old lady standing, fully illuminated, beneath a chandelier made of interlocking antlers. Although the woman's face had the grain of old leather, her thinning, impossibly bright gold hair spouted from a spangled doodad at the top of her head. The rhinestones at her ears were matched by a dozen glittering bangle bracelets equally divided between her bony wrists. She wore a T-shirt printed with a bottle of tequila and the words Eat the Worm, a short denim skirt, and new aerobic shoes that looked chunky at the end of her birdlike legs, legs that were dead-white except for wormy blue varicose veins.

"The name's Etta Sue Carson Wyatt Kopinski Lawless Frain, if you's wondering." She chortled at Molly's confusion. "I've had five no-good husbands and five hot-diggety divorces. Usually I don't bother with all them other names, so you kin jest call me Etta Sue. I run this place."

"I'm Molly Broome. I did come about the job, but

I thought Mrs. Peet—the woman who broke her leg—was the lodge manager.''

"Wail, I'm watcha call the exec-yew-tive house-keeper.''

Molly eyed the woman's cleaning cart. Although an array of spray bottles, sponges, mops and brooms were conspicuously arranged upon it, Molly was willing to wager that Etta Sue was more talk than action. The word *executive* was the clue, along with the fumes wafting off her. Fumes that were nearly as toxic as cleaning chemicals.

The kittens stirred more vigorously, making peeping sounds as they tried to climb out of their swaddling. Molly juggled the awkward bundle. "I found these kittens abandoned on the road.''

Etta Sue looked, then recoiled like a turtle pulling back into its shell. She resembled a turtle, in fact. A crotchety old snapping turtle. The skin on her worn face had surrendered to gravity some time ago and was draped in slack folds from her pugnacious jaw and the prominent cords in her scrawny neck.

"We ain't got need for cats at the Triple Eight," Etta Sue said. "Shoulda left 'em in the ditch.''

Molly cuddled the kittens protectively. "I would never do such a thing. I'm sure I can find homes for them.''

Etta Sue shrugged her bony shoulders and hollered "Sharleen!" up the stairs, her voice like the scrape of sandpaper. She took a broom off the cart and thumped it across the balusters as if playing a xylophone. "Sharleen Jackleen, getchyer lazy butt down here!" To Molly, she explained, "Sharleen's the housemaid. She works under me.''

The electric lights flickered. A girl's face appeared from above, hanging over the railing of the shadowed second-floor balcony. "Mom's cleaning Mr. Wyatt's bathroom."

Etta Sue arched her brows at Molly and muttered, "Sharleen works under Cord, too, if y'get my meaning." She raised her voice, waving the broom at the girl. "You go 'n' tell your ma we got us some lost kittens here."

The girl yelled "Mom!" over her shoulder as she galloped down the stairs. "Kittens?" she said, swerving to avoid the broom as Etta Sue stuck it into the cart at a cockeyed angle.

"Look." Molly lowered the bundle so the girl could see. "They were half drowned when I found them, but they're starting to dry off. We can probably brush most of the mud off."

"Ooh," the girl breathed. "Can I pet them?"

"Gently," Molly said. The child was about six or seven, with full pink cheeks and curly brown hair held back from her face by a bandanna tied into a jaunty bow. She patted the kittens with a plump little hand bearing chipped remnants of pink glitter nail polish.

She sighed happily. "What are their names? Could I hold them?"

"They don't have names, as far as I know." Molly picked up the kitten with the tan spot on its backside and handed it to the child. "I was calling this one Little Bit. Maybe you can name the other two."

"Oh...could I?"

"Pshaw," Etta Sue spat, although her tone wasn't as cross as it had been.

Molly looked up as Sharleen Jackleen arrived. The housemaid was a thirtyish buxom blonde with dark roots and long pink glittery fingernails that were an impractical choice in a profession that demanded scrub brushes. Her shiny satin blouse was tucked into a pair of jeans so tight Molly couldn't imagine how the woman had climbed into them without greasing herself up first. Was it too late for the Cowgirl Club to limit their request for tight jeans to the masculine version?

Etta Sue stood off to the side, staring through heavily lidded turtle eyes, her mouth firmly shut.

Molly introduced herself. "Hi. My name's Molly Broome. I was on my way to the ranch to see about a job when I found these kittens in the ditch. Could you spare some warm milk, maybe a towel…?"

She didn't have to finish. Sharleen Jackleen bent over her daughter and scooped up Little Bit. "Aren't you the cutest thing?" she squeaked in a baby-talk voice. "Itsy-bitsy-boo-boo!"

The girl bobbed up and down. "I wanna hold it, please, Mommy, can I hold it?"

"Not now, Jocelyn." Sharleen wiggled her way toward an open doorway on the right, making kissing sounds at the kitten as she fluffed at its fur with her sparkly nails.

Jocelyn tugged on Molly's sleeve. "The kitchen's this way, ma'am."

"You go on, then, Missy Sharleen Jackleen," Etta Sue called after them. "Don'tchew mind me none. I'll see to it that the house don't flood out from beneath us."

They passed through a large dining room furnished with a half-dozen bench-style tables. Extra chairs had been placed upside down on either end of each of them, making it obvious that the lodge didn't do much business during the off-season. Lilah Evers had told Molly as much, though apparently there would be an influx of tourists during the upcoming ski season.

Sharleen already had milk heating in the microwave when Jocelyn and Molly arrived. At a glance Molly could see that the kitchen had been built to serve large groups. There was an eight-burner stove, double refrigerators, a walk-in freezer and a central butcher-block table that was definitely an island unto itself. Plus an overhead rack hung with any number of industrial-size pots and pans, blackened and dinged with hard use. Aside from a few signs of neglect—peeling paint, rotting windowsills—the space appeared to be clean and organized. Though the view of a rain-soaked landscape was bleak, Molly was somewhat comforted. Sharleen confirmed Molly's suspicions when she said, "The kitchen's Mrs. Peet's domain." She stuck a knuckle into the steaming milk and winced. "Even in summer, when Cord hires a cook and a couple of assistants, Mrs. Peet runs things her way." Sharleen sucked her knuckle for a moment, Little Bit tucked into the crook of her elbow. She gave Molly a desultory smile. "Not that I care. I hate to cook."

"You hate to clean, too," Jocelyn blurted, then ducked her head as if she expected a swat. She busied herself with blowing on the milk.

Sharleen merely laughed. "Isn't that the truth."

Carefully Jocelyn set the bowl of milk on the linoleum floor. She glanced up as Molly unwrapped her coat and released the kittens. "My mom's going to be a singer."

"I'm already a singer," Sharleen snapped. She thrust Little Bit at her daughter and turned to Molly with a challenging tone. "What I'm going to be is a *famous* singer."

Molly offered a friendly smile. "Country western?"

"Of course." Sharleen patted her outdated peroxide bouffant. "Cord says I look a little bit like Faith Hill."

Dolly Parton at her gaudiest was more like it, but Molly maintained her noncommittal expression. She knelt beside Jocelyn. "Did you think of any names yet?"

The kittens were lapping at the milk, finally looking more like fluff balls than drowned rats. Jocelyn kept touching each of them in turn, little taps of reassurance. "I have to think of the best names first. I want them to be just right."

"Don't go making those kittens yours, now, Joss." Sharleen spoke offhandedly, more concerned with the sheen of her nail polish than the tears welling in her daughter's eyes. "You know Cord said no more pets after last time."

Jocelyn's head sank a little lower.

"You can name them anyway," Molly said. "And then even when they go to their new homes, they'll still belong to you...in a way."

"Yeah." Jocelyn picked up Little Bit, her shiny eyes sad even though she smiled bravely. "That's good, I guess."

Molly stood and gave the girl's shoulder a comforting pat. "The kittens may have caught a chill. Could you loan me a cardboard box and a heating pad?"

Sharleen had apparently lost interest in their plight. "No skin off my nose. Joss'll fix you up." Fingering her satin collar, she looked Molly up and down. "No offense, but you could use some fixing up yourself."

"Oh." Molly touched her face. Mud had dried on her forehead and in her hair. There was a damp patch on the seat of her pants. And one across the front of her blouse, too, from holding the rain-soaked kittens. Well, darn. She was accustomed to making a better impression on potential employers than this.

An unexpected thought struck her. Perhaps she and the Triple Eight were a match after all.

"You want a job with Cord Wyatt, you got to look

nice," Sharleen went on. She eyed the rain spots on Molly's plain white blouse and navy wool slacks, unimpressed. "One thing in your favor—Cord likes a woman with curves." She patted her own hourglass hips, her thin-lipped smile telling Molly that she'd best watch her step around Sharleen's man.

Molly blinked. Again, the job was sounding unappealing. "I'd prefer to rely on my experience and skill," she said coolly.

"Yeah, me, too!" Sharleen hooted. "Cripes, girlfriend, don't get your knickers in a knot."

A fork of lightning split the patch of gray sky visible through the kitchen windows, making Molly flinch. She recovered herself and reached for the pocketbook slung over her shoulder. "I brought my résumé."

Thunder rattled the windowpanes. The back door swung open to a gust of cold air and a strong odor of wet leather. Molly looked up from her open pocketbook and straight into the face of the movie cowboy. One glance at his handsome features, toothpaste-ad smile and the startling ice-blue shade of his eyes convinced her that he was without a doubt ready for his close-up. He was, in fact, ready for *her* close-up, but instead of sticking with a tried-and-true script, she went and lost her head and blurted, "It's you!" just as he said, his expression quizzical, his smile fading, "But you're not the right woman…"

And then—mercifully—the lights went out.

2

"EEEYEWWW!" In the first moment of pitch darkness, Sharleen Jackleen let out a piggy squeal and launched herself at Raleigh Tate. He knew because she slammed into his chest, torpedoes first. Her arms wound around his neck. "Please don't let me go, sugar," she breathed hotly into his ear. "I hate the dark."

"No one move," the other woman said evenly. "Jocelyn?"

The girl answered from the vicinity of the floor. "Yes, ma'am?"

"Do you have the kittens?"

"Only Little Bit."

Raleigh heard the stranger move cautiously in the dark as she said, "Let's see if we can find the others before they get stepped on." Already he liked her soothing tone and calm demeanor. But he was darn sure that she was not the Secret Service agent he'd been expecting.

"Kittens?" he asked, unwinding Sharleen's arms and setting her aside. In the gray light from the windows he could see vague shapes crawling over the floor—too big to be kittens, though.

"Abandoned kittens." A small splash was followed by a sound of disgust. "Found their milk," the woman said, her tone laced with wry humor.

Raleigh stepped closer, evading Sharleen's grab at his sleeve by a talon's breadth. He patted his pockets, found a matchbook and got down on his haunches to strike a match. The woman was on all fours several feet and one overturned bowl away from him. In the flickering light of the match flame, her round face appeared ghostly, its pretty features pooled with shadow, her eyes showing their whites, but staring levelly into his all the same.

They looked at each other wordlessly for a moment that stretched into another—long enough for Raleigh to wonder if she would greet his kiss with the same wide-eyed self-possession—and then the flame guttered out, stinging his fingertips. "Ouch," he said, dropping the match. It hit the spilled milk with a hiss.

"I found one of the kittens," Jocelyn called, from near the center of the kitchen. The woman swung around, following the sound of Joss's voice as the girl jabbered nonsense at the cat. What was it about babies that made females cluck and coo in an incomprehensible language that, as far as Raleigh could tell, served no purpose at all?

He struck another match, in time to see a nicely shaped derriere scoot across the kitchen floor. Sitting with Jocelyn in the shadow beneath the butcher-block table, the woman scooped up a white kitten and pressed her lips to the top of its head. She slanted a quick glance at Raleigh just before he snuffed out the second match. In the dark, he told himself that he was a big, bad, tough undercover agent; any twinges he'd felt were a result of his burned fingertips.

"I can't see," Sharleen wailed.

"There've got to be candles or flashlights around here somewhere." He hadn't been employed by the Triple Eight long enough to know where everything was, even though he'd already scoured every nook and cranny to which he'd gained access. The items on his search list were out of the ordinary compared to mundane household emergency supplies.

"There are flashlights by the cellar door," Jocelyn said helpfully. Raleigh's eyes had adjusted enough to track the girl's progress as she crawled out from beneath the table and felt her way along the cabinets toward the back door. He stood and followed her, placing a cautionary hand on her shoulder when she swung open the door opposite.

Raleigh looked inside, highly interested. He'd been having a heck of a time getting into the house alone; hence the female agent who was to take Mrs. Peet's place. Until this other woman had turned up in the agent's place, he'd thought he'd handled the switch very neatly, sending Mrs. Peet off to her son's house on an extended vacation and relaying to all concerned the story of her unfortunate "broken" leg.

Jocelyn removed four flashlights from a built-in shelf and handed them to Raleigh one by one. He took them absently, intent on the wooden plank steps that disappeared into the yawning black hole of the unexplored cellar. He switched on a light and gave it to the girl, letting her move away before he aimed his own heavy-duty flashlight down the stairway. Wooden beams, old stone walls, lots of moldering junk. Looked promising.

By the time he regretfully turned away, the females each had a flashlight. Their beams crisscrossed the worn linoleum, searching for other kittens. Sharleen passed by Raleigh closer than necessary, giving her breasts a little jiggle against his back in case he'd missed them. He hadn't—that was why he stepped away. If you were looking for a good time, Sharleen was your gal. While he had nothing against good times in general, Sharleen was still a suspect in the Triple

Eight counterfeiting case. As an accessory, at most. He didn't figure her for a mastermind.

On the pretext of aiding the search, he let the beam of his flashlight play across the other woman. Despite her dishevelment, there was an air of class about her. Though her shape was nearly as hoochie-coochie-mama as Sharleen's, the end result was a serene, voluptuous attractiveness that he found very enticing.

Make that distracting, he silently amended, and gave his head a shake. This case was crazy enough; the last thing he needed was another distraction.

She'd turned and was watching his face, her lips slightly parted. In a flash, he fixated on her luscious mouth, wanting her to whisper, to pucker, to crook her finger and beckon him with the promise of an all-nighter—and then some.

The blinding beam of her flashlight hit him square in the eye. "Mister, you'd better not budge."

Raleigh gritted his teeth and stood very still, hoping the direction of his thoughts wasn't as blatantly obvious as all that.

She strode toward him, her eyes narrowed. He gulped when she aimed her light lower, toward his fly. "Whoa, there, lady," he said. "I didn't mean any harm—"

She shot him a confused look. "There's a cat climbing up the side of your coat. Didn't you notice?"

He glanced down and sure enough, she was right. A cute little scrap of fur was clinging to the oilskin duster he'd bought off a cowboy on the street in Laramie. He plucked the black-faced kitten one-handed and held it up by its scruff, squirming and mewing, before plopping it into the woman's extended palms. "There you go, Miss...?"

"Ms. Broome. Molly Broome. I realize that you

weren't expecting me, but I heard about the job opening from Lilah Evers, so I came over to give you my résumé.'' She took a deep breath that did terrific things to her bosom. The damp patch on her flimsy white blouse worked like a modified wet T-shirt contest. The tops of her full breasts were pressed against the semi-transparent fabric, admirably filling out the cups of a lace-edged bra. "Unfortunately, what with the storm and the mud and the kittens, I'm in no shape to—"

"Your shape looks fine to me. Dang fine."

Molly made a choking sound. She leaned forward to peer into his eyes, then looked quickly away, her lashes throwing spiked shadows across her rosy cheeks. The ambient glow of their flashlights was very becoming on her.

"Sharleen warned me that you might think so," she said. Her shy glance had become a glower. "However, as I'm accustomed to winning jobs on my qualifications, perhaps we ought to call it a day."

Raleigh kept silent. He wanted to be rid of her. Right?

She spun away, hustling Jocelyn and the kittens toward the dining room, then just as suddenly halted and turned to face him, saying tartly, "A word of warning, Mr. Wyatt. You should watch your step. Sexual harassment is taken seriously these days. Not all applicants and, uh, employees—" she glanced at Sharleen Jackleen "—are quite so…magnanimous."

Molly swept out of the room. Sharleen set her hands on her hips and frowned after her, probably uncertain whether she'd been insulted or complimented.

Raleigh rubbed his prickly chin, grinning inside. Molly Broome was one hell of a woman. Awfully sweet and soft and pretty looking, but clearly no marshmallow. Hot damn, but she got his blood up!

He hurried after her. "Just a minute, Ms. Broome."
She whisked through the dining room without stopping.
He caught her in the doorway, his hand clasped around
her elbow. "Ms. Broome—you've made a mistake."

She whirled, shaking him off. "Oh, I sincerely doubt
that, Mr. Wyatt."

Even her pique was tantalizing. "The name's Raleigh Tate."

"Raleigh Tate?" she echoed, losing some of her fire.
"Who...?"

"I'm the head wrangler here at the Triple Eight.
Cord Wyatt's the owner. But you were right to come
to me for the job. Wyatt's given me hiring authority
while he's out of town."

Doubtfully Molly weighed his words. "The head
wrangler hires the lodge manager?"

"Yep." Raleigh leaned toward her, his voice lowered. "Would you leave the matter in the hands of Etta
Sue or Sharleen Jackleen?"

"Hmm." She drew back. "I'm confused. Etta Sue
did say an applicant was expected. I believe she mis-
took me for this other person."

"That so?" The incoming agent's identity was
known only to Raleigh, just as his would be known
only to her. "I did have an interview scheduled. The
storm may have caused a delay." He looked Molly
over, keeping his admiration in check this time. "Since
you're here, Ms. Broome, and threatening a lawsuit,
perhaps we should start over with a proper interview?
I believe you mentioned a résumé?" He cocked one
hip, arms folded across his abdomen. He had no intention of hiring her, but what was the harm in keeping
her a while longer, if only for appearances?

His, he reminded himself—his appearance as a

make-believe cowboy. Not hers, delectable though it was.

"I suppose it won't do any harm to talk." Molly shot him one more suspicious glance from beneath her lashes. "I'll just see to the kittens first."

"Joss will be glad to baby-sit," he volunteered as the girl came from the lobby with a cardboard box. Molly skimmed her light across its interior. The three kittens were nestled amongst a pile of tan corduroy, ready to nap.

"We can't use the electric heating pad," Jocelyn said, "so I found a hot water bottle instead. But I better fill it up before we lose our hot water, too."

"Good thinking," Molly replied. "I'm going to talk with Mr. Tate for a few minutes, Jocelyn. Would you take care of the kittens for me in the meantime?"

The girl's smile was enormous. "I sure will!" She ran off into the darkness, following the bobbing beam of her flashlight.

"She's quite a child," Molly murmured. "Very self-sufficient."

"Sure 'nuff." Raleigh hadn't given the girl much thought. He didn't know anything about kids, having grown up without siblings in a motherless household in Colorado. His father had been a small-town sheriff, more at ease with commanding deputies than coddling toddlers. By the time Raleigh was ten, he could shoot a rifle, ride a horse, drive a truck—on the Tates' small spread only, the sheriff being a stickler for the law—and even cook a tasty supper entirely from cans. He took Jocelyn's independence as a matter of course.

Molly drew herself up. "Well, then, let's get down to business." She held her light steady on Raleigh's face.

"Yes'm." He teased her with a slow smile. "Will

you accuse me of impropriety if I suggest we get comfortable first?''

She fingered the front of her blouse, peeling the fabric away from her skin. "Depends what you had in mind."

"More light, for one." He directed her into the lobby with a hand placed at the small of her back, keenly aware of the generous flare and sinuous movement of her hips. Apparently the woman couldn't walk without sashaying.

"Candles?" she said.

He aimed his flashlight at the enormous rustic stone fireplace centered on the wall opposite the check-in desk. "Firelight."

She hesitated. "Is that our only option?"

"Too romantic for you?" He glanced over his shoulder at her, then set his flashlight on the hearth, butt-end down. Without responding, Molly sank into one of the mission-style armchairs flanking the fireplace. He felt her gaze on him as he arranged kindling and logs in the andirons and took out his matchbook.

Molly rubbed her arms as the fire's warmth began to seep into the room. "I wonder what happened to Etta Sue. She was in the lobby ten minutes ago, setting out buckets to catch the drips."

Rain drummed the roof, working its way beneath the old cedar-shake shingles. Raleigh regretted seeing such a fine old place going to rack and ruin. "Etta Sue follows her own timetable," he said. "I've already learned never to expect her to show up when she's wanted. That way I'm pleasantly surprised if she does."

"Is she honestly the executive housekeeper?"

"In name only. Sharleen's the extent of the housekeeping staff for the time being. When business picks up, Wyatt hires more help.'' Raleigh took off his wet coat and hat and spread them across the hearth made of smooth rounded river stones. He added one more log to the crackling fire and went to sit beside Molly. She'd done something to her bedraggled hair while his back was turned. It was tucked behind her ears, the thick bangs smoothed over her forehead, burnished a deep chocolate brown by the firelight. Besides those luminous eyes and full lips of hers, she had a small straight nose, cheeks like apricots, a rounded chin with a slight cleft and a smooth ivory neck.

Raleigh believed that most folk's character eventually showed up on their face whether or not they wanted it to. Molly Broome's face told him that she was kind and honest, slow to anger, quick to forgive. Overly sentimental. Whereas he saw the world in simple blacks and whites, she probably looked for nuance and color and reason, and yet, like him, still believed in authority and justice. Unless it was his glands talking, he felt she might be a sensualist, though her experience was limited. There was something pure about her. She'd never known cruelty, sorrow or strife, he was certain.

"What about the cooking?" she asked, bringing him back to the moment with her crashing practicality.

Mentally Raleigh reset his strategy and goals into the straight lines that he preferred, hoping that his wayward thoughts would soon follow. All he needed to know about Molly Broome was that she was a complication, a zigzag, a way-out-of-bounds figure-eight *curve*.

"The cooking situation is dicey now that we're without Mrs. Peet. Besides me, Sharleen and Etta Sue, the off-season staff includes a couple of wranglers who work with the horses and other livestock. They live in the bunkhouse. We've all been getting by on canned food and sandwiches. I expect Wyatt will be forced to hire a real cook when the lodge reopens, the first of the year.''

Molly said winningly, ''I enjoy cooking.''

Raleigh stared till he had to remind himself that he wasn't hiring her. Even if she was ideal. ''The job isn't really about cooking, Ms. Broome, it's about managing. You'd have to run the lodge, see to guests, supervise staff...'' He raked his fingers through his hair. ''You ask me, it sounds like a hell of a lot of aggravation. For very little money.'' He named a salary that should put her off. Judging by her designer pocketbook and classic style, Ms. Molly Broome was accustomed to a certain standard of living.

She arched her brows. ''I assume that includes room and board.''

''You're still interested?'' Had she taken a good look at the lodge before the lights went out? Noticed Sharleen's fingernails? Gotten an eighty-proof whiff of Etta Sue?

''I need a job, Mr. Tate.'' She smoothed out her résumé and handed it to him. ''And I'm ready to start immediately.''

He skimmed the high points. She was only twenty-five. Single. Lived in New York City. *Whoa.* ''You're from New York?''

''You don't have to say it like that.'' Her eyes glittered in the firelight. ''I'm not some stereotypical man-eating bitch on wheels, if that's what you expect.''

He chuckled. ''That's apparent, Ms. Broome. I was astonished, is all. If I may ask, what in blue blazes are you doing all the way out here in Wyoming?''

''Call me Molly, please.'' She leaned back in the chair and rested her chin on her hand, her limpid gaze lingering on his face like a caress. Whether or not she knew it.

His voice lowered to an intimate tone. "We don't get many tourists here in November...Ms. Molly."

Her smile carved a dimple out of one plump cheek. "I'm not exactly a tourist. I came to Treetop to visit friends at the McHenrys' Goldstream Ranch. As it happened, I was unemployed, so when Lilah Evers mentioned an opening at a local dude ranch..." She shrugged.

He looked again at the résumé. Attached was a glowing recommendation letter from her supervisor. "Downsized you out of a job, did they, pretty lady?"

She fiddled with her collar. "The CEO earned a million-dollar bonus, but I'm afraid I was considered expendable, along with fifty other employees. They're hiring some of them back as 'temporary' workers. That didn't appeal to me."

Ah. Reason enough not to hire her. And just in time to stop him from making calf eyes at her like a lonesome, lovesick cowpoke fresh off the range. "Well, Molly, thanks for stopping by. Although your qualifications are adequate, I'm afraid it just wouldn't work out since this job is also temporary." He stood.

She didn't. The face she turned up toward his was disbelieving. "You're turning me down?"

"Sorry—"

Raleigh's apology was cut off by a heavy thud and banshee shriek that shook the rafters. Recognizing the voice, he gritted his teeth and silently asked the powers-that-be—in his case, the current director of the Secret Service—to grant him a few more weeks of forbearance.

Molly had leaped to her feet, startled. Raleigh waved off her concern. "That you, Etta Sue?" he called.

Another shriek sounded from near the balcony, this one mad rather than frightened, followed by a garbled moan that floated eerily in the dark cavernous space. "Grizzlegotme…"

Molly clutched Raleigh's arm. "We have to help her."

"Don't worry about it." Leave her alone and she'll sleep it off, is what he was thinking. "If she can scream that loud, she's not hurt."

Molly snatched his high-powered flashlight off the hearth. "I'll do it."

Since Raleigh was forced to accompany her up the steps, he allowed himself the pleasure of lagging several steps behind. Damn, but he wished the electricity would come back on so he could see if she was as fine in bright light as in shadow. At thirty-three, he was beyond the stage where how a woman looked at last call was all that mattered. More and more, he'd been feeling the need for a relationship that meant something. For the good old-fashioned TLC of a woman with smarts. With substance.

With figure-eight curves so generous a man could die in her arms and think he'd gone to centerfold heaven.

Molly had reached the top of the staircase. She flashed the light over bead-board paneling hung with a row of sepia-toned prints of settlers in covered wagons and cowboys on horseback. Three hallways opened off into different directions from the wide landing. Etta Sue's sepulchral moans and mutterings came from the one on the left. Tingly little shivers coursed through Molly's scalp.

Raleigh Tate, wrangler man, stomped off down the hallway, arms swinging. "What in tarnation did you get into now, Etta Sue?"

Molly froze, forgetting her wariness. Oh, come now. Had he actually said *tarnation?* She wasn't going to swallow that one!

Sure, tall, dark and handsome Raleigh Tate looked like the ideal cowboy, every worn inch of him—from his unshaved chin to the run-down heels on his boots—exactly right for a starring role in the movie that had been running in her dreams ever since she'd joined the Cowgirl Club. It was his act that she didn't buy. Half the time he spoke like a…a…like a lawyer, for pity's sake. But then he'd throw in some hokey country expression. Dang fine. Yes'm. Sure 'nuff.

Sure 'nuff!

What in tarnation was going on around this place?

In the darkened hallway, Raleigh grunted. Etta Sue yelled out another slurred phrase, something like, "Grizztickin'me!"

"Ms. Molly, you want to bring along that light?" Raleigh sounded aggrieved.

"Yes, of course," she said, holding it up to illuminate the puzzling situation. Raleigh was leaning over Etta Sue, who was laid out spread-eagle on the floor. On top of her, pinning her in place, was a…what looked like a…

Molly swallowed. "Tell me that's not a grizzly bear."

"Nope. It's a plain old black bear. Story goes Wyatt shot it off the back porch ten years ago and had it stuffed like he's the last of the great white hunters. Maybe you could untangle Etta Sue's hair from the claws when I roll ol' Grizzle off her."

Molly pushed aside the cleaning cart and knelt at the elderly housekeeper's head. "Don'tchew touch my cart," Etta Sue screeched, wriggling beneath the bear as if she were being attacked. One skinny arm waved in the air, bangle bracelets clinking.

"I only moved it," Molly soothed. She positioned the flashlight so it would shine on Etta Sue's face.

Her wrinkled lids snapped shut. "Keep that light outta my eyes and get this grizz off me afore I'm flattened like a pancake!"

Raleigh and Molly exchanged a wry glance and went to work. He looped his arms around the animal's molting midsection and hoisted it up as far as Etta Sue's ponytail would allow. She let out a screech to tell him when. Molly untangled the yellow strands, dealing with Etta Sue's grumblings and squirmings as best she could. The housekeeper was not forthcoming, but apparently she'd been pushing her cart through the hallway in the dark when her broom had speared behind the mounted bear and sent it crashing down on top of her. The beast's claws, affixed in an aggressive upraised position, had missed her face by a scratch.

"Thought I was a goner," she muttered as Raleigh set the bear upright. He shoved it back into its niche. "Coulda pierced my eyeball like a grape."

"You shouldn't have been wandering around in the dark."

Molly squelched Raleigh with a look. "We were all wandering around in the dark." She dabbed at an angry-looking scratch on Etta Sue's cheek. "You'll need disinfectant on this." With Raleigh's help, she got Etta Sue onto her feet and aimed toward the stairs. The woman smelled like a distillery, but she didn't seem particularly drunk. Just ornery.

"Howdeee!" Sharleen's soprano sang from below. "What's going on up there? Everybody okay?"

Etta Sue stopped and said, "My cart."

Molly assured Sharleen that they were fine. She took the housekeeper's bony elbow. "Come along now, Etta

Sue. I promise to go back for the cart as soon as your scrapes are cleaned up."

"Don't talk to me like I'm addled, missy." Etta Sue tucked her head into her shoulders and dug in her heels. "I ain't going nowheres without my cart."

Raleigh shook his head at Molly. "Never mind. I'll get it." He followed them down the stairs, bumping the heavily laden cleaning cart down one step at a time. How Etta Sue had managed the uphill climb was a mystery for the ages.

They were all settled in the kitchen with the flashlights arranged on the countertops to illuminate the medical procedure—Raleigh manned the antiseptic spray and Molly applied bandages—when a crash, a splash and a loud, angry yell came from the lobby.

Molly flinched and said, "Good Lord!" Raleigh muttered Wyatt's name with a tight edge to his voice that made her wonder. Jocelyn hugged the box of kittens. Sharleen grabbed a light and ran from the room, twittering assurances.

"Is it just the storm, or is it always like this?" Molly asked, packing up the first-aid kit. Add guests, she was thinking, and the Triple Eight could pass for a madhouse.

Raleigh ambled to the swinging door. "It's worse." From the lobby came a string of curses blazing enough to singe the tongue, along with a series of bumps and clangs. "That's the boss."

With a significant glance at Jocelyn's tender ears, Molly shooed Raleigh out the door. She stood to straighten her clothes and hair in preparation for meeting the ranch owner. Then again, why bother? Although her pride had been hurt by Raleigh's dismissal, what woman in her right mind would want such a job?

Etta Sue had slumped in her chair, dozing with her mouth open, one gnarled hand locked on the handle of her precious cleaning cart. Jocelyn agreed to stay and keep her company.

Now that the storm was letting up, the lodge wasn't as dark. Molly was sure that she could find the lobby without a flashlight. Still she hesitated, mentally listing all the reasons why she should be glad to get away from the Triple Eight with her résumé intact. One was a cranky housekeeper with an unused cleaning cart and a taste for booze. Two—a sex-bomb maid with grand delusions, big hair and oversize...fingernails. Three— a sad, sweet child who needed more love and attention than anyone but a parent should provide.

The fourth reason was Raleigh Tate himself. Raleigh Tate, movie cowboy.

No. She was better off leaving him entirely alone. The temptation was too great, the puzzle too involving. *Don't go there, Ms. Molly. Save yourself instead.*

Keeping a cautious eye on Etta Sue, Molly eased a mop out of the cart. She tiptoed from the kitchen to the dark dining room without making a sound. And walked straight into Raleigh Tate, wrangler man.

She staggered. Wow, he sure felt like a real cowboy. He had a presence as solid as stone, owing as much to his straight-shooting personality as his well-muscled frame. Come wind and rain, thunder and lightning, Sturm und Drang, Raleigh Tate would be a man to count on.

His hands were on her shoulders, holding her steady, but he wasn't saying a word. Molly couldn't, either. All she seemed capable of was hanging on to the mop for dear life.

In the dark, Raleigh touched her face with gentle fingertips, stroking her cheeks, her chin, her lips and even, when she closed them and swayed in his direction, her eyes. The caresses made her go weak with longing, but eventually she summoned up enough of a voice to whisper, "What are you doing?"

"Kissing you." His mouth seemed to have scarcely moved, but she could tell by his tone that he was smiling.

She bit her lip. "No, actually, you're not."

"I'm not?"

She shook her head.

"You're sure?"

She nodded emphatically.

He smoothed her hair back from her face. "Gol'darn it. I could have sworn I was kissing you."

"Y-you seem to have a perception problem." Her voice had cracked like a teacup in a tornado, but at least she'd gotten a few words out.

"Maybe it was just my imagination."

"Oh." When she inhaled, his scent—an amalgamation of wet leather, cold rain, resinous wood and musky male skin—went straight to her head. "So…does that mean you have been imagining kissing me?"

"'Bout a dozen times, each kiss better than the last." His husky chuckle sent a million thread-line crackles through her composure. "Makes me wonder if the real thing will live up to its billing."

She couldn't take the suspense any longer, even if that meant rising to his bait. "Well, then, go on and give it a try."

He smiled. He definitely smiled. "Try what?"

Sweet heaven! Even though Molly's chin was trembling and her head was whirling with the erotic images he'd invoked, she was able to speak words straight out of a movie script. Mainly because they were words she'd been waiting a lifetime to say. "Kiss me, cowboy," she whispered. "Please…kiss me."

"Well, now. Seeing as how you asked so nicely, Ms. Molly, I do believe that I will."

3

HIS WARM BREATH FANNED her face as his mouth lowered toward hers. In the suspended instant before the kiss, desire prickled at her nape and sank lower, tickling all along her spine, making her backside squirm. The room was so dark and she was so unlike her usual steady self that she was afraid she'd lose her balance altogether if she didn't put her hands on Raleigh's waist for support.

And just in time. He leaned closer. He kissed her...nose.

Her nose?

Probably a mistake, reasonable enough to understand in the dark. Nose-kissing didn't rate a paragraph in any sex manual she'd ever heard of, but Raleigh made it eligible, giving a little sucking kiss to the tip of her nose before he slid his pointed tongue around the side of it and down to the corner of her mouth. His lips touched hers there, his tongue making soft coaxing licks against her upper lip until she tilted her head back with a murmur of assent. Her fingers curled around his waistband, index fingers hooking onto the empty belt loops.

His arms swooped around her, his hands sliding everywhere at once as if he had only one chance to get the feel of her. His palms found her bottom and gave it a healthy squeeze. A goose! Her instinctive response was to flinch and go up on her toes, her cheeks—all four—washed with heat.

His mouth met hers then, right on target. *Oh, my.* Molly forgot her momentary self-consciousness. Raleigh Tate's full-on, four-square, openmouthed kiss was incredible, the sort that drove all other concerns from a woman's head. She was instantly infused with pleasure—hot, fierce, fire-breathing pleasure. Her only thought was that this kiss should never end.

The mop fell to the floor with a clatter.

Raleigh didn't hear it; he was in heaven. Molly's mouth was like warm honey, sweet and melting. He couldn't get enough of her.

But he was determined to try.

It was too dark to see her eyes. Every kiss, each caress, was its own world of sensation. He nibbled at her parted lips and she tugged on his belt loops, asking for more. He sucked at her lower lip; she moaned in her throat, pressing her soft, full breasts against his chest. He was driven to angle his mouth over hers and kiss her deeply, laving her tongue with his, filling his hands with her lush curves. The sense that an infinite passion had ignited between them was so mind expanding his head seemed to explode into brilliance.

It was the lights. They were blazing bright.

The electricity was on.

Molly bleated a startled "Oh!" and pulled out of his arms, flushing pink as she turned away, shading her eyes.

He blinked at the bright lights, greedily trying to take in the sight of her. If he hit the light switch fast enough, would she revert to the woman who'd gone so willingly into his arms instead of out of them? Probably not. Lightning rarely struck twice.

But some passions burned forever.

Cord Wyatt's voice boomed from the lobby. "Tate! Where are you, man?"

Raleigh looked at Molly and said, "Coming."

Her blush deepened. "We'll need this." She bent to retrieve the mop and defensively held it crosswise between them.

She was right. Arriving in the lobby, he saw that the wood floor was wet all over, many of the drip containers overturned. Cord Wyatt sat in a chair with his right leg propped up on an ottoman. One of his white crocodile size-thirteen cowboy boots was wedged into a bucket. Sharleen tugged at it ineffectually.

Wyatt waved her off. "Tate can do it."

"My pleasure, sir," the head wrangler said, not without a good helping of sarcasm.

While Raleigh forcibly removed the bucket from Cord Wyatt's foot—the boot went with it—Molly mopped up the spilled rainwater, watching through her hair when it swung loose to screen her face. Shaken by Raleigh's kiss, she forced herself to concentrate on the owner of the dude ranch. Looking at Raleigh was asking for trouble.

Cord Wyatt was a big man. Well over six feet tall and two hundred pounds, by the looks of it. Perched on the back of his head was a white cowboy hat with a rolled brim and an iridescent feather stuck in the silver hatband. A thick shock of iron-gray hair skimmed his brow. His face was large and florid, its features oversize to match his booming baritone. He dressed western-style, festooned with a silver-and-turquoise bolo tie, several matching rings and a heavily tooled belt that rode low below a firmly packed paunch. His sock had a hole in the toe.

Molly's lips curled. She'd bet anything his underwear was frayed at the edges, and dingy, too. She knew the type—concerned with outward appearances to the detriment of all else.

Simpering, Sharleen knelt at the rancher's feet to ease on the cowboy boot. Cord—who had to be fifty, minimum—gazed at her fondly, watching her minister to him with a certain smug satisfaction that was incredibly irritating to Molly. She supposed some women might see Cord Wyatt as a not unattractive older man— if they liked money and self-importance. Or at least the appearance of it.

Cord glanced her way. His brows went up. "And who might this be?" he trumpeted, evidently mistaking bombast for charm.

Molly tried to ignore her rising hackles. She put down the dented punch bowl and crossed the lobby, hand extended. They shook, Cord's grip strong enough to grind corn. "Molly Broome," she said, and swallowed her trepidation. "I've applied for Mrs. Peet's job, Mr. Wyatt."

"Ah." He laced his big hands over his stomach, lacking the good manners to stand. His gaze crept over her like a slithery snake until Sharleen started rubbing his thigh. Then he patted the housemaid's head and aimed a distracted question at Raleigh. "This the one, Tate?"

Raleigh had been standing off to the side, one leg crossed casually over the other even though his eyes had narrowed to slits as he watched Cord inspect Molly. At the question, he straightened up with a jerk. "No, sir. The woman who was so highly recommended to me didn't…ah…show up. The storm—"

Cord interrupted. "I like this one. She'll do."

Molly hesitated. She wanted a job, a new life, a chance for—her lashes flicked at Raleigh—romance. But she wasn't sure about the Triple Eight and its owner. Then again, living here would be like landing in the middle of a production of *City Slickers* or—saints preserve her—*The Best Little Whorehouse in Texas*. Her life would not be boring. And if she didn't like it, there was always Mrs. Peet's broken leg to fall back on. The woman was due to return in six months.

Why not take the plunge? The decision wasn't irrevocable.

"I'd love to work here, Mr. Wyatt," she said, regardless of Raleigh's scowl. Why would he kiss the stuffing out of her one moment and then thwart her employment the next? "And I promise that I'll do a very good job for you."

"Just a minute." Raleigh stepped toward them. "Wyatt, you gave me hiring authority."

"Only until I got back from the city," the rancher said, placid in his easy chair. "And I'm back early. You're hired...er, Molly, was it?" His gaze skipped up to her eyes, then lowered again to her breasts, so avidly her skin crawled.

Oh, dear.

"Molly Broome," she said heavily. *I'm up here.*

Raleigh, now the thwartee instead of the thwarter, was rankled enough to give her a smirk. She glared in return.

"Think it's time for your little speech?" he asked with a knowing grin. He slid his hands into the front pockets of his jeans, pulling the fly distractingly taut. She held her gaze steady. Wild kisses in the dark to the contrary, she would not sink to Cord Wyatt's level and ogle Raleigh as if he'd sold tickets to a sideshow. "The speech about relying on your qualifications?" he prodded. "The word of warning?"

Her smile was saccharine. "I'll keep it on tap for whenever—*whomever* it's needed."

Raleigh nodded, holding her gaze until her head was filled with thoughts of their kisses, which would have been fine if she'd concentrated on how inappropriate their actions had been, but she didn't. Not in the least. And, to tell the truth, the change from her usual well-behaved self was liberating. She felt light enough to float toward the ceiling like a helium balloon.

"Well, then, Ms. Molly," Raleigh finally said in a lazy cowboy drawl, "welcome to the Triple Eight Dude Ranch." His pale blue eyes bored into hers as if one string of fabulous kisses had let him in on all her wildest dreams. "I certainly hope your time here is all that you hope for."

"AND HE SAID IT AS THOUGH he has every intention of seeing to it that my time will be short and miserable," Molly said early that evening in her temporary quarters at Goldstream. For the past week she'd been sharing Ellie McHenry's small attic bedroom, tucked under the eaves of the family's sandstone ranch house. The tail end of the rainstorm pattered against the dormer window.

"Miserable?" Grace Farrow's nose crinkled. "Sounds to me like the opposite is more likely!"

"That's the thing." Molly took an armful of unworn garments out of the closet. "I can't figure him out. One moment he's this perfect movie cowboy, dialogue and all, and then he's…"

"Kissing you!" Grace shimmied with the thrill of it, practically bouncing on the twin bed.

Molly moved her suitcase to the opposite bed and dropped down beside her friend. Inside, whenever she thought about kissing Raleigh, she was like Grace—all pinwheels and firecrackers and exclamations. Outwardly she was leery of showing such great emotion when it all meant so very much to her. "Oh, Grace. I'm so—I'm just—" She pressed a hand over her mouth when it broke into a delighted smile all on its own.

Grace gave her a hug. "You found your cowboy, Mol! And such a hottie to boot!"

Molly laughed. "Let's not jump the gun. One kiss does not a romance make."

"It's a good start."

"There's the little matter of how eager he was *not* to hire me."

Grace nodded. "Yeah, that part's curious, all right. But tell me again about the kiss. First he said, what—?"

"Oh, you." Molly tossed a few sweaters at her friend to fold. "Occupy yourself. Get your mind off cowboys."

Grace chortled. "I will if you will." They packed in silence for only a few moments before Grace's green eyes clouded and she said with a dreamy sigh, "But did he have tight jeans, according to the Cowgirl Club mantra?"

Molly's expression was amazingly similar. "Not exactly tight. Formfitting. Bleached almost white, run out at the knees. No belt. He wore brown leather chaps when he was riding the Appaloosa, but he must have taken them off in the barn because—" She caught herself up short. "Listen to me. I've completely lost it."

"Aw, Molly, you used to be so sensible and calm, such a stabilizing influence on the Cowgirl Club. Look at you now. We're going to have to call Laramie in New York for advice. She's not yet under the influence." Laramie Jones was the third member of their small group, the purpose of which had always been more tongue-in-cheek than serious until rancher Shane

McHenry had shown up in Manhattan to sell Grace his horse. Within a week, Grace had chucked her previous life—and fiancé—to hitch a ride west with Shane. By the time they'd reached Treetop, Wyoming, they were engaged.

"You're so right, Grace. This isn't like me." Molly continued packing anyway. She zipped her dresses into a garment bag. Perhaps they'd be wearable in her new career, during the tourist season. Until then, there was a lot of work ahead of her to bring the lodge up to standard. Work she was looking forward to, she realized with a sense of relief. Wrangler Raleigh Tate was not the only reason she'd taken the job.

He was just the bonus.

What a bonus. *What a cowboy!*

"My parents are going to think I have a screw loose." Molly frowned as she sorted through her socks and underwear. "Moving to New York from Connecticut was understandable, but Wyoming? How can I ever explain Wyoming to them?"

"Invite them out next spring. Shane says the countryside's gorgeous as soon as it warms up. Your parents are reasonable, they'll adjust to the idea. Whereas mine…"

Molly smiled at Grace. "Are they over the shock of your broken engagement yet?"

"They've calmed down some, enough for us to have a reasonable discussion when I call. We've even reached a tentative agreement about them traveling out here in December for the wedding, though my mother insists on using the word 'quickie' every single time she mentions it. And she's still blaming me for ditching Michael and therefore practically forcing him into Caroline's ever-loving arms." Grace's lips twitched with amusement. "I'm not sure who was supposed to have forced them into the closet."

Molly couldn't hold back her giggle. "It was a sight to behold. First, you ran out on your engagement party, then your ex-fiancé disappears, too, and we're all frantic, thinking he's out on the ledge or something, out of his mind with heartbreak, until someone opens the coat closet and there's Michael and Caroline—" She waved her hands.

"Making out," sang Grace. "My ex-fiancé and my sister-in-law—Golden Boy and the Lemon-Sucker! The scandal, the shame! The horror!"

They collapsed in laughter. "I'll never forget the look of humiliation on Caroline's face. Michael didn't seem to mind as much—I think he felt vindicated after the ego-shattering blow of your breakup." Molly sobered, wiping the corners of her eyes. "It was Victor's reaction I cared about." Victor Farrow was Grace's brother, Caroline's husband, a good and decent man, a caring doctor.

Grace's small freckled face crumpled with concern. "I know. I've felt terrible that Victor was the innocent victim of my impulse, when all along he'd tried so hard to do everything right according to the Farrow code of behavior. Still, every time I think about what a narrow escape I made from that life, I grab on to Shane real tight and say a little prayer of thanks." She gave Molly a squeeze. "And that's what you should do, too, hon. If this Raleigh Tate is for real, hang on to him. I've been in Wyoming long enough now to know that not every cowboy is a keeper."

There was a soft knock at the open door. Eleanor McHenry hovered on the threshold. "Sorry to interrupt."

Grace waved her in. "Not at all. We're just talking about cowboys again—our favorite subject."

Ellie smiled shyly. She was a tall, slender young woman with wavy light brown hair, green eyes and a tremendous musical talent. She looked like the fragile type, and was treated as such by her mother and older brother, but Molly and Grace were in agreement that there was a core of strength in Ellie that ran deep. On her own, she had recently applied for—and won—a full scholarship to a music conservatory in San Francisco. She would be leaving in January to undergo intensive training as a pianist.

"Soon you'll have this room to yourself again," Molly said to Ellie. "I'm taking off tomorrow morning for my new job at the Triple Eight Dude Ranch."

"That was quick."

"I know." Molly zipped up her suitcase and pulled it off the second bed to make room for Ellie. Having a third party in on the discussion was the next best thing to benefiting from Laramie's wry observations. "Too quick, I guess. My head is spinning."

Grace nudged her in the ribs. "Time for straight talk, Cowgirl Club-style. It's plain as day who's got your head spinning. Ellie? Do you know a cowboy named Raleigh Tate? He's the head wrangler at the Triple Eight."

Shane's younger sister sat and looped her long fingers through a curlicue on the iron bedstead. "The name's not familiar. He can't be from Treetop. I know just about everybody who lives either in town or on the surrounding ranches." Having grown up in Wyoming, Ellie was not as gaga over cowboys as the members of the Cowgirl Club. Grace called it a proximity-as-immunization problem; she was working on an antidote.

"Somehow, I didn't get the impression that he was a local," Molly mused. She remembered her brief fantasy casting Raleigh as the mysterious stranger who rides into town and saves it from corruption. "I'm not sure why."

"The Triple Eight's had some problems holding on to their wranglers this past year. People are saying Cord Wyatt's in financial trouble. Maybe worse—something criminal. There's even talk about government agents asking questions around town. Could be the IRS." Ellie shrugged apologetically. "You know how rumors spread in a small town."

Grace straightened up. "That doesn't sound so good. Are you sure you know what you're getting into, Mol?"

Molly had to admit that she didn't. And that was what she found appealing. She was embarking on an adventure! Perhaps taking the first step by flying out to Wyoming had opened her to further change. It might even be that she was ready to break out of her role as the reliable, level headed good girl of their group and do something uncharacteristically wild.

Molly thought again of the wrangler with the pale blue eyes. Of how she'd said, "Kiss me, cowboy," in the dark.

She wouldn't mind if Raleigh Tate was her "something wild." She wouldn't mind at all.

"I COULDN'T AVOID IT. The pickup pulled out right in front of me. The road was slick. The brakes—the ditch…it wasn't my fault, Agent Tate, sir!"

"No," Raleigh agreed grudgingly. Although he couldn't abide whiners, he also couldn't lay blame on his colleague. "The blunder wasn't your fault." It was his. He'd been the one driven to distraction by Molly Broome's bountiful curves and big brown eyes.

Agent Melissa Stankle, a rookie to the job, looked as if she wanted to cry. Her face was pink and all scrunched up. Her chin quivered. Snuffling ominously, she cradled her heavily wrapped wrist against her chest like a holstered weapon. "I'm s-sorry that my accident messed up the case, sir."

"It'll work out. As soon as I figure out a way to get rid of Wyatt's new employee, we'll slide you into the vacant position as planned. Just be sure to stay out of ditches in the meantime, Stankle."

The rookie agent closed her eyes and sucked in a deep breath. "Yes, sir."

"And stop calling me sir. This isn't the military."

"Yes, sir. I mean, no, sir." She winced.

"Doc give you any pain pills?"

Stankle's chin shot up. "I don't need pain pills, sir. It's just a badly sprained wrist. I've dealt with worse."

"And the cut?"

She pressed her fingertips on the square white bandage affixed to her forehead. "A couple of stitches. Well, five. The doctor said I might have a scar." The moisture in her eyes became a gleam of pride.

Raleigh gave a silent groan. Even a slip of a girl like Melissa Stankle had bought into the Secret Service's gung ho, die-for-your-country mentality. He too remembered a time when acquiring an injury, or better yet, a scar—even one that came as a result of a fender bender—had felt like being pinned with a badge of honor. He'd hated desk work, craved the adrenaline rush of field assignments, no matter how tame. Now all of it seemed like just another day in the office.

Son of a gun. Was he a tired old warhorse at thirty-three? Was his weariness with the job and his growing susceptibility to soft women a sign that he'd lost his edge, that it was time for him to get out of the game for good?

He snorted. What would he do? Become a cowboy?

An absurd idea, but not as laughable as it might have been. He'd thought that the more ridiculous aspects of a Secret Service agent from the counterfeit division going undercover as a dude ranch wrangler were what had caused his misgivings about this assignment, but, surprisingly, he was enjoying the charade. Had to be a regression to playing cowboys-and-Indians, growing up. That he was country born and bred and could ride well enough to make a passable cowboy was why he'd been assigned to this job in the first place.

Raleigh's gaze crisscrossed the wet pavement and sparse sprinkling of parked cars. He and Stankle were sitting in the Jeep Cherokee he'd liberated from the Triple Eight's small fleet of two rust-riddled vehicles. Instead of picking up sacks of sweet feed at the Treetop feed store, he was parked in the farthest corner of the medical clinic's parking lot, hoping that none of the small town's residents would take note. Since Stankle was also incognito, there was no real reason to keep their acquaintance top secret. It just felt safer that way. One never knew when a casual observation might lead to a suspicion that brought down his case.

The rookie agent stirred, glancing with admiration at Raleigh's undercover cowboy getup. "Have there been any developments at the ranch?"

"I had a glimpse of the cellar. Seemed to me it would make a fine place for our suspect to conceal his contraband."

"Can you get a closer look, even though I'm not positioned inside the way we planned?" Stankle's features knotted at the ignominy of her recent failure to infiltrate the Triple Eight.

Warmth bloomed inside Raleigh every time he thought of Molly Broome, Stankle's unknowing spoiler. Though sabotaging Molly's employment would be a piece of cake, it would also be a tough mouthful to swallow. He didn't want to hurt such an innocent and good-hearted woman. The infamous Ollie North's flag-waving excuses to the contrary, Raleigh wasn't one to rationalize that the ends justified the means.

"I need a distraction to clear out the lodge so I can search it." That way he wouldn't have to dismiss—or part from—sweet Ms. Molly.

Stankle brightened. "I'll come up with a scheme." Her brows drew together. "How about a...tornado warning? Send them all to the storm shelter and the coast is clear."

"You have a personal in with the National Weather Service, Agent Stankle? Maybe even Mother Nature?" Raleigh smiled, imagining the hullabaloo of getting the ranch employees into a storm shelter all at the same time. Etta Sue would insist on taking her cleaning cart. Wyatt would need an easy chair and a six-pack. Molly Broome...well, *she* he wouldn't mind escorting into the dark.

"There doesn't actually have to be a tornado, sir."

"Too far-fetched. Let's work on getting you hired instead."

"I'm prepared to do what I must, sir. Anytime, anywhere, anyhow."

Raleigh tugged on his hat, pulling the brim lower over his face. Stankle had probably imagined her career with the Secret Service differently—investigating crazies, shooting bad guys, taking bullets for the president.

At the very least, being issued her own earpiece and pair of supercool Ray•Bans.

For Raleigh, a career that involved some form of law enforcement had been a given. You didn't stray from the straight and narrow when you were trained from birth by Sheriff Richard Tate, who was still in fighting trim and serving his fortieth year as small-town Colorado's cross between Joe Friday and Bat Masterson.

Then again, Raleigh wasn't supposed to crave the comfort of a soft, warm, cuddly woman, either. At least not for more than an occasional decadent romp. Men will be men, his father had once allowed, after delivering a lecture about uncomplicated physical desire versus the allure of females whose sentimental natures and generous attributes made them all the more treacherous. At the time, the volume of phone calls from giggly teenage girls had reached critical mass in the Tate household. On Raleigh's next birthday, his sixteenth, he'd received a box of condoms and a bundle of pamphlets about teen pregnancy and STDs. A sentimental man, the sheriff.

Stankle cleared her throat.

Raleigh blinked. His thoughts had jumped the tracks again. From the job at hand straight to sex. That wasn't good.

"What can I do in the meantime?" Stankle asked eagerly. She was a pretty girl, and brainy, too, with bright eyes, a wide mouth and a slender runner's frame wired with lean muscle.

She didn't attract Raleigh's interest one whit; curvy Molly Broome was still belly dancing across his fantasies.

Definitely not good.

"I could question the locals," Stankle offered.

"Yeah, sure, but that's already been done by an agent from the closest field office."

"I'll be questioning them unofficially. Undercover. It makes a difference. Sir." There was a prodding undertone to the agent's words. She'd noticed Raleigh's distraction.

He focused. With the exception of a few spiteful enemies and blabbermouth gossips who couldn't help themselves, the denizens of Treetop had been wary of his colleague's careful questions during the preliminary investigation. Even the proprietors of the businesses that had been passed the occasional fake bill seemed reluctant to name names; their losses had been negligible. The initial investigation had ended where it began—at the Triple Eight Dude Ranch, the apparent cynosure of the "funny money" that had first appeared in Treetop, but was now also connected to a complicated money-laundering scheme at a Laramie jewelry store.

While several of the Triple Eight occupants had interesting backgrounds, the main suspect remained Cord Wyatt. The rancher was juggling his holdings like a circus performer, desperate to maintain the appearance of a prosperous life-style while he waited for one of his dubious investments to pay off. The dude ranch was mortgaged to the hilt. Its business had begun to slough off as Wyatt's neglect became obvious to the guests. With no cash flow to speak of, he was left to scramble to meet payroll, mortgage and overhead expenses.

Keeping in mind both Cord Wyatt's community standing and the hot-running antigovernment trend, Raleigh's superiors were approaching an arrest with caution. His job was to nail down incontrovertible evidence of an ongoing counterfeiting operation so there'd be no chance of Wyatt and his accomplices wiggling out of prison sentences.

"Even undercover, Stankle, it's not likely you'd get anything from the locals except more gossip and innuendo. Wyatt may be considered a blowhard by some, but in the past he's also bankrolled the library expansion and Fourth of July fireworks. He's one of their own. In small towns like Treetop, that's a tough bond to break. Particularly for an outsider."

Melissa Stankle clenched her jaw. "Then what should I do?"

Raleigh started the truck. "I'll drive you back to the motel. You can interface with our agents in Laramie. See if anything new developed during Wyatt's most recent trip there. He came back early, and I want to know why."

"All right, sir." It was a crumb, but Melissa Stankle was the sort of dedicated agent who'd gather her crumbs until they formed a piece of the pie. "The body shop said I'll have my vehicle by tomorrow afternoon. Luckily there was only a smashed headlight and dented grill." She shook her head, then winced. "Women drivers," she sneered, rubbing her temples.

Raleigh grinned to himself as they coasted through the nearly empty parking lot, setting the details of their next rendezvous.

If he could quickly wrap up the evidence against Cord Wyatt, he'd be free and clear to approach the woman driver in question as himself rather than as a counterfeit cowboy. And then sweet Ms. Molly Broome could drive him to distraction as often as she darn well pleased.

4

SUDDENLY ALL WAS PANDEMONIUM.

The door swung open and Etta Sue barreled into the kitchen, hopping, hollering and flailing a dust mop. Molly was mystified until she saw the kittens. The senior housekeeper was trying to swat them across the floor as if they were a trio of fluffy white dust bunnies. Fortunately the kittens were nimble and Etta Sue was a bad aim, even when she hadn't been tippling.

"Heyah!" Molly stepped forward, waving her wooden spoon.

Jocelyn scrambled between the housekeeper's bowed legs, wailing like a fire alarm. The child snatched up one of the kittens an instant before the head of the mop pounded the floor beside it. A puff of dust rose in the air.

"Please stop," Joss cried, dropping the kitten down the front of her overalls. "It was my fault, Etta Sue."

"No-good varmints!" Etta Sue charged into the kitchen. Her mop swung wide, setting the hanging pots and pans clanging against each other like oversize wind chimes.

With a flour-dusted hand, Molly made a grab midway down the mop handle. "All right," she gasped. "What's going on?"

Joss rescued another kitten. "I'm sorry, I'm sorry."

"The varmints were at my brooms with their

claws." Etta Sue tugged at the mop, dirtying the front of Molly's apron. "Second time today."

Molly held on until Joss had retrieved the third kitten from beneath a chair. "Now, Etta Sue," she soothed, cautiously releasing the woman's weapon of destruction, "I'm sure the kittens did no real harm. Why don't we all calm down?" It was only her first day on the job and already she recognized that, like most of the crises at the Triple Eight, this one's clamor was worse than its cause. All the same, Etta Sue's screech, Sharleen Jackleen's twitter and Cord Wyatt's bellow gave good reason to invest in a pair of earmuffs.

"I'm warning you, little girly." Etta Sue shook a diamond-laden finger at Jocelyn. "Keep them scratchety cats away from my cleaning cart." Shouldering the mop with a jangle of her bangles, she strode from the room.

"The dining room needs dusting," Molly called after the "exec-yew-tive" housekeeper, knowing the heavy hint was probably futile. Etta Sue had spent the morning organizing her cleaning cart. Lunchtime, she'd nibbled at half a sandwich and slugged from what Molly suspected was a doctored mug of coffee, which had resulted in a three-hour afternoon nap on one of the couches in the lobby. Etta Sue's snores had been loud enough to rattle windowpanes.

Puzzling over when exactly the woman's mop had been introduced to dust, Molly brushed at her grimy apron. The gamboling kittens caught her eye. "The cardboard box isn't working, is it, Joss?"

"They climb out." The girl sat cross-legged on the newly scrubbed linoleum, trying to keep the kittens tucked into her overalls. Every time she nestled one into place, another squirmed out from the gaping denim bib and went skittering across the floor.

"Then I'm afraid we're going to have to confine the kittens to the kitchen for the time being." Molly knelt and scooped up Little Bit. "Mischief-maker," she said into his little face. The kitten batted at her nose.

Looking up, Jocelyn made the sad, wide-eyed, beseeching expression she was very good at. "Can't I have them in my room, too?"

"Maybe at night. If the door is kept closed so they're not wandering about the hallways." One day with Joss and the kittens and Molly knew she'd be a very lax mother when her time came, all hugs and sympathy instead of tough discipline.

"Ask your mom first," she said as an afterthought. Sharleen had made herself scarce since showing Molly to her room in the east wing. Molly had been left to her own devices, with no direction from her new boss. While scrubbing the kitchen floor, she'd decided that employee evaluations were high on her To Do list.

"I can't disturb her," Joss said offhandedly. "She's with Mr. Wyatt."

"Oh." Molly compressed her lips, hoping the situation wasn't what it sounded like. "In the, uh, office, you mean?"

Joss nodded. "The door's locked."

"I see."

The girl's button nose crinkled. "Mr. Wyatt yelled real loud at me about the kittens."

So that's what all the bellowing in the lobby had been about.

"He's allergic to cat hair," Joss continued. "Mom locked the office door to keep the kittens out."

As mischievous as Little Bit was, Molly doubted that his tiny paws could work a doorknob. Even one left unlocked. Her lips pursed with wry amusement. Sharleen must be waxing Cord's desk to a fare-thee-well.

"Then you and the kittens shall stay here. I'm glad to have the company." To keep Little Bit out of trouble, Molly settled him into the roomy pocket of her apron. "You can prepare the kittens' meal while I do ours."

"Yes, ma'am," Jocelyn said happily. She hopped up to find the dishes that had been designated for the cats' use. Earlier, Molly had called the nearest vet for an appointment, then made a run into town for kitten chow and a litter box.

Molly absently stroked the kitten's fur as she opened the oven to check on her baking powder biscuits. Not quite done. She wanted them light and fluffy and golden brown, the kind of biscuits that could make a cowboy's appetite sing.

She made a face at herself. One day on the job and she'd turned into a real Betty Crocker clone, a Total Woman for the millennium. But of course the fact that it would be Raleigh Tate sitting at her table, singing her praises, had absolutely everything to do with it.

The way to a man's heart...

The back door opened. Molly was becoming accustomed to raucous interruptions, but not yet to the sudden appearance of dude-ranch wranglers with the kind of movie-star looks that made her insides twitch as if she'd swallowed a handful of Mexican jumping beans. She bolted upright, letting the oven door slam harder than it ought to.

"How do," Raleigh said with a tip of his brim. He removed his hat, hanging it and a quilted vest on a hook by the door before turning to sniff the air audaciously, his pale eyes glowing like blue ice in the sunshine. "Sure smells good in here, Ms. Molly."

"Just Molly will do," she murmured, warmth rising in her face even as she backed away from the heat of the oven. Her rear end bumped into the table. "We're having chicken stew and biscuits."

Raleigh's spurs jangled as he walked to the stove and lifted a lid. "You weren't hired as a cook," he said, inhaling the scent of the rich chicken gravy she'd used to thicken her stew, "but I'm awful glad you're such a good one."

His smile renewed her quivers. She wound her arms behind her back, gripping the opposite wrists for leverage. "Well, thanks, but you're right—I won't always have time to cook. Today I'm still getting my bearings. Tomorrow I'm determined that Sharleen and I, and maybe even Etta Sue, are going to start cleaning this place from attic to cellar. We might be finished by the turn of the next century."

Raleigh took another step toward her, his brows knitting with concern. Despite the wintry chill outside, she could tell that he'd been perspiring. His nut-brown hair stood up in stiff peaks where he'd raked it with his hand. A bandanna hung limply around the strong column of his neck, tucked partway inside the open collar of a denim shirt. The dirt smudges that drew her gaze along the contours of his snug jeans made her wonder if he'd taken a spill. She'd learned at lunch that the wranglers were working some of the more high-spirited horses that day, keeping them tame enough so that the next tourist who stepped aboard in their designer jeans and fancy new spurs wouldn't find themselves sailing backward through space like a time machine. As a Cowgirl Clubber, Molly had wanted to go out to the corral to watch—Grace and Laramie would have probably insisted on *participating*—but she hadn't been prepared to desert the lodge on her first day. Sometimes her conscience was downright stifling.

Especially when she already knew that Raleigh looked like a dream come true on the back of a horse.

He'd turned on the spigots to wash up, but paused to look at her speculatively while water streamed into the sink. "You need another pair of helping hands."

Molly's gaze shot to his hands, big and strong, coated with grime, but still compelling enough to make her heart skip a beat. A tingly feeling, like the prick of a dozen tiny needles, tattooed her midriff. "Etta Sue..." she said, shaking her head. "Even Sharleen..."

Raleigh rolled up his sleeves, smiling to himself. "I'll see to hiring you an extra worker, at least on a short-term basis."

"Will Mr. Wyatt approve?"

Raleigh splashed as extravagantly as a seal pup while he washed. "He'll see the need." One brow lifted. "You'll back me up?"

"Um, sure." She did need the help. Sharleen was ineffectual; Etta Sue was, by the looks of it, inebriate.

"Then that's settled," he said, watching Molly closely as he dried his hands with a dish towel. Though she wondered why he looked so satisfied, she couldn't see reason to question him. His being involved in the running of the lodge worked to her advantage. As a woman more than an employee.

When Raleigh Tate was around, she was *all* woman. For maybe the first really significant time in her life.

His eyelids lowered. "Hey, there, little puss..."

Molly started. "What?"

Raleigh's grin was negligent. "Personally, I can work around the paw prints, but chewing on cat hair is where I draw the line."

Molly's confusion spun her in a circle. "No, no, Little Bit," she scolded, breathless with relief. Raleigh had been referring to the kitten—the rascal had crawled out of her apron pocket and prowled across the butcher-block surface without her noticing. She lifted Little Bit off the table before he could sink his paws into the glazed pineapples dotting her upside-down cake. The kitten clung to her and she recognized with embarrassment the needlelike prickles its claws made. The tingly feeling hadn't been a result of desire. Nor even the thrill of flirting. Just a kitten running interference. Was she so out of practice she couldn't tell the difference?

"Molly? Is something burning?" Jocelyn asked from her seat on the floor.

Molly's stomach lurched. "The biscuits!"

Wisps of smoke curled from the oven when Raleigh opened it. Wincing, Molly slid her hand into an oven mitt and pulled out a pan of hard brown discs. "This doesn't happen to me." She was flabbergasted. "This *never* happens to me. Honestly!"

"No big deal." Raleigh waved at the smoke. "We're carbon-based life forms. What's a little taste of charcoal?"

"You don't understand. I don't do disasters. I'm the calm, reasonable type. I clean up messes, not make them." Molly knew she was more distraught than the minor catastrophe called for, but it didn't seem like such a small thing to her. Raleigh had seen her muddy and rained on, down on her hands and knees wearing yellow rubber gloves, and now dusty and disheveled. All she had left was her ability to dazzle him with a home-cooked dinner. Other women had cover-girl looks or sparkling personalities. She had recipes.

He pried up one of the overdone biscuits. "Maybe they're salvageable." He ripped off the blackened bottom and took a bite out of the crunchy top. "Not too bad. Kinda hot."

"Oh, for goodness' sake." She snatched away the steaming biscuit and ran him a glass of cold water. "There's no need to burn your tongue just to prove that I'm not a complete failure. You didn't want to hire me in the first place."

He looked her up and down and smiled. "My mistake."

Molly tingled. She squeezed Little Bit through the oven mitt, but he was tucked under her chin, biting at the ends of her hair. The tingles were real. "Well, *I* thought so," she said to Raleigh, going for a saucy uptilt of her nose even though she couldn't hold back her answering smile.

He touched her cheek with one finger. "Cute dimple."

She bit the inside of her cheek. Raleigh was beyond cute. He was deep into gorgeous territory, though she wasn't the kind of woman who could straight-out say so.

"Nice eyes," he added.

She widened them. Okay, he was flirting. Definitely flirting. And he hadn't even tasted her pineapple upside-down cake.

His gaze lowered. "Plush…" He hesitated long enough for her to reflect that though she was plush all over, he seemed to think that was just fine—attractive, even. "…kitten," he finished with a teasing tone, taking the animal from her. "If I hold the little guy, would you please make another batch of those biscuits?"

Molly broke out of her momentary trance. Well! So Raleigh *did* want her for her recipes.

Be that as it may, she hummed to herself as she gathered the ingredients for a triple batch of biscuits. Inside she knew that a dessert other than pineapple upside-down cake was finally on her menu. It was called

Tingle-Me Cowboy, and all she had to do was flash her dimple and help herself to a big old slice of down-home country lovin'.

Molly nearly chuckled out loud at the thought. Gracious, she was falling for him faster than a soufflé in an earthquake!

By the time the second batch of biscuits had been baked, she'd set one of the big tables in the dining room and carried in most of the food. Raleigh had hung around, occupied by Jocelyn and the kittens except for when he rushed over to help Molly with the heavier items. A jug of milk. A stack of thick porcelain soup bowls. Finally, the hot soup tureen. She handed the butter dish to Jocelyn and followed Raleigh into the dining room with the basket of hot fluffy biscuits, her heart singing.

"I don't know what the usual procedure is," she said, glancing over the table, "but since this is my first night, I thought we—the staff—could all eat together. And Mr. Wyatt, if he's so inclined."

"I'll ring the dinner bell." Jocelyn ran from the dining room. A moment later, a loud clanging came from near the back door.

"Haven't heard that sound since Mrs. Peet was sent away," Raleigh said.

Molly looked up from rearranging a place setting. She'd used the plain but serviceable place mats and napkins she'd found in the sideboard. "I thought Mrs. Peet broke her leg."

Raleigh showed no expression. "Right. After she went away."

"Didn't you say *sent* away—"

Both of the dining room's doors swung inward at once. Joss and the two wranglers rushed in from the kitchen, Cord Wyatt, Sharleen and Etta Sue from the lobby. All of them were talking at once, obviously anticipating the home-cooked meal. Raleigh grinned at Molly. "Feeding time at the ranch," he said, over the scrape of chairs and benches being pulled away from the long pine table.

Having grown up in a household of seven, Molly was in her element. While the group passed around a dish of salad and the basket of biscuits—rapidly depleted—she ladled out the stew, overlooking the table with satisfaction.

Cord Wyatt sat at its head, his plate piled high, making loud jokes about smoky kitchens and charred profits. To his immediate right was Sharleen—as immediate as she could get without sitting in the rancher's lap. The other two wranglers came next, Rip Lawless and Nicky Peet, respectively, one as old as the other was young. Rip was grizzled and gruff, Nicky baby-faced and shy, but they both sneaked peeks down the front of Sharleen's scoop-necked top when she reached for the butter dish.

Raleigh was seated at Wyatt's left. He wasn't sneaking peeks at anything but the food, but then Molly already knew him to be the straightforward dang-you're-fine type. There was something to be said for a forthright stare of open admiration. Beside him, Etta Sue looked old and frail despite her jewels and peacock-colored outfit. She lifted a drooping stainless steel spoon to her mouth as if chasing the kittens with her mop had taken all the vinegar out of her. Scooted all the way down to the end nearest Molly was Joss, naughtily letting the kitten she'd smuggled inside her overalls lick gravy off her finger.

Pleased as Molly felt, it was a minute before she realized that all talking had stopped. All collective chewing and slurping, too. She looked up, about to sink her spoon into the stew, and saw that everyone had turned to her with strange expressions, their lips puckered.

Etta Sue was the first to unpucker. "Holy cripes, this stew bites the big one! Gaaack!"

Cord slammed down his spoon. "You don't expect me to eat this swill?"

Molly's face burned with a mixture of shame and outrage. Biting her lip, blinking hard, she stared into her soup bowl. The chicken stew looked all right to her. She'd made it the way her mother had taught her— simple, fresh ingredients, simmered over a low heat. Sure, the onions and potatoes were kind of mushy, and she wasn't sure about the age of the package of chicken she'd defrosted, but all the same...

She tasted the stew. And nearly gagged.

The diners' expectant silence was cut by Sharleen's high-pitched giggle. It sounded...malicious.

Salt, Molly thought, fuming. The stew was loaded with salt.

"I didn't do this," she said, her voice firm even though her brain swirled with questions.

She met Raleigh's eyes, aware that the denial sounded very much like her protest about the burned biscuits. "Look, I'm sure it was an innocent mistake," he said, aiming a glare at the sputtering Wyatt to keep him quiet. "It's a new kitchen. You got confused, reached for the wrong ingredient—"

"There's probably a cup of salt in this stew." Molly stirred up another spoonful and licked at it tentatively. *Gaaack* was the word. "Not an easy mistake to make."

Raleigh shrugged. "Then what...?"

"Sabotage," she said darkly, scanning the diners. Nicky, the young wrangler, was red in the face, unwilling to meet her eyes, but that might have been his shyness. Rip was unconcerned, gobbling biscuits and spearing extra slices of cucumber and tomato right from the serving bowl.

Neither Wyatt nor Etta Sue had been near the stove. That left Sharleen, who'd dropped in once or twice to fetch beer for the boss, and Jocelyn, who was occupied only with the kittens. Then there was Raleigh, of course, who...

Who hadn't wanted to hire her in the first place.

"Jocelyn?" Molly said, staring steadily at the opposite end of the table. Her eyes swerved between the gloating Sharleen and Raleigh, who scowled as he ran a hand through his hair. "Joss, honey, I'd understand if you had an accident, maybe with the kittens, and had knocked the saltshaker into the stew pot. I wouldn't be angry with you."

Joss ducked her head. "It wasn't me, ma'am." She let out a shaky breath and added very softly, "I didn't see who did it."

"Okay. I believe you."

Wyatt pounded the table. "I thought you said this woman was highly recommended," he roared at Raleigh. "I'm not paying wages for this...this...slop!" Like a spoiled toddler, Wyatt thrust the bowl away from himself, sending it skidding across the bare wood tabletop on a glop of congealing gravy.

Raleigh clenched his hands. "If you recall, I didn't recommend Molly. You chose her."

Thanks, Molly mouthed with silent sarcasm, even though Raleigh wasn't looking at her. His manner was suspect. Still, she couldn't see him ruining the stew just to foil her employment. Unless she'd entirely misjudged his character. Unless he was willing to go to any lengths to get her fired so he could hire his own *highly recommended* candidate. Unless—by now,

Molly's heart had long stopped singing—all his flirtatious compliments in the kitchen had been meant only as a distraction?

Trick me, cowboy?

She took a deep breath and stood. "Mr. Wyatt, I don't know what happened to the stew, but if you'll give me another chance, I'll prepare something else." The pickings in the walk-in freezer had been sparse, but she did remember seeing paper-wrapped packages labeled Chops.

Cord Wyatt merely grunted as she removed several of the soup bowls.

"Sharleen?" Molly said.

The housemaid blinked, her lipsticked smile disingenuous in its swift appearance. "Yes?"

"I could use your help." Molly stalked to the kitchen.

A moment later, the door swung inward to reveal Raleigh, carrying the contaminated tureen. He set it on the butcher-block table. "Sharleen's clearing the rest of the bowls."

Molly stepped out of the freezer, clutching two packages of pork chops. She gave him an accusing look. "Thanks for standing up for me in there."

He had the nerve to put his hand on her arm. "I meant to. I gave you an excuse—"

"Incompetence?" She sniffed and stepped away to slam shut the thick freezer door. "No thanks."

"Why would one of us..." He hesitated.

"Sabotage me?"

"Yes, sabotage you."

"Why don't you tell me, Raleigh Tate. Seeing as you're the one who so pointedly *did not* recommend me for this job."

His hands lifted in a blameless gesture. "There, Ms. Molly, I was only telling the truth."

She shook back her hair. "Hoping that the truth would set me free—straight to the unemployment line?"

Again he pressed his palm against her shoulder. She felt her traitorous body rising toward the tenderness of the touch. "I'm extremely pleased with the Triple Eight's new employee, whether or not she was my first choice." His voice was so smooth and velvety it soothed her hackles. His fingers moved, stroking her. And she reacted instinctively, rolling her shoulders like a cat looking for a caress.

"In spite of the oversalted stew?"

His mouth quirked. "It's not your cooking I'm all stewed up about, Ms. Molly."

Despite the warm glow building between them, she forced herself to step away. "Well, I'm baffled. Why would someone want to ruin my first dinner here?" Tamping down the feelings of attraction, she unwrapped the chops and stuck them in the microwave to defrost. "It's only my first day on the job. I haven't insulted anyone. I haven't stepped on their toes. Unless…" She glanced at Raleigh. "Was Sharleen after the position I got?"

"She has designs, all right, but winning a job that entails doing actual work is not Sharleen's goal."

Molly nodded. "That's obvious."

"Jealousy might be her motive. If she's seen the way Wyatt's eyeing you up."

Molly shuddered at the thought of being Cord Wyatt's object of affection. "Sharleen was in and out of the kitchen while the stew was simmering."

"Then again, so was I." Raleigh leaned against the island in a casual pose, toe to heel. He gave the star-shaped wheel on his spurs a lazy turn, watching Molly from the corners of his eyes as if testing her reaction.

Despite her earlier doubts, she wanted to trust him. "Technically, anyone could have salted the stew, even the wranglers. I was out of the kitchen for a few minutes now and then. The vandal could have slipped in behind my back." She rolled her bottom lip between her teeth. "But why?"

"You're sure you didn't accidenta—"

"Don't finish that sentence if you know what's good for you." Molly wanted to whack him with the heavy black iron skillet she unhooked from the wagon-wheel pot rack. "Remember? I don't do disasters." Certainly not until she'd arrived at the Triple Eight.

Raleigh grinned knowingly.

Her response was another blush. "The biscuits were an anomaly," she insisted, shaking a scolding finger at him. "You distracted me." The microwave beeped, giving her a reason to turn her back on the teasing gleam in his eyes. She was getting all funny-prickly inside again and it was very distracting. Nuking the chops to a crisp wasn't on her agenda.

Sharleen entered the kitchen, sauntering past Raleigh with the remaining soup bowls. She set them by the sink.

Molly glanced up from rubbing a mixture of spices into the defrosted chops. "It won't take a minute to scrape and rinse the bowls and put them in the dishwasher."

Sharleen buffed her nails on the front of her blouse. "I'm the housemaid, not the kitchen maid."

"You can share duties on occasion, Sharleen," Raleigh prodded. "The Triple Eight's an all-for-one operation."

That last bit sounded somewhat sarcastic to Molly's

ears, making her wonder what Raleigh's story was. Where was he from? Why was he here? Aside from the occasional tarnation and the sexy cowboy act he had down pat, he wasn't really very…cowpoke-ish. For instance, where had he learned about carbon-based life forms? The school of hard knocks? Ha!

"Yeah, sure." Sharleen's agreement was grudging. "But Cord said I don't have to get my hands wet if I don't want to. Do you know what I pay for these nails?" She flicked her flashy talons at Raleigh as she walked toward the door. "Too bad about the stew," she flung over her shoulder for Molly's benefit. "One more screwup and Cord'll boot you outta here on your keister."

Molly sank her fingertips into a flaccid chop, saying nothing. She wouldn't continue to work this way. Tomorrow morning, she and Sharleen were going to have a little talk. A dressing-down, she believed it was called. And if Cord Wyatt was such a fool that the result was Molly's termination, then so be it.

Raleigh drew her attention. Missing dessert, carbon-based cowboy-style, would be her one regret.

MOLLY BROOME SUSPECTED HIM. He knew it. And her instincts were correct, though not concerning the puzzle of the salty stew. He wouldn't stoop so low.

Raleigh dropped his jacket on a chair and bent to retrieve the kitten meowing at his heels. It was well past two in the morning. The lobby was dark and empty, though not silent. The creak of rafters contracting in the cold November air made the lodge seem like a living thing, a hulking beast whose bones were old and slow. Somewhere a shutter swung loose in the wind, battering a log wall. Overhead, the antler chandelier swayed ever so slightly, buffeted by the drafts that swirled beneath the ancient roof.

Raleigh shivered, chilled to the bone by his impulsive jaunt to the lodge. He waited for a minute, holding the kitten, listening for sounds from upstairs. Rip and Nicky stayed in the bunkhouse, closer to the barn. There were half a dozen small guest houses scattered in picturesque positions about the property; one of them was his own. The lodge itself had another twenty rooms available for guests, along with Cord Wyatt's master suite and the eastern wing of small bedrooms set aside for use by the household staff.

Molly was there. Tucked safely into bed. Wearing...

Raleigh's lusty imagination wanted to conjure up something skimpy and see-through, but his rational mind figured her for a flannel girl, through and no-see-through. Nevertheless, Molly in flannel would be quite a sight. He pictured her curled up in bed, skin all soft and warm and smooth as melted butter beneath her honeycombed layers of flannel. She was a sweet treat of a woman, built for indulgence, for comfort and cuddling on a cold winter's night.

Comfort? Cuddling?

Raleigh looked down at the kitten he'd been petting against his chest. Gosh darnit. He'd more than lost his edge. He'd lost his entire tough-guy attitude.

A small sound sent his instincts shooting back up where they belonged, on full alert. He searched the darkness. Covering the kitten's small black face to keep it quiet, he stepped toward the staircase. A ghost of a movement had caught his eye.

He nearly laughed out loud. So much for his instinct of danger. Another of the kittens was creeping comically down the curved steps. The risers were too high; the cat made a funny little leap from step to step, grabbing on to the worn carpet with its tiny claws, fuzzy tail twitching in time with its whiskers.

The pure-white kitten sat and looked at him and yawned, its tongue showing pink even in the darkness. He rescued it from the stairway, setting the pair of them on the floor. Joss might come in search of her pets, but it was a risk he'd have to take.

After the amazing Ms. Molly had saved dinnertime with her quick cooking, Cord Wyatt was in a better frame of mind. While the rancher stuffed his face with a third piece of cake, Raleigh had broached the possibility of hiring a temporary worker. Wyatt's refusal had been fast and firm. Three household employees would do for the off-season, even though two of them were Sharleen and Etta Sue. Time for Molly Broome to prove her mettle, he'd said, neglecting mention of what Raleigh knew to be the ranch's trickling cash flow. Molly—darn her—had agreed that she could handle her duties, as long as she was given the leeway to light a fire under Etta Sue and Sharleen.

Foiled again, Raleigh was left to his own devices.

He walked toward Wyatt's office, as quietly as the heels on his boots allowed. Such a surreptitious search was not strictly legit. But the mere knowledge of the existence of one piece of good strong evidence could be enough to convince his superiors to go after Wyatt with a search warrant. Once the rancher was arrested, Raleigh could end his cowboy charade.

He could court Molly properly.

Court? Hell and tarnation, that was nearly as foreign a word to him as *cuddling*. Or used to be.

He smiled in the dark.

Wyatt's office was unlocked, which soured Raleigh's mood. It wasn't likely he'd find anything incriminating behind an unlocked door, unless it was hidden extremely well.

He opened the door and paused to click on a discreet penlight. The kittens followed him inside, tumbling across the scatter rugs in high spirits. He thought of shooing them, then thought again. If he was caught red-handed where he wasn't supposed to be, the kittens would make for a good excuse.

Cord Wyatt's rolltop desk was placed against the outer wall. A computer and its components cluttered a second desk nearby, but Raleigh bypassed it with only a glance. It wasn't the sort of state-of-the-art equipment needed to produce counterfeit currency.

A cursory search of the desk confirmed what the bureau already knew. Wyatt's finances were a mess. He had overdrawn accounts with several Wyoming banks. A brokerage firm was calling in his margin on a recent raft of frantic stock buys. Colorful final-notice flags decorated the bills Raleigh found stuck way at the back of a drawer.

One of the kittens climbed up his pant leg, mewling softly. He switched off his flashlight and took the cat into his lap, sitting back to consider his next move. Time was running short. Up to now, the cash the bureau had recovered in town and tracked going in and out of the Laramie jewelry store amounted to mere drops in Wyatt's leaky bucket. If ever the man planned to proceed with the illegal scheme on a meaningful basis, it would be now, when he was dirt broke and desperate.

Raleigh scanned the room. Knotty-pine paneling, a stuffed-and-mounted rainbow trout, a leather easy chair, sagging in the middle like a swaybacked mare. Beside it was a table that held a faux Tiffany lamp and a cigar box. The only item of interest was the paper cutter on the desk—you needed a crisp cut on counterfeit currency. Otherwise, the office was a dead end.

Raleigh had leaned back in the desk chair to check behind the duck prints hung above him when he heard the soft but distinct sounds of slippered feet padding down the stairway. Hoping for Joss, hoping even more for Molly, he reached the door in a few long strides, stepped outside and closed it behind him as smoothly as you please.

A figure in white leaned over the banister. "Joss?" *Molly.* Raleigh exhaled.

"Joss?" she hissed. "Is that you?"

He stepped sideways toward the registration desk, sliding his backside along the wall. "It's Raleigh."

Molly hovered on the bottom step. "Raleigh? I can't see."

"Follow the sound of my voice."

He heard her suck in a quick breath. "Can't we have a light?"

"I like it in the dark."

His words dropped into the space between them like a stone in a deep black pool. Molly didn't speak; she didn't budge. Their silence grew thick, tamped by the creaking of the ceiling rafters. In the dim light filtering through the windows, Raleigh saw her reach for the newel post, her fingers closing around the finial for support. The ivory oval of her face was blurred, the edges feathered by her dark hair.

Deliberately she cleared her throat. "What, exactly, is it that you like…in the dark?"

He had to say it. "You."

"Me?" she peeped.

"Exactly you, Ms. Molly." He slid the slender flashlight into his back pocket and walked out of the shadows. Let her get a good look at him, take the quaver of fear out of her voice. He wore only boots and jeans and the shirt he'd hastily pulled on but left unbuttoned. Hopefully he looked dangerous to her peace of mind, but blameless otherwise.

"Wh-why are you here?" she asked, still quavering. "It's the middle of the night."

"That's the best time to do it."

He'd shocked her. Her eyes and mouth rounded. Deep eyes, honey lips, beckoning him to come closer.

"I had a craving," he said, stopping inches away.

Her face was soft with sleep. She wore sloppy gray wool socks and a white terry-cloth robe, hanging open over a pair of red-and-black buffalo plaid pajamas. He reached out, pinched a fold between his thumb and middle finger. Flannel? You betcha.

She shrank back, inhaling deeply. A gap opened between her buttons, giving him a glimpse of milky skin and the rounded underside of one bare breast. Suddenly all the oxygen was sucked out of his body. His leaden blood settled low, throbbing in his groin.

He released the pinch of fabric; the gap closed to a narrow sliver, equally tantalizing.

Her voice came faintly. "I don't know what you mean."

"Midnight snacks," he said off the top of his head, giving them both a reprieve. "Unless a craving for another piece of pineapple upside-down cake isn't what got *you* out of bed?"

"It was one of the kittens. Crying and scratching at my door." She frowned. "Rather loudly for one small kitten, come to think of it. Or even all three."

The kittens. Damn! He'd closed up two of them in the office. The third must have been Molly's midnight caller.

"But when I opened my door," she was saying, "it

was gone. I thought the kitten might have come downstairs. Joss was supposed to keep them in her room for the night.'' A split-second pause. ''Where did it—or they—go? Have you seen—no? You're sure? You see, I'm responsible for bringing them into the house. After today's troubles, Mr. Wyatt won't look kindly on—'' finally Molly ran out of words ''—any more mischief,'' she finished. Her hand lifted, hovering indecisively for a moment before going to the collar of her pajamas. She pressed a knuckle into the hollow of her throat. Exactly where Raleigh wanted his lips.

''We certainly don't want any more mischief,'' he said, unable to resist teasing her. He liked the catch in her voice. It told him that she was as affected by their proximity as he.

Her smile flickered shyly.

A thud came from the second-floor landing. A dozen thoughts shot through Raleigh's head, but chief among them was the likelihood that only Cord Wyatt—and Grizzle—thudded so heavily.

Raleigh reacted instantly, whether from professional instinct or intimate need, he wasn't sure.

Didn't care.

Molly's eyes flashed with alarm when he pulled her roughly into his arms. He covered her mouth with his own, making the kiss hot, urgent, demanding. Serious stuff. Down and dirty. Convincing.

Really convincing.

He pressed the small of her back with one hand and used the other to mold her plump derriere possessively. After the initial shock passed, Molly was surprisingly compliant. She allowed his tongue inside her mouth, even stroked it with her own, making crooning sounds in her throat. Her hips swayed. Her breasts pushed against his bare chest, the soft flannel of her pajamas sliding across his beaded nipples. Pleasure sizzled his nerve endings—a flash fire of desire.

All it had taken was a shy blink of Molly's eye, a sexy flick of her tongue. Acute desire had obliterated his initial intentions.

"Oh, Molly," he said, sliding his open mouth over her chin, finding the soft skin beneath it. Her head tilted back and he licked hot kisses along her throat, both hands cupping her buttocks now, kneading them through the terry cloth, pressing her toward his aching erection.

She wound her arms around his neck and he groaned out loud because the movement made her loose breasts sway against his chest and that was too much for a man to take in silence. He lifted her off the step. "C'mere."

She laughed. Her cheeks were pink and warm, her lips glistening with arousal. "I guess I do have a craving after all."

"We're not going to the kitchen."

He looked down. Several of her pajama buttons had come free. Her nipples were prominent, straining against the checkered flannel. All he had to do was slip a finger into the gap, give one good tug and her beautiful flesh would be released into his palms—

A stealthy sound from above cut through Raleigh's lust. He jerked around, his jaw clenched.

"Ahem," said Cord Wyatt as he backed away from the balustrade. "And just what is going on here?"

Molly slapped her hand over her mouth.

Raleigh seethed. "How long were you going to watch?" *You perv,* he might have added, except for the harsh truth that *he'd* been the one who'd begun the display. Silently cursing himself, he gave Molly's robe a tug, wrapping it securely across her breasts. "Sorry, Molly."

She fumbled for the belt. Her lips looked bruised. "It was me, too. I—I lost it."

My loss, Raleigh thought. *My fault.*

Wyatt was coming down the steps like a locomotive, steaming, chugging, wheezing. He wore a paisley silk dressing gown over a bare chest and sweatpants, his feet stuffed into the size-too-small white ostrich cowboy boots. "We'll have none of this," he huffed, working his brows up and down as he tried to ogle Molly while still looking stern. "The Triple Eight has a policy against fraternization between employees."

Raleigh stared at Wyatt, letting the man's own indiscretions with Sharleen remain unspoken.

Wyatt's face turned ruddy. "I'm the boss," he roared. "I make the rules!"

Molly was stricken. "There's no excuse." She shoved her trembling hands deep into her pockets. "But it won't happen again."

Raleigh's ego flared. *The hell it wouldn't!*

Wyatt allowed himself to be mollified. "That's all I need to hear. You have an important job here, mmm...*Molly,* and I wouldn't want to see you distracted from your duties." Smarm oozed from his pores as he patted her shoulder. "Stick with me and the Triple Eight and you'll go far, young lady."

All the way to a federal penitentiary. Raleigh scowled at the rancher's lingering paw.

Wyatt harrumphed as he turned to his head wrangler. "As for you, Tate..." Raleigh's eyes blazed; Wyatt faltered, then recovered, drawing himself up importantly. "You have no reason to be in the lodge at night. From now on, this place is off-limits to all the wranglers. I won't have randy cowboys carrying on beneath *my* roof, on *my* dime—'' Wyatt stopped suddenly. He frowned, squinting at the shadows. ''What the hell? Did either of you hear that?''

''What?'' Molly said, just as Raleigh said, ''No.''

''I heard whimpering. Scratching.''

''It's the wind,'' Raleigh suggested. ''In the branches.''

''No.'' Molly was earnest. ''I heard it, too, Mr. Wyatt. It's coming from your office and I think...'' She realized. ''Uh-oh.''

''My office?'' Wyatt stomped across the lobby, the silk dressing gown billowing behind him.

Molly moaned. ''I'm dead. Done for. Roadkill.'' She paused, working it out. Her eyes pierced Raleigh's. ''And I suspect that you, cowboy, have had a hand in my demise.''

5

MOLLY RUSHED TO THE OFFICE door, which was flung wide-open. Inside, Cord Wyatt—the beast—was roaring again.

No wonder. One of the kittens sat squarely in the middle of the computer keyboard, licking her fur. Shredded papers littered the desk and floor. The other kitten was sharpening her claws on an armchair; pinprick holes in the leather marked the progress.

Wyatt gripped the back of the chair. "Blasted cats," he raged, sounding like Etta Sue. He rocked the chair violently enough to fling the black-masked kitten over the side. The little creature let out a frightened yowl, clinging to the arm of the easy chair with one front paw.

Molly bolted into the room to rescue it. Supporting the kitten's hind end, she carefully plucked its claws from the leather. Wyatt supplied a steady stream of curses. And Raleigh...

Raleigh stayed in the lobby. Keeping his distance from the scene of the crime? Molly eyed him accusingly, positive that he had something to do with the kittens getting into the office in the first place.

Wyatt stalked the other kitten. For all his sound and fury, he actually seemed reluctant to touch the tiny animals. Molly wondered if he was afraid of them on some level, and all the loud blustering was his coping mechanism. But, really. Who could hate a fuzzy little kitty-cat?

Etta Sue.

Was her phobia contagious?

"Tate!" Wyatt bellowed, approaching the desk. Each deliberate footfall sounded like a thunderclap. "Get these animals out of—*unkh*." His eyes bulged. "What—?" He spun in a circle, looking behind him like a dog chasing its tail.

He'd moved too quickly—both feet slipped out from under him. His hands flew up, clutching at air as he went down hard. And loud.

Felled by a puddle of piddle.

Molly cringed. Aye-yi-yi! She really was a goner. And so were the kittens.

At first Wyatt rocked from side to side like an over-turned turtle, the smooth soles of his fancy cowboy boots sliding on the slickened wood floor. Finally he sat up, cussing and struggling with the robe that had become twisted around his torso, revealing a hairy jelly belly. Molly looked away.

Raleigh arrived to haul the rancher up off the floor. Realizing Wyatt was occupied, Molly leaped across the room to scoop up the second naughty kitten. Cradling both culprits in one arm, she blew stray cat hairs off the keyboard and hurriedly shuffled the scattered papers into a semblance of order.

"Don't touch a thing." Red faced, Wyatt belted his robe with tight, jerky motions. He was breathing heavily. "I want those sneaky varmints out of here. You take 'em, Tate. Tomorrow morning, sun up, drop 'em off at the Treetop Humane Society. If I see cats in the lodge ever again, I'll wring their puny necks!"

"You can't do that," Molly cried. "What about Joss? She'll be heartbroken."

"Jocelyn must learn that this is a ranch, not a petting zoo. Sharleen can handle the girl."

"They're my kittens." Molly tightened her hold on the squirming felines. "If they're banished, I'll leave with them."

Wyatt smoothed his crop of graying hair. "Now, Molly. Don't be hasty. There's no need to bother your pretty little head over a couple of mangy—"

"I'll keep the kittens."

Molly looked at Raleigh with surprise.

He nodded at her. "They'll stay in my cabin. You won't see so much as a hair of them, Wyatt."

The rancher wasn't in the mood to compromise. "Take them away as ordered. The Triple Eight doesn't need extra mouths to feed."

"Only until they're adopted elsewhere," Molly pleaded. "Please, Mr. Wyatt. It's important to me."

For a long moment Wyatt studied her, narrowing his eyes as they traced her figure. His expression softened. "All right. As long as they're kept strictly out of the lodge. I never want to see them again."

"Thank you, sir. And I'm sorry about the…you know." They all glanced at the wet floor, then away.

Since Wyatt seemed to be in a hurry, Molly managed only a quick wipe-up with tissues. At least the incident had served to divert the man's attention from his employees' make-out session. With only a few mild rebukes for form, Wyatt hustled them out of the office and said a gruff good-night as he stomped up the staircase. From below, Molly spotted what seemed to be a furtive movement in one of the dark hallways. When Wyatt responded with a rumbled greeting, she assumed that Sharleen was on twenty-four-hour call.

Molly turned to Raleigh. Her appreciation was tempered with her earlier suspicions, muddied further by the flagrant passion of their embrace—even the memory of which held enough heat to power a steamship. Losing her head in such a way wasn't her habit, but, she rationalized, it was the middle of the night. Her defenses were down. And willpower wasn't her strength in the first place. She'd been swept away by the fantasy of it all.

But what about Raleigh?

His head was cocked. The expression in his eyes was nowhere close to the confusion she felt. Clearly he wasn't shying away from the situation.

Men! Were they always so sure of themselves? Molly's lashes dipped in defense.

She blinked. *Holy cowboy.* Even though it was relatively dark, Raleigh's unbuttoned shirt gave her a great view of his chest. Shadows emphasized its sculpted contours; a pelt of curling brown hair obscured them. His hands were on his hips, dragging his unbelted jeans an enticing inch-and-a-half past his navel. His stomach was as flat as hers was curved, but instead of being self-conscious she thought only of how appropriate that seemed. They'd fit together perfectly, like a jigsaw, exactly as nature intended.

What was she thinking? Aware that she was already operating under a severe case of sensory overload, she scanned Raleigh once more, lingering over the denim molded to his calves and thighs, the virile bulge beneath his zipper. Her gaze drifted up to the indented knot of his belly button, the ridged abdomen, that curly pelt of hair above. Unfamiliar terrain. Incredibly tempting terrain.

One glance at Raleigh's face had her nuzzling the kittens again, stalling for time. She had questions, she had doubts, but how could she resist his handsome face and startling eyes? Framed by thick lashes, they were such a pure Arctic-blue that simply looking into them gave another shock to her system.

Most important, though, was the character they revealed. A character that seemed honest, good, *real*.

Even when the rest of him didn't.

"I appreciate you taking the kittens," she finally said. *Keep it simple,* she counseled herself. *Avoid mention of extraneous kissing. Get to the heart of the matter, even if your own heart is about to burst through your chest.* "Jocelyn's going to be disappointed. But not inconsolable, thanks to you."

"It was the least I could do."

"Meaning?" she blurted.

He shrugged. "Let's just say I owed you one."

Because he'd been the one to salt the stew? Impossible. Because, for some unfathomable reason, it was he who'd let the kittens into Wyatt's office? More likely.

Molly hesitated. There was a third option. Raleigh could be referring to their interrupted kiss.

Did she really want to find out?

"Here," she said, thrusting the two female kittens at him. She'd forget her misgivings for the moment. His motives—if he had them—might seem clearer tomorrow. "Hold on to these two. I'll go find Little Bit. He must have gone roaming around upstairs after scratching at my door. I don't want Mr. Wyatt stumbling upon him."

"Need any help?"

Molly stopped midway up the steps and slowly turned to face Raleigh. He certainly was a breathtaking hunk of a cowboy. And she was, without a doubt, smitten.

That still didn't make her dumb.

"I can do it," she said, then added in a dulcet tone, "Even in the dark."

"Is that so?" He was obviously amused by her spunk, willing to indulge her.

"Indeed." She summoned up a superior smile. "You wait here. Occupy yourself with thinking about how those kittens got inside a closed room all on their own. Personally, I'm finding the question quite puzzling."

Chuckling at how rewarding it was to overcome a deep craving—however temporarily—she turned and bounded up the stairs, every saucy, bouncy step telling him, *Indulge* this, *wrangler man.*

Oh, would that they could!

THE RANCH LOOKED WONDERFUL to Molly the next morning, perhaps because her mood was elevated higher than the mountain peaks. Exhilarated, she stepped outdoors dressed in boots, jeans and the corduroy coat she'd worn to rescue the kittens. The boots were thin leather Italian ankle-highs and the jeans were vintage 501s bought at dear Manhattan flea market prices, but that couldn't be helped. They'd get broken in, as had the coat. Wyoming was a matter of substance over style. Here, with her sturdy build and her old-fashioned integrity, she had a chance of fitting in.

"Won't you give me a clue?" she asked Jocelyn as they crossed the yard, their arms laden with cat supplies. Brittle brown grass and patches of crusty snow crunched beneath their boots. "I'm dying to know."

"You must be a cat," the girl teased. While Joss had been sad to learn that her temporary pets were now banished from the lodge, Molly's good cheer and Raleigh's invitation to visit the kittens anytime she pleased had buffered her disappointment. "'Cause, y'know..."

"Curiosity killed the cat?" Molly guessed.

Joss nodded, the tassel on her knitted cap swinging jauntily. "That's what Etta Sue says to me. All the time."

"Does she." Molly breathed deeply of the brisk air. It was a sunny day, warm for November at thirty-eight degrees Fahrenheit. The air was so clean and crisp she wanted to fill her lungs to capacity, purging the urban taint from her pores. On such a vividly beautiful morning, her previous city life seemed very far away.

"Personally, I think curiosity's an admirable character trait." Molly chuckled to herself. Of course she would! She was intensely curious about Raleigh; visiting the kittens at his log cabin was either going to satisfy her appetite or increase it. "We've all got to learn somehow."

"Yep." Joss smiled widely. Her chubby cheeks were ruddy with cold, her eyes bright blue in the sunshine. She'd begun to blossom under Molly's generous attention. "I already learned every bit of the ranch. Like an Indian scout."

"Ah, then lead on, Little Blue Feather. You shall be my tour guide."

"I thought that would be my job," Raleigh said, intercepting them on the path that wound past the big red barn and into a grove of slender aspen trees. He dipped his brim. "Ladies."

Molly nodded in kind. "Gentleman."

Standing before her on the path, he took the bundle of the kittens' bedclothes without lowering his piercing eyes from hers. The morning sun cast low rays through the tall bare trunks of the trees, striping him with light and shadow. His lashes lowered almost imperceptibly, just enough for her to know that he was looking at her mouth. If they'd been alone, he'd have kissed her. She was certain.

"I thought you're nearly as new to the ranch as me," she said, keenly aware of the movement of her lips. When Raleigh was around, her body was as attuned as a race car. It was her head that tried to slow things down.

"Been here less than a month," he said. "But I've made it my business to learn the lay of the land." He raised his brows, daring her to comment.

She borrowed one of his I'm-just-a-country-boy phrases. "That so?"

Joss tugged on Molly's sleeve. "C'mon. I want to see Little Bit and his sisters."

Molly took Raleigh's arm so they walked three abreast into the trees. "Joss is going to name the other two kittens today. But she won't give me even a hint as to what."

Raleigh suggested Topsy and Turvy.

Molly's head wagged. "After last night, Piddle and Puddle would be more fitting."

He glanced sideways. "Piss and Vinegar?"

She smothered her laugh. "That's going too far."

"You guys aren't even close," Joss said. "You'll see." She broke away and ran toward a small cabin perched halfway down the slope, situated to overlook the narrow creek coiled like a ribbon of silver amongst the flattened grasses and drifts of snow. Farther along, several other guest cabins studded the hillside.

"Door's open," Raleigh called. He crooked his arm, reaching for Molly's hand, tugging her to a halt. "Not so fast, Ms. Molly."

"I want to see." She pulled on his hand, not so much to hurry him along as to feel his grip on hers.

Even though they were both wearing gloves, delightful shivers ran up her arm.

"Give me a good-morning kiss," he said, his eyes coaxing her, "and then I'll let you go."

Her lips pursed. "Is this blackmail?"

"You can call it blackmail." He drew her closer, putting his face so close to hers she was sheltered beneath the brim of his brown felt cowboy hat. "I call it warm-up."

Warm-up? "Well…" Molly considered. "The wind *is* a bit cold."

"That's not the kind of warm-up I meant."

"Oh." She swayed toward him as he put his hands around her waist. "You're pretty sure of yourself, hmm, wrangler man?"

"When it's right, I don't fight it."

An easy warmth spread through her. Knowing she was wanted toasted her inside and out. "What about our boss? Isn't there now a rule against fraternization?"

Raleigh chuckled. "Shucks, ma'am, I don't call it fraternization, either."

"It?"

"This." He squeezed her waist. "Us. You and me."

The words filled Molly's heart to the brim. Just over two weeks in Wyoming and she'd found a ranch, a cowboy, a passel of kittens and one adorable little girl. She'd found three out of four of her Cowgirl Club goals—open skies, hard work and—she brushed her hand over Raleigh's iron-hard thigh—tight jeans.

As the recipient of such good fortune, she would be miserly not to give some back.

She closed her eyes to kiss him. It was a small kiss, a sweet kiss, a tender kiss. It landed mostly on his lower lip, and he smiled as her lips parted to pluck wetly, the rasp of his beard scraping her chin, his hands stroking her midriff, his chest pressing, pressing...

It was a small, sweet, tender kiss. It was a heartfelt kiss. And after one memorable moment, it was over.

She ran quickly down the path, blood pumping, heart hammering. Her nostrils flared as she stepped into the log cabin; she stopped and took a good deep breath. The scent of cedar was strong even though the cabin was old, its gaps filled in with chinking. White stripes alternated with the dark honey of the rounded logs.

Senses sharply tuned, Molly absorbed the place in a glance. The cabin was small, just one room, with a nook for cooking and another for sleeping. A wedding ring quilt covered the corner of the bed that showed behind a partially drawn curtain. The rest of the furniture looked old but comfortable, of the grandma's attic variety. There was a black cast-iron woodstove, a farmhouse table and a trio of nine-over-nine pane windows set all in a row, their sashes slightly warped but offering a breathtaking view. Looming over the fresh-running stream and a thick piney forest, snowy mountain peaks made a jagged outline against the rich blue sky. Absolutely majestic. Nearly overwhelming.

Raleigh entered the cabin, slapping his hat against his thigh. Absolutely masculine. Molly's intoxication rose, bubbling in her bloodstream as though she'd mainlined champagne. Definitely overwhelming.

Fighting to contain her runaway emotions, she turned her attention to Jocelyn. The girl was lying on her back on a large round braided rag rug, giggling while two of the kittens crawled all over her and the third sat on her chest, licking her cheek.

Molly shook her head. "Oh, Joss, honey. Please remember that the kittens aren't yours to keep."

The girl sat up, clutching the black-faced kitten under her chin. "I wish…" She sighed loudly.

"I know." Molly sympathized. She knew about wishing. And now she even knew how tantalizing it was to have your wishes come true, to have them spread out before you, so near, so dazzlingly within reach, if only you could believe it was true…

"There's not much around here for the cats to get into," Raleigh said, bringing her back to the present problem with a jolt, "but I can't keep them for long. Eventually, they'll have to go."

Molly leaned down to pat the pretty white kitten that had toddled over to sit on her boot. "I'll find them good homes."

Joss looked up, her lower lip quivering. "You promised they can keep their names."

"Yes." Molly knelt and picked up the kitten. It squirmed in her grasp, trying to get free. "Have you decided?" she asked Joss, giving the feline her thumb to gnaw on.

The girl nodded. "The white kitten is Holly." She got to her feet and gave the kitten with the black mask to Raleigh. "And this one is Dolly."

"Holly?" Molly squeaked. "Dolly?"

Raleigh chuckled. "By golly."

"YOU'VE GOT A FAN, you know," Raleigh said as they slowed the horses to a walk for the last leg home. He was riding the spirited Appaloosa again. He'd put Molly on one of the beginners' trail horses, an obedient strawberry roan gelding with a thick winter coat. Though he'd had his doubts when she said she rode in Central Park with her girlfriends, she'd turned out to be a proficient equestrian. Her explanation was that she'd learned how to ride at a summer camp in Maine, and had further studied her technique by watching westerns with her late grandfather. No joke.

Molly patted the gelding's neck. "You mean Joss. Is she getting too attached?"

"To both you and the kittens."

"I was afraid of that." Molly sighed to herself; a puff of steam rose from her mouth. The red woolen scarf wrapped around her head brought out the rosy color of her cheeks and lips. She wasn't cover-girl glamorous, but she sure was pretty enough to turn a cowboy's head. "So what's Sharleen's story?" she asked.

"For one, her real name's Charlene Brodsky." Although he was relating what he'd learned from the bureau's background checks, the information was readily available, even from Sharleen herself. "Grew up in Washington State, got married at twenty, had Joss a few years later. After her divorce, she changed her name to Sharleen Jackleen, packed up and headed to Nashville to become a country singer. Got as far as the border before her car broke down. Money ran out in Boise. She's been at the Triple Eight for about a year now, still talking about going to Nashville every time she gets mad at Wyatt for not offering marriage."

"Wow." Molly rested her rein hand on the saddle horn. "You know her whole life story."

"Uh, she's cornered me a few times. She likes to talk." He'd held back plenty of details—such as Sharleen's habit of cutting corners with the law and taking up with men who had shady means of support. Her life at the Triple Eight with Cord Wyatt was the most legitimate she'd known. Until someone at the ranch had started turning out funny money.

"We had our own discussion this morning," Molly said. "I'm not sure that she's going to give me any respect, but she did agree to do better work. I left her mopping the floors. We'll see how it goes.''

Raleigh caught her eyes. ''Hey. Get the cleaning cart away from Etta Sue and you'll really be in business.''

She giggled. ''What's up with that? Is Etta Sue the old, faithful family retainer, or what?''

''Something like that, I reckon.'' He wasn't ready to get into the Etta Sue complications.

''I reckon,'' Molly echoed, narrowing her eyes at him as the horses topped the pine-crested ridge. They looked down over the shallow bowl of hilly land that cupped the dude ranch, with the twisting stream at its base. The cobalt sky had grown cloudy during their horseback ride, casting changeable shadows across the grass that had been so green in summer, but was now dried to a dozen soft shades of brown. Much of the snow that had fallen earlier in the month had been scoured away by the winds.

The temperate chinook breeze ruffled the Appaloosa's mane. The horse snorted restlessly and worked its hooves, eager for home, but Raleigh's hands on the reins kept the gelding dancing in place like the figurine on a music box.

''You look good on a horse,'' Molly observed. ''How is it you've come to work on a dude ranch?''

''Destiny,'' he said, being glib. And, just possibly, honest. Finding Molly, sweet, desirable Molly, was a twist he hadn't expected. If he was very lucky, she would agree to fulfill his destiny.

''That's no answer,'' she said, but he'd given his horse a signal and they were moving down the slope at a brisk walk, following one of the many trails that crisscrossed the ranch and surrounding acreage. The strawberry roan followed as it had been trained to do.

Molly was boiling with questions by the time they

arrived at the barn. So that Cord Wyatt wouldn't deem their outing a pleasure ride, Raleigh had taken along the wire-splicing gear and called their tour of the ranch riding fence. He'd even stopped now and then to shore up a weak spot in the barbed wire, explaining that the Triple Eight sustained a small herd of cattle for an authentic feel. Moving them in a roundabout route from a Triple Eight pasture to another leased from the state provided the guests with an overnight "cattle drive" experience. While it sounded like fun to Molly, it was also the type of thing that Shane McHenry—who took ranching very seriously—scoffed at.

Molly dismounted. Her afternoon with Raleigh had seemed genuine. Then why did she suspect that she'd been taken for a ride?

They led their horses into the barn. It was an immense structure, stained a faded brick-red, with stone walls sunk into the earth so that the entrance was below grade. Inside were box stalls, tie stalls, stanchions, feed and tack rooms. It smelled homey, earthy, elemental.

Rip Lawless took Molly's horse. "Sharleen was in here lookin' for you, madder 'n a wet hen. Etta Sue rolled her cart 'cross Sharleen's clean floor." Cackling, he scratched the white prickles of his unshaved beard. "The woman's a hellcat."

Molly nodded. "Yeah, Sharleen's tough to deal with. I'll smooth things over."

"Not her. Etta Sue." The wizened wrangler lifted down the heavy saddle and tossed it over a partition. "I shoulda seen she was too mean to marry."

"You and Etta Sue were *married?*"

"I was number four. Fresh outta lockup and too dad-blamed jackrabbit-jumpy to think straight or I mighta, whatchamacallit, reconsidered my options."

Molly thought back to her first meeting with the

crotchety housekeeper. "Uh-huh. Etta Sue mentioned her husbands to me. But she reeled their names off so fast I missed most of them."

Raleigh came over, leading the Appaloosa. "Lawless, take the horses and turn them out with the others. Don't get lost, we're feeding soon."

"So Lawless is a name to be taken literally," Molly said when the wrangler had left the barn leading the riding horses. "Does everyone on the Triple Eight have a colorful past?"

"Not me." Raleigh unzipped his jacket. "I'm as straight as a branding iron."

Molly stepped closer. Between the snaps of his chambray work shirt, she traced the curvy three-digit design that was the Triple Eight's brand. "Not so-o-o very straight," she said, and gave him a playful push with the flat of her hand.

He caught her elbow. "I'll break Wyatt's rules anytime you give me the go-ahead, Ms. Molly."

She stood tall, her head tilted back. "Are you ever going to call me just Molly?"

"I'm saving that for an intimate occasion."

She lifted her gaze beyond his face so she wouldn't succumb to the allure of his eyes. "You're definitely too sure of yourself. Or maybe I should say you're too sure of *me*." Spotting a distraction, she wrested her arm from his grip with a small tug and pointed toward the peaked roof. "Goodness, is that an authentic haymow?"

Raleigh's brows shot upward. "Yep. Would you like to see it?"

"I don't know if that's wise. Even in New York, we've heard of what goes on in haymows."

"Want to find out if it's true?"

Molly was tempted. She tried to think of what Laramie or Grace would do, but that didn't help. Laramie was too cool, Grace too excitable; if a cowboy was involved, they'd find their own inimitable ways up into that haymow, ways that Molly couldn't pull off in a million years.

Luckily for her wavering willpower, it was late afternoon. Soon she had to get back in the lodge to start dinner. Not much could happen in ten minutes, even in a haymow. "I admit I'm curious," she said.

Raleigh gestured with his head. "There's the ladder."

Molly went to it. "Just a peek." She looked over her shoulder after climbing several rungs. "I have to get back to work."

"There isn't much to see anyway."

Molly smiled to herself, thinking, *Not unless you follow me.*

6

"IT'S WARM," Molly said, having learned that warmth was a relative concept in Wyoming. A November day was called warm when its temperature passed the freezing point. Her bedroom in the lodge was chilly, but sleeping under a down comforter made her warm and cozy. Horseback riding with a movie-star cowboy could be hot-hot-*hot* even in winter.

She unbuttoned her coat, looking around her. The light was dim, the air thickly scented with ripe alfalfa. The mow encircled the upper reaches of the barn, with a wide opening in the middle so she could see down to the center aisle and the stalls on either side. A couple of horses hung their heads over the Dutch doors, twitching their ears, looking for oats.

"Heat rises," Raleigh said. "This place is a steam bath in summer."

"You've been here less than a month."

"But I'm haymow experienced."

Her smile came out crooked. "I'll bet."

The winter's supply of hay bales filled the vast space almost to the rafters. There was little room to move about; the opening yawned, unguarded. She put her hand on a pitchfork sticking out of a broken bale and maneuvered around it, leaning into the long handle for support.

The fork pitched, as it was wont to do, and her foot

skidded on the loose hay. "Yipes," she gasped, and then Raleigh had his arm around her waist.

"Careful," he murmured. "Watch your step, city girl."

"I'm fine." She plopped onto a short stack of two bales and peered over the edge. "Did you ever have your life flash before your eyes?"

"Once, sort of."

"Was it a good life?"

Raleigh propped his boot on a bale. "At the time, I thought it was." He rocked his head at her, the corners of his eyes crinkling. "You don't miss what you've never had."

"Oh, that's not true. Not for me. I have a wonderful family and good friends and my life has been blessed, but still…" She gnawed her lower lip. "I always knew I wanted…" Her hands opened and spread, palms up; it was a gesture of emptiness, but also of searching.

Raleigh sat beside her, straddling the hay bale. He knocked his hat off and leaned closer, intent on her face. "You wanted…?"

What Molly wanted was a loving relationship—put plainly, a husband—but as a veteran of the Manhattan dating wars she was realistic enough to know that she couldn't say that to a man, straight out. The committed relationship talk invariably made New York's perennial-eligible-bachelor types turn tail and run. Molly didn't know about real-life cowboys, but movie cowboys sure weren't much good at sticking around, either.

So, instead she said, "Many years ago, my friends Grace Farrow and Laramie Jones and I formed this group. It's a silly thing, really. Even embarrassing, now that I'm actually here in Wyoming. I shouldn't tell you." She hesitated, but only for a moment. Her feelings for Raleigh were growing to a point where she wanted to be forthcoming, whatever the consequences.

"We call ourselves the Cowgirl Club. It started as a lark—we were horse-crazy ten-year-olds—but over the years other members came and went and we three still maintained the club as a social thing for...for...women who love cowboys, I guess you'd say. But not just cowboys. All things western—ranches, mountains, horses, food, fashion." *But cowboys above all else.*

Raleigh looked bemused.

Not amused.

Bemused. As if...

"Are you an attorney in disguise?" she blurted. "A stockbroker, an investment banker?"

Surprise lit his face. "Of course not." He scowled. "Why would you think so?"

She shrugged. Oh, this was humiliating! She put her face in her hands, not wanting to look at him. "I read this book. A romance novel. The heroine thought she was marrying a cowboy, but he was really a millionaire masquerading as a cowboy because of a kidnapping plot gone wrong and—but that's not important. What I mean is...sometimes I wonder about you."

"I don't understand." He sounded cautious.

"It's little things," she said. "Aside from Grace's fiancé, Shane, all I know about cowboys is what I've seen in movies. So I'm no expert. Just the same, my female intuition keeps telling me that maybe you're not entirely..." She squeezed her features together and said tentatively, "Genuine?"

Slowly Raleigh bent over and picked up his hat. He plucked a blade of hay from the crown, raked his hair back and slid the hat on, settling it low over his forehead. His Adam's apple bobbed. "Molly, I grew up on a ranch. A small operation, true. My dad was a sheriff, he ranched part-time. But it was an honest-to-goodness ranch. With cattle and tractors and corrals and hay-mows.''

''Oh. Well. A girl can always be wrong. As I said, I'm no expert.'' Aside from fifteen years' membership in the Cowgirl Club, she added silently. Which qualified her for precious little.

A strain of lockjaw grit made her persist. ''So then why were you wandering around the lodge last night?''

He stiffened. ''I don't see the connection.''

''Neither do I, exactly. But I do know that the kittens were found on the wrong side of a closed door and you were the only one around. Mr. Wyatt might not have noticed, but I did. And it made me wonder.'' She peered closely at Raleigh. ''Why were you inside our boss's office?''

Raleigh shook his head. ''You're asking too many questions.''

''Meaning you don't want to answer them.''

He stood. ''Stick to your job, Molly, and let me do mine.''

Well! She shuffled her feet on the chaff-dusted plank floor. Below, Rip and Nicky Peet were rolling out the wheelbarrow filled with oats and sweet feed. The half-dozen horses that had been kept inside banged their hooves on the stalls in anticipation, stretching their heads into the aisle and whinnying excitedly. Without warning, Raleigh tossed a couple of bales from the mow. One of them bounced hard, splitting into thick flakes.

''I have to go,'' Molly murmured, feeling awkward inside as she stepped carefully past Raleigh to get to the ladder. Her haymow experience hadn't been as intimate as she'd hoped. No movie fantasy, certainly.

Raleigh surprised her by taking her hand, guiding

her to the first rung. His hand was strong and sure. Warm. In any climate.

She looked into his eyes as she slowly descended. For a long moment he said nothing, gave no sign of concession, but then, like a half-swallowed sigh, she heard her name. *Molly.*

Just Molly.

And she realized that their interlude in the haymow might have been intimate after all.

NEARLY A WEEK LATER, Molly was humming in the kitchen as she wrapped Christmas cookies for the freezer. Though her family was still perplexed by her sudden decision to stay in Wyoming, she'd been pleased to discover that she'd had little difficulty assimilating to ranch life.

Looking back, she could see that she'd always been an anachronism in New York City. Laramie and Grace had sometimes teased her about that, about how she usually managed to transcend the nastier realities of city life by keeping up her goodwill and general air of girl-next-door niceness. They said she was too soft for the Big Apple—the Sour Apple, she sometimes called the city on bad days. Now Molly knew her friends had been right.

Oddly enough, it had turned out that she wasn't too soft for life in remote, bone-chilling, hardscrabble, small-town Wyoming.

In the past week, she'd learned to drive the Cherokee over icy washboard roads. She'd weathered her first mountain blizzard, though Raleigh had insisted the blizzard was a mere flurry. She'd changed fuses, rousted layabouts, used her hair dryer to unfreeze water pipes, handled her boss's clumsy passes without a lawsuit and even arm-wrestled Etta Sue for possession of the dust mop.

Instead of being exhausted, Molly was ready for more. True, the housework and cooking were starting to wear on her, but now that the place was set to rights she could begin on her real job—managing the running of the lodge and its guest cabins. While her first look at the books had been daunting, given time she was sure that she could turn a profit.

Meanwhile, Raleigh said Mrs. Peet was still in traction.

Etta Sue had taken to schlepping around the lodge in five pounds of costume jewelry, spending much of her time canoodling with Rip Lawless in the wranglers' bunkhouse.

Every day Sharleen went into town for voice lessons and stayed away long enough to pick her daughter up from school.

Best of all, Cord Wyatt had been off the ranch for two long, lovely, relaxing days.

Molly had peace and quiet, she had work, she had Christmas cookies. Sometimes she even had Raleigh. Life was good.

"Have a Holly, Dolly Christmas," she sang off-key to the kittens, who were batting several pieces of crumpled paper across the linoleum. Ever since Jocelyn had bought them new collars with bells, they were easier to keep track of. However, as the boss was due back this evening, Molly wasn't taking any chances—Raleigh had promised to drop in and remove the kittens to his cabin before he started the evening chores.

Which may have had *something* to do with her good cheer.

Since she was alone in the lodge, it didn't matter that her voice stank on ice. She threw herself into another chorus. "O-o-o-oh, by golly, have a Holly, Dolly Christmaaaas—" Inspiration struck. "Holly," she said, putting down a cookie and picking up a pencil to add a notation to her long list of chores. They must have holly.

The second week of December, the Triple Eight was hosting the major event of Treetop's social season—a wedding reception for Shane McHenry and Grace Farrow. Molly was doing double duty as both bridesmaid and party planner. She was determined that the reception would go off without a hitch. Providing that she could get the shingles repaired, install and decorate a twelve-foot Christmas tree and oh, yes, there was the continuing problem with blown fuses. She turned a page and made another note.

Call Electrician.

On cue, the wind howled and the lights flickered. Molly added an exclamation point. Grace would approve.

Downy flakes of snow were collecting in the corners of the windowpanes. Molly peered out at the leaden white winter sky, shivering over the contrast between it and the warm, cinnamon-scented kitchen. She hoped everyone made it back to the ranch safely.

Raleigh appeared on the path that led from the barn to the lodge. Molly's pulse trip-hammered even though she knew he was only coming for the kittens. She dug her hands into the deep pockets of her sweater, her stomach tightening in anticipation.

The past week, she hadn't seen much of Raleigh. Occasionally she wondered if he was avoiding her. True, Wyatt had sent him to a livestock sale in Sheridan to have a few of the trail horses auctioned off. Then there'd been all that snow-shoveling. And feeding livestock at ten below had to be hell. Half the time she sent the wranglers thermoses of soup or thick meat-loaf sandwiches to be gobbled in the bitter cold while Cord Wyatt relaxed in his easy chair, coaxing Sharleen into massaging his feet.

Raleigh came inside, bringing the stinging cold with him. He pulled off his gloves and jacket, knocked snow from his hat. Molly went to pour a mug of coffee. The motor of the fridge suddenly kicked in. Her hand shook. Coffee sloshed out of the mug onto the warming pad; spattered droplets sizzled into steam. The scent of burnt caffeine hung in the air.

"Coffee?" she said, offering the mug.

"Yeah, thanks." Raleigh's cold fingertips pressed against her knuckles.

The heavy lobby doors banged open. She snatched her hand away. "Who's back? Mr. Wyatt?" Dolly pounced on Little Bit; they wrestled to the jingle-jangle of tiny bells.

"Sharleen," Raleigh said. He leaned against a cabinet. "I saw her fishtail into the driveway in her little compact."

"That's okay, then. But don't forget to take the kittens out of here." Molly looked around, harried. "I've got to get this kitchen cleaned up before I can start dinner." She grabbed a bunch of the packets she'd prepared, dozens upon dozens of cookies wrapped in foil, and shoved open the door to the walk-in freezer.

Raleigh entered behind her, his wide shoulders filling the doorway. She took the last few packets from him and set them neatly on a top shelf, trying to ignore the thrill of having him standing so close. "Thank you."

"My pleasure," he said, holding her gaze with his, smiling a little at the advantages of their tight quarters.

The freezer door slammed shut.

Raleigh whipped around. He grasped the handle and tugged, then beat on the heavy door. "Hey. We're in here." He slammed his shoulder into the door; it bucked but didn't open. "Open up!"

"God, no," Molly said, disbelieving. She pushed up next to Raleigh and hammered her fist on the door's stainless-steel facing. "Sharleen, let us out! Sharleen! This isn't funny!"

Raleigh joined her shouts.

They heard a scraping sound and stopped, pressing their ears against the cold steel to listen. Another scrape, followed by a heavy-sounding thunk that jolted the door. Molly flinched.

Raleigh's brows drew together. "The table?"

"Too heavy," she said, but it wasn't true. The butcher-block table was on casters, though they were normally locked in place. It was heavy, but it could be moved. One really good shove and it would block shut the freezer door. The thought inspired her to attack the door again, pounding and hollering until her throat was sore.

There was no response. She turned off the temperature-control dial, aware that it wouldn't do them much immediate good. Unless the door was opened to let warm air in, the freezer compartment would hold its frigid temperature for a very long time.

She buttoned her sweater up to her chin. The cold was already creeping into her bones. Knowing they were trapped made it seem all the worse.

Raleigh examined the mechanics of the freezer door. The simple latch opened outward, putting the hinges on the other side of the door. "I thought this thing doesn't lock."

"It's made not to, as a safety precaution." She let out a nervous, sickly giggle. "So no one accidentally gets stuck inside, you see. Somebody does it to you on purpose, of course, and sorry, buddy, you're on your own.''

"Maybe I can unscrew the latch." Five minutes later, Raleigh gave up, his fingers raw at the tips. The latch was ice-cold, impossible to unscrew without the proper tools.

Molly expelled the breath she'd been holding, making a cloud of vapor in the small room. "I'm cold," she blurted, recognizing that it was one of those stupid things a person says to distract themselves.

Raleigh gave her arm a squeeze. "Do jumping jacks." He suggested they take inventory of the small room, but there wasn't much to see. A narrow strip of solid floor, two racks, partly filled. A couple of small vents, but no windows. Idly he picked up bags of frozen peas and cauliflower, weighing them. "If I were MacGyver…"

Molly shivered. "I'm really cold."

He dropped the vegetables and put his arms around her. "Say something warm."

"Steaming mounds of mashed potatoes with melting butter." She burrowed her face against his chest. "Gravy boats, filled to the brim with hot, thick gravy." Very slowly his body heat began to seep beneath her skin. "Twenty-pound Thanksgiving turkeys, straight from the oven, all crisp and brown."

"Barbecue," he said, eyeing a side of frozen beef. "Sizzling steaks, charred burgers, hot baked potatoes, a whole roast pig on a spit."

"Hot chocolate that warms you from the inside out." She swallowed, her stomach churning. "Maybe we should eat the cookies before they're frozen."

He rubbed her back. "We're not going to starve.

We're not even going to freeze. Someone will come into the kitchen soon enough, looking for supper.''

"Of course! You're right. But in the meantime, I am so-o-o cold." She had to grit her jaw to stop the chattering of her teeth.

Raleigh stroked her hair, the one part of her that wasn't cold. "Tell me about the hottest, sweatiest, most miserably scorching day of your life."

"Um, I'm still stuck on Thanksgiving with all the food. You tell me. But hold me tighter, because I'm still cold."

He spread his legs a little and unabashedly tucked her against the length of him, enfolding her torso in a bear hug. They were so close she could feel the seam on the inside of his jeans through her thin jersey pants. The hard metal teeth of his zipper pressed into her belly; her cheek and breasts molded to his chest. The embrace wasn't sexual, she told herself.

At least not yet.

Making love would warm them up. *Holy cowboy,* she thought. *What a glorious way to stave off hypothermia.*

"Hottest day," he said. "Okay. I was fifteen, working my dad's ranch. It was sweltering. Hot enough to broil beef on the hoof."

"Ugh."

"Ranching isn't pretty, especially when you're branding calves. They're running around bawling, the air's thick with panic and sweat and the scent of blood and burning hair. Corral's hot and dusty, fire's roaring like hell, branding iron's too hot to touch. My clothes are stuck to my body, sweat's streaming down my face, stinging my eyes, but I've got to wrestle a hot, twisting calf to the ground and pin him there, his belly heaving…"

"Enough. I get the picture."

"Still cold?"

She hugged his ribs. "Yeah, but now I'm cold *and* queasy."

"So. Your turn, Ms. Molly."

Her mind flipped through broiling summers in Connecticut, sultry August days in the city when you'd swear steam was rising off the pavement. "Well, there was one day when I was about thirteen. I'd argued with my mom about something so crucial to my existence that I can't remember it now. I ran upstairs in a fury, all the way to the attic, and, jeez, talk about heat rising—that place was as hot as a sauna. Within seconds I was dripping wet. I was too stubborn to go back down, so I wound up crying myself to sleep on a pile of rolled-up sleeping bags. Hours later, my grandpa found me there. Poached like an egg."

"What happened then?"

"Mom put me into a cool bath until I started to recover. Then she emptied all her ice trays—and all the neighbor's ice trays—into it to bring my temperature down further." Molly turned her head to the other side to warm her right cheek against Raleigh's chest. "I remember feeling embarrassed and grateful and still a little mad all at the same time. Afterward, my mom let me eat a pint of Ben & Jerry's ice cream and Grandpa Joe rented *Jeremiah Johnson* for us to watch because it had snowy winter scenes in it. For weeks, my brothers called me the 'Boiled Shrimp' because I'd been cooked pink."

They held each other for another ten minutes, shuffling around every once in a while to keep their blood moving, breaking apart only to pound on the door and yell for help.

"What's the purpose?" Molly asked at one point.

Blowing on her fingers didn't help because it made her colder to see her breath. "What would Sharleen gain from locking us in the freezer?"

"If it was Sharleen," Raleigh said, his tone foreboding.

"Who else? I think Etta Sue's still in the bunkhouse with Rip. They're rekindling their romance."

"Oh?" Raleigh's suspicions spiked. When he'd left the barn to come up to the lodge for the kittens, Rip had been shoveling out stalls. Alone. Either Molly was mistaken or Etta Sue was lying. "Is that what she told you?"

"It's obvious, Raleigh. She's been wearing more makeup and jewelry than normal, and even breaking out her special bottle of peppermint schnapps to lure him into a nightcap. They've always got their heads together, whispering. It's sort of cute."

"Hmm." Raleigh made a mental note. Etta Sue's connection to Wyatt had already made her a possible—though unlikely—accomplice.

"You know they were married," Molly continued. "Sharleen told me Etta Sue's decided to ignite the old flame."

"I didn't know," he said, keeping his interest mild even though Molly's innocent remark had him springing to attention like a bird dog. A previous marriage between Rip Lawless and Etta Sue Frain was definitely something to check into, particularly if it had occurred around the time that Rip's cell mate had been Lawrence Pratt. Pratt, aka Leonardo, was a notorious forger whose record had been compiled during the days when engraving plates and printing presses were the illegal tool of the counterfeiter's choice rather than high-tech laser printers.

Another little job for Stankle, he thought. She would be so thrilled.

Molly looked up at him. Her lips were pale. He fought the urge to kiss her till the pleasure of it heated their blood. She should be just as soft and pink and warm as she wanted. Ever since she'd questioned him in the haymow, though, he'd battled to scale back his interest in her for the sake of the case.

"It had to be Sharleen who locked us in," Molly said. "You saw her drive up, right? So she was the only one home."

He decided to keep the question of Etta Sue's whereabouts to himself. A ninety-pound weakling, she wasn't capable of shoving the heavy table an inch, let alone a foot.

"Plus…" Molly put her head down on his chest and wiggled against him. "Sharleen's my number-one suspect for all the incidents. I guess she thinks we're competing for Cord Wyatt's affection. Eeewww. As if!"

"What do you mean—*all* the incidents? What's happened aside from the salted stew?"

"Um, not much." Molly lowered her voice. "I went into the cellar to change a fuse and as soon as the electricity came on, someone shut off the lights from the upstairs switch. It didn't mean anything—I had a flashlight."

The cellar? Invisible icy fingers that had nothing to do with the temperature lifted every hair on Raleigh's nape. "What else?"

"Oh, Etta Sue and I did battle over the newspapers she'd collected in the lobby. I put them out for recycling. She hauled them inside again. Sharleen egged her on. Who knows why."

"There's more?"

"Yesterday, Sharleen knew I wanted her to dust the

upstairs halls. Grizzle's turned gray. By strange coincidence, Etta Sue's cart disappeared—along with all the cleaning supplies." Molly shrugged. "Nagging annoyances—that's all."

Maybe, maybe not. Raleigh set her back a step. "Listen. I want you to keep your suspicions about Sharleen to yourself. Don't confront—"

"Hallo," boomed Wyatt's voice from the other side of the freezer door. The greeting was cut off. After an instant of silence, the rancher snorted like a bull. "What in the world...?"

Molly and Raleigh banged on the door, shouting in unison. With a grunt, Wyatt shoved aside the table. A second later, he flung the freezer door open and they burst into the kitchen.

Wyatt stood before them in a cowboy hat and thick sheepskin coat, holding a broom. His wide nostrils flared. "I'd like an explanation."

"So would I," said Raleigh.

Molly stated the obvious. "Someone locked us in the freezer." She rubbed her hands together, shivering more violently than she had in the cold. The kitchen was blessedly warm, but it would take a while to feel it all the way through.

Raleigh shut the freezer door. Wyatt thrust the broom through its handle. "The broom was like this," he said, "and the table was pushed right up against it. Why would anyone—" He stopped and looked from Raleigh to Molly with narrowed eyes. "And why were you both inside the freezer?" Angry color stained his cheeks. "I warned you, Tate..."

"Wyatt, if Molly and I were going to rendezvous, it wouldn't be inside a freezer."

"No," the rancher huffed. "I suppose not."

A soft jingle reminded Molly of the kittens' presence. "What I want to know," she blurted, glancing furtively for the contraband kittens while trying to distract her boss, "is who trapped us and why. We could have been frozen into icicles. Brr." She pointed one of the kittens out to Raleigh, then smiled when Wyatt turned to look at her. "Let's go build a fire and get warm," she said, reaching for his arm. Dolly's little black face peeped out from behind the stove; Molly smiled warmly at her boss, maintaining eye contact. She jogged his arm. "Coming, sir?" According to Joss, he loved to be called "sir."

A satisfied expression broadened his features as he escorted her to the door. He covered her hand with his own. "Of course, Molly, my dear. Let's get you as snug as a bug in a rug. Or shall we make that a bedbug, hmm?" He chuckled with insinuation and pushed through the swinging door.

Sharleen stood on the other side, arms crossed, tapping the toe of one pink suede boot in agitation. Her chest heaved. "I *detest* bugs!" she exclaimed, her voice pitched high and weepy.

Molly wanted to explain her compromising position, but before she could, Sharleen had spun on her spike heel and flounced from the room.

7

WHEN A GLOWERING SHARLEEN next approached Molly, she could not have been in a more vulnerable position.

That morning, the Triple Eight's towering white spruce Christmas tree had entered the lobby trunk-first, inch by prickly inch. Molly had gently pointed out that she'd asked for a twelve-footer, not a twenty-footer. After much comment and wrangling—by Raleigh, Nicky and Rip, appropriately enough—the tree was maneuvered into a stand, straightened, toppled, repositioned, checked with a level and finally wired to the staircase for stability. By that time the chandelier had stopped swinging.

Decorating it was Molly's job. Raleigh was quite helpful, insisting that she stay in the lobby while he carried innumerable boxes of decorations down from the attic. It took him a long time, until Etta Sue began loudly supervising. Then he couldn't finish fast enough.

Now Raleigh had gone to the barn and Etta Sue had once again made herself scarce. Molly was alone, perched at the top of a ladder, draped with the increasingly tangled lengths of holiday lights. She was supposed to be transferring them to the tree. Instead, she was perspiring. She was frazzled. She was on the verge of cussing out her usually boundless Christmas cheer.

It was not a good time to deal with Sharleen's absurd jealousy over Cord.

The housemaid sidled up to the bottom of the ladder and put her hands on a rung. Molly said a prayer instead of a curse, leaned sideways and threw a loop of lights over the top of the tree like a lariat. The ladder swayed. Miraculously, the lights settled into place, strung from branch to branch. Even more miraculously, the ladder steadied.

Molly looked down through the branches to meet the other woman's eyes. "I've got you," Sharleen said, her smile hovering halfway between menacing and helpful, as if she—and the ladder—could go either way.

With a clinking of colored lightbulbs, Molly climbed down a rung. "That's o—" she balanced precariously to wind another length around the tree "—kay. Uh, thanks, Sharleen. You can let go now."

Sharleen didn't. "You should have strung the bulbs lengthwise. It's easier."

"Now you tell me." Molly plugged two cords together and tucked the connection at the back of the tree. As quickly as possible, she draped the remaining strings of lights around the spruce, doing a haphazard job of it because the ladder seemed to wobble every time Sharleen "steadied" it. She was waiting when Molly stepped down, breathing hard.

Sharleen's eyes narrowed to slits, making her mascara-clogged lashes stick together. "I coulda got rid of you," she said, blinking but petulant. "One push would have done it."

This is all I need, Molly thought as she warily backed toward the thick tree, *a housemaid with homicidal tendencies.* A sharp-needled branch slapped the back of her head and she yipped with alarm, her nerves jangling.

She faced Sharleen. Maybe they should have it out. "Then it was you who trapped me in the freezer?"

Sharleen advanced. "Don't try to pin that one on me, sister. I told you I went right upstairs when I got home—Joss backed me up on that. You heard her."

Molly ducked under a string of lights, retreating even farther into the tree. Joss had gone along with her mother's alibi, all right, but it was debatable whether or not she'd admit to the truth. Since no real harm had been done, none of them had wanted to press the issue with the child.

"I caught you making time with Cord," Sharleen accused shrilly, stabbing one of her talons at Molly. "Don't think I've forgotten just because my sugar bear bought a pair of diamond earrings to make it up to me." She tilted her head so the rocks in her lobes would catch the light.

Molly pressed backward into the branches. Her fingers were sticky with sap; pungent evergreen needles ground beneath her shoes. "I have no personal interest in Cord Wyatt," she insisted, for about the fiftieth time. "He's my boss—nothing more."

"You had your hands all over him!"

"I was cold." Molly swallowed thickly. "He was...helping me to warm up." That didn't sound so good.

Sharleen peered through the bushy tree, her hands set on her hips. "Keep away from him from now on."

"Absolutely." It was the easiest promise Molly had ever made.

Sharleen seemed satisfied. "And just to prove how cooperative I can be, I'll tell Raleigh there's no use in making any moves on me," she said, being oh so selfless. "He's cute, but looks don't count for nothing when the wallet's empty."

Molly couldn't resist saying dryly, "I imagine Raleigh will contain his disappointment."

"Yep, I'm a one-man woman." Sharleen giggled. "Form a line, boys. One at a time!"

Molly exhaled. What was she doing, hiding behind—practically *inside*—a giant spruce tree? Sharleen had cockeyed values and a colorful self-image, but she was harmless. Molly even felt some sympathy for the woman's tenuous position—fending for herself, raising a daughter alone, trying to keep Cord Wyatt happy.

Molly understood that although Sharleen coveted money and fame while Molly wished for a silver-screen love affair, what they both really wanted was security.

"Molly," Sharleen said, almost tentative, "will you come to the talent show tonight?" She'd abandoned her Betty-Boop-on-steroids persona, but was totally fine with talking to a Christmas tree. "I need lots of clappers—Punch picks the winner with an applause-o-meter."

Molly hesitated. Sharleen had announced plans to sing at the Thunderhead Saloon's Annual Holiday Amateur Talent Show. Top prize was two tickets to the Rotary's Cold-Hands Hot-Dish supper.

"Um." Molly imagined Cord Wyatt's sweaty hands roaming loose under the table…in search of a hot dish, one might say. "I'll go if Raleigh goes," she offered. He could be her bodyguard.

"Swell. Two clappers for the price of one."

Sharleen departed, leaving Molly stuck in the tree. It wasn't the kind of intimate embrace she had in mind these days. Dang if there weren't spruce needles inside her bra!

Needing a lift other than the kind provided by an underwire, Molly picked up the dangling cords, recalling as she did every year that, after all the struggle, there was nothing as cheering to the spirit as the lighting of the Christmas tree. She lifted a branch, found an outlet and plugged in the lights.

The tree stayed dark. Even when she wiggled the plugs back and forth vigorously enough to produce a spark.

"Why me?" she asked the huge, sticky spruce. It didn't answer. The thing was beautiful, but it had no personality.

Molly gave up. She slumped to the floor, completely baffled. Before she'd come to the Triple Eight, she'd been a Mary, not a Rhoda, at least professionally. Her recipes worked like a charm, neither burned nor over-salted. Her To Do lists never grew beyond a page without the items getting crossed off. And her Christmas trees always lit up on cue.

Now she was living a life straight out of a bad sitcom and gosh darnit, she'd never been happier. Wasn't that something?

Molly was about to crawl out from beneath the tree when the sound of creaking wheels warned her of Etta Sue's approach. The woman pushed her cleaning cart out of Wyatt's office at an unusually brisk pace, stopping once to surreptitiously glance around the lobby.

Molly, down on her hands and knees and therefore out of sight, chose to keep silent. For such a loud-mouthed broad, Etta Sue's furtive behavior seemed awfully suspicious.

She rummaged around in her cart and pulled out a bottle of cheap booze. Molly had a mouse's-eye view from her position beneath the tree as Etta Sue took a small swig, then liberally patted liquor on her pulse points as if it were perfume. Strange habit. No wonder the woman went around smelling like a distillery.

Etta Sue replaced the bottle and continued on her way. Molly stayed hidden, puzzling over what she had seen. Like a lot of what happened at the Triple Eight, it made no sense at all.

THE THUNDERHEAD SALOON was Treetop's one and only hot spot. Wagon wheels flanked the entrance. The interior featured knotty pine in abundance. A polished bar took up the crook of the L-shaped room. Its stools were occupied by genuine cowboys downing genuine shots. Molly counted six silver rodeo buckles, two handlebar mustaches and one golf-ball-sized wad of chewing tobacco.

The folks from the Triple Eight occupied one of the big round tables. Cord Wyatt was playing the expansive host, overseeing conversation, calling for another round of beer before the previous one was consumed, continually standing to hail old friends from across the crowded room. Sharleen was primping for her superstar turn. Nicky Peet was eyeing one of the waitresses. Etta Sue and Rip were eyeing each other.

Molly was grateful when Raleigh finally asked her to dance. Hoping that he'd get the hint, she'd turned down the handlebar-mustached cowboy who'd approached her, ten-gallon hat in hand. Grace, of course, wouldn't have hesitated—she'd have stood right up and dragged her cowboy onto the dance floor. Laramie would have engaged the most intriguing cowboy in the place with one long, intense look. Molly, as usual, was stuck being nice, sweet, meek, patient. Yuk!

"Looking good, Ms. Molly," Raleigh said as they squeezed into a space on the dance floor, a too-small clearing amongst the maze of tables.

"Thanks." Molly wiped her hand on her flared suede skirt before giving it to Raleigh. She'd never two-stepped before, but once they started, she felt the rollicking gait take hold. Around them, couples shuffled, dipped, occasionally spun. The music was lively; spirits were high. Twinkling lights and fresh evergreen garlands swagged the ceiling.

"You, too," she said. Raleigh wore black under a buckskin vest with a long fringe. He'd even buffed his boots and shaved his square chin. Whiffs of sandalwood aftershave tickled her nostrils.

He pulled her a little closer, looping his arms around her waist as their two-step turned into a hip-swinging shuffle. "This is almost like a date."

"Almost," she agreed. They'd shared a ride with Nicky, Rip and Etta Sue, the whole group enlisted by Sharleen as audience. "But does it qualify as fraternization?"

"Don't worry about that." Raleigh smoothed his palms across her derriere. She leaned against his chest. Her eyes closed. Heaven.

Heaven got even better when he started nuzzling her neck. She leaned her chin on his shoulder and smiled in bliss, unconcerned with who might be staring. That wasn't like her, she realized distantly. How wonderful.

"Watch the earring," she breathed when Raleigh's tongue stroked toward her ear. He lipped her lobe, sucking the pearl button earring into his mouth. The warm, wet pressure made her completely lose track of her inhibitions. He could swallow the earring for all she cared, just as long as he swallowed her along with it. She wanted his mouth everywhere on her, doing things that could drive a cowgirl plumb loco.

"Someone's smiling at you," Raleigh murmured.

"Yeah, me." She was all lit up inside.

"A little gal with crazy red hair. Let's ignore her."

"That's Grace," Molly said without opening her eyes.

The muscles in Raleigh's shoulders flexed when he

craned his neck. "The infamous Grace? The stowaway who rode a horse trailer out of Manhattan?"

After she'd leaked the story of the Cowgirl Club in the haymow, he'd been curious, so she'd told him all about Laramie and Grace and their quest for cowboys and adventure. He thought it was hilarious—completely missing the point, as far as Molly was concerned.

Squinting, she gave a little wave in Grace's direction. They called each other practically every night to discuss wedding details—and coincidentally provide updates on activities at Goldstream and the Triple Eight. She was looking forward to talking to Grace in person…eventually.

Molly pressed her cheek to Raleigh's leather-clad shoulder, her fingers tangled in his fringe. Grace would be the first to understand that tearing yourself out of the arms of a cowboy was not an option.

Raleigh wasn't up on the ins and outs of Cowgirl Club etiquette. He broke their embrace and directed Molly toward Grace and her fiancé, Shane McHenry. Although the two men were close to the same height, Shane was lean and rugged, a contrast to Raleigh's classic good looks. Raleigh was smooth. Shane was serious and sincere in what he said and what he promised—the rock to Grace's butterfly. It was a good match.

Molly and Grace hugged hello and exchanged fevered whispers, leaving the men to introduce themselves. "Cow-girrrl," Grace purred. "Was that dancin' or was that romancin'?"

"Cloud nine time," Molly admitted.

"This is so great! Now, if only Laramie was here—" Grace stood on tiptoe to check out the cowboys lined up at the bar "—she could have her pick."

"Then she's definitely coming for the wedding?"

"Of course! You know she's a bridesmaid. Since you're taken care of, I'm planning to throw her the bouquet. Even though she'll kill me. Should we scout the eligible cowboys and set her up with someone good? What about Raleigh?" Grace shot him an admiring glance. "Does he have any brothers?"

"Gosh, I don't know." Molly frowned. "Aside from the basic facts that his mother's dead and his father's a sheriff and he grew up on a ranch, I don't really know anything about his personal life." Considering her conservative nature, it was strange, then, that she should feel so comfortable with him. She should be more concerned with who, precisely, she was falling in love with.

Wow. *Was* she falling in love?

Raleigh smiled as he placed his hand at the small of her back. "Let's get back to the table. Looks like the talent show's about to begin."

"Sure." Molly reached for Grace's hand, as if to pull her along. Actually, it was Molly who needed the support, because suddenly it was crystal clear that she was falling for Raleigh Tate like an avalanche. Disaster—the manmade kind—was turning into her middle name.

The amateur talent show was exactly as billed. Sharleen was fourth up on the stage, right after a magician called Mack the Mysterious, who used a hamster named Harry instead of a rabbit. The only mystery about Mack's act was when it would end.

Sharleen sang "Don't It Turn My Brown Eyes...*Green,*" which was obviously a none-too-subtle message to Molly. Otherwise, she was better than expected. Clearly she'd watched Marilyn Monroe sing "Happy Birthday, Mr. President" one too many times, and her voice got reedy when she tried to work in a Mariah Carey high note. But the cowboys loved how she blew them kisses, wiggling in her sequined blouse and skintight Wranglers. Their hooting, hollering and wolf whistles were plenty loud enough to put Sharleen in the finals without the help of the Triple Eight's designated clappers.

After a baton twirler—the front row learned to duck—a flame swallower—at whom Punch Fiorelli, owner of the Thunderhead, waved a raw steak—a terrible ukulele rendition of "Jingle Bell Rock," and the eye-opening sight of three church choir members getting funky with it, Molly was ready for a break. She and Grace used the standard ladies' room ploy to make their escape.

"Couple of months ago we were in Manhattan, thinking the only nightlife worth having was mixing with the beautiful people," Grace said when it was their turn inside the tiny bathroom. "Did you ever think...?"

"Is this an improvement?"

"Sure it is, Mol. I'll take wacky over well-to-do any day of the week. At least these people aren't too blasé to admit they're having fun."

"You're right. I was just this morning thinking that I'd never been happier. Couldn't put my finger on why, though."

"From what I saw on that dance floor, your fingers know exactly where to go."

Molly blushed. "Right again, Gracie."

"Mmm-hmm. And just how far have they gone...Ms. Molly?"

"Not so far that he's stopped calling me Ms. Molly." Even though she was trying to reapply her lipstick, Molly smiled at herself in the mirror. "But far enough. Remember the time we went to the U.S. Open and Pete Sampras took his shirt off?''

"I remember it fondly—me and a few thousand-million other women.'' Grace thought it over, then whistled softly. "Woo. You're saying that Raleigh's chest is...?'' She fanned herself.

Molly nodded. "Not to brag, but yes.''

"Ah.''

"QUICK, THIS WAY.'' Raleigh took Melissa Stankle by the elbow and steered her away from the rest rooms toward a nook upholstered with sheepskin jackets and Gore-Tex parkas. "Stay back,'' he said. As Stankle pressed herself in amongst the outerwear, a fur-lined hood knocked off her pristine new cowboy hat. "I'm with people,'' Raleigh explained, catching it. "I can't risk them seeing you.''

"But why are you here?'' whispered the rookie agent. "With everyone off the ranch, it's the perfect opportunity to—''

"Change of plans.'' Raleigh wasn't about to explain that when Molly had asked him to join her at the talent show, he'd agreed before the professional part of his brain was up to speed. "Besides, I've got a new lead. It's urgent.''

Stankle snapped to. "Yes, sir!''

He put his hand against the wall and leaned in to whisper to her about Etta Sue's probable marriage to— and divorce from—Rip Lawless. About their current rapprochement. Rip had always been the likely connection between Cord Wyatt and Leonardo's counterfeiting know-how. Etta Sue's involvement solidified the bureau's suspicions.

Stankle licked her lips in anticipation. "I'll get on it, sir, right away.''

Several women walked by on their way to the ladies' room; they looked into the nook and giggled, making assumptions about Raleigh's compromising position. He tried to keep his face turned away.

His glance fell on Stankle's shiny boots, indigo jeans and western-style blouse. "Going native, Agent Stankle?"

"Cover," she mumbled. "I'm blending in."

Raleigh touched her silver-and-turquoise bracelet. "Expense account?"

"But you bought that oilskin duster right off a cowboy's back!" Her freckled face darkened. "Paid two hundred bucks for it. I don't see why you're the only one who gets to wear a disguise."

He popped her hat back on her head. "Go easy, Stankle. I'm only teasing."

She straightened, batting away the sleeve of a camouflage army jacket. "Yes, sir. Of course. I'll leave at once to get on the new lead. Soon as I tell Nicky— *whoa*." She'd glanced past Raleigh's shoulder; her head reared back in surprise.

He turned in what felt like slow motion. A wave was flying at him. No time to avoid it. The contents of a tall cold drink splashed squarely in his face, including an overripe cherry and a lemon twist. He sucked in a breath, tasting sweetened liquor.

"Take this, too!" Molly cocked her arm and pelted him with a toothpick-speared chunk of pineapple. A tiny paper parasol whizzed past his ear.

He swiped his face, disbelieving, even though the bottom had dropped out of his stomach. "Molly?" The cherry slid slowly down the side of his jaw.

"That's Ms. Broome to you." Sweet, meek Molly slammed the empty old-fashioned glass onto a surprised waitress's tray, snarled, "What are you looking at?'' at Stankle, and charged off into the crowded saloon, shoving unceremoniously past rough-and-tumble cowboys and choir members alike.

Grace Farrow caught a drop from the end of Raleigh's nose. "Don't worry, cowboy. If you made Molly Broome act like a witch, it's gotta be love."

"THE NIGHT WAS AS BLACK as her mood," Molly intoned, looking out the kitchen window. Sounded like a mystery novel. She raised the knife threateningly, watching her reflection in the glass. Molly Broome, murderess.

She stabbed a loaf of homemade bread and started sawing. Something wrong with her motor reflexes. Every piece she cut was either mangled or lopsided.

Oh, well. She dipped the sharp tip of the knife into the one-gallon can of peanut butter and scooped out a dollop to spread across one of the deformed slices. The bread tore. She folded it in half. Dropped it on a plate. Took a seat.

One bite was all she managed. Her usual response to emotional turmoil was to eat, but for once she had no midnight snack follow-through. A churning remorse had filled the hollow space in her stomach.

Remorse and...*jealousy*.

The remorse was expected. She wasn't accustomed to flying off the handle with livid rage. Honestly— throwing a drink in a man's face? Straight out of a soap opera!

She smiled.

Perhaps her remorse wasn't as complete as expected from that nice girl, that good girl, Molly what's-her-name. You know, the quiet one. So easy to overlook.

The jealousy, though. That was another matter.

She still felt it, like a hot charge of electricity

plugged into her fingertips, her navel, her toes. Every time she thought of Raleigh, straight-arming the wall, leaning close enough to nuzzle his little girlfriend as they exchanged cozy whispers, intimate jokes…

High-voltage jealousy.

He'd touched that woman's hand, he'd smiled into her eyes.

He danced with me, he sucked my ear.

The girl was cute. Young and slim, decked out like a cowgirl. Shining eyes that had looked up at Raleigh as if he were a heartthrob hero of the silver screen.

Same way Molly looked at him.

The man's ego must be the size of Texas if he dared to try and hook up with two women on the same night. Molly wondered if the other woman was the backup. Or was she?

She picked up the knife and speared it through the loaf of bread crosswise. A senseless gesture, but she felt better. After a while, her thoughts cooled enough to acknowledge that it was possible that what she'd seen at the Thunderhead wasn't what it looked like.

But wasn't that what a cheater always cried? *It's not what it looks like!*

Molly snorted. Nine times out of ten, it was exactly what it looked like. Bet your boots. Bet your soul.

Hell, no. She'd wager her heart.

She already had.

And now she was in misery.

"Ah, Molly, there you are," Cord Wyatt said as he came through the swinging door. He was wearing the silk dressing gown again, with cowboy boots, but no pajama bottoms. His legs were thick, lumpy, hairy. "We missed you at the Thunderhead. What happened?"

"I left early. With my friends, Grace and Shane. Sorry. I should have let you know."

Wyatt pushed his belly into the edge of the butcher block, invading her space without compunction. "The rest of the evening wasn't the same without you, dear Molly."

She took her plate to the trash can and dumped the sandwich, keeping her back turned. "Did Sharleen win?"

"Alas, no. Second place. The crowd took a liking to a young gal in a leotard. A contortionist." He laughed loudly, clearly relishing the memory. "That girl could do a backbend around a pool cue. It was unbelievable."

"I can imagine."

"Don't be that way. Gymnastics aren't necessary as far as I'm concerned. I'm an easy man to please."

Molly's teeth clicked. "What did—whatever do you—what—" No, she didn't want to know.

Wyatt walked toward her, his bulk swaying from side to side. She backed up until she was pressed against a cabinet with nowhere else to go. He was between her and the swinging doors. Suddenly the kitchen—her haven—seemed miles away from safety.

"Molly," Cord murmured. "I must say you're doing excellent work. I've been—" he rubbed a palm across his paunch, revealing a sparse patch of steel-gray chest hair "—watching you."

Which didn't sound like a comment on her job performance. She pretended it was. "I'm enjoying the work, Mr. Wyatt."

"Wonderful." His heavy eyelids lowered. "But there's so much more you can do for me."

"Of course. Once we have guests, we'll be busier."

"That's not what I meant, sweet thing."

Molly choked on the insinuation. Impossible to

brush this off as just another of his clumsy attempts at flattery. She filled her voice with censure. "Really, Mr. Wyatt."

He loomed over her. "It's time you called me Cord."

"This is inappropriate. It's making me extremely uncomfortable." Try sick to her stomach.

"Then let's find a way to make you happy." Cord gripped her upper arms in his big paws and pulled her against his chest. His broad face came rushing toward her, a monolith. Enormous. Hard. Rapacious.

"No." She struggled. "Let me go."

Held tight, she could only throw her head back to avoid the kiss; his wet mouth grazed her cheek. He was slightly off balance, searching for a place to plant his lips. She twisted out of his grasp. He fell forward, bonking his head against the edge of the cabinet. His bellow filled the kitchen.

Molly wasn't about to wait to see if he was injured. She fled to the back door, flinging it open so hard the knob slammed into the wall. She didn't stop, just ran pell-mell into the cold black night.

Her slippers had no traction in the snow. She slid, stumbled, went down on her hands and knees in a snowbank. Scrambling up, she threw a quick glance over her shoulder. The illuminated window and open door cast golden patches of light across the snow. Inside, Wyatt was bellowing, telling her to come back. He was sorry if he'd gone too far. He'd leave her alone. Whatever she liked, just come back.

Ha. She'd rather risk black-toe frostbite.

Molly found her bearings. The barn was closest, with the wranglers' bunkhouse nearby. She could go there, if she wanted to.

She didn't.

A narrow path to Raleigh's cabin had been carved out of the snow. She hurried along it, slipping on the hard-packed snow. Momentum kept her up. The frigid air cut through her robe and pajamas, quick-froze her nose and cheeks and fingertips, filled her aching lungs with every breath. She focused on Raleigh. He would make her warm.

The hillside was a toboggan run—she took most of it sliding on her rump, grateful that there was a light on in the cabin. Smoke rose from its chimney, white against the starry black sky.

"Raleigh!" She pounded on the door, only now remembering that he might not be alone. Her fists stopped. What if…?

The door opened before she could retreat. "Molly?"

She tried to take a deep breath, forgetting that her lungs were filled with ice crystals. What to say, what to say?

Even though her voice creaked like the bare frozen tree trunks, she settled on a simple "May I come in?"

"Of course." Raleigh nearly lifted her across the threshold. "What are you wearing? God, Molly, you're freezing. Are you crazy, going out in the snow like this?"

Her teeth chattered. "Ca-ca-cowgirl Ca-club didn't pre-prepare me for twenty-below."

He hustled her to the fire that crackled inside the potbellied stove. "What's going on?"

She held her hands toward the radiating heat, not answering immediately. Jealousy and outrage were powerful emotions—she'd just gutted a loaf of bread and qualified for the Winter Olympics to prove it. If Raleigh knew about Wyatt's harassment, he'd probably retaliate in a way that was sure to get him fired.

Though she wanted Raleigh in her life with a need

that ached worse than a zillion midnight cravings, she could fight her own fights. He didn't have to be her savior.

He didn't have to be her cowboy hero.

The man was more important to her than the myth.

8

"I KNOW WHY YOU'RE ANGRY," Raleigh said when she refused to answer. There was a strange look on her face. He wondered if she'd come to the cabin on impulse, intending to confront him, and then thought better of it. For sure, something specific had fired her up hot enough to carry her this far. In a robe and pajamas, no less.

Knowing the excuse would sound lame, he said, "It wasn't what it looked like."

Molly closed her eyes, her expression one of great sufferance. "Is it ever?"

"Can I explain?"

Her lids cracked. "Can you?"

Not really.

"That's what I thought," she snapped when he hesitated. She turned, offering her backside to the woodstove. Her expression was closed.

Raleigh dragged the quilt off his bed and wrapped it around her. For a fleeting moment, Molly's eyes met his, dark chocolate, bittersweet, vulnerable. He saw that in spite of her anger, she wanted him to explain, needed to believe.

He refused to lie. But could he trust her with the truth? Should he tell it, knowing that it might endanger her?

"Molly..." He searched for words that would tiptoe

him through the minefield of his obligation to the bureau versus his deepening feelings for her.

"It's simple," she said. "Who's the girl?"

"I can't tell you that."

Molly made a motion to drop the quilt, but he caught it and pulled it back up around her shoulders. He brought her to the couch and sat beside her. "It's not that way," he said, holding her hand. "She means nothing to me."

Distastefully Molly slid her hand away. "Well, if that's true, then the situation's worse than I thought. Men who can substitute one woman for another like interchangeable Barbie dolls, and it means *nothing* to them—" Her entire body shuddered. "You're all despicable."

Guilty, he thought. Not concerning Stankle, but in the past, he hadn't always cared…enough. He respected his partners; he wasn't wildly indiscriminate; he tried to be up-front about offering only a short-term relationship. And still he was guilty.

"Okay," he conceded. "Maybe you're right. I suppose I can tell you that the girl's name is Melissa. She does mean something to me, just not what you've assumed."

"She's your twin sister." Molly's voice was laced with irony. "Your mother? Your long-lost daughter?"

"She's my colleague."

Molly closed her mouth on another sarcastic retort. Her chin dipped into the folds of the quilt. "I don't understand what you mean by—"

He interrupted, hoping to salvage some degree of confidentiality. "We were conferring." Maybe he could get by if he glossed over the situation. Distracted Molly from the crucial questions.

"You were conferring. Sure, I'll buy that one. Conferring with a cowgirl in the Thunderhead Saloon—why not?'' Suddenly Molly stood and flung the quilt over his head. Her slippered feet stamped across the floor. ''Conferring!'' he heard her spit.

Discarding the quilt, he caught her by the door. ''Don't go.'' Engaged as he was by her high color and heaving breasts, by the unexpected sting in her spirited response, he was smart enough to focus on practical issues. ''You'll freeze.''

Molly slumped, resting her forehead against the door. ''I should apologize for throwing a drink in your face.'' Her voice started out wooden, then softened to silk. ''I *should*...'' Her lips curved bewitchingly. ''But I don't believe I will.''

She turned to face him, tossing her dark hair back from her face. ''You deserved worse, Raleigh Tate.'' It was some sort of challenge.

So he kissed her. Call it an impulse—an inspiration. Heck, call it succumbing to the primitive desire that had already consumed most of his misgivings.

All he knew was that it was right.

Molly knew it, too. She didn't resist, only came into his arms with a heat that matched his own, almost aggressive—definitely aggressive—her mouth open, her teeth sharp on his lip, her tongue fluent with the strength and depth of her need. Raleigh was rightly astonished. And humbled.

''Whoa,'' was all he could say when they broke apart, panting heavily. It had been more of a liberation than a kiss, releasing the tension and highly charged emotion that coursed between them. The dam was broken. Their mutual lust was rampant.

They surged toward each other like forces of nature. Wild kisses became reckless caresses.

Molly gave a short, sharp cry when he pushed aside

her robe and ripped open the buffalo plaid pajama top. For one instant, he hesitated, then swept her voluptuous body into his arms and carried her to the bed. *"Raleigh!"* she said, laughing, flushing pink, her open hands pushing his face away from her exposed breasts.

He sat her gently on the edge of the bed and knelt before her to remove her slippers. She sat tall, breathing hard, her eyes glittering as she watched him. He reached around her and caught the elastic waistband of her pajama bottoms, saying, "Please," as he dragged them over her bare behind. She lifted up and the bottoms slipped off, revealing ivory thighs, girlish kneecaps, rounded calves.

"Raleigh…" she said again, suddenly wary.

Their pace had slowed, but the desire was still there, so strong he could taste it. "You're so beautiful," he murmured, tracing his fingertips along the seam of her thighs. "Don't back out now."

Her eyes widened, but she arched into the caress. "Who's backing out?"

"Good." He gazed at her breasts, erotically cradled in the open slash of the pajama top. She scooted up on the bed, still a little shy but fighting it. "No, c'mere," he said, following her so he could suck one of her erect beige nipples into his mouth, tasting her sweet flesh with his tongue as her thighs parted and he stroked between them with an intimacy that made them both draw breath and collapse flat upon the bed, braided together like lengths of rope, doubled in strength, twice as profound.

MOLLY LET HERSELF GO. It was a conscious decision.

She might regret it, she knew. She wasn't sure she believed Raleigh—about anything. And yet she trusted him, she did. He was a good man; he'd never intend to hurt her, even though in the end she feared he might have to.

But, oh, she needed this. She wanted it.

And so she surrendered her inhibitions. She let herself go.

His mouth was hot and wet on her breast, the suction great, sending tremors quaking through her body. Too much. As if he knew, he slowed, his tongue just grazing her sensitive nipple, circling the areola until she relaxed into the pleasure of it and said, so softly he shouldn't have heard, "More."

Possessive hands covered her breasts. He rose above her on his elbows and knees. She crooked her leg, pressing a thigh firmly against his erection, trapped inside jeans grown tight enough to please any cowgirl. He closed his eyes, sucked in a breath of air, his jaw clamped tight. Her thigh moved sensuously. A little torture, she thought, served him right.

"More?" she asked, most pleasantly.

"You're bad."

"That's a new one." She rubbed her palms on his furry chest. He dropped his hips, pushing into her with a pressure that was divine. "Yes, more of that," she pleaded. "But deeper."

Obligingly he shed his jeans. She was wanton, shameless, shocking—rolling over and taking his condom and stroking him with both her hands before applying it. "You surprise me," he said huskily, finding her breasts again and pushing them together and then apart with a circular rubbing motion. He kissed and licked at her cleavage. "I thought you were shy."

She held his head, letting her own loll as a satisfied purr vibrated in her throat. "Often I am." He wrapped his hands around her waist. Her head swung forward again and their lips met, making kisses that were tender and needy, that, truth be known, plucked at every one of her heartstrings. "But I'm no virgin."

He cocked a brow. "Neither am I." His raspy chuckle tickled her senses like sandpaper.

Finally he eased her down onto the bed and she lay quiet for a moment, watching him with her body on fire and her heart melting in the heat. The sheer recklessness of her behavior *was* extraordinary. She wasn't prepared to have him know it, though. Playing the eager, experienced lover for him felt like her last protection against...tomorrow.

He'd said, "You're so beautiful," and she'd believed it. He inspired her confidence. When he looked at her, she was a sensuous goddess, not a plump, ordinary, glorified housekeeper. Which was marvelous. Fantasy time.

The quilt was gone, so he pulled the sheet and a fluffy blanket around them to hold in their body heat. He stroked every inch of her until she was begging and then finally moved gingerly atop her. "Don't be gentle now," she said, adding, "I'm not fragile," though she loved that he would think so. "I won't break."

"What a woman," he breathed, spreading her thighs, pushing himself slowly inside her.

She almost regretted the words. He was quite large, and it had been a while for her. The pressure was acute, but it was good. And in the next instant it was better. She moved beneath him, rocking her hips, her flesh clasping his. Agony was pleasure was passion.

He thrust, then paused to savor the moment. His breath fanned her face. "Deeper?"

She raised her knees and took hold of the iron bars of the headboard. "Yes. Deeper. All the way." *This time,* she promised herself, *all the way.*

Raleigh's eyes were both fire and ice. "Trust me, Molly."

Her lashes lowered. "I..."

He touched her face. "Trust me."

She could only nod.

He ground against her in just the right spot and a cry ripped loose from her throat. "Yes." *I trust you.*

She arched, again and again, meeting each one of his thrusts. A climax boiled inside her. Let go, let go, she chanted to herself, the pleasure peaking, her muscles quivering, all of it part of the primal rhythm. *Let go!*

And she did. A wondrous, reckless, shattering surrender—so intense she would forever be grateful that when it happened she was held safely in Raleigh's arms.

HE WAS CAREFUL to do everything right. He stayed inside her, and around her, holding on until the pulsing heat gradually receded. Once she'd recovered, he shifted, relieving her of his weight. He whispered sweet nothings in her ear. With his lips and fingers he soothed away any female-type regret or embarrassment she might entertain.

And still she withdrew.

A suitable irony, he thought. His comeuppance. How many women had wanted more from him, had done everything right and still he'd withdrawn?

This time, it was he who wanted promises of love.

"Molly?" he said.

She was wrapped in her white terry-cloth robe, covered from neck to ankles. Worse, she hadn't come back to bed. She'd gone from the bathroom to the couch, and stayed there, knees drawn up to her chin, worrying her lip with her teeth as she thought deep thoughts that didn't seem to include him.

He cleared his throat. "Unless I'm mistaken, that was pretty stupendous."

Her big brown eyes regarded him warily.

He climbed out of bed, into his jeans. "Hell and tarnation, woman—what's wrong?"

She winced. "Okay. Yes, it was stupendous."

"Too much for you?"

"No. It was great. I'm indebted. That was, you know, my, um, first one."

"Honestly?"

She brushed her bangs into her eyes, then shook them away again. "Well, I've had them with a man in the same bed. But not actually 'in the moment,' if you get my drift. I have this problem with trusting a partner enough to really let myself go...."

Was that all she fretted over? His chest expanded at least half an inch as he crossed the room. "No longer a problem," he boasted, pounding his chest like a he-man to make her laugh.

"At least not with you." Her smile quavered.

"Another easy fix," he said. "Stay with me."

There it was.

Her startled gaze rose to meet his. She knew he meant it.

"But I don't even know who you are," she protested, and all his high hopes fell to earth with a thunderous shebang.

"Then I'll tell you," he heard himself say with barely a pause. "I'll tell you everything."

"YOU'RE AN UNDERCOVER COWBOY." Molly said it again, just to be sure. She didn't know how she felt about his revelation, but at least it was a relief to know the truth. "You work for the U.S. Treasury."

"Secret Service," he said. "It's an agency of the U.S. Treasury."

"Not a wrangler man," she wondered. "A Secret Service man." Raleigh watched her closely, his expression cautious. She narrowed her eyes. "I *knew* all those tarnations and dang fine, ma'ams were a put-on."

"Not completely," he said, rubbing the shadow of his beard. "I did grow up on a ranch, like I said. My father has the habit of talking that way. He's strictly against the cruder styles of cursing, particularly in the presence of ladies. Probably I reverted unconsciously to play this part—my dad's an old-fashioned true West lawman."

Molly shook her head. "This is amazing."

"I want you to meet him."

She put her hand up. "Slow down. I haven't decided if I trust you. What if—"

Suddenly Raleigh's arms were around her. "You trust me," he said into her ear. He nipped the lobe. "You trust me all the way, sweetheart."

"You *are* too sure of yourself." She pushed him away, blushing with the knowledge that he had reason to be, no matter what his profession. A man is a man is a hero. "I want to hear more about this case you're working on."

"I don't want you involved."

"I'm already involved. Up to my neck."

"That's true. But I don't want to endanger you."

"Come on," she scoffed. "No one at the Triple Eight's a killer."

"A criminal's liable to do near anything when he's cornered." Raleigh left for a moment, then returned with his wallet. Head down, he fingered through its contents.

Molly's mouth was dry. Her vision was laser-focused, but, God, it hurt her heart to look at him for too long. Yet she felt this overwhelming need to memorize him.

His hair was ruffled; his chest and feet were bare. There was a small white scar near his collarbone, a mole in the crook of one elbow. Each frown furrowed a line across his forehead, deeper above his right eyebrow. His jeans were worn, a little baggy in the seat, frayed at the hem. His nose leaned just a fraction to the left, a small imperfection that kept him merely breathtakingly handsome rather than impossibly unattainable.

Her poignant longing over every detail was disturbing.

Was she afraid of losing him? Did she trust him or not?

He handed her a twenty-dollar bill. "No thanks," she said, trying to crack a joke. "I'm free."

"This is serious, Molly."

With a sigh, she took the money. She couldn't quite get her mind around the evening's developments. First Wyatt, then Raleigh, now this. Counterfeiting at the Triple Eight? It was laughable.

"Can you tell if it's real?"

She examined the bill, front and back. "Looks real."

"It's fake. Wyatt passed one just like it at a gas station in Treetop. The clerk had been trained to spot counterfeits, but didn't notice Wyatt's until after he'd left. There had already been a few bad bills spotted elsewhere in the area. The Secret Service launched an investigation."

"If that's true, why haven't you arrested him?"

"Right now, Wyatt would probably get off with a small fine. We want to know if there's more where this bill came from, and exactly who's involved in the scheme. There's a good chance this twenty is a drop in the bucket. We see a big jump in counterfeit currency during the holidays because retailers are busier than normal and temporary workers aren't adept at spotting the fakes."

She smoothed the twenty. "How do you tell?"

"The paper. It's close, but not quite right. And look at the outside border. See how the tiny lines are smudged?"

She held it up to the light. "So's the portrait of Jackson."

"Good eye. If we had a magnifying glass, I'd show you other giveaways as well. There are polyester threads and microprinting that a copier can't reproduce."

Molly blinked. "A copier? A plain old photocopier?"

"Not exactly. Today's counterfeiter needs a state-of-the-art computer setup and a laser jet printer. Have you seen anything like that in the lodge?"

"No, but…"

Raleigh's eyes switched on to high beams. "What?"

She snapped her fingers. "Of course. That was why you were checking out the office in the middle of the night." She pondered the situation with her chin resting on her knees, trying to add up all the small inconsistencies. "Hmm. Here I thought all the little tricks and nuisances were directed at me—Sharleen wanting to get me out of the house. But maybe the counterfeiter wanted to freeze *you* off the ranch."

"There's no way Wyatt could know. The only person I'm in contact with is Stankle, and she's—"

"Stankle?" Molly interrupted.

"Forget you heard that. You don't need details."

"She's the girl at the Thunderhead." Relief swept through Molly, blasting every hint of jealousy from her brain. "Okay. I get it now." She smiled. And couldn't stop smiling. Even when Raleigh responded with his own wicked smile and cupped his hand around her breast and licked his tongue over her dimple, working toward her lips...

A stirring near the woodstove distracted Molly from the kiss. One of the kittens meowed softly as it crawled out from its bed and spotted Molly and Raleigh on the couch.

"Back to bed, Dolly," Raleigh said with exasperation when the kitten wended toward them. "Or Holly. I lose track."

Molly took the kitten into her lap. "Pure white— she's Holly." The kitten rubbed her head on Molly's palm, then rolled over, batting the air with her paws, playfully attacking Molly's fingers. Molly sent Raleigh an apologetic look. "I know I should be finding the kittens a home. But I keep thinking about Jocelyn and hoping that somehow..."

Raleigh folded his arms behind his head and stretched out his legs, crossing one over the other. "Once Wyatt's in jail, Joss can have all the kittens she wants." He sounded very confident.

Molly, having learned that everything was complicated at the Triple Eight, wasn't so sure.

TICKLING HIS TOES.

Raleigh drifted slowly upward from a soporific sleep, missing Molly's warmth. Where was she?

Beneath layers of bedclothes, his toes twitched.

"Cats," he groaned, feeling whiskers, soft silken

fur. "Holly," he said, nudging the kittens with his foot. "Dolly. Little Bit. Get outta there." He felt for Molly, found an empty pillow.

The tickling resumed.

A sandpapery tongue licked at his toe. Chuckling quietly, he searched for Molly, stretching an arm into the emptiness on her side of the bed. The phrase made him smile. *Her side.*

The black-faced kitten crawled from beneath the blanket and pounced on Raleigh's curled fingers with unsheathed claws. The pain made his entire body jerk involuntarily.

"Ouch."

Who said that? Raleigh sat up. "Molly?"

There was a lump at the foot of the bed. Molly's round pink face appeared from beneath the covers. She was rubbing her nose.

"Is this a fetish I should know about?" he asked.

She reached under the blanket and tickled his toes. "The kittens woke me up by licking my feet. We all discussed it and decided to do the same for you."

He settled back. "There are worse ways to wake up." He thought of falling asleep with her bare breasts pressed against his chest. "Better ones, too."

Molly dived back under the covers and started kissing her way up his body. The ends of her hair tickled. Her fingertips rubbed pleasure deep into his relaxed muscles. Her luxuriant body pressed its soft weight into his. "I can't stay all night," she warned.

"Then don't start up with me."

She didn't stop. Thank heaven. "I guess I can stay a little bit longer," she mumbled, and her mouth was so warm and wet on him that he knew he'd do anything to make sure she never ever went away again.

THE NEXT AFTERNOON, Molly was posing in a mulberry A-line bridesmaid's dress, finding herself quietly amused by the anxiety in Grace's eyes. Who'd have believed it? Grace Farrow, who was as likely to jump out of a cake as to cut it, was in a tizzy over color-coordinated garter belts and wedding-cake etiquette. She'd started out planning a fast, simple—some might say quickie—wedding, but Lu McHenry, Shane's mother, had put the pressure on and now Grace had an extravaganza—Treetop-style—on her hands. And less than a week to finalize the details.

"Laramie says she's allergic to bridesmaid's dresses. What do you think, Molly? Will she hate it?" Nervously Grace twisted a lock of her curly hair around a finger, corkscrewing the corkscrew. "I know the matching hats and boots are sorta cheesy, but I decided what the heck, we're the Cowgirl Club, why not shoot the works."

"I like them." Molly set her cowboy hat at a jaunty angle. For the wedding, it would be decked out with a tulle bow and a nosegay of mistletoe. She lifted the hem of the midlength western-cut dress. "And boots are much more comfortable and practical than high heels."

"Well, my mother's definitely going to spazz. She thinks velvet is for drapes. Her heart was set on Vera Wang. And when she finds out that we're having a deejay for the dance..." Grace tugged on her hair, a nervous habit. "The fur will fly. But it was either that or the Ukulele Minstrels."

"Sharleen Jackleen could sing," Ellie McHenry, the maid of honor, suggested from her position atop a dining-room chair. Her dress was the same as Grace's, in a soft shade of pine-green velvet. Miss Lettice Bellew,

Treetop's primo seamstress—who doubled as owner of the local boardinghouse—pinned the hem.

"I can see it." Molly giggled. "A hoochie-coochie version of 'White Lace and Promises,' sung at C above high C."

Grace handed Miss Bellew another pin. "Jeez. No, thanks. I'll take a pass." She glanced at Molly. "Speaking of passes. Back to your tale of woe."

Molly removed the cowboy hat and carefully lifted the dress off over her head before answering. "It wasn't pleasant, but it was only a kiss. An attempted kiss, I guess. I mean, Cord was groveling this morning, begging me to forgive his crude behavior, swearing it wouldn't happen again. What could I do?"

"You could sue his ass," said Grace. "That's probably what he was afraid of."

Ellie twirled for the seamstress. "That or the wrath of Sharleen's fingernails."

"Last night, I was upset. But today..." Molly shrugged. "I'm used to men acting like morons around me. Large breasts short-circuit their brains. They get so they can't think of anything else."

"Yep, it's a scientific fact." Grace peeped into the bodice of her wedding gown. "Not that I'm personally acquainted with the phenomenon, you understand."

Their laughter was the perfect conclusion to the final fitting appointment. The women changed clothes, piled on boots, coats and hats, then exited the boardinghouse to a pretty wintry scene right out of a storybook. Range Street was lined with modest bungalows and two-story frame homes, decorated for the holidays. Thick clumps of snow frosted the evergreens; the bare branches of deciduous trees were traced with a white and silver filigree.

Grace caught a drifting snowflake on her tongue. "More snow. Isn't this great?"

Ellie knotted her scarf and shivered. "I can't wait to get to San Francisco."

"Christmas shopping first. Sure you can't come, Molly?"

"I have a long grocery list. And a million things to do at the lodge if we're going to be ready for your wedding party."

Grace asked Ellie if she'd warm up their car, then linked arms to accompany Molly to her vehicle. "Listen up, girlfriend," she said. "If the fact of my party being booked at the lodge has anything whatsoever to do with you not busting Cord Wyatt's chops for sexual harassment, don't hesitate on my account. Your well-being is more important than—"

"No, Grace. That's not it. Honestly."

"Well, I'm worried. Are you safe around that horn dog? Even if you don't want to quit, you can always come and stay nights with us at Goldstream. It's a bit of a rough commute, but..."

"No, Grace." Molly patted her friend's gloved hand. "Really. I'll be fine. Cord's learned his lesson."

"There is Raleigh, I suppose."

"I can take care of myself."

Grace crinkled her nose. "But that's no fun."

Molly smiled to herself as she opened the Cherokee's door. "You got that right." She was still on an endorphin high from last night.

"Hold on." Grace waved at Ellie, motioning to wait another few minutes while she climbed into the passenger side of Molly's vehicle. "Now," she said, settling herself in, "even though Laramie calls the look on your face the ride-'em-cowgirl expression, I'm sensing there's even more to the story. Is there a problem?

Aside from the little Miss Sweetheart of the Rodeo Raleigh was getting cozy with at the Thunderhead."

"He explained that. It wasn't what it looked like."

Grace put on a woman-of-the-world air. "Honey, that's what they all say."

"This time it's true." Molly couldn't explain further, so she veered off in another direction, even though it was still all of a piece. Her problem was that the pieces fit together like a crazy quilt—taken individually, they made no sense. "Remember how I told you about the salted stew and the freezer incident?"

"Revenge for Dummies, by Sharleen Jackleen."

"Maybe not. There have been other odd occurrences."

For instance, Molly realized, the way she'd been conveniently awakened just in time to interrupt Raleigh's visit to Wyatt's office. She turned the key and switched on the heat before continuing. "I have reason to believe that there's a motive that doesn't involve me personally."

Grace's face scrunched with confusion. "How could it not? You were the victim."

"This is true," Molly mused. Except for the freezer lockup, she'd been the sole victim. As if the plan was to either scare her off or get her fired. But how could that play into the cockeyed counterfeit money scam?

Last night, Raleigh had confessed that he'd intended to remove her from the scene, but then hadn't gone through with it. Was he telling the truth?

He wasn't a cowboy.

Maybe he wasn't a Secret Service agent, either.

Molly groaned. She was so perplexed, she wasn't thinking straight. Of course Raleigh was being honest. She trusted him.

Because he'd given her an orgasm? Or because she loved him?

"Molly?" Grace prodded. "Want to clue me in?"

Molly gripped the steering wheel and stared straight out the windshield at the snowflakes wafting from the endless blue-gray sky. "Oh, Gracie. I'm in a fix." She turned to her friend. "What do you do when everything's so mixed up you can't tell up from down? When the man you might be in love with turns into a stranger before your eyes? When he kisses you senseless, tells you a far-fetched story but skimps on the details—for your own protection, mind you—and then has the audacity to ask you to trust him? What do you do, Grace?"

Grace blinked. "I guess that depends."

"On what?"

"The man."

After a long moment, Molly nodded. *Back to a matter of trust,* she thought. *Back to the counterfeit cowboy.*

9

GRIZZLE WAS LIT UP like a…well, like a Christmas tree. Molly stopped and looked even though she was pressed for time. With so much to do in the days preceding the wedding, she'd persuaded Sharleen and Jocelyn to finish the decorating. Now the stuffed bear was draped with tinsel and blinking lights. Candy canes hung from his upraised claws.

Molly shrugged. If it made Jocelyn happy…

She picked up her velvet skirts and trotted down the stairs. Imagine—Shane and Grace were married. The wedding had taken place in a picturesque white church in the countryside, with both families in attendance. Plus a few of Grace's closest friends from New York and several dozen celebrant Treetoppers. All of whom were about to descend on the Triple Eight.

Aye-yi-yi.

Etta Sue met Molly beneath the garland-draped antler chandelier. ''Ree-dick-yew-luss,'' she crowed, waving her arms at the lit fireplace, the organized registration desk, the shining floors, the extravagant tree. ''The whole darn thing is ridiculous!''

''This party is going to produce the first profit the ranch has seen in a year.'' Molly had grown immune to Etta Sue's complaints. Like Cord Wyatt, the woman was mostly bluster. Besides, she'd dressed up in a gaudy gold lamé ensemble with candy-cane-striped tights, all her jewels in evidence. She should be grateful for the excuse.

"This is your fault, Molly Broome." Etta Sue flicked the spout of her bleached ponytail and raised a knobby fist to the sky like Scarlett O'Hara. "If anyone comes near my cart, there'll be hell to pay."

"Then I suggest you lock it up somewhere safe." Molly went on to the kitchen before Etta Sue could continue the argument. She had more important things on her mind than baby-sitting cleaning supplies.

The log-walled dining room was rustic but festive. She'd found long white tablecloths for the tables. A florist from Rawlins had delivered centerpieces—simple bunches of holly, glossy leaves and red berries set in a lacy cloud of baby's breath. Strings of beads and tiny twinkling lights were twined through evergreen boughs and looped garlands.

So far, so good. Molly took a deep breath and pushed through the swinging door.

The kitchen was bustling. Though Molly had been prepared to hire extra workers, kitchen volunteers had begun popping out of the snowbanks as soon as the wedding invitations had gone out. The women of Treetop knew how to put on a buffet.

"Hot-dish heaven," Molly murmured as she wandered through the kitchen. Early arrivals were ripping foil covers off their edible donations, slicing lasagna—six pans!—making coffee and buttering rolls. A blue-haired woman in a Martha By Mail apron looked at Molly and said, "You shouldn't be here in that pretty velvet dress," and soon others had taken up the refrain. "You're a bridesmaid—go and enjoy the party," they said, pushing her toward the door. "We've got everything under control."

Molly found herself back in the dining room.

Male hands caught her by the elbows, spun her around. "Hey, Ms. Molly."

"Don't go in there," she warned Raleigh. "The Betty Crocker chorus has it going on."

He kissed her.

She melted into his arms. His lips were cold; the kiss tasted of sugar and spice. "You've been sampling," she accused, her hands resting on the fine woolen lapels of his conservative dark blue suit. For the first time he looked more like a G-man than a cowboy. She tried not to care.

"I came to the back door, looking for you. A woman handed me a cookie and sent me on my way. I felt about five."

Molly tested out the theory by slipping her hands inside his suit coat and running them over his rockhard chest. "Nope. You still feel pretty adult to me."

"Do that again, Ms. Molly, and my rating will be *X*." He nibbled at her lips. "Can we make a date for tonight? I'll show you how to put the *X* into Xmas."

"Gee, I have all these guests to take care of." The Farrows and the rest of the New York contingent had all checked into the Triple Eight the past night. She patted his shoulder. "But hold the thought."

He groaned. "My thoughts aren't what needs holding."

Molly was rather frustrated herself. She'd been so busy for the past week, they'd only been together once, late at night in his cabin, and had spent much of their time going over Raleigh's case, trying to connect the seemingly random events. Well, *some* of their time.

"I've been thinking," he said in a low voice that was somehow different than the husky whisper that made her toes curl. "As there's been no illegal movement from our suspect lately, my superiors are ready to pull the plug on this assignment. Tonight might be my last chance to prove my case.''

"This is a wedding party," Molly protested. "I don't want it ruined by undercover operations."

"Hush." He touched a fingertip to her lips. "I'll be discreet."

"No, Raleigh. Please."

"I never should have told you the truth in the first place. It was unprofessional. But you bamboozled me."

Her arms crossed defensively; she wasn't sure if that was a compliment or a complaint. Raleigh started to kiss her again. "What's that for?" she said, warding him off.

He doffed the brim of her mulberry-colored cowboy hat. "Mistletoe. I can't help it." The hat was festooned with a nosegay of the stuff, which was why Molly intended to avoid Cord Wyatt like the plague.

"Go on," she said, smiling but pushing Raleigh away. "Get out of here. Just don't expect me to help you play your spy games."

"Isn't this the season for reindeer games?" Laramie Jones sauntered into the dining room with her own hat tucked under one arm. She stopped and tilted her head, regarding Raleigh curiously. "You must be Raleigh Tate."

"Laramie, Raleigh." Molly smoothed her dress over her hips. Whereas she felt round as a berry in her bridesmaid getup, Laramie looked fashionably slender and stylish in the same dress in silver-gray, her raven hair glossed by the reflection of the starry lights. "Raleigh, Laramie Jones. My fellow bridesmaid, and the third member of the Cowgirl Club."

With a little curtsy, Laramie heel-to-toed her matching cowboy boots, showing them off. "As if you couldn't tell." She smiled at Molly. "Shane and Grace have arrived, along with the Farrows."

Molly gave her friend a quick squeeze and then departed to greet the rest of the wedding party. Laramie turned immediately to Raleigh, her sloe eyes narrowing to slivers. "Here's the deal, *cowboy*. I've known Molly for fifteen years. She's the kindest, warmest person on earth, too trusting and generous by far. I don't know what your story is, bucko, but you're as phony as a nine-dollar bill. If you hurt Molly, I'll hunt you down and truss you up and use a red-hot branding iron on every inch of your sorry hide. You'll regret the day you ever strapped on a pair of chaps and called yourself a cowboy."

She stopped to measure his response.

Raleigh nodded. What else could he do?

Laramie put on her fancy-dress Stetson. "Then if that's settled," she said airily, "shall we join the wedding party?"

THANK HEAVEN Sharleen was monopolizing Wyatt. As it was, Molly danced with Arthur Farrow, who quizzed her on summer rates; Grace's friend Troy Kazjakian, who swung her wildly, do-si-do-style; Rip Lawless, who kept calling Laramie "one fine filly"; Victor Farrow, who related news of his separation from Caroline, aka the Lemon-Sucker; and Nicky Peet. The young wrangler blushed when he requested a dance, blushed again when he put his arm around Molly's waist, and blushed even more when she asked about his date—a familiar young woman with a conservative suit, a wide-brimmed cowboy hat and a keen pair of eyes, going by the name Melissa Stankle. When Hank Evers cut in, Molly begged off with the excuses that her new boots were giving her blisters—true—and that she had to check on how supplies were holding out. Patently untrue. She intended to have a word with Mr. Raleigh Tate. How dare he turn Grace's wedding party into an undercover sting operation without permission!

"OKAY, STANKLE, WHAT GIVES?"

"Hello, sir. Er, hello, *Tate,* sir. Nice party."

"I don't remember asking you to attend."

Stankle waved in the direction of the dance floor. "Nicky Peet did. I met him at the Thunderhead. He's a cute kid."

"So were you. Before you sneaked onto the Triple Eight."

Stankle gave Raleigh a blank look. "I thought you wanted me here, sir."

"Not tonight," he growled. Dadburn son of a gun— as his father would say. He'd definitely lost his edge if he could no longer intimidate Stankle.

"*Especially* tonight," she said. "Something's going down. I can taste it."

"That so?" he replied, ultracasual. The hell of it was, she was right. He could taste it, too, and having all these people around was making him jumpy.

"I've confirmed Etta Sue Frain's marriage to Rip Lawless. Occurred straight out of prison, lasted only sixteen months, but it establishes a direct pipeline to Leonardo. With that man's know-how, they could counterfeit the Declaration of Independence if they wanted to."

"Then why wait all these years?"

"No need to risk it till now. You know what a bind Wyatt's in financially."

Raleigh nodded. "And as it happens, Rip arrived at the ranch only weeks before the first reports of counterfeit currency reached our field office."

Stankle smacked her lips. "We've got us a counterfeiting ring, sir. A *gang*."

Raleigh wasn't so sure. "Maybe," was all he said.

OUT ON THE DANCE FLOOR previously known as the lobby, Cord Wyatt's partner was pressing hard. "It's time for more jewels. Get me something flashy—a big fat emerald ring surrounded by diamonds. A real sparkler."

Wyatt chuffed; his partner's fingernails dug through his suede jacket and into the flesh of his upper arms. "I can't afford to go on another of your shopping trips."

"You can't afford *not* to, little big man."

"There's not enough payoff. You're going to put me in the poorhouse, woman."

"Wrong." She tossed her blond hair; the diamonds in her lobes glittered. "I'm going to save you from it. You'll see."

"WHAT'S WITH YOUR FRIEND Laramie?" Raleigh asked Molly when she finally caught up to him.

"What do you mean?"

"She's fierce."

"She's being very convivial. Look at her, slow-dancing with Rip Lawless. Etta Sue had better stay on her toes."

"Right. Have you told Laramie about me?"

"Raleigh! You swore me to secrecy. I wouldn't—"

"Then she's just whip-smart." *And ferociously protective.*

"Oh, yes. Laramie's quite the woman. Smart, beautiful and mysterious. As a rule, men are captivated, but she's really quite choosy. I've seen three-hundred-pound football players wither under her disdain."

"She moves like a cat."

Molly said in a small tight voice, "Glad you noticed. I did so want you two to get along."

"Aw, Molly. You know you're my sweetheart."

"Maybe I'm just a convenience. You decided you needed me to gain access to the lodge."

"Wait a minute. I thought you suspected me of being your prankster. You can't have it both ways."

She gasped. "How did you know that?"

"Your face is an open book."

She covered it with her hands. "I didn't truly suspect you, Raleigh. I just…wondered. Now and then. When I wasn't thinking straight."

"Hey, fine by me. You shouldn't be trusting *anyone* here at the Triple Eight."

"Surely Joss and Sharleen and Etta Sue…"

"Either Sharleen or Etta Sue could be involved."

"There's no way Cord would—"

"Careful," Raleigh interrupted, shushing her again. None of the wedding guests seemed to be paying them any mind, but you couldn't be too cautious.

Molly whispered. "He wouldn't trust Etta Sue. She's loudmouthed, unreliable and half-drunk most of the— *oh*."

"What?"

"I just remembered something suspicious I saw. Involving Etta Sue's liquor consumption. You know, I don't think she's as tipsy as she makes out. Or as weak. Look at how she wheels that heavy cart through every room in the lodge. Up and down the stairs, even."

"You're right. I've noticed that myself."

"Still, why would Cord share—"

"Because Etta Sue is his mother."

Molly's jaw dropped.

Raleigh put a finger under her chin. "Zip up. You don't want to attract attention."

"You could have told me sooner," she said hotly. "It explains a lot. Like why Etta Sue's on the payroll even though she does no work." Molly's eyes searched the dancers. "Humph. I guess the family that bellows together, et cetera. And they're both afraid of the kittens, too."

"Can you see now why I warned you to keep away from confrontations? Watch what you say. Don't question them. That's my job."

"Yours and Melissa Stankle's. Did you think I wouldn't notice how you sneaked her in here?"

"Gosh darnit, Molly. You shouldn't even know who Stankle is. Keep it to yourself, huh? Please?"

Molly watched the newlyweds in silence, her expressive face revealing her turmoil. "If you two wreck Grace's reception," she warned, "I'll—I'll—"

"You'll what?"

"I'll never tickle your toes again!"

"HOLLY? YOU OKAY? Little Bit, shh. You'll get me in trouble." With the kittens cradled in her long skirt, Jocelyn tiptoed past the dancers. Nobody noticed, not even her mom when she slipped out of the crowd. Joss pressed herself against the banister, sure she was gonna get caught, but her mom went by without glancing up the stairway. Only over her shoulder, back at the crowd.

Joss peeped at the kittens. "Let's get upstairs. Quick. You can stay in my room tonight."

"WHAT'S WITH THAT GUY Raleigh?" Laramie asked when she was finally able to corner Grace and Shane.

''What do you mean?'' they said, married for mere hours and already speaking as one.

''He's leading Molly on.''

''Oh, Laramie.'' Grace tried to shove some of her flyaway hair back under her beaded headpiece; she'd ripped off the veil right after the ceremony. ''You're too cynical. Raleigh's a perfectly nice guy—I like him a lot.''

''You don't buy his cowboy act, do you?''

Grace and Shane exchanged a look.

Impatiently Laramie tapped the floor with the silver metal tip of her boots. ''If he's a cowboy, I'm Debutante of the Year.''

Grace gazed up at Shane. ''What do you think, my dear husband?''

''He knows his stuff,'' Shane said, adding an out-of-character lovey-doveyish ''my little wife,'' for Grace's benefit. He squeezed her waist.

''Newlyweds,'' Laramie scoffed. Her smile was indulgent. ''Save it for the honeymoon, guys. I need the straight dope.''

''I wouldn't swear to it, but I figure this is his first job as a wrangler. His hands aren't beat-up enough.'' Shane held up his own hand—worn, weather-beaten, scarred, sporting a shiny gold marriage band. Grace's eyes glistened at the sight; with a soft exclamation, she took her new husband's hand in hers and covered it with kisses.

Laramie felt vindicated. ''That's what I thought,'' she said, mostly to herself. ''But telling Molly's gonna be the killer.''

RALEIGH FOLLOWED his suspect from the lobby, through the dining room, into the kitchen. He was waylaid there by the worker bees. The ladies clucked and cooed and pressed enough leftovers on him to last a week. Finally he escaped into the cellar, letting them think what they would about his impending rendezvous. Molly would understand.

At first he thought he'd lost the trail. The cellar seemed pitch-black. He took a flashlight off the shelf, but didn't turn it on as he descended the plank steps by feel, treading lightly to avoid giveaway creaks. Once at the bottom, he spotted a light shining in a far corner—the dim, wavering glow of another flashlight. Also movement among the shadows. The rustle of paper.

Raleigh circled around piles of junk, peering through the darkness. Aha.

He crept closer. The suspect's greed was palpable.

He switched on his light. Sharleen Jackleen spun around and he aimed it dead in her eye. She gave a surprised cry, her hands flying up to protect her face. "I didn't take any. I swear, I didn't. I swear."

Raleigh saw what she'd been doing. A dusty tarpaulin had been flung aside, revealing bundles of newspapers—much like those Molly had once commented on—piled on an old treadle sewing machine. Sharleen had cut the twine on the top bundle and gone through half the stack, separating random sheets of uncut currency from alternate layers of printed newspaper and plain paper. Raleigh edged closer and tested a corner of one of the blank sheets. It was a good quality of paper, a nice match to the special linen-and-cotton blend used by the Bureau of Engraving and Printing.

Sharleen squinted into the glare of his flashlight. "Oh, it's only you. You're not allowed in the cellar." Her shrill laugh scraped his eardrums. "What are you doing here, Raleigh? Did you follow me?"

"There's a better question. What are you doing with all this counterfeit currency?"

Sharleen's mouth opened and closed like a goldfish. "Is that what this stuff is?"

She was no actress. "Yep," he said. "Imagine that. And you're caught red-handed."

"But I only found it! By accident! I didn't make it."

"Then you're in luck. Testify against your cohort and you'll probably get off with a fine. How does five thousand strike you?"

"What!" she screeched. "I can't afford—" She pulled her wrist out of his grasp. "Lemme go. Who do you think you are, anyhow?"

He flashed his badge. "Secret Service. And I'm placing you under arrest for possession of counterfeit currency. We can talk about the forgery and distribution charges later. Your cooperation will be duly appreciated."

"You got me all wrong," Sharleen was weakly protesting when suddenly she shut up and looked overhead. As did Raleigh. Dust filtered down upon his face. The rafters shook as what sounded like a herd of buffalo crossed the floor above them, accompanied by panicky exclamations and distant shouts of "Fire!"

"FIRE!"
Molly's gaze traveled up the sparkling Christmas tree. Jocelyn leaned over the balustrade near the tree's metallic star, her face bathed in its golden light. Her eyes were round with fright. "There's smoke," she called down to the wedding guests. Her small voice shook. "I think it's a fire."

For an instant, nobody moved. Then a mild panic set in as people rushed either toward the doors, into the adjacent rooms, or up the stairs. Molly was the first to choose the stairs.

Wisps of pale smoke hung near the ceiling of the second-floor balcony. "Joss," Molly gasped as she reached the top of the staircase, "go to the lobby. Hurry. We may have to evacuate the building."

Shane stepped in. He hustled Joss over to Grace, who had gathered up the voluminous fur-trimmed skirt of her wedding dress with both hands. "I want you both downstairs. Go now."

"Wait!" Grace dropped the gown and gave him a quick hug and kiss. "Stay safe."

Thick smoke was pouring from the hallway on the left. Molly yanked a fire extinguisher from a glass box set against the wall.

"The kittens!" Joss struggled against Grace's embracing arms. "Molly—help," she cried. "The kittens are in my bedroom."

"I'll get them, Joss, I promise, but you have to go now." Molly turned to confront the smoke and heat.

Shane caught her by the shoulder. "Let me go first."

The east wing was filled with a gray haze. "All I can see is smoke," she said, tasting it on her tongue.

Shane coughed. "Smells like burning hair."

They kept near the wall, crouching low where the air wasn't as thick. Molly spotted the source—flames flickered in the built-in niche, forming a recognizable upright form. "Grizzle?" she said hoarsely, choked by the stinking smoke. Her eyes teared; the shape blurred.

Shane grabbed the extinguisher from her and aimed it at the flames, dousing them with shots of white foam. Molly became aware of several others joining the rescue squad just before a dense cloud of smoke belched from the bear's niche, obscuring her vision. She covered her nose and mouth with a hand, fighting through the acrid smoke, trying to get to Joss's bedroom to save the kittens.

Raleigh appeared beside her. "Molly!"

She fell into his arms. "Raleigh. This is a disaster."

"Fire's out," he said, holding her tight. "You're okay."

The smoke was rising, coating the upper reaches of the ceiling with a thick fog. Through a dull haze, she saw Shane and the others inspecting the blackened niche. "And Grizzle?"

"I'm afraid he's charcoal."

"The bear was draped with holiday lights," she remembered. "They must have ignited his fur." She coughed violently. "Let's rescue the kittens for Joss and then get some fresh air. This awful stink is sickening."

When they emerged from the bedroom with the kittens, Nicky Peet and Melissa Stankle were already setting up a fan to clear the air. Arthur Farrow was directing traffic near the staircase. The kittens were passed on to Laramie, who nodded at Raleigh with grudging respect and then promised Molly she'd take the pets downstairs to Joss.

Something about the ruined bear had caught Raleigh's attention. "Give me a hand, will you?" he asked Shane, and together they maneuvered the charred hulk farther out into the hallway.

Poor Grizzle was a wreck. His snout had melted into his teeth; the remainder of his head was burned beyond recognition. The bulk of his body was black with soot and twined with sad remnants of the holiday lights. The scorched hide had split open in several places to reveal its stuffing. Raleigh poked at it curiously.

Molly touched a blackened, melted candy cane. "Yipes. Still hot."

The bear's pedestal must have been unstable. When Raleigh reached behind the misshapen creature, it fell without warning, crashing face-first into the opposite wall. Molly jumped out of the way just in time.

"Stay back." Raleigh put his arm in front of her and gave Grizzle a kick. The bear lurched sideways, its blackened claws gouging scratches into the wall before finally tipping over and landing with a thud on the dingy carpet runner.

"Down he goes," an onlooker said.

Molly's eyes widened as she leaned in for a closer look. "Raleigh? Is that...?"

"Don't touch them. I want to preserve fingerprints."

"But those are—"

"Diamonds," said Melissa Stankle. "And rubies too."

A clear plastic pouch had fallen partway out of one of the rips in the bear's mangled hide, spilling forth a tangle of jewelry—earrings, bracelets, rings—encrusted with gems. "They don't even look real to me," Molly said. "But they must be worth a fortune."

Raleigh knelt and carefully poked deeper into the stuffing. With the tip of a pen he eased out a wad of cash that had been rolled and secured with a rubber band. Then another.

"Counterfeit?" Molly breathed.

He tipped one of the rolls upright on the singed rug. "I can't be sure till I examine it, but something tells me we've found a stash of the real thing."

Cord Wyatt shoved his way through the crowd, stopping only when he ran belly-first into petite Melissa Stankle, who set her feet and stood her ground, hands on hips, chest thrust against the rancher's. "What is going on here?" he roared, looking past Stankle to the smoky, buckled walls and overturned bear. "Sharleen's being held against her will by a group of madwomen in the kitchen, there are cats crawling up the Christmas tree and apparently someone has set fire to my house! Don't you people realize that my insurance has lapsed?''

Raleigh stood and took out his badge. ''That, Mr. Wyatt, is the least of your troubles.''

10

MOLLY WAS UP AT SIX the next morning, making breakfast and smoothing her ruffled feathers with clichés. Ah, that was one: ruffled feathers. And, of course, the show must go on. Watched pots. Too many cooks. Make lemonade. Don't count your eggs.

She cracked hers two at a time into a mixing bowl. Too many to count. Despite the wedding party's disastrous finale, many of the lodge's guest rooms were filled. As the smoke and fire damage had been contained to the hallway of the staff's wing, the guests weren't terribly inconvenienced…except by the acrid scent of Grizzle's demise, which still lingered this morning despite Molly's efforts with superstrength Mr. Clean, sandalwood incense sticks and cinnamon-scented air freshener.

"Morning." Laramie shuffled into the kitchen wearing a knee-length Jets jersey over leggings, her long hair pulled back in a sloppy ponytail. "I smell burnt bear and coffee."

Molly said good-morning and pointed toward the latter.

Laramie yawned as she filled a mug. She topped off Molly's as well. "Raleigh get back yet?"

"Nope." Molly tried to sound jaunty. "Neither did Cord or Sharleen. I guess that means they're officially in custody."

"Wow. What a mess."

Molly whisked the eggs. "I don't know what to tell Joss, Sharleen's daughter. With all of last night's confusion, explanations were easy to avoid when I put her to bed in one of the guest rooms. She was more concerned with the kittens. But this morning..."

Laramie put her elbows on the butcher block. "It shouldn't be your problem, Mol. I know you have a strong nurturing instinct, but in this case maybe you should let Sharleen sort it out for herself. She's responsible, not you."

"If I hadn't made Raleigh suspicious about the newspapers, he wouldn't have followed Sharleen to the cellar. I know she was breaking the law and all, but when I think of her daughter..." Molly sniffed. "Joss needs attention, not more neglect."

"You've got to know none of this is your fault. Thinking that way's just plain dumb."

Molly continued nonetheless. "I figure that was also why Sharleen—or whoever—was trying to get rid of me. As soon as I was hired, I was in a position to see too much."

The caffeine had perked Laramie up. "What did you see? I understand that Sharleen and Cord Wyatt were running a counterfeit scam, but where does all the jewelry come in? Grace and I overheard Sweetheart of the Rodeo say that she didn't even think it was real."

Molly's smile surfaced. "You mean Melissa Stankle. Raleigh's colleague from the Secret Service. We should ask her to join the Cowgirl Club."

"The Secret Service!" Laramie whooped, slapping the table. "A counterfeit cowboy! Now there's one for the annals of our club. Unbelievable."

"Did you honestly threaten Raleigh with a branding iron?"

"The guy was playing fast and loose with a sister

cowgirl's heart. No way could I let that go unchallenged.''

"Well, thanks for defending me, Laramie." Molly put the mixing bowl in the fridge and went to the freezer—giving a little shiver as she always did—for packages of bacon and sausage. She was planning an old-fashioned hearty country breakfast, with oatmeal and flapjacks, too. Surely frying bacon would mask Grizzle's odorous memory.

Molly returned to the conversation. "*However*, I would like to point out that I'm not as trusting as you assume. I recognized that Raleigh wasn't being straight with me and even so I chose to…" Her voice trailed off; unconsciously, she brushed her fingertips across her smiling lips.

Laramie looked askance. "Take a walk on the wild side?"

Molly returned to the moment. "Turns out that even when I'm bad, I'm law-abiding," she admitted, feeling sheepish. "There's no getting past it. Even in the midst of swindlers and counterfeiters, I'm stuck being the nice and normal one."

"Such a shame."

Molly looked directly into Laramie's eyes, and so saw them widen when she confessed, "I've always secretly wanted to be unique and exotic like you."

"And I've always wanted to be nice and normal, so there you go." Laramie's smile was rueful.

"Is it too late for us to run away and become cowgirls?"

They laughed, agreeing that though they'd made it as far as Wyoming, their cowboy fantasies were turning out to be more complicated than they'd imagined. Even Grace, who in many ways was living out her fondest dream, had been forced to deal with all her old issues first. And then new problems arrived, just to keep life bumpy. But so very interesting.

Creaking floorboards and plumbing sounds signaled that the guests had begun to stir. Molly speeded up her breakfast preparations while she and Laramie pondered her prospects at the Triple Eight, which didn't look too good if Cord Wyatt was indeed a counterfeiter. No solution presented itself, so they moved on to discuss Laramie's job as a travel agent, which led to their curiosity about Shane and Grace's choice of honeymoon. Having developed a certain unexplained fondness for road trips, they'd turned down Hawaii and Barbados to travel the Pacific Coast Highway by pickup truck, continuing all the way to Mexico, which at least sounded warm. Horse trailer not necessary, according to Grace.

Laramie helped arrange the sideboard in the dining room and then went up to change. Molly fed the crowd buffet-style, turning out scrambled eggs and countless flapjacks. Her only kitchen helper was the silent and solemn Joss, who'd brought the kittens downstairs in a closed cardboard box and seemed intent on establishing perfect behavior—a reaction Molly remembered from her own childhood. She'd believed that if she did everything within her control exactly right, surely all that was out of her control would step in line. It was a hard habit to break.

Molly gave Jocelyn a hug and went to chat up the guests. Nicky Peet was offering trail rides in the snow; Laramie and a few of Grace's New York friends were game. The Farrows were leaving within the hour—skiing at Aspen. Molly assigned Rip to chauffeur them to the airport.

Only Etta Sue was noticeably absent.

Molly returned to the kitchen. "Jocelyn, have you seen Etta Sue?"

The girl looked up from feeding the cats. "Yes, ma'am. She's in her room. The stink doesn't bother her, she said."

"But she's not sick? Maybe I should bring her a breakfast tray." *And thus satisfy my curiosity.*

"I think…" Joss's eyes were huge, wary. She ducked her head. "I think she's drinking."

Which was precisely what Etta Sue wanted them to believe. "It was Etta Sue who put salt in the chicken stew," Molly said, sounding certain even though she was taking a flying leap.

Joss cringed. "I'm not s'posed to tell."

Molly reassured her. "You don't have to say a word, honey." *I already know.*

The back door opened and a harried Sharleen stepped inside, wearing yesterday's clothes under an unzipped pink patent leather jacket. She slammed the door, put her hands in her lopsided bouffant and let out a huge, dramatic sigh. Jocelyn cried, "Mommy!" and ran to hug her waist, further crushing the crumpled skirt.

"Well." Molly was astonished. "Welcome back. Is Raleigh with you?"

Sharleen ignored the question. She patted her daughter's back with one hand and held the other out before her, fingers spread. "They broke one of my nails," she wailed. She felt for her lobes. "And confiscated my diamond earrings!"

"But are you—" Molly stopped; she couldn't say the words *under arrest* in front of Jocelyn.

"They questioned me. For hours. It was terrible— terrible!" Tears had carved tracks through Sharleen's makeup, washing much of it away. She'd peeled off her extra set of eyelashes and forgotten to reapply lipstick. Her face seemed young, naked and vulnerable.

Molly's soft heart filled with sympathy, especially when Joss pressed her face in Sharleen's midriff and pleaded, "Don't leave me, Mommy. I'll be good. I won't play with the kittens anymore—I promise."

"Oh, my little sugar baby." Sharleen knelt and hugged her daughter. "Don't you worry about your momma. I'm a fighter." She looked up at Molly. "No one's gonna frame me for something I didn't do." She let out one of her high-pitched laughs, but it didn't sound too confident. "I've done enough wrong in my life. This time I'm innocent. I swear."

Molly believed her. In essence. "Then why were you...uh, you know?"

"Well, I knew you and Etta Sue had argued over those newspaper bundles. And then she went to all the trouble of hauling them into the cellar. Didn't add up, y'know? So a couple days ago, I checked them out and found all that money. Like winning the lottery."

"You should have told someone right then," Molly said.

Sharleen shrugged. "I figured Etta Sue for one of those crazy old dames, the kind who keep fifty cats and sleep on a mattress stuffed with twenties." Her eyes shifted. "How was I supposed to know the darn stuff was funny money? It looked real enough to me."

And then, under cover of the wedding party, Sharleen had decided to give her bank account a boost, Molly thought, filling out the scenario herself. The woman was guilty of stealing the counterfeit currency, not making it. And technically not even that, because Raleigh had stopped her in the middle of the crime.

"This is good," Molly mused. "What's the story with Cord, though?"

Sharleen's face creased with worry. She actually cared about the guy, Molly realized. But then, she'd have to; she'd rubbed his feet. A woman didn't do that unless—

Molly blanched. Holy cowboy. Why, she herself had tickled Raleigh Tate's toes!

"I don't know what's happening with Cord. Agent Stankle drove me back and she wouldn't say a word. Is he in trouble? Were my earrings—" Sharleen covered Joss's ears and whispered, *"Stolen goods?"*

"I don't think so," Molly said slowly. Chances were the diamonds weren't genuine, either.

Although the pieces still didn't fit neatly, she was beginning to believe she knew why. "Sharleen, will you and Joss take the kittens out to Raleigh's cabin? It might be better if they're—" Molly pointed at Jocelyn, hoping Sharleen would get the hint "—out of the way."

For once, Sharleen was compliant. "Sure." She gave her daughter a little push. "Get your coat and boots, sugar."

"Just a minute, Joss." Molly weighed her words. "You once told me that you'd explored every inch of the ranch. By chance, did that include Etta Sue's cleaning cart?"

Joss shook her head vigorously. "No, ma'am. I don't ever touch the cart. Etta Sue's real mean about it."

Molly let out her breath. "Okay." *Too bad.*

Joss stopped at the door and said in a small voice, "I know where she keeps it when she doesn't want to drag it up the steps." She looked guilty. "There's a little closet. Under the steps. Sometimes I play there when Etta Sue's not using it."

"Okay!" Molly said, exultant.

Joss hunched her shoulders. "It's always locked."

I'll break in, Molly decided, but then Joss, bless her

inquisitive little heart, added, "But I know where there's an extra key."

IT WAS FITTING, Molly decided as she opened the narrow closet door. In more ways than one—Jocelyn had unerringly picked the correct key from the discards forgotten at the bottom of a kitchen junk drawer.

Considering the circumstances of Molly's glorified housekeeping job, it truly was fitting that a cleaning cart should provide the denouement. Perhaps.

The tiny closet was tucked into the space beneath the curved angle of the steps. Etta Sue's cart had been parked inside, wedged deep, as far as the slanted ceiling allowed. Molly grabbed the handles and eased the heavy cart incrementally through the narrow doorway. The broad bushy head of a sweep broom clunked against the jamb. The wheels squeaked, not loudly, but enough to make her heart jump into her throat. She didn't want to find out how Etta Sue would defend her territory. If this mess played out like the final scene of a western, a shotgun was sure to be involved.

"Get a grip," Molly whispered to herself. "It's only a cleaning cart. Even I know how to pull the trigger on a bottle of Windex."

At first glance, the contents were innocuous. At second glance, she picked out the near-empty liquor bottles salted among the cleaning supplies. Sharleen had said that Cord supplied his mother's booze; ergo, Etta Sue must want even her own son to think of her as a good-for-nothing boozehound. But why?

Molly lifted out a few of the cleaning supplies, saw nothing suspicious, then knelt to examine the bottom shelf and underside of the cart. She had to push aside several filthy rags that were hung from the sides. It seemed the perfect hiding place, but all she found was an empty bucket, a few ratty scrub brushes and a sponge that had grown enough mold to supply a junior high science fair.

Out of frustration, Molly gave the cart a shove. The thing barely moved. It had to be weighed down with something that she was missing.

Screwing up her face with disgust, she picked over the contents of the rectangular garbage can attached to the front of the cart. It wasn't so bad. In fact, the trash was the cleanest she'd ever come across—nothing but crumpled sheets of newspaper. She smoothed one out. It was only the *Sweetwater County Sampler,* where the area's criminal activities were printed in the police blotter, such as it was: "Tuesday, 8:15 a.m., Deputy Ryan responded to a call from 112 Balsam Road— Dog, 6, bit boy, also 6, on big toe. Pedigree unknown, pending veterinary report. Deputy Ryan dispensed lollipop and leash."

Molly reached through the rest of the balled newspapers, feeling for the bottom of the can. The distance was minimal. Odd.

A false bottom? Ah, now that would be a naughty trick.

She emptied the can and reached inside again, concentrating on the edges. There was give on one side; she worked her fingertips under the false bottom, gave it a good tug and lifted the piece out.

She peered into the trash can. Yes, there it was, the crucial element of the contemporary counterfeiter's modus operandi, according to Raleigh: a top-notch laser printer, the Spectrum Platinum 6000, professional series. The artists' choice, Spectrum ads boasted.

Also, apparently, the con-artist's choice.

Molly frowned. She was no legal expert, but it seemed to her that merely owning a laser printer was proof of very little. Even when you kept it at the bottom of a trash can.

Which admittedly seemed rather suspicious. Better to put everything back where she'd found it and call Raleigh at the Treetop police department.

She didn't get the chance.

A terrible, ululating cry cleaved the silence. *"Ay-eeeiiiahhh!"*

So there really is such a thing as a bloodcurdling scream, Molly thought in the instant before she looked up. Etta Sue hung over the balustrade of the second-floor balcony, her unnaturally bright hair falling into her face. Her arms flailed. "Don'tchew touch my cart. Don'tchew—dare—touch—"

Molly dodged the glittery glass ball ornament that Etta Sue hurled at her head. It shattered on the floor, followed by several others in quick succession. Smash, smash, smash.

The gold star tree-topper came next, spinning fast, its points lethally blurred, the end of its cord stripped to the wires. Molly ducked behind the cart. The star crashed directly into it, puncturing an aerosol spray can with a hiss. Bottles toppled; brooms rattled.

Molly risked a quick peek. Etta Sue was reaching down into the decorated tree for more ammunition, drawing up a length of jangling metallic beads. The huge spruce swayed in place, tethered by wires. Ornaments dropped through the branches, smashing on the wood floor and rolling off in all directions. The lopsided loops of holiday lights flickered off and on, emitting sparks somewhere at the back of the tree.

The lobby doors banged open. Raleigh stood on the doorstep with his feet planted wide, his heroic figure silhouetted against the blue sky and snowcapped mountain peaks beyond.

He spoke in a deeply masculine, no-nonsense voice that sent a thrill rippling through Molly. His command filled the space up to the rafters: "Drop the beads, Etta Sue."

Raleigh's oilskin duster was open, as was the jacket of his tailored suit; his hands hung easily at his sides, fingers tensile—prepared.

If he draws a six-gun, Molly thought, *I'm turning in my video card.*

Etta Sue must have seen too many westerns herself. She stared Raleigh straight in the eye, spat with contempt and deliberately reached down into the tree to jerk the rope of beads free. Electricity crackled. Sparks flew.

Etta Sue stiffened, mouth agape, one hand clenched on the copper beads. For several seconds she was riveted in place by the shock. Then she let out a high-voltage, smoke-detector "*Eep!*" and fell straight backward like a broken ironing board, landing with a thud on the carpeted balcony.

The flames that had burst from the electric cords gathered at the back of the tree sputtered out. A scent of sizzling ozone and singed spruce needles hung in the air. Etta Sue twitched, groaned, muttered inaudibly.

Another Triple Eight crisis had passed.

Molly stood and walked toward Raleigh, crunching bits of glass underfoot. "My hero," she sang out in a clear soprano, silly with relief, giddy in love. "I know it's a cliché, but what in tarnation's wrong with a good cliché?"

Raleigh, no slouch in the romantic hero department, took her into his arms. His expression was quizzical, but his eyes were focused on Molly's face with a sincerity that meant everything to her. He grinned and said, "If the boot fits…"

There was no avoiding it. Molly didn't even try. "If the *cowboy* boot fits," she said with double his sincerity, "wear it, Raleigh Tate. Wear it."

11

TIRED OF WAITING, Molly opened the doors one more time and stepped outside into the cold. A fringed fleece blanket was wrapped around her like a shawl; she pulled it tighter. The air was chillier than before. The sun had gone down. Deep clear cold filled the shallow valley like liquid ice.

She imagined the ranch encased in the clear dome of a snow globe. Tidy, quaint, picturesque—the log lodge and cabins, the barn, corrals, the ridge of pines. One shake and snowflakes would swirl, spiraling around the woman posed on the doorstep, waiting forever for her cowboy to come home.

Not a snow globe, she thought. A movie. The finale. Of course.

Had it already ended? With Raleigh riding off into the distance in the sheriff's car, not alone but just as good since Etta Sue had recovered enough to demand a lawyer and then stubbornly clamped her big mouth shut?

It looked like things would work out for Cord Wyatt, after a fashion. He'd been released on bail a few hours ago and had come back to the ranch with his tail between his legs. Sharleen had given him the cold shoulder but was already showing signs of warming, especially since Cord was so eager to make apologies that he'd allowed Jocelyn to choose one of the kittens to keep as a pet.

The tip of Molly's nose was ice-cold. She waited another minute, gazing up at the stars. It seemed that they had different stars in Wyoming—radiant, glittering ones, sprinkled thickly across the dark sky with a depth and brilliance that was breathtaking.

Headlights cut through the night. Molly's heart leaped.

She watched the sheriff's vehicle plow through the powdery snow. Raleigh was home. Maybe she would get a Technicolor happy-ever-after yet.

He strode toward the lodge with a bare head, naked hands. She said, "You must be freezing," and enveloped him in her blanket. Her arms. Winter had its advantages.

Raleigh wrapped his arms around her as well, rubbing his cold hands up and down the back of her fisherman's sweater. The vapor from their mouths mingled. She jittered up and down, laughing softly. He inhaled, his eyes aglow even in the dark. Especially in the dark.

"Come inside," she murmured.

He kissed her; she'd known he would. And by the time the kiss had ended, her whole being was suffused with its endless pleasure and enduring promise.

"Inside you," he whispered against her hair. "That's where I want to be."

"The house first, lover boy." They linked arms and went inside, shutting the door behind them. The lobby was as big and drafty as ever, but somehow homier. The fire was lit. The tree was dark except for the glimmer of silver tinsel and restrung copper beads that reflected the dancing flames. Sharleen had swept up the broken ornaments; the floor shone, an unbroken expanse the color of maple syrup.

Two armchairs were drawn up to the fireplace. Molly sat Raleigh in one, started to turn away, then found herself pulled into his lap, her feet kicking up in the air. "All right for you," she said, snuggling against him. "Tell me when your legs go numb."

"Why, Ms. Molly, it should be perfectly obvious by now that you couldn't make me numb if you tried."

"You were numb in the freezer."

"I was a gentleman in the freezer."

"Maybe I don't want a gentleman."

His lashes dipped, darkening his eyes. "You want a cowboy?"

"In a manner of speaking." She rubbed a finger across his prickly whiskers. "I want a cowboy attitude."

"Which constitutes?"

"Pride. Courage. Humility. Integrity. Wit. Strength…tempered with gentleness."

"You've been thinking about this."

"For about fifteen years."

"Daunting," he said. "How's a mortal man—let alone one of your vaunted cowboys—supposed to meet such expectations?"

She pressed her cheek to his. "Don't worry. You qualify."

He stroked her hair. "Even though I don't normally wear chaps and spurs?"

"Mere trappings," she said, and it was true. She could even get used to the straitlaced blue-suit-white-shirt-and-tie look if she had to.

His kiss was sweet and tender and filled with affection. "I love you, Molly."

Her lucky stars were shining tonight. "And I love you."

"Will you come with me when I go?"

Her breath caught short. "You're already planning to leave?"

"Soon. My part of this investigation will be wrapped up within a day or two. The case goes to federal prosecutors."

Molly got up and walked back and forth in front of the stone fireplace, worrying her lip. Her thoughts churned. She wanted to be with Raleigh above all else, but the prospect of leaving Wyoming when she'd begun to think of it as home gave her the slightest pause. What she really, truly wanted was for her and Raleigh to stay the way they were, together at the Triple Eight. Although the wish may have borne a trace of her longing for cowboys, it was mostly rooted in her old insecurity about change. Too much, too fast, too new.

Still, it was Raleigh. She loved him. More than enough.

"You'll probably have to leave the Triple Eight in any case," he said, feeling desire tighten his voice.

More than a physical desire. An emotional, spiritual need for Molly had gripped his heart in a vise. His father had said that love made a man go soft, but what Raleigh felt was tight and painful and gut-wrenching. If he didn't win her, he might well die.

Molly sat on the stone hearth. Her eyes were round, dark, bottomless. "How's that?"

Raleigh tried to concentrate on the straight and narrow path that he'd known so well before Molly Broome had thrown him for a loop. "I can only guess, but Wyatt's going to be leveled with a large fine, at the very least. Apparently Etta Sue was the instigator of the counterfeiting operation. Wyatt was her errand boy. However, considering his tenuous financial position, any fine at all is likely to force him into bankruptcy. The Triple Eight—and your job—will become casualties. I'm sorry for that."

"I'd expected as much." Molly's face was sad as

she glanced around the room. "As many troubles as I've had here, I've grown to love the old place. I hate to say goodbye."

"I know." He felt himself smile fondly. "I'm going to miss it myself. This ranch brought back a lot of good memories for me."

Molly drew her gaze across his face contemplatively. "Tell me about the case. From the beginning. I still don't understand the details."

Raleigh swallowed. All this delaying was torture. "Etta Sue's not being very cooperative, so we're still working out the details. But it started when Wyatt passed a counterfeit twenty at a Treetop gas station, then at a few other local businesses. Once he'd come to our attention, we connected him with an operation we'd had under surveillance in Laramie. A jewelry store."

"Aha. Jewelry—Etta Sue's partiality."

"The shop owner had been, in essence, laundering counterfeit currency. Knowingly taking the fakes, giving good money for bad."

"But how would that profit him?"

"Her. Exactly what the bureau wondered. Until we realized that she was selling her co-conspirators costume jewelry at retail gemstone prices. She passed them a relatively small amount of good money as change, 'ate' the counterfeit cash, then turned around and cooked her books so that the store could use the supposedly legitimate receipts to launder money from an illegal gambling operation. The IRS, the feds and the local police are going to tussle over who gets first crack at prosecuting that mess."

"Oh, gosh," Molly breathed. "Then Etta Sue's jewelry—and the stash in Grizzle—was all fake? And she knew it?"

"Absolutely. Every week or so, she was sending Cord to Laramie with the currency she'd printed up at home. Thus far, their actual profit was small potatoes, but it would have gradually added up...if Wyatt hadn't gotten greedy and tried spending the counterfeit bills elsewhere. He claims the entire scheme was Etta Sue's idea, she says it was his." Raleigh shrugged. "Who knows?"

"How will you prove any of this?"

"We have Wyatt at the jewelry store on surveillance video. I figure Etta Sue's fingerprints are all over the printer, the special inks she used and the uncut currency we've confiscated. It's enough."

Molly started pacing again. "What was the point of the liquor bottles in her cart? And why did Etta Sue go after me?"

"The liquor—I don't know. Could be she's crazy like a fox, since I have to admit it was one of the reasons I overlooked her. At least until I realized that Sharleen was being honest when she claimed to have merely blundered onto the forged currency." On his first mad drive back to the ranch, Raleigh had beat himself up over that. He was thankful that his mistake hadn't resulted in worse than a Christmas tree shoot-out, and determined that Molly would never be at risk again. Even if that meant he had to quit the bureau and turn himself into a cowboy.

"Also," he continued, trying to move the discussion on to what was most important, "Etta Sue may have wanted to appear addled so Wyatt would believe he was the boss even as she manipulated him to do her bidding. He seems to be contrite now that he's faced with punishment, but he also has an aggrandized ego that rivals the Rockies in scale."

Molly's lips pursed. "Tell me about it."

"The motive of her vendetta against you was perfectly simple. She saw you were far more competent than Sharleen, and didn't want to risk that you'd discover what she was up to."

"Why not save the bother and just tell Cord to fire me?"

"Maybe she did. But he liked you, right? And, remember, he was operating under the assumption that he was the boss."

"This is too convoluted." Molly shook her head. "So it was Etta Sue who let the kittens into Cord's office and then scratched at my door to wake me up?"

"I don't know about the scratching. But your suspicions about me—in that instance—were on the money. I let the kittens in during a midnight scouting expedition. Not intentionally. You came downstairs in your flannel pajamas and distracted me, remember?" He leaned forward to catch her around the knees. "You make a very nice distraction."

Molly came closer and rested her hands on his shoulders. "Did you ever notice that Etta Sue and Sharleen share quite a few similarities? The hair, the gaudy jewels, the piercing voices?"

"They say that men often marry their mothers. Figuratively speaking." Raleigh nuzzled the curve of Molly's stomach. He reached around and squeezed her lush bottom, wishing that she would get off the subject and onto his lap. If love was going to make him soft, then luckily Molly was at hand to get him hard again.

"Raleigh?" she said. Her fingertips brushed at the ends of his hair, touching lightly on his face now and then until finally he took his nose out of her navel and his teeth off her zipper and looked up. "Tell me I don't look like your mother."

He laughed and dragged her into his lap. "It's true

that your particular nurturing female touch supplies what's been missing in my life for a very long time. But, no, Molly, you do not look even remotely like my mother.''

A smile curled across her lips, sweet and pink, punctuated by the comma of her dimple. "This is good."

"Does that smile mean you'll come away with me?"

Her nod became a sigh. "Yes. But, oh, Raleigh, the ranch…"

"I'm asking you to marry me. Even if the cowboy boot doesn't fit."

"I think you've proved that you're plenty cowboy enough for me," she said. "Yes, Raleigh, I'll marry you." She nestled herself against his chest. "There's no reason I can't wear the boots in the family."

He kissed her hair. "And I can always request a transfer to one of the field offices in Colorado or Wyoming."

"I'll marry you either way." She tilted her head back and offered him her kiss, her future, her boundless love. "I'm a sucker for happy endings."

MAITLAND MATERNITY

Where the luckiest babies are born!

Join Harlequin® and Silhouette® for a special 12-book series about the world-renowned Maitland Maternity Clinic, owned and operated by the prominent Maitland family of Austin, Texas, where romances are born, secrets are revealed…and bundles of joy are delivered!

Look for

MAITLAND MATERNITY

titles at your favorite retail outlet, starting in August 2000

HARLEQUIN®
Makes any time special ™

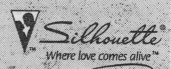

Silhouette®
Where love comes alive ™

COMING NEXT MONTH

HARLEQUIN Duets™

#33

THE SHERIFF AND THE E-MAIL BRIDE by Liz Ireland
Lone Star Lawmen: Book 1

Sheriff Sam Weston refuses to believe the crazy notion that Heartbreak Ridge has a romance curse…but he isn't taking any chances, either. On the Internet, he rounds himself up a lady far from his tiny hometown. In fact, the lonesome lawman thinks he's found himself a foolproof courting method—until his cyber-fiancée arrives on his doorstep *eight months pregnant!*

STRAY HEARTS by Jane Sullivan

Legal secretary Kay Ramsey wants her ex-fiancé to pay for cheating on her, so she shaves his prizewinning cocker spaniels! *Her punishment?* A hundred hours of community service at a local animal shelter. No problem—except that Kay is scared silly of anything with four legs and fur! But when she sees veterinarian Matt Forester, she knows one hundred hours isn't nearly long enough….

#34

THE WRONG MR. RIGHT by Tina Wainscott

Marisa Cerini is tired of being the screwup of the Cerini clan. She'll do anything to make her family proud—including going along with a *really* outdated Italian tradition! Everybody in her family has found their true love at the annual Amore festival—and now it's Marisa's turn. But the only man Marisa meets is a clumsy Scotsman who knocks her over and breaks her ankle. Barrie McKenzie is gruff, opinionated…and very sexy. He may be Mr. Wrong, but to Marisa, he's looking pretty right!

NEVER SAY NEVER! by Barbara Daly

Heiress Tish Seldon is convinced that her fiancé is head-over-heels in love—with her money! Fleeing her wedding, she lands squarely in the lap of gorgeous Sheriff Zeke Thorne, who knew women meant trouble even before Tish came along to prove it. But an unwise kiss from unwillingly smitten Zeke gives Tish her first taste of passion, and she wants to pursue it—if only he'd stop fighting her off!

CNM0700